The Wife at the Last House Before the Sea

BOOKS BY LIZ EELES

Heaven's Cove series
Secrets at the Last House Before the Sea
A Letter to the Last House Before the Sea
The Girl at the Last House Before the Sea
The Key to the Last House Before the Sea
The Path to the Last House Before the Sea
The Sisters at the Last House Before the Sea
The Diary at the Last House Before the Sea

The Cosy Kettle series
New Starts and Cherry Tarts at the Cosy Kettle
A Summer Escape and Strawberry Cake at the Cosy Kettle
A Christmas Wish and a Cranberry Kiss at the Cosy Kettle

Salt Bay series
Annie's Holiday by the Sea
Annie's Christmas by the Sea
Annie's Summer by the Sea

LIZ EELES

The Wife at the Last House Before the Sea

bookouture

Published by Bookouture in 2025

An imprint of Storyfire Ltd.
Carmelite House
50 Victoria Embankment
London EC4Y 0DZ

www.bookouture.com

The authorised representative in the EEA is Hachette Ireland
8 Castlecourt Centre
Dublin 15 D15 XTP3
Ireland
(email: info@hbgi.ie)

Copyright © Liz Eeles, 2025

Liz Eeles has asserted her right to be identified as the author of this work.

All rights reserved. No part of this publication may be reproduced, stored in any retrieval system, or transmitted, in any form or by any means, electronic, mechanical, photocopying, recording or otherwise, without the prior written permission of the publishers.

ISBN: 978-1-83618-372-3
eBook ISBN: 978-1-83618-371-6

This book is a work of fiction. Names, characters, businesses, organizations, places and events other than those clearly in the public domain, are either the product of the author's imagination or are used fictitiously. Any resemblance to actual persons, living or dead, events or locales is entirely coincidental.

PROLOGUE

Beatrice ran her fingers over the ivory silk. The delicate fabric was five decades old yet it had retained its soft sheen, thanks to being wrapped in tissue and hidden from the light.

The beautiful dress looked as good as new, marvelled Beatrice, and parting with it would be difficult. But she had to harden her heart because everything was changing and it was time to let go of the past.

'Move on,' she murmured to herself, pushing the dress into the vintage leather holdall at her feet. But the past was not so easily left behind, and memories started coming at her, thick and fast.

It was the most amazing dress, and there were gasps from guests as she'd passed them in the church on that autumn morning. Sharp intakes of breath, and murmured asides: 'What a stunning gown! I dread to think how much it cost.'

A small fortune, as it turned out, with no expense spared for the wedding of Colonel and Mrs Farleigh-Addison's only child.

Plump, white peonies had adorned every pew at St Augustine's Church in Heaven's Cove, and the altar was laden with hot-house blooms. Only the best was acceptable... the best ceremony and reception, the best speeches, the best dress. If only he had been the very best of husbands.

Beatrice remembered her journey to the church in a sleek car almost too wide for the village's narrow lanes. She'd never forget that the driver had stopped so she could drop a coin into the ancient well that stood not far from the quayside.

The cool air had been laced with the sharp tang of the sea, and she'd heard boats chugging into harbour as her money fell into the darkness and she made her wish.

It was a tradition in Heaven's Cove that every bride stopped here on their way to the church, to wish for a long and happy marriage and, perhaps, for children.

But her wish had been different that bright morning so long ago. Her sole wish had been for courage – the courage to do what surely had to be done. But it hadn't come true that day. Wishes never did, did they? Not when fallible people were involved.

Beatrice took a deep breath and pushed the dress farther into the holdall. This was the bag her father had used when she was a child, and he and her mother would go to London for a 'break'.

A break from me, thought Beatrice, even though she'd always been a good girl who was quiet, undemanding and obedient. So very obedient when it came to her parents.

Beatrice pulled her shoulders up to her ears and let them drop.

'Just let it go,' she muttered, shoving the dress to the very bottom of the bag where it bunched into a puffy mound of fabric and broken dreams.

Then, she piled other clothes on top – the velvet jacket she no longer wore, the skirt she'd never really liked, the jumpers and blouses that had once filled her wardrobe.

Many of them swamped her now because she'd lost weight over the last few months, since she'd finally found her backbone and made an irreversible decision. And she was glad to see the clothes go. They belonged to another life, when she'd felt like someone else entirely.

Beatrice blinked to bring herself back to the present, and zipped the bag shut.

Some people took unwanted clothes to the tip but she couldn't bear to throw them out. She tried to recycle when she could, and the clothes were still in good condition.

They might suit someone else. And perhaps another woman – one madly in love who couldn't afford a grand wedding – would make good use of the beautiful silk dress.

Maybe it was time to bring it back into the light and give it another chance to help make dreams come true.

Beatrice carried the bag through the house where she'd grown up, and out into the front garden. She would drop the holdall off tonight, when the lights had dimmed in Heaven's Cove and there was no village gossip to see what she was doing.

'You make your bed and you lie in it.' Her mother's words echoed in Beatrice's mind as she swung the bag into the back of her car and waited for darkness to fall.

1

EMMA

The wishing well sat in the middle of a small, cobbled square, surrounded by whitewashed cottages.

It looked pretty, with its circular stone wall and red-tiled roof. But Emma peered into the darkness and shivered, wondering how deep the drop was. How far she would fall before hitting the bottom.

Years ago, the well had provided fresh water for the inhabitants of Heaven's Cove. And now, though redundant, no one had the heart to remove it because it had become a part of local folklore: a place where dreams might come true, if you wished hard enough.

That's what Emma had been told anyway, on her first day in the village almost three weeks ago, by a middle-aged woman named Belinda who'd made a beeline for her in the pub and regaled her with her life story.

Tourists mostly overlooked the well because it was behind the main street that ran through the village – tucked away behind the gift shops, cafés and ice cream parlour that faced the picturesque harbour.

But Emma had noticed locals lobbing in spare change as

they passed. And she was a local now so, after re-reading her solicitor's upsetting email and shoving her phone back into her pocket, she fished in her purse for a handful of coins.

Would the wishing well gods think she was a cheapskate? she wondered, frowning at the coppers in her palm. But it was either a handful of change, or the two-pound coin still in her purse, and throwing that away seemed over the top when money was tight.

There was always the gold wedding ring that she was still wearing. Emma twirled it round and round on her finger, thinking hard.

Hurling the ring into the depths might feel therapeutic, especially on today of all days. But after it had been swallowed by the water far below, she'd probably have regrets.

Emma uncurled her fingers and let the copper coins fall into the well.

'I wish,' she murmured under her breath. 'I wish...'

But her mind was too muddled to make any sort of coherent wish. There was too much going on in her life that needed fixing. Too much about her that needed to be put right.

She finally decided on *I wish I'd made more of my life*, but immediately changed her mind because that was too over-arching. Everyone had some regrets, and she had *loads*. The wishing well gods wouldn't stand a chance.

How about *I wish my daughter needed me more*? Though it was good, wasn't it, that Thea was living an independent life?

Yes, it was very good, Emma told herself firmly, even though her heart lurched at the thought of Thea hours away in London.

'Come on,' she murmured to herself. 'Focus! What do you want?' And then, what she really needed right now popped into her head.

I wish I knew how to feel now that I am, as of today, officially divorced.

Having feelings wasn't the problem. Emma had more of

them than she could handle, including apprehension, agitation, fear, and a deep, deep sadness that blunted the beauty of this coastal Devon village.

But shouldn't she also be feeling some excitement as a new chapter of her life began? A whole world was waiting for her, as a footloose divorcee. Well, the whole of Heaven's Cove, at least, and that, Emma decided, was about all she could cope with at the moment. Excitement would have to wait.

Emma turned her back on the well, deciding not to make a wish at all because it was pointless – though at least throwing coins into the well had made her feel more like a local. Like someone who deserved to be here – a member of the Heaven's Cove community, running a village business.

Talking of which... Emma glanced at her watch and, realising it was almost half past eight, began striding quickly towards the middle of the village.

As she walked, she glanced up at Driftwood House where she was staying until she got herself sorted out. The isolated guesthouse was a white smudge from here, perched on top of the cliff that rose high above Heaven's Cove.

It was good of Rosie to take her in even though the guesthouse was officially closed for a while. It was great that she remembered the long-ago link between her family and Emma's that had prompted her to extend an invitation to stay.

But Emma also suspected that Rosie, who ran Driftwood House with her husband, Liam, had felt sorry for her: an unremarkable middle-aged woman who was starting over.

As she walked on, Emma relived her decision to up sticks and move to a different county that was so unfamiliar. To a tiny village by the sea.

Emma wasn't a spontaneous type of person. Journeys were usually worked out days in advance, holidays planned in detail months before heading off.

But moving to Heaven's Cove, on little more than a whim,

had seemed the best way to make a point. To prove that she was more than Carl's cast-off wife. More than a mum who wasn't needed any more.

To prove that she might be forty-six, with dodgy eyesight and the menopause beckoning, but she had courage.

Though now she was here, she didn't feel brave at all. And even the fabulous view that she woke up to every morning at Driftwood House couldn't quell the panic that had taken root in the pit of her stomach.

Fluttery panic persisted, even when the sight that greeted her on pulling back the bedroom curtains made her catch her breath in wonder.

On sunny mornings, white horses topped rolling waves and brightly coloured fishing boats bobbed. While on windy, greyer days, waves pounded into the cliff, sending plumes of spray high into the air.

It was all very different from the traffic and power station chimney beyond the bedroom curtains of her London family home. The home that had now been sold so that Carl could shack up with his new girlfriend elsewhere in the city.

Emma decided to change her wish.

My wish is that I'll never tire of the magnificent view from Driftwood House, or take it for granted, she thought, walking on towards her shop.

That was probably an easy wish to grant, but maybe easy was all you got for a handful of coppers.

Emma dodged the tables on the pavement outside The Heavenly Tea Shop, and hopped to one side as the fishmonger sloshed a bucket of water and ice across the cobbles.

Carl and Thea thought she was crazy to move here. To a place she'd only visited once before, on a family holiday. And she'd been wondering if they were right ever since she'd arrived. Even on a day like today, when the sun was shining in a china-blue sky and seagulls were wheeling on a sea breeze.

It would be so easy to give it all up and return to London. It would be so much less stressful to go back to a life that felt more familiar.

'I need to change my wish,' she said out loud, then winced as the fishmonger gave her a strange look.

She lowered her voice to a murmur. 'I'd like to wish for courage instead. That is, if you don't mind,' she added, presumably to the wishing well gods who could magically hear what she was saying.

She shook her head – maybe she *was* going crazy – and hurried on, towards the shop she'd opened just over a fortnight earlier.

She could see it in the distance now. Heavenly Vintage Vavoom, selling carefully selected, pre-loved clothing at affordable prices.

Pre-loved. A little like her, mused Emma. Once valued but now a cast-aside divorcee.

Which was such a maudlin thought, she gave a rueful smile at her current capacity for self-pity.

Emma was usually a glass-half-full kind of person, but her divorce and those coins thrown into the wishing well had sparked a cascade of memories and feelings today that she'd rather have left alone.

A hard day's work in the shop, boosting her brand-new business, would banish them and help her to build her new life, she decided. It was important to remember that she was living her dream, even if it didn't always feel like it.

Emma reached into her pocket for the shop key and glanced at the large leather holdall lying near the doorstep. A cardboard luggage label was attached, on which was written FOR THE CHILDREN'S CENTRE.

But before she could investigate the holdall any further, a low male voice sounded behind her.

'I'd rather not have tatty old bags left outside my business. It's not a great look, is it.'

Emma groaned quietly and turned to face her neighbour.

They'd never actually spoken before, but she'd seen him going in and out of his shop that was next to hers – an old-fashioned gentlemen's outfitters whose large, plate-glass window was edged in dark wood.

He couldn't be much older than her. His chestnut-brown hair was lightly peppered with grey and there was only a smattering of lines on his face. His eyes, she noticed, were hazel, verging on green, and his jaw was tight, presumably with annoyance. As usual, he was dressed in a formal dark suit, a white shirt and sombre tie. He wore it well but always looked as if he was on his way to a funeral.

Emma forced herself to smile at the man who was waiting for her reply with his arms folded.

'Hello,' she said, extending her hand. 'My name's Emma and I've just opened Heavenly Vintage Vavoom.'

'Yes, I'd gathered that,' said the man coolly. He gripped her hand firmly but gave it the briefest of shakes. 'I'm Leo Jacobson-Jones and I run the outfitters next door.'

'Yes, I'd rather gathered that too,' said Emma, her smile slipping. She wasn't in the mood for being overly nice to someone whose first ever words to her had been a complaint. Not on today of all days.

'Right.' Leo cleared his throat. 'Anyway, I'd like it if you could move the bag as soon as possible.'

'Of course. I do ask that people don't leave charity donations outside,' said Emma, pointing at the large notice printed in her window. 'But I'm afraid that the message doesn't always get through.'

'You'd think donation etiquette would be common knowledge, seeing as Heaven's Cove seems to be awash with charity shops selling second-hand goods already.'

'Awash? I don't think so. I've only seen two others in the village, and mine isn't a charity shop anyway. I sell carefully selected vintage clothing.'

'Which is second-hand.'

'Yes,' said Emma, feeling a flash of annoyance. 'The clothing I sell is second-hand. Not everyone wants to buy or can afford the brand-new suits that you sell. But everything I stock is in excellent condition and I carry a number of respected labels, from Lanvin and Givenchy to Dior.'

'Yet people still dump charity donations on the pavement.'

Emma resisted an urge to tell him to push off.

'They dump… they *leave* donations outside *my* business because a small section of my shop is allocated for donated clothing, with all the money raised from that going to the local children's centre. As I'm a newcomer, it's good to support a village initiative, don't you think?'

'It's one way of ingratiating yourself, I suppose.'

Ingratiating herself? She was raising money for a great cause, not sucking up to local bigwigs. Emma could feel her heart thumping as she tried to hide quite how irritating she was finding Leo double-barrelled Jones.

She'd had quite enough of difficult men recently, and didn't need another on her first day as a divorcee.

Leo glanced at her and ran a finger beneath the collar of his white shirt. As Emma's eyes flickered down to his chest she caught a glimpse of a slim silver chain against his collarbone. The chain seemed out of place, somehow, on such a staid man.

'Anyway, if you could get the bag moved before my customers start arriving,' he snapped, pulling his lips into a tight line. It was the same expression she'd seen yesterday through his shop window when she'd had the temerity to pause outside Jacobson-Jones Gentlemen's Outfitters and talk on her phone.

When Emma opened the shop door and bent to pick up the bag, which was surprisingly heavy, Leo stepped forward.

'Do you need a hand with that?'

'I'm sure I can manage,' said Emma crisply, but Leo had already grabbed the bag from her and deposited it on the floor inside Heavenly Vintage Vavoom.

'There you go. Right, I'll let you get on.'

With that, he turned on his heel, strode off and disappeared into his presumably terribly upmarket, non-second-hand shop.

'Whatever,' muttered Emma through clenched teeth, channelling Thea as a teenager.

She stepped inside, took a deep breath to shake off the last few minutes, then looked around her and grinned. Setting up this business was scary, and the man next door was patently an arse. But the shop still made her smile, because it was all hers.

She'd dreamed of running her own fashion business when Thea was small but she'd had no time, particularly because Carl's career was taking off and he was always home late.

Then, when Thea got older, Carl hadn't been keen on Emma 'wasting money' on a venture that he reckoned would never succeed.

So she'd parked her dreams and thought that was it. Until Carl had lit a fire under them by running off with a woman not that much older than his daughter.

Apparently, some women marked being dumped for a younger model by changing their hairstyle. Emma had kept the fair bob that grazed her shoulders but had moved across the country and opened a clothing shop instead.

Perhaps a visit to the hairdresser would have been more sensible, she thought, hit by a sudden wave of anxiety.

What if the shop failed and Carl and Thea were proved right? What if she had to leave Heaven's Cove in disgrace? What if the arsey man next door made her life a misery?

Emma pulled back her shoulders and breathed out slowly. 'Courage,' she murmured to herself before looking around the shop to make herself feel better.

The stone walls she'd whitewashed were hung with antique mirrors and countryside prints by Old Masters, in gilt frames. And there were two rose-pink wingback armchairs near the changing room, so people could wait in comfort.

The wide range of vintage clothing she stocked was arranged in sections – blouses, shirts and jumpers, dresses, skirts and jackets – and then by size.

Most of the clothing and accessories in the shop had been sourced by Emma online. By scouring clothing resale sites and wholesalers, or visiting vintage fairs to find the right pieces.

Spotting a navy velvet size 12 skirt amongst the size 14s, Emma plucked it from its rail and placed it where it should be.

The skirt wasn't the only piece of clothing that was in the wrong place. Maisie, the teenager she'd hired to help out, was supposed to be keeping the shop in order, but her concentration was erratic.

Emma often found her with her head in her phone, and she was beginning to regret her hasty decision to take the girl on – a decision swayed by Maisie's resemblance to a younger Thea.

Maisie had marched into the shop a week ago and asked for part-time work.

Emma was doing OK on her own. She hadn't been exactly overrun with customers in the first week she'd spent running the shop alone. But she'd looked at Maisie's expectant face, imagined Thea's disappointment at being turned down for a similar job, and said 'yes' on the spot.

It was rash and, so far, the spontaneous hiring hadn't been a rip-roaring success.

Emma turned over the 'Closed' sign, pushed the door wide open to encourage browsers, and dragged the heavy holdall to the back of the shop. She might as well go through it before the first customers arrived.

Sitting cross-legged on the floor, she began to pull clothes from the bag: good-quality jackets and trousers, elegant tailored skirts, silky blouses, and two good winter coats. But there was nothing to say who had left them outside.

Emma peered at the clothing labels which held a treasure trove of information, if you knew what to look for.

They were all expensive, stylish pieces, some of them decades old, which suggested that the donor was a mature woman with money, taste and a flair for fashion.

Suddenly, Maisie came rushing into the shop. She'd been hired to work weekends only, but was helping out more during her Easter break from school.

'Sorry I'm late,' she declared, pushing her long, dark hair over her shoulder. 'Caitlin didn't wake me up, even though she promised. Honestly, ever since she's been loved up' – Maisie rolled her eyes – 'she's, like, totally unreliable. If that's what love does to you, turns you into a brainless idiot, I'll give it a swerve, thanks very much. What's that?'

Emma, blinking under the onslaught, looked down at the last piece of clothing she'd just pulled from the leather bag. A froth of silk and lace lay in a puddle on the wooden floor.

The fabric felt smooth and luxurious under her fingers, and it caught the light when she got to her feet and let the garment unravel.

'Oh,' said Emma.

It was a wedding dress. An exquisite wedding dress made of the lightest ivory silk, with an intricate lace overlay across the bodice. The full skirt fell in ripples to the hem that moved in the sea breeze coming through the door.

Maisie's big brown eyes opened wide. 'I don't agree with the patriarchal and misogynistic concept of marriage that keeps women in their place, but that's, like, awesome. It's well lush.'

Emma had been told that Maisie was often monosyllabic on first arriving in Heaven's Cove with her stepmother, Caitlin, not that long ago. But she'd certainly found her voice since starting at the local school and making friends.

'It's wonderful, isn't it?' said Emma, brushing her palm across the fabric which seemed to glow in the morning light. 'The most beautiful dress I've ever seen.'

'Who does it belong to?' Maisie asked, stepping forward.

Spotting flakes of croissant from breakfast stuck to Maisie's fingers, Emma gathered the dress close.

'I have no idea. It was in this bag of clothing that was left on the doorstep this morning, much to Leo Jacobson-Jones's disapproval.'

'That grumpy dude next door?' Maisie turned up her nose. 'He looks well weird in that boring suit. My friend Beth says he wears it all the time, even when there's a heatwave and everyone else is in shorts. And his dad's even worse.'

'He's just following a dress code that fits with his shop,' said Emma, not sure why she was sticking up for Leo, and concerned by Maisie's assertion that his father was 'even worse'.

Worse as regards grumpiness or fashion sense? She'd yet to meet Mr Jacobson-Jones Senior, who was, apparently, a VIP in Heaven's Cove. Or so Belinda had told her during their lengthy pub chat, which had felt more like a grilling.

Maisie sniffed and, without another word, headed for the back of the shop where there was a small kitchen area, a toilet, and hooks for jackets and coats.

Emma carefully placed the amazing wedding dress across a clothes rail, picked up the holdall and turned the attached luggage label over.

She was hoping that whoever had left the clothing on her doorstep had also left contact details. Emma would love to get in touch to thank her, and to see if she had any other vintage treasures in her wardrobe. But the back of the label was blank.

Perhaps there's a note inside the bag, thought Emma, turning it upside down.

There was a clang as something metallic hit the floor and, when Emma bent to pick the object up, she realised that it was a ring.

She placed the ring in her palm and studied it. Made of warm-yellow gold, it was a plain band. A wedding band.

Emma's thumb automatically went to the wedding ring on her fourth finger. The ring that she'd contemplated hurling into the wishing well less than an hour ago.

Had someone thrown their wedding ring into the holdall, along with their wedding dress?

Emma turned the ring over and noticed an engraving inside, opposite the hallmark which was almost worn away. The engraving was faint too but – she brought it up to her face and squinted – it looked like *B & R Aeternum*.

Emma dredged up remnants of the Latin she'd taken at school. *Aeternum*. That meant 'for ever', which was an optimistic word for a wedding ring. Emma, as a brand-new divorcee, might even say hubristic. But what if, for the owner of this ring, it had been true?

Just because her own long marriage had crashed and burned, that didn't mean everyone's did.

Emma turned the ring over and over in her hand, thinking hard. Perhaps the gold band had fallen into the bag, and somewhere out there, the woman who'd kindly donated clothing to help the local children's centre was mourning its loss.

'A'right?' said Maisie loudly, appearing from the back of the shop. 'What do you want me to do, then?'

'Um...' Emma curled her fingers into the palm of her hand and focused on the teenager in front of her. 'There's a pile of clothing over there that needs to be steam-cleaned. Could you get on with that?'

'I s'pose,' said Maisie with a scowl. 'Though that steam makes my fringe go frizzy.'

As she wandered slowly off, Emma unfurled her fingers and stared at the wedding ring.

Who on earth did it belong to? And was the long-ago bride distraught at its loss, or glad to see the back of it?

2

LEO

Leo shut the door of his shop behind him and closed his eyes for a moment. He'd just realised that sometimes he sounded exactly like his father.

It's one way of ingratiating yourself. That's what he'd said to the woman next door about her raising money for a local charity.

He hadn't meant to sound quite so... mean. But he had. And she'd assumed that he was casting aspersions on her motives.

It was a pain that people were leaving battered bags in the street outside. *Anything* that might put off his customers was to be avoided. Especially now, when business was so worryingly slow.

And Emma – a name he'd always liked – had been quick to take offence. So it wasn't *all* his fault.

But he had to admit that he could have handled their first meeting better. Particularly as they were going to be neighbours. Although his father, Robert, reckoned she wouldn't last long.

'She's going round saying she sells pre-loved clothing. Pre-loved!' he'd added with a snort. 'That's code, that is, for a load of old tat that, unfortunately, attracts exactly the wrong kind of customer for us. Our clientele is top-end.'

His father, a self-made man and proud of it, could be rather a snob at times. And Leo hadn't had the heart to tell him that the 'top-end clientele' that he valued so highly were pretty thin on the ground right now.

Robert had set up this business from scratch and built it up with hard work and sacrifice – Leo had heard *many* stories of how hard he'd grafted to become a pillar of the local community.

So what a shame if this shop went under just as his father finally got round to retiring, and the business became Leo's responsibility. Following in his father's footsteps was hard enough. Failing would be unthinkable.

Leo adjusted the jacket on the mannequin near the door that sported a black suit and bow tie. He needed to get the shop shipshape, ready for the day, but his mind kept flitting back to his new neighbour.

He'd spotted Emma earlier that morning while he was walking to work. She'd been staring into the old wishing well with a thoughtful look on her face. Then she'd twirled the wedding ring on her finger round and round before throwing a handful of coins into the darkness.

What had she been wishing for? he wondered. He knew what he would wish for – but, as he didn't believe in any of that wishing well nonsense, his wish was immaterial.

And the fact that his new neighbour had time for all that hocus-pocus was another black mark against her.

Leo took off his jacket and had begun to tidy round when the bell above the shop door clanged and his father bowled in.

'Have Cyril Clarkson's new suit trousers arrived?' he asked, his cheeks ruddy from the walk down the hill towards the sea.

'Good morning to you, too,' said Leo, raising an eyebrow. 'They arrived late yesterday.'

His father was supposed to be easing into retirement but he couldn't let go and trust Leo to get things right.

'Have you informed him? He was insistent that he needs them by this coming weekend, for his great-niece's christening, up country.'

'Yes, of course I have,' said Leo, stung anew by his father's lack of confidence in him. 'I rang him yesterday afternoon and he said he'd call in for them later today.'

'Good.'

Robert picked a speck of dust from a jacket draped across a nearby mannequin. A rather spooky headless mannequin that had given Leo nightmares as a child.

'Oh,' said Leo, keen to share some good news. 'You know James Collis, who farms out past Heaven's Brook? He said he'd be in this weekend to choose suits for his wedding. He's after matching morning dress for himself, his best man, the father of the bride and a couple of ushers, so that could be a significant hire. I saw him in the pub and persuaded him that we'd be a good option.'

'Hmm. A hire's not as good as a sale, but better than nothing, I suppose.'

Would it kill his father to say 'good job' to him once in a while? Leo wondered.

'By the way,' Robert continued, 'did I see you talking to that woman next door as I was coming down the hill?'

'Yes, I had a quick word with her.'

'About what?'

'Nothing much.'

'What's she like?'

Leo shrugged. 'Fine. About my age. Married. Quite attractive.'

Why had he commented on her appearance? She *was* quite attractive, and she'd seemed stylish in a dark blue dress with a nipped-in waist and sweetheart neckline. But his father was now giving him an odd look.

'Annoying,' Leo added as a deflection. 'She was fine but annoying.'

Robert agreed with his son's opinion, that the woman was annoying. Although he'd never actually met Emma, he'd taken a dislike to her. This was partly because of what she was selling, but mostly because he didn't approve of renting the shop to a village 'outsider'.

'And you talked about nothing much, you say?' he continued.

'We exchanged pleasantries. That's all.'

Pleasantries was far from the truth but Leo decided not to mention the dumped holdall if his father hadn't spotted it. There was no point in antagonising him about his new neighbour even further.

Robert sniffed. 'Did I tell you that I've been asked to open the village's midsummer fair?'

'You did mention it, but what an honour!' said Leo, relieved by the swift change of subject. 'You're a real VIP around here,' he added teasingly.

'Yes, I am,' said Robert, who was unhindered by modesty when it came to his standing in Heaven's Cove.

Leo found his attitude trying at times but he did admire what his father had achieved. Born into a poor family a few miles away, he'd built himself up to be, as he liked to describe himself, 'someone'.

'I'm surprised they haven't asked me to open it before,' Robert continued. 'I mean, I chair umpteen organisations, I'm a trustee on countless others, and I represent the village at district council level. I'm thinking of standing for the county council when I'm fully retired. What more could anyone possibly want of me?'

Time, thought Leo, remembering how busy his father had

always been when he was growing up. Always far too busy on some committee or other to play football, read bedtime stories or simply sit and chat about school.

But that was all a long time ago and his mother had filled the gap as best she could.

Leo blinked hard as he remembered his mum, who had died exactly two years ago this week. Now was not a good time to be floored by the waves of grief that came less regularly these days but took him more by surprise because of their infrequency.

He'd already told his father that the woman next door was attractive, and he'd only get another quizzical look if he seemed upset.

'Anyway.' His father clapped his hands together. 'I might as well check Cyril's new trousers while I'm here and see if the stitching on them is up to par.'

'It is,' said Leo. 'I've already checked.'

'I just want to make sure. Our business lives and dies on its reputation for quality. And, when I've done that' – he looked at Leo, his eyes shining – 'I have something else rather exciting to tell you.'

When Robert walked towards the stock room, Leo sighed. His father had many honourable qualities and was hugely respected. But, as his son, he'd always been expected to live up to his exacting standards.

An envelope had fallen from his father's jacket and Leo picked it up and placed it on the counter. Then, he decided to check in the till that there was enough of a cash float. Most people used plastic these days but the customers of this store, in keeping with the old-fashioned ambience of the place, often preferred to use notes and coins.

He'd asked one customer a few days ago if he'd like his receipt emailed to him, and the man had stared at him aghast, as if he'd suggested stapling the receipt to his forehead.

Leo pressed the button on the till but the money drawer

didn't slide open. He switched the till off and on again at the mains. That usually worked, but not this time. The till was still dead. And when Leo went to the light switch by the front door and flicked it down, the lights above the counter remained unlit.

As Leo flicked the switch back up, Robert called from the back of the shop. 'Is the power out again? I can't see much back here.'

It might be the twenty-first century, but Heaven's Cove still had occasional power cuts. Leo had loved them as a child – reading by candlelight and walking through a pitch-black village with only torchlight to show the way. It was like being a pirate smuggling contraband under cover of darkness.

However now, although the outages were fewer and farther between, he found them frustrating. How was a business supposed to run with no power? At least the lights usually came back on quite quickly.

'What on earth is going on?'

The bellow made Leo jump. What now? Had his father found a missed stitch in a trouser hem?

Leo hurried towards Robert, being careful not to trip over anything in the gloom.

'What's the matter?' he called out.

His father shouted back: 'The light in the stock room suddenly cut out and now nothing's working.'

'What the hell?' murmured Leo.

He looked down because something cold was soaking into his socks. His ankles were sodden.

Pulling his phone from his pocket, Leo turned on the torch and gasped when he realised he was walking in water. The spillage was black like tar on the floor tiles.

'There's a flood,' his father declared, appearing from the kitchen. 'Mind you don't slip. I thought you'd left the kitchen taps on but the water's not coming from them.'

'The till and lights at the front of the shop aren't working either. Maybe the water has shorted the electrics.'

'Oh, for goodness' sake. Where's it coming from?'

When Leo bent down and trained torchlight on the bottom of the wall, he was horrified to see water coming over the top of the skirting board. It swelled and bubbled above the wood before trickling to join the growing lake.

'I think I know exactly where it's coming from,' he said, his heart beginning to pound.

'Where?' Robert demanded, his face looming out of the gloom.

'From the shop next door. It looks like it's coming through the party wall.'

'From that infernal woman who's selling tat?'

Usually, Leo tried to rein in his father's tendency to erupt. But he felt pretty close to losing his cool himself.

This was all too much. Their business was hanging by a thread, it was the second anniversary of his mother's death – although his father had failed to mention it. And now water was pouring into their shop from next door, which was far more damaging than an abandoned holdall in the street. Their electrics, already in dire need of updating, were probably toast.

'We need to get this sorted out right away,' said Robert, splashing towards the front door.

Leo rubbed his temples which were beginning to throb. 'I know. I'll deal with it.'

He quickly splashed after his father because he didn't want him rushing into Emma's shop in a filthy mood.

He caught up with him outside Heavenly Vintage Vavoom and took hold of his father's arm.

'Wait a minute, Dad, please. I said I'd deal with it.'

Robert stopped and turned towards his son.

'If she's caused this flood, it's not acceptable.'

'Obviously not.'

'Will you tell her that?'

'Of course I will.'

'Only I need to know that you're fully invested in making our business work.'

The implication in his father's words, the injustice of them, made Leo's breath catch in his throat. Much of his youth had been spent behind the counter at Jacobson-Jones Gentlemen's Outfitters, selling suits to wealthy local landowners.

And when his peers had left Heaven's Cove for exciting pastures new, he'd stayed behind for the sake of the family business. He'd thrown himself into it with no complaint and had come to love this beautiful village. Yet his father still questioned his loyalty and suitability.

Today, it felt like the final straw.

Leo's jaw set into a tight line as he stepped in front of his father and hurried ahead, prepared to do battle with their nightmare neighbour.

3

EMMA

Emma pushed the discarded wedding ring into the pocket of her dress, wondering why she hadn't mentioned it to Maisie.

Probably because anything to do with weddings felt a little raw today, and she couldn't handle a teenager making more wisecracks about matrimony.

But, even though she felt bruised by the institution, she had to admit there was something romantic about *B & R Aeternum* – the lovers' initials for ever nestling against the skin of the long-ago bride.

But B & R gave her very little to go on, if she wanted to return the ring to its rightful owner who surely hadn't meant to simply give it away. Carl had betrayed her, yet she still wouldn't put her wedding ring into a charity bag. At the moment, she couldn't even bear to take it off her finger.

The dress was different. Emma placed it on a padded clothes hanger and then carefully smoothed out the creases in the delicate fabric.

Giving this away was more understandable, even though it must have been hard to part with such an exquisite gown.

Fancy finding a wedding dress *and* a wedding ring on the

very same day that her divorce became official. Emma groaned with exasperation. Those wishing well gods were having a right old laugh, at her expense.

But there was no time to mope around.

'Maisie, are you all right back there?' Emma called. 'Don't forget I asked you to steam-clean some of the new stock, if you don't mind.'

Or even if she did mind. Emma wasn't finding it easy to adjust to the role of employer. She had a tendency to feel like a surrogate parent when it came to Maisie. But, just because she was missing her own daughter, she couldn't be too soft on her.

She'd just decided to go and see where Maisie was lurking when she was dismayed to spot Leo from next door standing outside her window, giving her his hazel-eyed stare. What had she done wrong now?

And she was even more dismayed when he rushed in, closely followed by a man she took to be his father.

There was a resemblance between them, from their straight noses and square jawlines, to the formal suits they were both wearing. Though the older man – sporting a gold clip on his tie and a silk handkerchief in his jacket pocket – was less lean than his son and currently very red in the face.

'Is everything all right?' Emma asked, looking past them to see if there was an emergency happening in the street.

'No, everything's not all right,' said Leo, his cheeks now flushing too. 'You appear to have flooded our shop and knocked out our electrics.'

Emma blinked at him. 'I don't know what you're talking about. I don't know anything about a flood.'

'Are you quite sure about that?'

'Yes, I'm very sure.'

Emma could feel her hackles rising. Leo was speaking to her in a similar patronising tone of voice to the one that Carl sometimes used.

'Frankly, it's rather akin to sabotage,' the older man said.

Was he joking?

Leo put his hand on the older man's shoulder. 'I've got this, Dad.'

'Have you, though?' said the man, shaking off Leo's hand.

'Yes, I have.'

These words from Leo were through gritted teeth and he looked very close to losing it.

Emma narrowed her eyes. There was a family dynamic going on here that was making this whole ridiculous situation even worse. But, quite frankly, she didn't have the time or inclination to get involved in it. Her own dysfunctional family was quite enough to deal with.

'I truly don't know what you're both going on about,' she said briskly. 'If you do have a flood, it's nothing to do with me.'

'It patently is because water's coming through the wall, from your side,' said Leo, his eyes cold.

Emma swallowed, suddenly feeling nervous.

'Might there be a burst pipe? The only water source we have that's close to our dividing wall is in the bathroom.'

'Which is where?'

'Follow me,' said Emma wearily, tired of being harangued in her own shop. This was worse than being accosted outside about the holdall. And customers could turn up at any minute and be put off by an argument happening on the shop floor.

She led the way to the back of the shop, past Maisie, who had finally appeared and was watching with her mouth open.

There were three deep steps down to the tiny bathroom which housed a toilet and basin and, as Emma's feet reached the bottom step, cold water whooshed over the tops of her trainers.

'Oh!' she exclaimed. 'Oh, bugger.'

The place was swimming in water. She pushed open the bathroom door and quickly sized up what had happened.

The basin tap hadn't been turned off properly and the plug

was in, which meant the basin was full and water was dribbling onto the floor. Her footsteps sent a mini wave towards the stone wall that separated her shop from Leo's next door.

Emma gave the tap a swift turn and plunged her hand into freezing cold water to pull out the plug. Inexplicably – and making matters far worse – a sodden hand towel had been left in the basin and was blocking the overflow. The flood had been caused by a catalogue of stupid errors.

Emma breathed out slowly and then turned to Leo, who was watching her with his arms folded.

'I'm so very sorry. I have no idea how this has happened.'

Leo glared at her disbelievingly, but it was the truth. She always washed her hands under a running tap and never put the plug in.

Over Leo's shoulder, Emma spotted Maisie, who had two bright spots of colour in her cheeks. Her eyes met Emma's before she quickly looked away.

'It's clear what's happened,' said Leo. 'You failed to turn off the tap properly and now we're under water and unable to trade. The flood in my shop *is* your fault.'

There was no denying it and, even though it killed Emma to apologise to such a sarcastic and unhelpful man, there was no other option.

She took a deep breath. 'I'm extremely sorry for what's happened. It was obviously a complete accident.'

When he said nothing, Emma splashed back through the water and climbed the steps into the dry. 'But it's happened, and what we need to do now is work out how best we can get this sorted out.'

Leo turned without a word and headed back onto the shop floor. Emma bent and took off her soaking shoes and padded after him, leaving damp footprints on the wooden floor.

While Leo had a quiet word with his father, Emma realised her heart was thumping. What if her dream was over before it had even properly begun? She didn't have much money left after setting up the shop. And paying out for flood damage could swallow a good chunk of what there was. Her shop insurance wouldn't cover it – not when it was user error.

'I really am sorry,' she called out.

The two men stopped conferring and looked across at her.

'I'm sure you are sorry, but I'm afraid your apology doesn't help,' said Leo. 'We're going to lose trade because we can't open for business with no electrics and the place smelling of damp. Heaven knows how long it will take for the electrics to dry out.'

When he closed his eyes and grimaced, Emma began to feel sick. She hadn't meant to cause such a fuss.

Perhaps Thea had been right when she'd railed against her plan to move to Heaven's Cove and open this shop. Carl had openly laughed at the 'ridiculous' idea and said she needed to act her age – which was rich from a man who'd recently taken to wearing a friendship bracelet and a Taylor Swift T-shirt.

She'd gone ahead anyway, but it was only the beginning of week three and she was already in trouble.

'It's just not good enough,' the older man suddenly declared, his cheeks puffing out with indignation.

'Dad,' said Leo quietly, but his father wasn't going to be shut down.

'You're dragging down our business,' he railed. 'Day after day.'

Emma folded her arms, her chest feeling tight.

'How is my shop dragging you down?' she asked, keeping her voice as level as she could.

'I'm Robert Jacobson-Jones, founder of the gentlemen's outfitters next door. It was established by me decades ago and has been attracting a particular clientele ever since. Though God knows, the gift shops and ice cream parlours in the village don't help. I've spoken out against them, as chair of the village residents' association. Did you know that I'm the chair?'

Emma shook her head – though she had a vague recollection of Belinda in the pub going on about a man called Robert who was a local bigwig. He was also full of himself, it seemed, seeing as he hadn't answered Emma's question and had simply used the opportunity to talk about himself.

'Well,' Robert continued. 'I do chair it, along with a number of other organisations. And I spoke against you opening this charity shop for second-hand clothing.'

'My clothing is pre-loved,' Emma murmured, feeling as if she'd been punched.

She'd jumped through hoops and had worked so hard to get this shop open and finding out that local people – her neighbours, in fact – had actively tried to stop her was upsetting.

'Your clothing is second-hand, tatty and unwanted,' Robert insisted.

Emma wasn't going to let that pass. She pulled herself up tall.

'The clothing I sell is vintage and I can assure you that none of it is tatty or unwanted. I give my customers a chance to own a variety of garments, some produced by iconic fashion houses, that they could never have afforded new. We're also raising money for the local children's centre with our charity sales.'

'Vintage?' he huffed. 'Really?'

'Yes, really.'

'Come on,' insisted Leo, putting a hand on his father's arm. 'You've had your say.'

But Robert brushed off his son's hand. '*You* might call it vintage, but that's simply a weasel word for second-hand and tatty, in my book.'

Emma glanced at Leo, who was now staring at the floor, as if he'd washed his hands of the whole situation.

'Actually,' she said, hearing a wobble of indignation in her voice. 'We had some clothes donated just today, for our charity section, that are exquisite.'

She pointed at the clothing that was still in a pile on the floor. The leather holdall was lying nearby and she noticed Leo look at it and then glance at her. His expression was hard to read. Was he still angry, like his father? Or was that embarrassment she glimpsed on his face?

'I wouldn't class that bundle as exquisite. I don't think that... that—' Robert stumbled over his words and started again. 'I don't think... I don't—'

Robert stopped speaking. His mouth was open but no sound was coming out.

'Are you all right, Dad?'

Leo stepped forward and placed his hand beneath his father's elbow. Emma stepped forward too, her anger overtaken by concern.

But Robert ignored them, and Emma followed his gaze. He was staring at the beautiful silk wedding dress that she'd placed on the hanger. Sunshine was streaming through the open shop door and catching the delicate embroidery at the hem of the skirt.

The dress appeared to be glowing, and Robert was caught in its light and seemingly dazzled by it.

'Come on, Dad,' murmured Leo. 'You've had your say so let's get back. The water's stopped coming through the wall now so we can start sorting out the mess.'

But Robert didn't move. He glanced at Emma. He looked stunned, frightened even.

'Dad,' said Leo more forcefully, glancing at the wedding dress. 'I said come on. Now.'

Robert allowed himself to be led out of the shop by his son, and neither of the men looked back.

Emma sat down heavily on the stool near the till because her legs were feeling like jelly.

What a complete and utter mess. She was only just keeping her head above water financially. Emotionally too. And now she was in some sort of feud with the unwelcoming man next door, and his father, who was downright rude.

In fact, his father was odd. Emma thought about the man's bizarre reaction to the wedding dress that was currently wafting in the breeze coming through the open shop door. He'd seemed bewitched by it.

But that was the least of her concerns at the moment, Emma realised. She felt she should offer to go and help next door but she couldn't face it after that showdown. Anyway, there was still a flood on this side of the party wall to sort out.

'Welcome to your first exciting day as a divorcee,' she said ruefully, getting to her feet and going in search of Maisie and a mop.

4

EMMA

Emma finally found Maisie loitering in the garden at the back of the shop. Though 'garden' was pushing it. The small rectangular space was paved over and the terracotta pots that Emma had inherited from the shop's last inhabitant were filled with very dead plants. Emma meant to re-plant the pots, to provide a splash of colour during the summer months – if she lasted that long in Heaven's Cove.

'Here you are. I've been looking for you.' Maisie muttered something in reply that Emma didn't catch. 'I wondered if there was something you wanted to tell me.'

'Nope.' Emma heard that all right.

'Are you quite sure there's nothing you wanted to talk to me about?'

'Like what?'

Maisie raised her head and glared at Emma defiantly. Emma knew that look from her own experience of raising a teenager. It meant that Maisie was going to brazen out her mistake.

'Like the fact that the tap in the bathroom was definitely

turned off properly, the last time I used it yesterday. And I never, ever put the plug in the basin.'

Maisie pulled in a breath and doubled down on her glare, as if she was about to deny everything. Then her shoulders slumped.

'Look, I'm not saying it *was* me, but there's a chance, a *small* possibility, that I might have forgotten to take out the plug when I was washing my trainers in the basin, just before I left yesterday.'

'Why were you washing your trainers in the basin?'

'Foundation,' Maisie declared. 'I was re-doing my make-up 'cos I was meeting friends at the ice cream parlour. Not that I think it's, like, obligatory to wear make-up, just 'cos you're a woman. No one should have to fit in with the patriarchal dogma of what constitutes feminine beauty. But I had a zit on my chin which I wanted to—'

'So, are you saying you got foundation on your shoes?' interrupted Emma.

Maisie blinked. 'That's right.'

'And you were washing it off.'

'Yep,' said Maisie with a flick of her long, dark hair.

'And using the hand towel for… what, exactly?'

'Uh, drying my trainers, obvs,' said Maisie, with an expression that implied Emma was being incredibly dense.

'Of course,' she replied wearily.

'Anyway, I didn't mean to leave the plug in.'

'Or the tap on.'

'The tap was only ever so slightly on,' said Maisie. Then, clocking Emma's expression, she looked down again at the floor and hair swished across her face. 'Sorry,' she mumbled. 'It was an accident.'

'An avoidable accident that's caused no end of trouble.'

Maisie bit at her lip and shifted from foot to foot. 'Did you tell them it was me?'

'No, I didn't.'

Maisie looked up at that, surprise written across her face.

'Are you going to tell them?'

'Probably not.'

'Why?'

'What's the point? They'd taken against me already.'

'Thanks. That's, like, pretty decent.' Maisie's eyes suddenly opened wide. 'I'm not sacked, am I? Only I really like this job.'

Did she like the job? She turned up late and was keen to leave early though, to be fair, she did occasionally work quite hard in between.

Carl never had any time for people who didn't measure up at the company where he worked as a director. He'd fired loads of people who were surplus to requirements, with no hint of remorse. Which, Emma suddenly realised, had been excellent practice for dispatching his wife.

She pushed the thought away. 'No, you're not sacked, Maisie. I'm not happy about what's happened. It's made my life very difficult. But we all make mistakes.'

Some of them far worse than causing a minor flood. Some involved marrying the wrong man and only realising it two decades down the line.

'Thanks,' said Maisie gruffly. 'I 'preciate it. My stepmum would lose her sh—' She checked herself. 'She'd go nuts if I had trouble here too.'

'Too?' asked Emma, raising an eyebrow and wondering what Maisie had failed to tell her about her past.

Maisie folded her arms. 'It's just I had some trouble at my school in London, before we came to live in Heaven's Cove with my aunt.'

Emma imagined a tsunami washing through Maisie's old classrooms.

'Nothing involving a flood, I hope?'

'Nope. It was nothing like that. I played a practical joke, that's all. But it went wrong and no one stood up for me.'

'I see,' said Emma, noticing a wobble in the teenager's voice. 'So what's school like here? Is it better?'

Maisie began to kick her foot against a hefty terracotta pot. 'Yeah, it's good, thanks. The boys are mostly idiots, but I've made some proper friends here. Not like before when people only pretended.'

She stuck out her bottom lip as Emma thought back to Thea's problems with false friends and bullies at school. Like Maisie, she'd put on a grumpy, outspoken front but it had masked vulnerability.

'Look, why don't you put the kettle on?' Emma suggested. 'I think we could both do with a drink.'

While Maisie scuttled off towards the kitchen, Emma pictured her daughter, now all grown up.

Thea had a nice boyfriend and was happy working at a nursery in London. But, like Maisie, she had her vulnerabilities, and Emma often worried that she'd been more adversely affected by the divorce than she'd let on.

Would she start to blame Emma even more for the split and become ever more distant? Emma felt a stab of anticipatory grief at the prospect, but she took a deep breath. All she could do was support Thea and be as good a mum as possible.

'As long as Thea's happy,' she murmured to herself. 'As long as she's happy, that's all that matters.'

It had been a mantra she'd repeated so many times over the years, as her daughter's life had expanded and her own had got smaller. That was the way of things, of course: Thea becoming a teenager with her own friends and her own life, then hitting her twenties, moving out and getting a boyfriend. It was right that she didn't need her mum so much any more. But that didn't mean Emma didn't sometimes feel left behind and redundant.

There was a sudden crash from the kitchen as crockery hit

floor tiles and shattered. Emma sighed and pushed her hand into her pocket where the gold ring was nestling. She ran her fingers along its smooth curves before going to help Maisie, whose swearing could be heard in the yard.

It could be heard on the shop floor too, Emma realised when she spotted a woman standing near the 1980s bomber jackets she had on sale.

The woman had her hands over the ears of the young girl who was with her.

'Shush, Maisie,' Emma hissed, poking her head around the kitchen door.

She ignored the shards of crockery at Maisie's feet and continued on into the shop.

'I do apologise for the language,' she said brightly, relieved that the stream of curses had stopped. 'I'm afraid my assistant has had a small mishap in the kitchen.'

'Nothing too serious, I hope,' said the woman, uncovering the little girl's ears.

'No, just a couple of broken plates.'

Which was far better than a shop under water. Emma's heart sank anew as she pictured Leo and Robert paddling next door. Should she have offered to help them clear up? Probably not, after Robert's comments about her dragging his business down. If that was what he thought, she'd hardly be welcomed.

'You're new here, aren't you?' The woman held out her hand. 'I'm Nessa. I'm friends with Rosie, who you're staying with at Driftwood House. And this is Lily, my daughter.'

'It's lovely to meet you, Nessa, and you too, Lily.'

Emma shook the woman's hand, grateful for her friendliness. It had been a trying morning so far.

'How are you finding Heaven's Cove?'

'It's a beautiful village,' said Emma. 'Wonderful. Lovely.' She could feel the smile slipping from her face. 'Just, you know, a bit unfamiliar at the moment. I've never lived in such a small place before.'

'It can feel rather claustrophobic at times, with everyone knowing your business.' Nessa tilted her head to one side. 'It takes a while to settle in.'

'And for people to accept you,' Emma blurted out and then regretted it.

Honestly, one shred of kindness and her defences were immediately shattered. This woman had come here to shop. She didn't want a sob story.

But Nessa smiled sympathetically. 'Some of the locals are a bit "us" and "them" with newcomers to the village. My partner isn't from round here and he often comments on it. But you'll be accepted after a while, by everyone.'

'Except my neighbours,' murmured Emma.

'Who are your—' Nessa glanced into the street and grinned as realisation dawned. 'Ah, you're next to Robert and Leo. Robert's got a finger in every pie around here and an opinion on everything that's happening.'

'Including me opening a vintage clothing store right next to his business.'

And flooding out his premises. Emma decided not to add that piece of information. She wanted to find out how bad the damage was before news of it spread around the village.

'Oh dear.' Nessa winced. 'He'll come round, I'm sure. Ask Rosie about him. She'll tell you that his bark is worse than his bite, and he's done a lot for the village. Leo must find it hard to—'

'Mummy, look!'

Nessa was distracted by the ear-splitting squeal from her daughter.

'Leo must find it hard to... what?' asked Emma, but Lily was jumping up and down and taking all of Nessa's attention.

'Look at the princess dress!' said Lily, pointing at the wedding gown. Her eyes were wide open in wonder.

'Oh, my. That dress is absolutely beautiful,' Nessa declared, turning back to Emma. 'Where on earth did it come from?'

'I'm not sure. It was left outside in a bag of charity donations. I think it's pretty old, and a one-off, made to measure. There's no label in it.'

'It was donated?' Nessa whistled through her teeth. 'That's unbelievable. It looks like a real family heirloom and must have cost a fortune new. Look at the quality of it!' She stretched out a hand and brushed her finger across the delicate silk. 'I wonder who wore this down the aisle years ago. Whoever it was, she must have looked amazing.'

'Just like a princess,' said Lily, stretching out her hand.

'Absolutely.' Nessa grabbed the child's hand before it reached the fabric, and she winked at Emma. 'Lily's been eating chocolate so probably best not to touch. Now, tell me. Do you have any leather jackets in stock? I'm looking for something gorgeously soft but' – she gave a sheepish grin – 'not too expensive.'

Emma smiled. 'I might have just what you're looking for.'

While Nessa browsed through the small range of leather jackets in stock, Emma stood beside the wedding dress, guarding it from sticky-fingered Lily.

Why had Robert reacted so strangely to the dress? she wondered, thinking back to that awkward moment. Perhaps, like Lily and Nessa, he was awestruck by the delicate beauty of the exquisite garment.

But, though Emma didn't know him at all, she doubted that. He was obviously well-known round here and had seemed rather pompous and abrasive during their brief acquaintance. Seemingly not the sort of man to be rendered speechless by a 'second-hand' dress.

And what about his son? Emma felt frustrated that Nessa

had been interrupted before she'd finished her observation: Leo must find it hard to... what? Be pleasant to people he was meeting for the first time, perhaps?

'I've found quite a few things I like. Can I try them on?' asked Nessa, wandering over with several garments flung over her arm.

She might have come in looking for a leather jacket, but a lime-green dress from the 1960s, a 1980s blue jacket with shoulder pads, and a full skirt in bubble-gum pink had taken her fancy. A battered brown biker jacket was hanging over her shoulder.

'Yes, of course. There's a changing room in the corner. Would you like me to keep an eye on Lily while you try them on?'

'No thanks. Lily's going to help me choose,' said Nessa, giving her daughter a wink.

After they'd disappeared into the changing room, Emma sat waiting with her fingers crossed that Nessa would buy something. Every sale gave her dream a boost – a dream that she'd waited so long to achieve.

Her fashion degree had been a casualty when she'd unexpectedly fallen pregnant with Thea. At first she'd tried to combine her studies with a young child. But her life–work balance was always on a knife edge, and a brutal bout of chicken pox which hit Thea for six had been the final straw. Emma had thought the spots would never disappear.

Carl had encouraged her to give up her studies and become a 'proper mum', and she'd loved her little girl so much – and had been so exhausted – that it had seemed the best option at the time.

Later, she'd regretted not pushing through and finishing her degree. But she'd been comforted by Carl's assertion that she could go back later. Though 'later' had never come.

She'd never lost her love of fashion and, when Thea was

small and money was tight, she'd enjoyed searching out bargains in charity shops.

A beautiful old pair of Jaeger black silk trousers, jumbled together with faded corduroy and old cargo pants in a hospice shop, had sparked her interest in vintage clothing. And it had grown with every exciting discovery.

As Carl was promoted and their income increased, he'd disapproved of her fashion choices. She could hear his voice in her head right now: *'What will people say if my wife's walking around in second-hand clothes? They'll think I don't earn enough to support my family.'*

But mostly she got compliments from others about her outfits, and she became more knowledgeable about vintage fashion. She learned about fabric, silhouettes, stitching, care labels and even zips that could help to date clothing, and she realised how much she loved the vintage world.

That was when she'd first suggested opening her own business. But it was mothballed when Carl scoffed and told her she was selfish to focus on doing something for herself. It was much better to think of her family and be a stay-at-home mum. Though he'd been perfectly happy for her to boost the family finances by working part-time for a local office supplies company.

It was a boring job, and Carl had made occasional digs about *her* being boring as her life had shrunk to cooking, cleaning, and selling box files and printer ink.

A trickle of anger made Emma's shoulders tighten. Looking back, it seemed so unfair. But she took a deep breath and berated herself for being so dramatic.

Carl was trying to do the best for all of us, she told herself as Nessa and Lily emerged from the changing room. And here she was, running a vintage fashion business at last.

Better late than never, her time had come, though not in the way that she'd expected. She finally had her vintage clothing store, but there was no husband or daughter nearby to cheer her on.

Emma gave Nessa a smile and let her shoulders drop. This dream had been a long time in the making and it would take more than an unsupportive family, weird neighbours and unwelcoming locals to make her give it all up.

Very weird and unwelcoming neighbours, as it turned out. But they wouldn't get the better of her, and neither would a lost wedding ring.

Emma pushed her hand into her dress pocket, where the inscribed gold was nestling, and vowed that she would do her best to reunite the ring with its owner – whether unfriendly locals like Leo and Robert helped or not.

5

ROBERT

Robert despaired of his son as they went back into their dark, damp shop. Leo should have insisted that the woman next door come round, so she could see the damage that her thoughtlessness had caused, including water pooled across the floor and light switches that no longer worked.

But he'd let her get away with it, more or less. Robert felt he should say something, to point out the error of his son's ways. But he no longer had the heart for it. Not since he'd seen that dress caught in the sunlight.

'I have a headache,' he told Leo as he stood in the open shop doorway. 'Can you deal with things on your own?'

'Of course,' said Leo, concern etched across his face. 'Are you all right? You didn't seem yourself back there. I can take you home if you like.'

Robert knew he was lucky to have a son who gave two figs about him. A son to uphold the family name and the successes that he had built up. But Leo's concern made him feel even more disorientated.

Had his son realised what had spooked him in that woman's shop?

'No, I don't want you to come with me,' Robert snapped. 'There's plenty for you to be getting on with here.'

He regretted his impatience immediately when the concern in his son's eyes was replaced with... what was it? A hardness, that he was seeing more and more in his son's expression. As if a shutter had come down.

'I'll see you later,' he told his son more softly. 'Call the electrician and get him to come out today, will you?'

'Yes, Dad. What else would I do?'

Robert opened his mouth but decided against speaking. He seemed to have upset his son again, and he didn't trust himself to say anything else. He feared he'd already given too much of himself away, and in front of that woman, too.

He would walk home, he decided. Back to his large stone-built house at the top of Heaven's Cove. It was an impressive house, carefully chosen for the impression it gave to visitors and villagers, rather than for comfort.

However, its four bedrooms, two bathrooms, and conservatory which boasted a magnificent view across the village and down to the sea, were comfortable enough.

The only downside was constantly having to go up and down the steep hill which led up from the seafront. As a younger man, it hadn't bothered him. But recently the climb had started playing havoc with his knees.

He was halfway up the hill now and in need of a rest. So he sank down onto the bench that stood where a gap between the cottages lining the hill gave the best view.

There was a strong smell of the sea as he sat and massaged his kneecaps through his trousers. A seagull nearby ignored him while it ate the fish head it had probably snatched from a fishing boat at the quayside.

Another five minutes' walk and he would be home. The house would be empty and he'd rattle around the place which was far too big for one man.

But living there made him the envy of people with poky little cottages in the centre of Heaven's Cove – cottages similar to the one in which he'd been born and brought up.

When a vivid memory of himself at his mother's knee in their tiny back kitchen swam into his mind, he pushed it away – as he always did when remembrances of childhood inconveniently ambushed him.

It hadn't happened for a while. Not now childhood was so far behind him. But seeing that dress out of the blue this morning had momentarily catapulted him back several decades. Could it be the same dress? he wondered. It looked just like the one he remembered, with its unusual design and intricate embroidery. What if...

'Good day, Robert,' said a voice behind him.

When he looked up, he fought to keep his expression neutral because it was Belinda, who was pleasant enough but always spreading gossip.

What would she tell people about you if she knew the truth?

Robert swallowed as the thought made his throat constrict.

'Will you be at the residents' association AGM on Friday?' Belinda asked, smoothing down her steel-grey hair.

'Of course. When do I ever miss an important meeting?'

Robert stopped rubbing his knees because he didn't want Belinda telling people he couldn't manage the climb to his own house.

'I'll be there too,' she said. 'I don't think they'd get anything sorted without us. Especially you. You really are the backbone of this village, Robert.'

Robert smiled, his mind still elsewhere.

'How are you getting on with that woman who's opened the shop next to yours?' she asked, waving away a persistent fly.

Her question snapped him fully into the present. 'Why do you ask?'

He leaned back languidly on the bench as he spoke, trying

to give off an aura of nonchalance. There was no way that Belinda, even with her seemingly superhuman ability to wheedle out gossip, could know what had happened in that woman's shop half an hour ago… unless she'd been passing by at the time.

Robert frantically scoured his memory. She hadn't been around when he and Leo had marched into the shop. But he'd been distracted and disorientated when he'd left. Had she been loitering nearby and spotted his reaction to the wedding dress?

'I'm simply interested to know how she's settling in,' said Belinda. 'We had a long chat in the pub and it's very sad. Between you and me, she and her husband are getting divorced and she's moved to Heaven's Cove for a fresh start. Or to mend a broken heart, more like. She didn't specifically say so, but I got the impression that the divorce wasn't her idea. She seemed rather lost.'

In spite of his annoyance with Emma, Robert couldn't help feeling some sympathy for her. Starting over was hard – he should know. And being ambushed by Belinda in the pub must have been overwhelming.

He glanced at Belinda with alarm when she put her shopping bag on the ground and sat down beside him. He couldn't face being Belinda-ed today.

Robert stood up quickly, wincing as his knees complained.

'Anyway, I must get on. Lots to do.'

'Really?' Belinda's face crumpled into dismay. 'I was hoping to talk to you about the anti-social behaviour that's happening outside the village hall on Saturday nights, and the planning application for a new build on the site of the old wash house.'

'Maybe we could have a chat about that after the AGM?' Belinda's face brightened at the prospect. 'A brief chat.'

'I'll look forward to it, and I'm sure you can work your magic on these issues, as usual. This village is lucky to have you.'

'That's kind of you to say,' murmured Robert, starting to walk away.

He had a standing in this village that he'd worked long and hard for. But it had all been worth it.

He suddenly remembered the letter in his pocket that had caused such excitement after landing on his doormat this morning. The letter that contained an offer which would mark the pinnacle of his achievements in Heaven's Cove. An offer that proved all of his sacrifices had been worthwhile.

He'd meant to tell Leo all about it but he'd been sidetracked by the water flooding through from Emma's shop, and blindsided by the dress.

A memory of the ivory silk gown rippling on a hanger in her shop jolted into his mind. He closed his eyes in a bid to banish it, but the image remained sharp. Like a photograph.

What was it doing in that woman's shop? And if it was the dress he believed it to be, why had it been discarded?

Memories began to tumble through Robert's mind. Memories that he'd worked so hard to eradicate. But it seemed they were still there, lurking in the recesses and ready to strike when his defences were down.

Robert walked on, ignoring the persisting ache in his knees. The sight of his big house would settle his mind. The house that he'd earned through hard work and innovation. He'd made something of himself and that was all that mattered. He'd showed them all.

Though it was a good job that they didn't know the true story behind his success.

A cold rush of shame washed through Robert and he stumbled over a loose cobblestone.

It was no good, he realised with a sickening lurch. He'd been deceiving himself, thinking he could accept the offer that had dropped through his letterbox that morning. He would have to turn it down, even though doing so would break his heart.

But that was the only option after what he'd done so long ago. Accepting would turn a spotlight on his whole life and who knew what stones might be upturned and dark secrets released?

Robert felt tears pricking at the corners of his eyes but he kept on walking towards his grand, imposing house. Now was the time to hold his resolve and not cry about what had been lost in the past, or what he was about to lose in the future.

No one but him knew what he was capable of. And it had to stay that way.

6

EMMA

It was so beautiful up here, high above the village. Emma pulled in a breath of sea air and drank in the view: white-tipped waves curling towards the land, seagulls wheeling in a powder-blue sky and, below her, Heaven's Cove.

The village was a huddle of thatched cottages and narrow, meandering lanes, with an ancient church at its centre, surrounded by greenery.

It was much as it had been for centuries, which was comforting somehow. It suggested that current challenges – divorce, uninterested children, accidental floods and surly neighbours – were merely fleeting blips in an eternal universe.

Emma gave a rueful smile at her change of heart and turned towards Driftwood House which stood alone on top of the cliff.

It was a handsome house, with its tiled roof and white walls, and picture-perfect on a lovely evening like this. But it must seem bleak and lonely up here, when winter storms blew in and the ocean was a choppy slate grey.

Would she still be here in Heaven's Cove when winter drew in? she wondered. Maybe not if relations with her flooded neighbours soured to the point that her business was affected.

It was just her luck that the grumpy neighbours in question were part of a respected local dynasty.

How to make yourself popular with the local community – irritate the hell out of its VIPs. 'Go, Emma!' she murmured.

But this was her dream and she was determined to see it through, come hell or flood water.

Emma perched on a large boulder that edged the cliff path, put down her shopping bag and allowed herself a breather. If only Thea was here to enjoy this stunning view. She claimed to be a city girl through and through, but surely she'd be won over by the sun-kissed water and the endless sky?

Thinking of her daughter made Emma feel homesick and she pulled her phone from her shoulder bag, after checking the time.

Thea should be home in her flat by now and maybe she could fit in a call before meeting up with her boyfriend.

'Mum,' said Thea, picking up after three rings. 'Can't talk now 'cos I'm rushing. I got held up at work so left late and I'm supposed to be going out this evening, with Henry.'

'Somewhere nice?'

'Yeah, the theatre. I'll ring you tomorrow and tell you all about it.'

'OK,' said Emma, although she knew her daughter was unlikely to keep her word.

Emma had fallen into the role of 'the one who rings' and she suspected that was unlikely to change. Even though her long-term roles of loving wife, always-there mum and general family dogsbody had undergone a recent upheaval.

'How's work going?' she asked.

'Not great, but it's a job, I guess.'

'What's the problem with it?'

'Nothing. Where are you?' Thea demanded. 'What's that noise?'

Emma glanced up at the birds circling high above, surfing the air currents.

'It's birds – gulls. I'm sitting on a cliff, above the sea, in the sunshine. It's really beautiful here. You should come and visit.'

'Mmm. If I get a chance.' Emma could make out the sound of her daughter's kitchen cupboard doors opening and banging shut. 'Did you ring about anything specific? Only I need to eat soon.'

'No, nothing really. I just... well, I just wanted to make sure you're all right and to say hello.'

'Which you could do face to face if you came back to London.'

'Maybe I will one day but not for a while.'

There was a silence then Thea asked: 'How was your day?'

'Good, thanks.' Emma decided to say nothing about the flood and the run-in with Leo and his father. 'Someone left a bag of clothing outside and it included the most beautiful wedding dress I've ever seen.'

'Cool.'

'And a wedding ring.'

'Random.' There was more banging and crashing in a London kitchen far away. 'How are things going with your little charity shop?'

'It's actually a store for pre-loved vintage fashion.' Emma said it lightly because this was a battle she had no chance of winning. 'But yeah, it's going well. Early days, and all that. But I had a few people in today, looking around.'

'Did they buy anything?'

Emma pictured the lime-green dress and leather jacket that Nessa had purchased.

'Yeah, I had a few sales.'

'But not enough to keep you going.'

'Like I said, it's early days.'

Emma tried to quell the churning in her stomach. Her fledgling business had to succeed or what did she have left?

She'd rung her daughter to make herself feel better but so far that wasn't working.

Far away, in Thea's flat, a saucepan was banged onto a hob. 'You do know that Dad thinks you've lost your mind, don't you?'

Emma winced at her daughter's penchant – much like Carl's – for *telling it like it is*.

'I am aware of that fact, seeing as he said as much to me, the last time we met. How is your father?'

'Yeah, fine.' There was a silence.

Emma took a deep breath. 'Has he moved in with Selena?'

Even saying the name of the woman Carl had been having an affair with made Emma's stomach flip but, as of today, he was no longer her husband and she needed to be adult about the situation.

'Um... yeah, he has. But he's told me it's mainly for practical reasons now he doesn't have the family home to live in. It's cheaper than renting somewhere on his own.'

Carl, the last of the great romantics. Emma rolled her eyes, though there was no one around to see it. Only a circling seagull who landed at her feet and began to peck at the ground, close to her toes.

'I'm going to be late for Henry so I really do have to go now, Mum. If you're sure you're all right and there's nothing else?'

'I'm fine. I only wanted to ring to say that I love you and miss you.'

'You, too,' said Thea distractedly as her microwave oven began to beep. 'Gotta go.'

'OK, love. I'll ring' – Thea ended the call – 'you again soon.'

Emma blinked and looked towards the horizon as a breeze cooled her face. She was careful not to blame Carl for the split when she spoke about it with Thea. After all, a divorce was never completely one-sided.

But it had been Carl who'd smashed everything with his infidelity, and smashed her self-esteem in the process.

Fortunately, there were some benefits to her new situation, Emma realised. This view for one. She looked around her, at the grass bending gently in the breeze and sunlight glistening on the sea.

Thea wanted her back in London, but being here right now was more soothing for her soul. Even though her new neighbour's bizarre reaction to a donated wedding gown, and his son's high-handed manner, were playing on her mind.

7

EMMA

Emma let herself into Driftwood House and walked quietly across the tiled hall. A large grandfather clock was standing in the corner and a wide staircase led to the upper floor.

It was kind of Rosie to let her stay while she searched for more permanent accommodation in the village. Especially as Rosie had only recently become a new mum and the guesthouse was closed to guests while she adapted to her new responsibilities.

She was finding it tough, thought Emma, surprised that the house, for once, was deathly quiet – so quiet that the wind could be heard blowing around the eaves.

Emma tiptoed into the cosy living room and smiled. Rosie was slumped on the sofa, fast asleep, with baby Alfie snoring softly on her chest. He looked adorable in a bright blue babygro.

Emma went into the kitchen, put on the kettle and began to unpack the carrier bag she'd carried up from the village: fresh mackerel from the fishmonger's, dark green kale and potatoes from the mini-supermarket, and a large bar of milk chocolate. She deserved it after the day she'd had.

Emma twirled the wedding ring on her finger that Carl had placed there more than twenty years ago. Even though, as of today, she was no longer married, she couldn't face taking it off. And even if she did, there was no way she could ever give it away.

So how could the bride who'd donated her wonderful wedding dress have given away such a precious piece of jewellery? The dress was one thing, but the ring too? It must have been a mistake.

Emma put her hand in her pocket and, feeling the smooth coldness of the lost ring, vowed to return it to its owner.

Although her own love story had imploded, maybe she could play a part in someone else's. And while her ex-husband and daughter no longer needed her, this long-ago bride did – even if she didn't yet know it.

'Oh, hello. I didn't realise you were back.'

Emma pulled her hand from her pocket and spun round. Rosie had padded into the kitchen, with Alfie still snuggled into her shoulder.

'I left a little early. It's been quite a day.' Emma gestured at the kettle which was wafting curls of steam towards the ceiling. 'Would you like a cup of tea?'

Rosie nodded, her eyes huge in her pale face. 'That would be fabulous! It sounds ridiculous but I don't seem to have had time to drink today.'

Or eat either, thought Emma, noticing dark shadows under Rosie's eyes. New motherhood was exhausting. She remembered how it had been with colicky Thea. Eating, drinking, even snatching time for a two-minute loo break had seemed impossible sometimes. Life had been hectic and overwhelming. And yet the memory of that time, when she and Carl had been bleary-eyed but blissfully happy, was so bitter-sweet it made her catch her breath.

'Did you get much sleep last night?' she asked, deliberately focusing on the here and now.

When Rosie shook her head, dark, unbrushed hair fell across her shoulders.

'Not much. It wasn't Alfie's fault. He only woke up twice for a feed but, even when he was asleep, I couldn't settle. I had to keep checking on him, you know?' She bit her lip. 'Just in case he'd stopped breathing, because he's had a bit of a cold and sounds so snuffly. Daft, huh?'

'No, not daft at all. It's simply a case of understandable mum anxiety,' said Emma with a smile. But she felt a niggle of worry. Driftwood House was a beautiful place to live, but Rosie was quite isolated up here.

'I saw a notice for a mother and baby group that's held in the village hall on Wednesday mornings. Have you tried it out?' she asked, pouring hot water into the teapot.

'Not yet, but I will do,' said Rosie, wincing when Alfie stirred in his sleep. 'It still takes so long to get out of the door these days and I don't have the energy after so many broken nights.' She scanned the food on the worktop. 'That's a lot of fish, just for you.'

'I thought I could cook tonight for you and Liam, if you'd like.'

'That's really kind but you don't have to. Liam can cook for me when he gets back from the farm. His parents can't cope without him at the moment.'

'It must be very difficult for his mum.'

Rosie nodded. Her father-in-law's dementia was getting worse and Liam was spending more and more time at the farm, near Heaven's Cove beach, that his family had run for decades.

'Liam might not be back until late and you look as if you could do with a meal now.'

'I am quite hungry. I don't think I had lunch.' Rosie's eyes suddenly filled with tears and she brushed them away angrily. 'Sorry. So sorry. I'm not usually such a wimp.'

'You've got a few-months-old baby,' said Emma softly, pouring tea into Rosie's cup and placing it on the table in front of her. 'And sleep deprivation can be brutal.'

'I know, but women all over the world have babies every day, and it's not as if we didn't want to become parents. Me and Liam, we love little Alfie so much. Being a mum is great. It's wonderful. It's just…'

Rosie swallowed and bent her head over Alfie's sleeping body.

'It's just that motherhood is exhausting and occasionally terrifying.'

'That about sums it up.' When Rosie properly smiled, her eyes lit up and Emma saw her as she must usually be – full of life and drive. 'No one tells you about that side of it. Well, to be fair, people do tell you. Sort of. In code. But I didn't believe them.'

'First-time mums never do.' Emma went round the side of the table and put her arm around Rosie's shoulders. 'All I can say is that it does get easier. But it takes a while to adjust to a different kind of life. It did for me, anyway.'

'How was your life as a new mum?'

'Hard work, and I was pretty clueless when my daughter arrived. I kind of made it up as I went along.'

'I know the feeling.' Rosie smiled ruefully. 'How soon did you go back to your job after the birth?'

'I was at college in London, studying fashion and textiles, when I had Thea. In my second year.' She wrinkled her nose. 'Getting pregnant wasn't part of my plan but these things happen. Anyway, I always meant to go back and finish my studies but, you know how it is, life gets in the way and I never did.'

'That's a shame.'

'It is.'

Emma picked up her own cup of tea and took a sip. It was well over twenty years since she'd made the decision to leave college, and she was surprised by how long the tendrils of regret had persisted. She'd so wanted to return but Carl had been against it, and she'd needed his help with childcare to make it work.

'That explains your venture into vintage clothing' – Rosie waved a hand at Emma – 'and your fabulous fashion sense. Where did you get that amazing dress?'

Emma ran her hands across the navy-blue crepe. 'It's from the 1940s. I found it in a flea market in east London a while ago. And the belt is 1950s, I think. I like to mix and match different decades.'

'You always look fabulous, whereas I, at the moment...' Rosie glanced down at her sweatshirt and tracksuit bottoms.

'You look like a tired new mum, but that will change. I promise you.'

'I know.' Rosie planted a soft kiss on Alfie's bald head. 'Anyway, I'm glad that you finally managed to put the studies that you did complete to good use and open the shop in the village.'

'Better late than never. Though today was a bit of a disaster.'

'Tell me. Anything to take my mind off of milk and nappies.'

Emma recounted the tale of the flooding, being careful not to blame Maisie. If people in Heaven's Cove thought Emma was the one who'd been daft enough to leave the plug in and the tap on, so be it. She could take the hit, whereas Maisie... maybe not so much.

'Oops, that sounds stressful,' said Rosie as Emma's story came to a close.

'It was a very stressful day.'

And you don't know the half of it. Emma pushed her wedding ring round and round on her finger. She was tempted to blurt out to Rosie, *Also, I am officially divorced as of today*. But the poor girl had enough on her plate without hearing about Emma's marital failure, and Emma wasn't sure that she could say it out loud without crying, anyway.

So, instead she said: 'I feel terrible about the damage to the shop next door.'

'I imagine that Robert took it well,' said Rosie, raising an eyebrow.

'He was absolutely delighted.' Emma attempted a sardonic grin. 'What do you know about him and his son? Nessa said you were a good person to ask about them.'

'When did you see Nessa?'

'She came into the shop this morning with her daughter and bought a dress and a jacket. Are you good friends?'

'The best, and she knows about kids so I feel very safe when she's around. She was so helpful during Alfie's early days but she has Lily and a job and a partner so I insisted that she spend less time here.'

Rosie winced when Alfie stirred and checked he was still asleep before continuing.

'Anyway, back to your new neighbours, Robert is a bigwig in the village. A self-made man, as he never fails to mention, who's involved in just about everything that goes on around here. Just between you and me, he can be a little overbearing at times, but he's fine.

'Leo is gentler but I don't know a lot about him. I've missed out on a lot of gossip because I moved away from Heaven's Cove for a few years. But I think he was married or engaged or something, though he isn't now.

'That's all I know because his father is so... I don't know... *everywhere* and larger than life, Leo seems a bit in his shadow. He's kind though, I think.'

Not when he's haranguing people about bags left in the

street. Emma took another sip of tea. 'What's their background then? Have he and his dad always lived around here?'

'Robert was brought up a few miles away, in a tiny hamlet called Heaven's Brook. In a very modest cottage, according to Belinda. He's got an amazing house now at the top of the village. Have you met Belinda yet?' When Emma nodded, Rosie smiled. 'Of course you have. She'd have made a beeline for you, as a newbie in the village.'

'It was Belinda who told me that Robert's wife had died a while ago.'

'That's right. I went to her funeral at the local church, although I didn't know her that well. Leo looked distraught, poor man, and I felt so sorry for him. I know what it feels like to lose a mum.' Rosie stopped and cleared her throat. 'Robert didn't seem as distressed, though it's hard to tell, isn't it? People don't always show emotion in the same way. Though, by all accounts, their marriage wasn't terribly—' Rosie broke off, her face flushing. 'Sorry. I'm turning into Belinda. I shouldn't gossip.'

'Don't say anything you're not comfortable with sharing,' said Emma, although she desperately wanted to know what gossip Rosie had been about to impart.

Their marriage wasn't terribly... what? Terribly happy, presumably. Emma knew what that felt like, but Robert and his wife had stuck it out until the end. Presumably she'd never discovered flirty texts from a much younger woman on his phone.

'Are you sure you don't mind cooking?'

Emma blinked, too caught up in her memories to take in what Rosie was saying. 'Sorry? I didn't catch that.'

'I said that you really don't need to cook for all of us.'

'I know, but I'd like to, as a thank you. It's so good of you to take me in while I'm looking for somewhere to live in the village. Especially when you've got your hands full at the moment.'

Rosie shrugged – gently, so as not to wake Alfie. 'You're welcome. To be honest, there's some selfishness involved because I feel safer having another mum around. Plus, it's such a lovely story, how you chose Heaven's Cove for your new business.'

Not so much lovely as potentially crazy, thought Emma.

When she was growing up in London, a friend's mother had often waxed lyrical about Heaven's Cove which was where her family came from. She'd talked about the village's cliff, topped by a single house, and its sandy beach and thatched cottages. And young Emma had become quite obsessed with the place.

She'd found a book about Devon in the library and would stare for ages at the photos of stormy seas, cottage gardens and sweeping moors.

Her obsession had faded over the years, however it had lingered enough that, when Thea was small, Emma had brought her here, to Heaven's Cove, on holiday. And, in a bizarre way, it had felt like coming home.

She and Thea had enjoyed a wonderfully happy time. But Carl had complained that the village was 'claustrophobic and boring' so they'd never returned as a family, and Emma had put the place out of her mind... until her marriage imploded and her dream of running a vintage clothing business had resurfaced.

That was when vivid images of Heaven's Cove began to pop into her mind and, keen to distract herself from heartbreak, she'd hatched a plan to move to the village.

It was spontaneous and impulsive, and her family had thought she was having a breakdown. But she'd seen the move as a breakthrough – a way of distancing herself from London and heartbreak and thwarted ambitions.

And when a search online had revealed that a shop in

Herring Lane, Heaven's Cove, was vacant and in need of a tenant, it had seemed like a sign. Fate was pushing her forward.

'Tell me again about how you met my mum,' said Rosie. 'I know I was there, but no one ever talks about Mum any more, which is sad. Sorry, do you mind?'

'Not at all,' said Emma, who could see how Rosie felt the loss of her mother ever more keenly now that she was a mum herself.

She thought back to that halcyon family holiday twenty years ago.

'I was walking with Thea, just out there' – she tilted her head towards the kitchen window. 'I'd gone in search of the house on the cliff that I'd heard so much about, and we were having a lovely time, but then it began to rain. And when it rains up here…'

'Oh, it rains.' Rosie laughed. 'It comes at you horizontally and there's no escape. You must have been soaked.'

'We were, but your mum was here, at Driftwood House, and she offered us shelter. We were drenched so she got us towels and made us drinks and she and I sat and chatted for ages. She was such a lovely woman.'

'She really was,' said Rosie, blinking back more tears.

'Then, when we'd dried off, she drove us back to our holiday flat in the middle of the village. She was incredibly kind.'

'I remember that day so well,' said Rosie, stroking her infant's head. 'A young girl suddenly appearing on my doorstep was very exciting. I got a bit lonely up here sometimes.'

Emma remembered Rosie back then, too – a beautiful child, with serious, russet-brown eyes, showing her and Thea around her amazing house that sat alone on top of the cliff.

'Your mum and I kept in touch for a while, and I never forgot her or this stunning house. I googled it when I decided to return to Heaven's Cove and saw it had been turned into a guesthouse. I hoped I might see your mum again.'

'Wouldn't that have been lovely.'

'It would. I was so shocked to hear that she'd passed away.' Emma reached across the table and patted Rosie's hand. 'It's really kind of you to take me in, just like your mum did all those years ago, though for longer this time. I promise I'll be out of your hair soon.'

'There's no rush. I really like the company, and you feel like a link with my mum.'

Emma swallowed. It was so sad that Rosie's mum, Sofia, was missing out on the joy of being a grandparent to Alfie, and was not around to help her daughter through the early months of motherhood.

Emma would like to repay Sofia's kindness to her all those years ago by supporting Rosie now. Though the advice she could offer, and cooking the occasional meal, seemed inadequate.

'I'm sure your mum would be very proud of how you're coping,' she said.

Rosie's eyes brimmed over with tears, but she smiled, and Emma felt glad that she was here. She could never take the place of Sofia, but it felt good to be useful again.

When Alfie began to stir, Rosie went off to change his nappy, and Emma began to cook.

As she sliced and boiled the kale and fried the fish in butter, she tried not to think about work tomorrow.

She felt awful about the flood and prayed that the shop next door wouldn't have to close while repairs were made. She would feel obliged to help out as much as she could, even though that might mean spending more time with Leo and his unpleasant father. It was all getting very complicated.

'Dad thinks you've lost your mind.' Thea's words echoed through her head, and Emma couldn't help but wonder if maybe her ex-husband might have a point.

She slid browned mackerel onto Rosie's plate and thought

again about Robert and Leo. The shock and fear on Robert's face when he'd seen the donated wedding dress had been visceral – it was as if he'd seen a ghost.

But whatever had spooked him so much was none of her business, Emma told herself firmly as she drained the vegetables. She had quite enough to cope with in her new life without getting embroiled in another family's secrets. Robert's intriguing reaction to the beautiful dress would have to remain a mystery.

8
LEO

Leo knelt down and placed both palms on the wooden floorboards. They felt damp and there was a slight aroma of mildew, but they seemed drier than they'd been yesterday, after he'd mopped up the last of the water.

'It's not great, mate, is it?' called Terry, the electrician, from the back of the shop. 'But I don't think it has been for some time. I've had a look at your fuse box and let's just say that things are not looking peachy.'

'Just do the best you can,' said Leo, wishing he'd found a less pessimistic electrician. Terry had a reputation for approaching every job as an insurmountable problem. Though, on the plus side, he was good at his job and he'd been available at short notice.

'That flood's done a right number on you,' shouted Terry, following this declaration with a tsunami of tuts.

Leo got to his feet and wiped the knees of his jeans which now sported damp patches. The sooner Terry was done, the better.

As he wiped at his legs, his hand knocked against the letter his father had left behind yesterday, and it fluttered to the floor.

Leo picked it up and glanced at the envelope. His father's address was typed and the envelope had been opened. It was another bill, no doubt, which would need to be paid quickly. Shop finances were already iffy and they couldn't afford any late payment penalties.

Leo pulled a folded piece of thick, cream paper from the envelope and swiftly realised it wasn't a bill at all – it was a letter. He scanned it quickly and then read it again, more slowly this time as his jaw dropped.

Rather than a demand for money, this letter was putting a proposition to his father. One that he could not refuse.

Leo read it for the third time, properly taking in the information. It seemed that his father was being awarded an MBE for the extensive voluntary work he'd carried out over the years and the difference he'd made to his local community. Someone must have nominated him for the prestigious award, and now his father would be included in the King's Birthday Honours.

Leo whistled through his teeth. Robert would receive his Member of the Order of the British Empire award from the royal family at an investiture at Buckingham Palace, and Leo could already picture how proud he would look on the day.

'Wow, well done, Dad,' he breathed.

He did a quick search online on his phone and discovered that his father's nomination would have been one of many approved by an honours committee, with the final list of recipients going to the Prime Minister and the King.

Medals didn't mean much to him, but his father would be over the moon with the official recognition.

The part of the letter that asked if his father would accept the award made Leo grin. His father would be champing at the bit to get his hands on it.

A picture of the medal online showed a silver cross with a red ribbon, which Leo could imagine his father wearing pinned to his suit during Remembrance Day activities in the village.

Actually, he could imagine his father wearing it every day. He'd probably pin it to his pyjamas before bed.

And he'd relish being able to put 'MBE' after his name when he signed letters and documents. His father had always stressed the importance of 'being someone', and this award would be the icing on the cake for him.

Such good news seemed like a ray of sunshine amongst a gloomy few days and Leo's grin widened. He was surprised his father hadn't mentioned the honour, though it was probably the exciting 'something else' he'd been about to tell Leo about yesterday, before he was side-tracked by the flood.

The locked door of the shop suddenly rattled.

'We're closed,' Leo called out. 'The sign's up saying that we're closed following a flood.'

But the person at the door went on rattling until he put the letter down and went to investigate. He peered through the glass and breathed out slowly.

Emma, that annoying woman from next door, the one who'd caused this whole problem, was standing outside, and she was holding a mop and bucket. He opened the door a crack.

'Yes? Can I help you?'

Emma shifted from foot to foot. 'I was wondering if I might be able to help with the clean-up. I assumed you wouldn't want my help yesterday, not after things got a little... heated between us. But I wanted to offer my services today. I'm here and ready to help.'

'You really don't need to.'

'I know, but I'd like to.'

Leo was minded to refuse and close the door. It would only wind his father up if Emma got involved. But there was something about her standing on the doorstep, looking so earnest in jeans and a '60s-style psychedelic-print top, that got under his skin. Plus, he'd just had good news which had knocked some of the grump out of him.

He opened the door wide.

'OK. Come on in. Who's looking after your shop while you're here?'

'Maisie.' Emma grimaced. 'She's promised to come and get me if there are any problems. Um… is your father here?'

'Not at the moment,' said Leo, noticing a flicker of relief in Emma's blue eyes.

The day's early sun had disappeared behind cloud, making the shop extra gloomy, and he flicked the light switch before remembering it was a waste of time.

'I didn't realise that you didn't have any electricity at all,' said Emma, a deep line appearing between her eyebrows.

Before Leo could reply, a shout reverberated from the back of the shop: 'They're completely wrecked.'

'That's Terry,' he explained. 'The electrician. He's not the cheeriest of sorts.'

Emma's face was now creased with concern. 'I'm so sorry. I feel terrible about what's happened and the effect it's going to have on your business.'

And she looked so distraught, Leo felt a flash of sympathy for her.

'Our electrics were outdated anyway and needed a revamp,' he confessed. 'So it's given us a push, I suppose.'

Emma gave him a grateful smile. 'Though I don't suppose you'd have had the electrical work done during trading hours.'

'No, that's not ideal.'

When he noticed that Emma was glancing at the honours letter to his father, that he'd left out on the side, he grabbed it quickly.

'Anyway,' he said, folding the letter back into its envelope, 'the water's gone now but there's still cleaning up to do.'

'OK. Where shall I start?'

When Emma looked around, Leo's heart sank as he saw this shop that he knew so well through her eyes. It was old-fashioned, with its dark-wood counter, old-style mannequins dressed in formal suits and open drawers of cashmere socks and silk ties of every hue.

It had been like this for decades. He remembered being in here as a child. Sometimes it had been the only way to connect with his father, who was working seven days a week to make the business a success.

'I've not been in here yet, though I've put my nose to the window. It's very traditional and...' Emma looked around, her eyes wide, 'cultured.'

Leo suppressed a smile because his father would love that review of his life's work. He liked to think of himself as a cultured man.

'Are you kept busy?' asked Emma, running her fingers across a pair of moss-green socks. 'Do you have a lot of customers?'

The truth was, not so many these days. The clientele was gradually dying off. Literally, in many cases, which meant Robert and Leo were spending an increasing amount of time attending the funerals of long-time customers. People Leo had known since childhood.

And the gap they left wasn't being filled. Younger people didn't want to frequent such an outdated store and, despite Leo's entreaties, his father was doing his best to ignore the online shopping revolution completely. But Robert wouldn't thank him for spreading that about.

'We have enough customers,' Leo told Emma enigmatically.

Though enough for what? Enough to run him off his feet? Enough to keep abreast of the hideously high business rates? Enough to keep him from pondering on the different routes that his life might have taken?

The answer to all three was no, but Emma had accepted his answer and was sweeping her hand across the floorboards.

'Oh dear. They're still damp,' she said, straightening up, her forehead pinched. How old was she? he wondered. Probably a little younger than him – early forties maybe? 'So where did the water come through from my shop?'

'Follow me and I'll show you.'

They made their way to the back of the store and Leo pointed out the corner where water had bubbled over the skirting board.

'That's where we noticed the water coming in, though not, unfortunately, before it got into the electrics.'

'You can say that again, mate,' grumbled Terry, who was in the corner, on his hands and knees, with his head in the fuse box. 'I haven't seen anything this bad since...' He sat back on his haunches to think about it. 'Yeah, it must be 2022, at old Bert's place near the castle ruins. His electrics were totally fried when water breached the sea wall and flooded his basement.' He tutted. 'Not that your electrics are far off, mate.'

'All I can say, again, is that I'm very sorry,' said Emma beside him.

'Which is all well and good, but it doesn't actually help much.'

He knew he sounded sharp, but Terry was winding him up, and anxiety about how he would make his end-of-month figures with the shop closed for a few days meant he was mega cranky.

Emma's expression darkened and she folded her arms. 'I appreciate that my apology doesn't help in any practical sense, which is why I'm here in person offering my help. I'm afraid I can't rewind time and make what's happened not happen. It was a mistake, at the end of the day.'

'I just don't get how you could leave the plug in the basin, the tap on, and a towel blocking the overflow pipe.'

Emma looked at him as if she had something important to say. Another fulsome but useless apology perhaps? But then she shook her head.

'It's happened and I'll do whatever I can to help sort it out.' She swallowed. 'Will it cost much to put right, do you think?'

'I have no idea. It depends on the extent of the damage that Terry discovers.'

'I'll pay for it, obviously.'

'That goes without saying.'

Leo didn't like the tone he was taking with Emma, and he presumed she wasn't swimming in cash, having just opened a brand-new business. But he was so worried about the impact of prolonged closure on sales.

Emma pursed her lips, her cheeks going pink. 'Look, there's no need to be like that. I appreciate this makes life difficult for you, but you're not the only one who's not having the best of times right now.'

When Emma's bottom lip wobbled, Leo felt ashamed for making her cry. He wanted to step forward and say that none of it mattered. But there was too much awkwardness between them, and the truth was that it did matter. A lot.

But what was happening in her life, he wondered, that meant she wasn't having 'the best of times'? He suddenly noticed that her left hand was bare. There was no longer a wedding ring on her fourth finger, the one she'd been fiddling with yesterday by the wishing well.

'Let's leave it,' he said. 'Like you said, it was an accident that can't be undone, so it's a case of managing the aftermath.'

Emma nodded. 'Sure. Put me to work.'

An hour later, between the two of them, they'd scrubbed tide marks off skirting boards, checked stock for damp and opened windows to air away the musty smell.

The hard work made him hot and, after a while, Leo pulled off the Aran sweater he'd thrown on that morning. When he noticed Emma staring at him, he tugged at the bottom of his T-shirt, worried it had ridden up, revealing bare skin.

'Is that a Metallica T-shirt?' she asked, leaning her mop against the wall.

Leo glanced down at the faded black T-shirt, one of his favourites even though it was ancient. 'Yeah, that's right.'

'Do you like them?'

Leo folded his arms. 'Don't I look like a Metallica fan?'

'Not at all. I'd put you down as more a fan of Beethoven's Symphony Number Five.'

'Then you'd be surprised,' he said, wondering if Emma viewed him as old-fashioned and boring. If that was the case, it was disappointing, though he wasn't sure why he cared.

Emma went back to work but, after ten minutes, she stopped again and brushed hair from her eyes.

'How long have you worked with your father?'

'Ever since I left university.'

'What did you study?'

'Economics.'

'Didn't you want to become a fancy economist or something similar?'

Leo was growing tired of Emma asking lots of questions.

'That would have been nice,' he admitted. 'But my father needed help in the shop and it was sort of understood that I would take over the business long-term one day. This business is his pride and joy. What about you?' he asked, feeling he should probably show some interest.

'I worked part-time for years, for an office supplies company.'

'Really?'

Emma stopped wiping down paintwork and stared at him. 'Yeah, really. Why?'

Leo wasn't sure why his remark had hit a nerve. 'I thought you'd be doing something more creative. In the arts perhaps. It's quite a leap from office supplies to running a second-hand clothes shop.'

Emma frowned at him. 'Pre-loved vintage clothing. I've always loved fashion. I studied it at college.'

'That would explain your individual fashion sense.'

Emma smiled. 'You say individual fashion sense. My daughter, Thea, describes it as my perimenopausal cry for help.'

Leo laughed at that. 'Charming! Actually, I think you look —' Leo swallowed because, although Emma looked attractive in her faded blue jeans and vibrant vintage top, it would be far too personal to say so. 'Nice,' he finished lamely.

'Nice?' Emma raised an eyebrow. 'That's faint praise worthy of Thea.'

'How many children do you have?' asked Leo, keen to move the conversation on.

'Just the one, who's grown up now. Thea lives in London and works in a nursery. I live here now and I'm div—' She stumbled over her words and tried again. 'I'm divorced.'

Leo gestured at her hand. 'I noticed that you were wearing a ring yesterday and now you're not.'

He immediately kicked himself for mentioning that. Did it look odd that he'd noticed her wedding ring? As if he went round, sizing up women according to their marital status?

But Emma simply shrugged. 'I finally got round to taking it off last night. Thought I might as well, seeing as my divorce became final yesterday.'

'Yesterday?'

When Emma nodded, Leo had a pang of regret about marching into her shop, with his father in tow. That must have been the last thing she'd needed on such a difficult day. Though what else could they have done, with water coming through their dividing wall?

'Anyway,' Emma said briskly. 'Thea and my ex-husband are off doing their own things so now seemed a good time to make my dream come true.'

'The dream being...?'

'The shop,' said Emma, her forehead creasing as if he was being particularly obtuse.

Which he probably was. His head was too filled with business worries, excitement over his father's award, sad memories of his mum, and Terry's incessant grumbling to concentrate properly.

'I wish that I was getting a few more customers in,' Emma added. 'Though I know it's early days.'

She was probably wishing for an influx of customers when he'd seen her at the old well yesterday morning, thought Leo. So that her dream of running a shop and living happily ever after could fully come true.

He looked around him at the dark, varnished wood and spooky mannequins, and the pile of bills to be paid in the corner. Well, good luck with that.

'Do you remember the beautiful wedding dress that was hanging in my shop when you and your father came round yesterday?' she asked suddenly. Leo nodded, thrown by the swift change of subject. 'It was amongst the clothes left in the leather holdall that you complained about.'

'Who does it belong to?' Leo inquired, his interest piqued. He knew nothing about wedding gowns but it was clear to anyone that this dress was something special.

'That's just it. I have no idea. There was no name left with the bag and nothing in any of the other clothes to give me a clue.' She pressed her lips together. 'Actually, I thought that maybe your dad recognised it? He reacted very oddly when he saw it.'

'Not really. He was fine,' said Leo, even though his father's bizarre reaction had been impossible to miss, and he'd been wondering about it ever since. 'My mum died two years ago this week, so maybe the dress brought back memories of her.'

He didn't think that was the reason at all – his parents'

marriage hadn't been a particularly close or happy one. But talking about it didn't feel right.

'If that's the case, I hope it didn't upset him too much.'

Not as much as a shop floor covered in water, thought Leo. But he'd made enough digs for one morning, and clearly Emma was dealing with her own problems. So he kept his mouth shut.

'Actually...' Emma bit her lip. 'I found something else unusual in that bag.' She pushed her hand into her pocket and pulled something from it. 'Look.'

Leo stared at the yellow-gold ring lying in the palm of her hand.

'Did you say that was in the bag too?'

'Yes, at the bottom.'

'May I?'

Leo picked up the ring which felt heavier than he was expecting. The gold was worn and smooth and, inside, the hallmark had almost been rubbed away. But an inscription was just visible: *B & R Aeternum*.

B & R, the initials of his parents: Barbara and Robert.

'It looks like a wedding ring,' said Emma, standing close. 'But I can't believe that whoever donated the dress meant to donate the ring as well. It must have fallen into the bag by mistake but I have no idea how to return it.' She hesitated. 'Do you think that maybe your dad might know who the ring belongs to?'

'Why would he?'

'I thought he might know who the ring's owner is if, perhaps, he *did* recognise the dress?'

'My father can recognise a Savile Row suit at thirty paces but I'm not sure that wedding dresses are his thing. Anyway, don't you think the woman this ring belongs to would have come looking for it by now, if she'd dropped it into the bag by accident?'

'Maybe, but there was nothing in the bag to say who she is

and the bag appeared outside my shop overnight. Maybe she doesn't want anyone to know who she is. Perhaps it's a secret.'

Leo snorted out loud at that. He couldn't help it.

'A secret?'

Honestly, this strange woman who'd suddenly appeared in their lives had her head in the clouds, with her talk of dreams and secrets, and her visits to the wishing well.

Emma's cheeks flushed pink as she took back the ring and pushed it deep into her trouser pocket.

'I can help for a little longer and then I'd better get back to my shop.'

They worked in silence for several minutes until the phone rang. It was a call from a customer who'd heard via the grapevine – no doubt Belinda, who'd stuck her nose to the glass and peered inside earlier – that the shop was closed.

Leo reassured his customer that the closure was likely to be short-lived. But there was bad news when Terry finally stopped fiddling around at the back of the shop and marched through to the front.

Emma got up from her knees where she'd been wiping the floor and brushed dust from her jeans.

'What's the verdict on the electrics?' Leo asked.

'Just like I thought, they're kaput,' said Terry. He pushed a hand through his thinning hair and gave a loud sniff. 'Knackered. Wrecked. Completely zapped.'

Leo was taken aback. Even by Terry's pessimistic standards, this was more depressing than usual.

'How long will it take to put right?'

Terry sucked air through his teeth. 'Well, I'm going to need to replace a fair bit of the ancient stuff so... a week—'

'A week!' exclaimed Leo. 'I can't be out of action for a week. I have outstanding orders to fulfil and new orders to bring in. I can't close the shop for a whole week.'

Terry shook his head. 'What I was about to say was that the

work would take a week *or so*. It might be just over a week actually. Once you start a job like this, you're never sure what you might find along the way. And this is a very old shop with electrics to match so who knows what horrors are lurking.'

Leo stared at him, trying to gauge if this was Terry's usual pessimism talking, or a sensible estimation of the problem and the time it would take.

'I'll get Perry's lad in to help me,' Terry continued. 'I can put together an estimate for you. To be fair, this work is long overdue. Your electrics are in a shocking state.' He paused, his face deadpan. 'No pun intended.'

Leo rubbed his temples because his head was beginning to ache. His father would be incandescent at the thought of the business closing for so long. The two of them even took holidays at different times so trading never ceased.

'Couldn't the shop remain open while the work is being done?' Emma asked.

Leo had forgotten she was still there. He glared at her, suddenly furious anew about the trouble she'd caused.

'I wouldn't recommend it,' said Terry. 'We'll need to pull down parts of the ceiling so there's going to be noise and dust. And, it goes without saying, no electricity.'

'Which means you're going to lose custom,' said Emma, turning to Leo, who tried to keep his face neutral, even though she was now stating the obvious.

'I'm afraid so,' he said levelly. 'Plus, the book containing all the numbers for our customers who are due to collect items has been soaked and the writing is mostly illegible.'

'Surely you've got that information backed up on computer.'

Yes! That's what he'd suggested to his father so many times. But Robert was adamant: 'We're not the sort of business that stores information in the cloud, whatever that is. Businesses get hacked, but that will never happen to us.'

He'd insisted they write everything down on paper which

was fine... until it wasn't. Until a woman leaving a bathroom tap on overnight managed to wreak the havoc that keyboard hackers never could.

'No,' said Leo deliberately. 'We don't have that information on computer.'

'I see. And how will not having that information impact on your business?'

'It means we have people booked in for fittings and to collect items and we don't know who or when so can't let them know that the shop is closed.'

Emma stared at her feet for a moment while Leo silently berated himself for not insisting that his father become more computer savvy. Leo had been planning to shift over to a completely computer-based system as soon as his father retired.

'Could you run your business out of my shop for a few days?'

Emma's question took Leo by surprise.

'How would that work?'

'You could move stock into my store and be there for your customers. A notice put up in your shop window would point them to mine. And they wouldn't exactly have far to go.'

She gave him a weak smile while Leo took in her offer.

It might work. He tapped his toe on the damp floor, thinking. His father wouldn't like it but what other options did they have? It would keep the business ticking over while the repair work was happening. And it would only be for a few days. Plus, she owed them big time.

'I guess that might be acceptable,' he said slowly.

It would mean working in close proximity to a woman who didn't much like him, but they could keep themselves to themselves. As much as they could in a relatively small space.

Emma pulled back her shoulders. 'Great. Let's do that then. I can help you move your stock next door. I just need a couple of hours to make some space for you.'

'Right,' said Leo, still thinking hard. *Right* sounded rather ungracious so he managed to add 'thanks', still wondering how to break the news to his father, who would see it as consorting with the enemy.

Though, fortunately, Robert Jacobson-Jones MBE would be so cock-a-hoop about his award, that might take the sting out of it.

'Yes,' he said. 'Let's do it. I hope it'll only be for a week, tops.'

Emma swallowed. 'Great. Maisie's been worryingly quiet so I'd better get back.'

Her face had paled. She was apparently regretting her offer to share shop space but, after causing the flood, she'd have to put up with it. And so, thought Leo, would he.

'Shall we begin our arrangement tomorrow?' he asked.

'Yes, OK. That'll give me time to sort things out.' She collected her bucket and mop and looked back as she got to the shop door. 'What about meeting here at eight o'clock tomorrow morning? I can let you in and help you to get set up, before we have any customers.'

'Eight it is, then,' said Leo, crossing his fingers that it would only be for a week, however pessimistic Terry was being. He felt quite sure that neither he nor Emma would be able to stand any longer than that in each other's company.

9

EMMA

'I hope it'll only be for a week, tops.' Me too, mate. Me too, thought Emma, stopping at the wishing well on her way home. After fishing in her purse, she dropped a pound coin into the water far below and backed up her hope with a wish.

'My wish is that Terry gets a move on so Leo ends up sharing my shop space for as little time as possible.'

She walked away a few steps before doubling back. 'Oh, and also, I wish that the electrical work doesn't cost loads of money or I'll be out of business before my shop's been open a month. I'll never live it down with Carl or Thea, who already think I've lost the plot.

'And finally' – although three wishes was excessive for a pound – 'I wish I could find the owner of the lost wedding ring.'

That last wish was because Emma didn't have a clue where to start searching.

She looked around her nervously. It would be just her luck for Leo to be loitering nearby. She could still hear his snort of disbelief when she'd suggested that the owner of the ring and wedding dress might be trying to keep her identity a secret. He'd clearly thought she was being ridiculous.

Fortunately, there was no one in sight, but Emma still felt foolish. She'd just spent time pleading with the gods of a wishing well in a tiny Devon village. Maybe her family was right about her and she'd soon be returning to London, with her tail between her legs.

Money-wise, she'd definitely be in big trouble if Robert and Leo made her pay for all of the electrical work being done in their shop.

Leo had intimated that a lot of the work had needed doing anyway, because their electrics were so out of date. She didn't want to end up paying for that too, but the thought of arguing about her share with the Jacobson-Jones duo made her heart sink. They weren't easy people to talk to, let alone reason with.

Emma walked on through the village, focusing on the sights and sounds around her: waves lapping against the stone quayside, a sharp aroma of vinegar as she passed the fish and chip shop, blobs of melting ice cream on the pavement.

But her thoughts kept returning to her encounter with Leo earlier that day. She'd felt so nervous knocking on the door of his shop, mop in hand and ready to help clear up the mess that Maisie had made.

She'd considered sending Maisie to do it but she didn't have any faith that the teenager would do a good job. And the last thing she needed was to antagonise Leo and his father any further.

So she'd left Maisie in charge of her shop instead, which could have been disastrous but, as it turned out, had been fine. Maisie had even made a couple of sales which perhaps proved that she worked better when left to her own devices.

Leo's shop had been a revelation: a gloomy space with ghostly mannequins in tailored suits, with no features on their freakishly smooth faces.

And Leo had been rather a revelation himself. Having not seen him in anything but a full suit, including waistcoat, today he'd been rocking faded blue jeans and a burgundy Aran jumper.

Obviously he didn't wear a suit at all times. He'd hardly wear one to bed. But seeing him in casual jeans had given her a jolt. And they weren't dad jeans either. They fitted well in all the right places, she couldn't help but notice.

What *did* he wear to bed? Emma wondered. Pyjamas, perhaps, like Carl always did. Or just underpants, maybe.

'Stop thinking!' she told herself as she began to climb the path that led up the cliff, towards Driftwood House. But images of Leo were tumbling through her brain. She pictured his dark hair, usually carefully brushed away from his face, becoming increasingly unkempt as he cleaned the shop. A large lock had fallen across his face and he'd pushed it away with the back of his hand.

And then there was the T-shirt – black, faded and sporting a Metallica logo which had surprised her even more than the jeans. He was the last person she'd have taken for a heavy metal fan. Apart from his father, who – Emma would put money on it – had never been near a mosh pit in his life.

She'd been relieved that Robert wasn't around this morning, but maybe he was somewhere celebrating his good news. She hadn't meant to pry into the older man's business but it wasn't her fault that the letter was left lying around and she'd caught sight of it.

Robert Jacobson-Jones MBE. It was impressive, Emma had to admit, but he was still a peculiar man. Leo had been less than forthcoming about his father's reaction to the wedding dress in her shop. But he'd thought it was odd, too. She'd seen that in his hazel eyes.

Emma stumbled slightly as loose stones shifted underfoot. She needed to stop thinking about Leo and his father and pay more attention to the cliff path or she might slip and fall into the sea far below.

Though that might be preferable to spending the next week sharing shop space with good-looking Leo. Emma stopped walking and finally admitted it to herself. Yes, Leo Jacobson-Jones was good-looking, albeit in a rather grumpy way.

That might prove distracting, but fortunately she was a peri-menopausal divorcee who was off men for life.

Instead, Leo's stay in her shop would only be distracting because he was likely to snipe and be moody and get on Maisie's nerves. It would be like trying to keep the peace with two teenagers around. But there was nothing else for it.

'I will survive,' said Emma out loud, before launching into a chorus of the song which startled a passing seagull that screeched in alarm.

She'd scurried away from work this afternoon because she hadn't wanted to bump into either Leo or his father. She couldn't face them which was ridiculous seeing as she was a grown woman.

There were echoes in the way she was dealing with the two men, Emma realised. Echoes of her old life during which she'd placated and accommodated and rarely stood her ground.

She'd vowed that this new start would be different. She would be different. Yet here she was, falling into old patterns from the start.

Emma came to a halt and looked out across the churning ocean which was banded shades of blue, from indigo at the horizon to pale aqua near land.

The vastness of the seascape and its enduring regularity – the tide came in and the tide went out, whatever madness was happening in the world – made her feel calmer. And braver.

She'd wished for courage yesterday at the village well but there was no point waiting for bravery to magically descend upon her. The only person who could make that happen was her.

The change starts now, she thought, shielding her eyes from the sun which had just peeped through cloud and was lighting a golden path across the water.

She would stand up to Leo and Robert, pay for the flood damage out of her meagre savings, and then have as little as possible to do with them.

She would also, somehow, track down the owner of the lost ring and maybe, in the process, find out what had spooked Robert so much about the wedding dress. However much she'd tried to forget his reaction, it still intrigued her.

But first, and foremost, there was the next week to get through. That was likely to be challenging enough.

10

ROBERT

Robert pushed his plate across the table and sat back in his chair. The house was very quiet this evening. Usually he had Radio 4 on in the background but he didn't have the heart for a comedy show or documentary tonight.

He missed Barbara. It was funny because they'd driven each other mad when the two of them were in the house together. Their marriage, though convenient in many ways, hadn't been the happiest.

Yet, now she was gone, he found himself hankering after even the things that had once irritated him about her: her love for loud, discordant jazz music, her stiletto shoes that made dents in the parquet flooring, the way she licked her finger and used it to pick up crumbs on her plate.

His mother had picked up crumbs that way too. And perhaps it was the similarity that had got under his skin. But his mother was gone now as well.

Robert steepled his fingers beneath his chin and thought about the whirlwind of emotion he'd experienced since receiving that letter, and then unexpectedly spotting the wedding dress that he would never forget.

Deliberately blocking out the dress, Robert relived the moment he'd opened the fateful letter after it had dropped onto his doormat.

Barbara would have been over the moon to know that he was being awarded an MBE, just as he'd been overjoyed on first reading about it.

So what a shame that he had to turn down such a prestigious honour. What a tragedy that transgressions from the past were never truly eradicated, however hard you worked and however much of a success you made of your life.

Robert got to his feet and started clearing away his half-eaten meal. He didn't want to sit here thinking about things long gone that could not be changed.

The sound of the front door closing made him jump and the plate he was putting into the dishwasher clattered down, onto the food-smeared cutlery.

'Dad?' Leo's voice echoed from the hall. 'Where are you?'

'Kitchen!' Robert called out, bending over to dab flecks of mashed potato from his slipper with a piece of kitchen towel. He straightened up as his son came into the room. 'What are you doing here, so late?'

'I wanted to call round, to see you.'

'You could have had dinner with me if you'd come round earlier.'

Leo glanced at the remnants of Robert's meal that he'd scraped into a plastic container, ready for the food-waste bin. 'It doesn't look as if you ate much.'

'Not hungry,' said Robert brusquely, wondering why his son had really called in.

Leo's cottage was on the other side of the village and he rarely made unplanned visits. He'd called by regularly after Barbara's death but had soon realised that Robert was coping well and his visits had tailed off. There was no particular need when they saw each other at work anyway.

'Shall I put the kettle on?' Leo asked. 'Then we can have a coffee and a chat. We have a lot to talk about.'

That sounded ominous but, when he smiled, Robert's shoulders relaxed. His son couldn't be here with bad news, could he, if he was smiling? Perhaps the damage from the flood wasn't as bad as he'd feared. It would be lovely to have some good news.

Robert made two cups of instant coffee and then the two men retired to the conservatory which looked out over the village and down to the sea.

Barbara had always loved this room for its brightness. South-facing, it caught the sun and would have been unbearably hot in summer if not for the ceiling fan which wafted a gentle breeze when Heaven's Cove sweltered.

The conservatory was gloomy now, as night approached, but Robert, flicking on the light, didn't mind because he loved the conservatory for the way it made him feel – which was, basically, king of all he surveyed.

That was ridiculous, of course, because all he physically owned was this house and the shop in Herring Lane.

But in Heaven's Cove he owned something without price: status. He had a standing in this village that belied his impoverished upbringing. A respect that transcended his beginnings and acknowledged how far he'd come. That showed anyone who'd doubted him exactly what he was made of.

Robert sat down on the comfy sofa and placed his mug of coffee on the table beside him.

'So, why are you really here?'

Leo eased himself into the wing-backed chair that faced the garden and laughed. 'Straight to the point as always, hey, Dad?'

'It's the only way to do business.'

When Leo's laugh faltered, Robert wanted to say, *Not that you're business of course. You're my son and I love you.*

But declarations of love were hard to come by in the Jacobson-Jones family and the moment passed.

Leo reached into the pocket of his trousers and pulled out an envelope.

'I came by to tell you that you dropped this in the shop, and I'm afraid I read it.' He held up his hand as Robert recognised the envelope and his stomach lurched. 'I'm really sorry. I know I shouldn't have. But I thought it was a bill that needed paying and didn't realise it was personal. So I'm sorry that I've spoiled the surprise, but it's amazing, Dad. An MBE! You're going to have trouble keeping this quiet. As soon as Belinda gets wind of it, she'll be all over you like a rash.'

Robert looked away from his son's excited face and stared out of the window. At the glow of lamplight from cottage windows that led down to the blackness of the sea. He mentally kicked himself for being so careless.

'I wish I hadn't dropped the letter. You shouldn't have read it.'

'I know but, like I said, I thought it was a boring bill.' Leo grinned. 'Look, I'm sorry I found out your awesome news that way, but you were going to tell me about it anyway.'

'I was, but, since then, I'd decided not to tell you at all.'

'Come on, Dad,' said Leo. He sounded surprised, hurt even. 'It's not the sort of thing you can keep quiet. The honours list will be made public soon enough, the media will pick up on it, and then everyone will know what you've achieved.'

Everyone will know. Robert flinched at the idea. He liked being a big fish in a small pond. But this would bring his name to a wider audience and might rekindle memories best left forgotten.

Robert took a deep breath. 'Everyone will *not* know because I've decided not to accept the MBE.'

When Leo was silent, Robert turned and looked at him. His son was staring at him with his mouth open.

'I-I don't understand,' he gabbled. 'Why wouldn't you accept the honour?'

'I don't deserve it.'

Leo laughed incredulously. 'You definitely deserve it. You've worked hard for this community. You belong to just about every organisation going and everyone knows who you are. It was probably someone in the village who nominated you for the honour in the first place.'

'I just don't want the fuss, all right? I don't want to go up to London to receive the award—'

'From a member of the royal family.'

Robert briefly closed his eyes, imagining how Barbara would have loved dressing up for the investiture ceremony at Buckingham Palace. How it would have felt like the culmination of everything he'd worked so hard to achieve.

But he couldn't go back to London, where it had all begun. He needed to keep his head down, even after all these years. Or the shame would overwhelm him.

'Just leave it, Leo,' he said sharply. 'I'm not accepting the award and that's that. As I said, I don't want the fuss, and I can't stand London. I haven't been back there since I worked in the hotel years ago, and that's not about to change.'

'London's not so bad,' said Leo mildly. 'Was it the city itself or the hotel that you couldn't stand?'

'Both,' Robert snapped, before regretting his harsh tone. He'd got himself into a mess, but none of it was his son's fault. 'Look, I worked at a hotel in Hamswood Grove from autumn 1970 and got the money I needed to return to Heaven's Cove and start a business. So my time there served a purpose, but I just didn't much enjoy it. London wasn't the place for me.'

'Fair enough.' Leo hugged his coffee close to his chest. 'What job did you do at the hotel?'

'I worked as a butler to the VIP guests.'

'That sounds interesting. What was the hotel called?'

'I can't remember,' said Robert, rubbing his forehead. He

could feel the beginnings of a migraine prickling. 'I think it was named after an exotic flower or something like that.'

'An exotic—'

Robert cut him off. 'Something purple, but it was a long time ago and I can't see the point in rehashing it.' He breathed out slowly and said more gently: 'Now, can I have the letter back, please?' When he held out his hand, Leo passed over the envelope. 'So, tell me about the shop and how much damage that infernal woman has inflicted.'

Leo's eyes were still fixed on the envelope that Robert had placed in his lap. Was he going to try to persuade him again to accept the honour? Robert braced himself but, thankfully, his son moved on.

'Terry is sending us a quote for the work that needs doing on the electrics.'

'For goodness' sake, that woman!' Robert huffed, glad to be focusing on someone else's mistakes, rather than attempting to hide his own. 'We'll have to make sure she pays for the damage.'

'Sure. She should pay for what damage the water has actually caused,' said Leo. 'But our electrics have been in need of a major upgrade for some time.'

'Are you standing up for her?'

'No, not at all. I'm simply trying to make sure she doesn't pay over the odds – I'm trying to be fair.'

'Well, unfortunately, life isn't fair.'

Robert picked up his coffee and took a sip as a bat swooped low by the picture-glass window.

'So how long will the shop be in upheaval?' he asked.

'A few days. Well, actually, more like a week.'

'A *week*?' Robert's jaw dropped. 'So what happens to our business and our customers?'

'You don't need to worry about it, Dad, because I'm sorting things out. You're supposed to be retiring, remember?'

Robert opened his mouth and then closed it again. His son

was right. It was time for him to step back, as hard as that might be, and let Leo forge his own path. He had enough to think about as it was.

Robert got to his feet and put his largely undrunk coffee back down on the table, along with the honours letter.

'Please don't think me rude, Leo, but time's marching on and I'm getting tired.'

'Then, you'd better get to bed.' Leo stood up and grabbed his father's cup. 'I'll put both of these in the dishwasher on the way out.'

They'd almost reached the front door when Leo said, 'That wedding dress in Emma's shop. The one that was donated by somebody, but she doesn't know who.'

Robert took a deep breath. 'Yes? What about it?'

'You seemed rattled by it.'

'Rattled? I don't do rattled, as you well know.'

Robert tried to keep any tension out of his voice. He'd figured this moment might be coming from the puzzled look Leo had given him when he'd left that woman's shop so abruptly.

'OK. It's just that the dress was donated anonymously, as you know, and Emma found a ring with it.'

'What sort of ring?'

'A wedding ring, with *B & R Aeternum* inscribed inside it.'

'Really?' Robert was suddenly aware of his own heartbeat. It was so loud, surely Leo could hear it too. 'How interesting,' he managed.

'I wondered if you had any idea who the ring might belong to.' Robert shook his head vigorously. 'It's just that Emma seems determined to return it. She thinks it must have fallen into the bag by accident.'

'I have absolutely no idea who either the dress or ring belong to,' said Robert. He didn't like lying to his son but it wasn't as if he hadn't lied before. 'And it seems a waste of everyone's time to look for the owner of a ring which has clearly been given away. Quite frankly, I have better things to do than talk about some lost piece of jewellery that no one cares about.'

Was that too much? Robert was almost beyond caring. He opened the front door wide. 'Thank you for calling by, Leo. I'd best get on now – I have a few things to do before bed.'

'I'd better leave you to it then. Sleep well, Dad.'

There was a moment of awkwardness, as if Leo was waiting for something – a hug or a handshake. But then he walked out of the door and disappeared into the gloom.

Robert did have things to do before bed but, first, he went back into the conservatory and stood looking out over the village.

More lamps were coming on in the cottages that descended in rows down the hillside. But out to sea, the lights of fishing boats had been turned to faint smudges by a mist that was rolling in.

The view from here was amazing, even when the sun had disappeared over the horizon. But this evening, he didn't feel like the king of all he surveyed.

Too many memories were surfacing and dragging him back towards the past. Back to when he was known as Bob. Before he made his own good fortune, married well and became someone.

It had been a hard slog. And one that was now at risk because of an unforgettable wedding dress and an inscribed ring made of the best Welsh gold.

'Where are you?' he murmured softly, his cheek so close to the window, his breath misted the glass. 'Have you come home at last?'

He could find out for sure. He could go to the house and, if she was there, beg for her forgiveness. But that would only alert her to what he had done.

And though there was a time when he'd longed to see her, now he wasn't sure that he could face it. Not after all this time.

Robert pulled himself up tall and thought about his next move. The biggest risk to the life and reputation he'd built through blood, sweat and tears was that woman in the shop next door. She was infecting his son with dangerous doubts, and didn't know when to stop digging into a past that needed to remain hidden.

Robert drummed his fingers on the glass and closed his eyes. He hadn't come this far to be scuppered by a woman who sold second-hand clothes.

11
___

LEO

Leo hurried home, under a darkening sky scudded with navy clouds. Light was spilling from The Smugglers Haunt pub and a couple of people drinking outside – old friends from school – called him over.

But Leo waved and declined their offer to join them. He had far too much on his mind.

The visit to his father hadn't gone how he'd expected. He'd thought his father would be cock-a-hoop about his fantastic award. A little miffed, perhaps, that Leo had found out before he'd had a chance to reveal the exciting news. But far too excited to berate his son too much.

However, as it turned out, his father wasn't excited at all. Instead, he'd seemed – Leo thought back to Robert's dour expression – mostly sad. Robert Jacobson-Jones had been offered a coveted MBE and, for some inexplicable reason, he was turning it down.

He claimed he didn't deserve it, which was rubbish because his father had never appeared to suffer from a lack of self-esteem.

Perhaps, thought Leo, turning into a narrow, cobbled lane,

not wanting to go to London to receive the award was the real reason. His father certainly had a peculiar relationship with the city. He rarely spoke about his time there as a young man, and became agitated if anyone asked about it.

And he'd certainly seemed on edge this evening. Especially when Leo had mentioned the ring that Emma had found.

His father had tried to appear nonchalant but Leo knew him well enough to spot when he was being evasive.

The castle ruins were ahead and Leo slowed down as he approached the tumbled stones which appeared ghostly in the mist coming in off the sea.

There was no one about. The damp air seemed to have seen off the local teenagers who often congregated here during the evening. So Leo sat for a while, on a ruined wall that had once marked the boundary of the castle. And he asked himself a question that he could not answer: why was his father keeping secrets?

Everyone had something they never spoke about. For Leo, it was the heartbreak of realising that he and his fiancée, Anna, would never marry and grow old together. A tragedy can make or break a relationship and, in their case, it had caused fractures that had eventually splintered everything that was good.

No, that's not what I hide away, thought Leo in the gloom descending on the fallen stones. He occasionally did talk about what had happened to him and Anna. It wasn't something he always shied away from. But what he never mentioned, and rarely even admitted to himself, was how dissatisfied he felt with himself.

He was doing OK, he supposed. He had his own home, and he was no monk. He'd had occasional relationships that warded off the loneliness he might otherwise feel. But he felt like a failure.

Everything had been handed to him on a plate: a comfortable upbringing, a job in the family firm, and reflected glory from a respected parent. Yet he'd still made a mess of things.

His long-term love with Anna had ended, his relationship with his parents hadn't been easy, and he was about to take over a business that was set to fail, as far as he could see.

In short, he was more or less alone and, compared to his saintly father, rather a disappointment to everyone.

'Poor little Leo,' he murmured, berating himself for his self-pity when he had so much. He was lucky and it was about time he remembered that.

Leo got to his feet and walked on, through the thickening mist which wrapped itself around him.

Heaven's Cove looked dreamlike in the smudgy haze and Leo found himself wondering about years gone by and the woman who'd lost the wedding ring that Emma had found.

Had she been happy with her life on the day that she'd worn the beautiful wedding dress that was now hanging in Emma's shop?

Thinking of the dress reminded Leo that he hadn't told his dad about his arrangement with Emma, to share her shop space. He'd meant to, after celebrating his father's MBE. But the atmosphere had been so strained, after his dad's shocking announcement that he was turning the honour down, he'd kept his agreement with Emma quiet. His father would find out soon enough.

A lot had happened since Emma had pitched up in Heaven's Cove, Leo realised. The appearance of a mysterious ring and dress whose owner remained anonymous, his father's behaviour which hinted at secrets being kept, and his own increasing dissatisfaction with his life.

Things are changing, he thought, as the fog thickened and shrouded him completely.

12

EMMA

Emma rolled over in bed, yawned and stretched her arms above her head. She felt tired and groggy because Alfie's cries had echoed through the house in the early hours, keeping her awake.

For such a little person, he had a very loud yell. His cries had reached the converted attic room where she was trying to sleep. And poor Rosie and Liam, on the front line, must be exhausted.

Emma snuggled back under the duvet, happy that her days of baby rearing were long past. All those midnight feeds, dirty nappies and never-ending colic. There were challenges involved in having an adult child – Emma was learning that you never stopped worrying about your kids, however old they were. But at least she could sleep in these days, until roused by her alarm.

Emma glanced over at the alarm clock on the bedside table and was jolted wide awake. It was five to eight – five minutes before she was supposed to be meeting Leo at her shop. He was probably already standing there – he seemed the kind of man who'd be annoyingly early – with his arms full of stock and his heart full of irritation.

'Damn!' Emma exclaimed, jumping out of bed so quickly it made her head spin.

She sat back down on the duvet, picked up the clock and shook it – though that didn't help. She must have been so tired after Alfie's early morning din that she'd slept through her alarm. Or she hadn't set it properly in the first place.

Either way, she was going to be hideously late, and she didn't have Leo's mobile number so she could ring and apologise.

Emma briefly closed her eyes. *Another* apology. Leo already didn't like her. That was plain enough. And his father, having accused her of dragging his business down, would go ballistic at this latest transgression.

Throwing off her pyjamas, Emma grabbed her towel and headed for the en suite shower, pausing only to find the number of Leo's shop and call it.

But no one answered – probably because Leo was standing outside Heavenly Vintage Vavoom right now, banging on the glass and cursing her. He would think she was totally flaky. Oh well, he could join the queue behind her daughter and her ex.

The warm water was soothing and Emma felt less stressed by the time she'd got dressed. Leo and his horrible father, she'd decided, would just have to wait.

'It's not my fault if the alarm didn't go off,' she muttered to herself, picking up the lost wedding ring which had spent the night on her dressing table. 'Not really. And it's definitely not my fault that their stupid shop was flooded and can't be used for a week.'

Though they don't know that it wasn't me who left the tap running, thought Emma, shoving the ring into her handbag and heading down the steep attic stairs. *And I did hire Maisie in the first place so the buck ultimately stops with me. This whole business venture of yours, Emma, is going to rack and ruin from the start.*

'Stop!' she said loudly, emerging onto the first-floor landing. 'Please, just shut up!'

'Oh gosh. Could you hear him upstairs? I'm so sorry.'

Rosie was standing outside the door of the nursery with Alfie in her arms. There were dark shadows beneath her eyes and she was still in her dressing gown.

'No. I mean yes, I did hear him,' gabbled Emma. 'But I wasn't saying shut up to Alfie. I was saying shut up to my brain which is driving me mad this morning. You wouldn't believe what I've done now. I—' She stopped talking and took a deep breath because Rosie didn't want to hear about her missed alarm. 'Tough night, huh?'

'Not the best.' Rosie gave a wan smile. 'He was up almost every hour. Liam and I took it in turns to soothe him but Liam's headed off for the farm now and Alfie still won't sleep, even though he's fed and changed and he must be as tired as I am. Do you think I'm doing something wrong?'

'No, absolutely not.' Emma walked over to Rosie and stroked Alfie's silky head. He gazed back at her, eyes wide open. 'He could be teething, I suppose, but some babies just need less sleep than others. I swear Thea was nocturnal. She loved being up all night, every night. But it did change. By the time she reached her teens, I could never get her out of bed.'

'Her teens?' Rosie looked aghast. 'What, like thirteen years away? I'll have died of sleep deprivation long before that.'

'No. Thea started sleeping through the night *long* before that,' Emma assured her.

'When she was still a baby?'

'Absolutely,' she lied, remembering the broken nights that had persisted until her daughter was three years old and Emma was half dead with exhaustion.

Carl had rarely helped out. In fact, he'd moved into the spare room so that his nights wouldn't be disturbed. And she'd simply accepted his absence because she was too tired to argue.

At least it sounded as if Liam was stepping up to his responsibilities as a father. And maybe Alfie would turn a corner and sleep through more swiftly than Thea had.

Alfie startled at the sound of Emma's mobile phone ringing and she scrabbled to grab it from the bag over her shoulder.

'Sorry my phone's so loud,' she mouthed, as her fingers closed around it.

'Don't worry.' Rosie leaned her weary head back against the wall. 'It's not as if the baby was asleep.'

Emma hurried along the landing and jabbed at her phone screen to answer the call.

'I'm sorry that I'm late, Leo. I'll be with you as soon as I can.'

There was a pause and then a familiar voice said: 'Who the hell is Leo?'

Emma's breathing grew shallow as she realised that the man on the other end of the line was Carl. They hadn't been in touch for weeks, other than an occasional text exchange about Thea.

She'd contemplated texting him the day before yesterday, after the divorce became final, but had wimped out because what could she say? *Happy Divorce Day! I hope that you and Selena will be very happy?*

In the end, she'd said nothing at all and had waited for him to make the first move. She'd hoped, after all they'd shared, that he might at least check she was OK, all alone on such a sad day.

However, there had been no word from him, so, at midnight on 'Divorce Day', she'd taken off her wedding ring and packed it away in her suitcase. Thea and Selena were Carl's world now and she didn't feature in it.

But now here he was, calling her out of the blue.

'Is Thea all right?' she asked, suddenly anxious. 'She seemed a bit down about her job when I last spoke to her.'

'She's fine, I think. We saw her a few nights ago, with Henry, and they seemed the same as normal.'

We saw her. Emma's heart hurt at the thought of Thea and Selena cosying up, but at least she was still seeing her father.

'So how are you doing, Carl?' she managed.

'Oh, you know.' She didn't know – how could she? Carl cleared his throat. 'Are you still in Devon?'

'Yes, after all the planning, I've actually opened my vintage clothing store.' When Carl made no comment on her new venture she added: 'Everything's going brilliantly, so far.'

That was putting an absurdly positive spin on things, but Emma wasn't about to tell him the truth. That she felt lonely and sad and out of her depth. She still had some dignity left.

'What do you—' Carl broke off abruptly. 'Is that a baby crying?'

'Yes.' Emma moved further down the landing, away from Alfie's insistent cries. 'The woman who owns the place where I'm staying has a little boy.'

'Where *are* you staying?'

'In Heaven's Cove.'

'That tiny place where we had that godawful holiday when Thea was young?'

'I enjoyed the holiday, actually. I've got lots of happy memories of it.' Carl mumbled something she didn't catch. 'So why are you ringing?' she asked, finding the whole conversation horribly awkward.

'It's about storage.'

'Storage?'

Emma was baffled. What on earth was he talking about?

'Yeah. Selena and I have moved to a new place in Hamsell Green, not far from the Tube station, and I was wondering if I could grab a few things out of storage to help fill the flat. I mean, I know lots of the stuff belongs to you, too, but it's just sitting there in a warehouse and costing us a fortune in storage fees. So I thought...'

You thought you'd use it to furnish your love nest.

Emma's heart sank. Carl hadn't rung up to check she was OK after the finality of their divorce, or to talk about their shared child. He'd rung her because dipping into their storage facility for furniture was cheaper than going to IKEA.

'Just do what you like,' she said. 'Anyway, I've got to go because Leo will be waiting.'

'Again, who is Leo?'

'Just a man I've met. See you sometime, Carl. Bye.'

Emma ended the call and dug her nails into her palms so she wouldn't cry and make her mascara run.

She shouldn't have been so enigmatic about Leo but she couldn't resist it. Everything had been on Carl's terms for long enough.

'Who was that ringing you so early?' asked Rosie, coming to the door of the nursery with Alfie, still wide awake, in her arms.

'It was Carl, my ex-husband. I assumed it was Leo at first, though thinking logically, I'm not sure how he would have got my phone number.'

'The village grapevine is a fount of knowledge. You'll soon learn that the locals know almost everything about everyone in Heaven's Cove.'

'Is it impossible to keep a secret round here?'

Rosie's face clouded over. 'Not impossible, but secrets do have a habit of coming back to bite you.' She gave Emma a sympathetic smile. 'Are you all right after the chat with your ex?'

'Yes, thanks. We're divorced now and, therefore, I am completely over him.'

Emma laughed to show that she meant what she said, even though she didn't.

She couldn't help envying Rosie, who, in spite of lack of sleep, had so much: a child who needed her and a husband who adored her.

But at least she had her new business to boost her spirits.

Thinking of her shop turned her mind to Leo, and she groaned as she checked her watch.

She was so late now, there was almost no point in hurrying at all.

13

LEO

Leo rapped on the glass door and checked his watch again. It was gone eight o'clock but there was still no sign of Emma. Surely she hadn't forgotten that they were moving his stock into her shop so that he could continue to trade?

Terry, and whoever he'd roped in to help him, would be turning up at eight thirty and starting work – which would mean noise and dust and endless requests for cups of tea.

Leo wanted to avoid all of that. But mostly he wanted to avoid his father, who would throw a fit if he saw his couture suits being moved into a shop that, in his view, sold 'tat'.

It would be far better if the whole thing was a fait accompli by the time Robert cottoned on to what was happening.

'Good morning, Leo,' said Belinda, from over his shoulder.

He turned around and plastered on a smile. 'Morning. You're out early.'

'I like to get my morning constitutional in as soon as I'm up and dressed these days. Before the hordes descend. Tourism is all well and good for the local economy, but getting around the village takes twice as long when the pavements are clogged with people eating ice creams. Don't you think?'

'Mmm,' said Leo noncommittally.

'So, what are you doing outside Emma's shop at this hour?' Belinda peered through the glass. 'Is she around?'

'Nope, I don't think so,' said Leo through gritted teeth.

It was just his luck that Belinda had to be passing right now, while he was loitering outside Emma's empty shop feeling stood up and stupid. But Belinda was like a bloodhound who'd picked up a scent. If there was something out of the ordinary going on in Heaven's Cove, she was inexorably drawn to it.

Belinda stared at the armful of suits he was carrying.

'You're not donating those suits to her shop, are you?'

'No, definitely not. These are brand new.'

There was a silence while Belinda waited for him to explain further. When Leo said nothing, her eyes narrowed.

'I hope Emma's shop is doing well. I've heard that she's newly divorced and it was all rather acrimonious.'

'Then you've heard more than me,' said Leo levelly, wondering if that was true.

A combative divorce might explain why she seemed stressed all the time. Though he supposed that flooding out a neighbouring shop when you'd only been in the village for a couple of weeks might raise your cortisol levels.

'I also heard that it's going to take at least a week for your damp electrics to be sorted out.'

'Who told y—'

'Terry,' said Belinda briskly. 'I saw him in the pub last night and he told me all about it. He said your ancient electrics were in a terrible state. Though I don't think he should be talking about other people's business like that.'

'Probably not,' said Leo, gobsmacked by gossipy Belinda's hypocrisy, 'but it doesn't matter. It's not a state secret.'

'Good. Well, I suppose I'd best be getting on. I hope Emma turns up soon, if that's who you're waiting for. I guess being newly divorced means that she's single. Like you.'

'I guess so,' said Leo, not keen on pursuing Belinda's train of thought. If she saw the two of them together, she'd realise that any attempt at matchmaking would be sorely inappropriate.

Emma thought so little of him, she couldn't even be bothered to turn up on time to meet him.

'Right, then. I'm off,' said Belinda, having another peer into the shop. 'Good heavens! That's a beautiful wedding dress hanging in the corner over there. It looks rather old. Who on earth did that belong to?'

'I've no idea, and I don't think Emma knows either.'

'Someone rather well off, I'd wager. The embroidery looks exquisite, even from here. Anyway, must be going.'

She gave Leo a wave and marched off towards the quay.

Leo glanced again at his watch and felt his shoulder muscles tense. It was now almost quarter past eight and Emma was still nowhere to be seen.

Leo dumped the armful of suits back on the counter of his shop and began hurrying through Heaven's Cove. Past the wishing well and towards the cliff that towered above the village.

He'd tried to be adult about the situation. But after flooding his shop, Emma's no-show was the final straw and he felt furious.

Deep within him, Leo realised that fury was too extreme a reaction to what was, basically, being forgotten by a woman he hardly knew. Deep irritation would be more appropriate in the circumstances.

A therapist might say he'd felt forgotten as a child, while his parents were bickering or his father was constantly in the shop or doing 'good works'. And he sometimes felt forgotten still, as his father was lauded by locals, and he tried – in vain – to measure up to Robert's reputation.

But Leo didn't have much truck with therapy and had always prided himself on being able to manage.

So he breathed deeply and dialled down his fury. But, as he reached the top of the cliff and strode across the grass towards Driftwood House, he still felt angry at the havoc a newcomer to the village appeared to be wreaking on his business and personal equilibrium.

14

ROBERT

The sun was low in the sky, mostly obscured by thin cloud, and the sea was dove grey. A sharp breeze was blowing in across the waves and it was chilly up here on the cliffs so early.

Robert pulled up the collar on his jacket and wished he'd wrapped his cashmere scarf round his neck before venturing out.

He rarely climbed the cliff these days. There didn't seem much point when he'd seen the view dozens of times before. Plus, his knees weren't what they once were.

But he'd woken this morning needing space and fresh air. Somewhere to breathe and to think.

He'd considered coming up here at 3 a.m., when demons from the past had kept him from sleep. But he'd probably have fallen over in the darkness and broken his leg. Or his neck after falling off the cliff.

Robert peered over the edge and felt his stomach flip as he surveyed the jagged rocks far below. They were visible with the tide out but they'd disappear beneath the waves again when the water rose.

A long time ago, he'd stood in this exact spot and felt the

same pull towards the edge of the land. The same urge to step into space and experience a moment of complete freedom before gravity took over and he plummeted down.

But life had been different then, and so had he.

For a start, he'd never have dreamed that, one day, he would be offered an MBE. And never in a million years would he have believed that he would turn it down.

Robert took another step towards the cliff edge before turning his back on the sea and looking across the grass and wild flowers that dotted the top of the cliff.

There, in the distance, stood Driftwood House. It was a handsome building, battered by decades of winter weather and sea spray that was lifted high by the wind on stormy days.

He'd once thought it the poshest house he'd ever seen. It was certainly a stark contrast to the tiny rented cottage in which he'd grown up. A two-up, two-down thatched cottage which, from the first moment he could remember, had seemed too small.

His bedroom was so cramped it only just accommodated a single bed and he'd slept on the sofa for years after he grew so fast his feet scrunched up against the bedroom wall. That cottage, that life, had never been enough for him.

Robert craned his neck but the hamlet of Heaven's Brook couldn't be seen from here. He'd have to walk past Driftwood House to see its huddle of homes, a couple of miles inland.

But there was no point. The cottage was still there but his parents weren't. They'd died years ago which, though sad, had relieved him of his obligation to visit them occasionally.

Robert breathed out slowly to ease the tightness in his chest. He was a different man now from the one who'd disappointed his parents so very badly.

Leo was under the mistaken belief that it was Robert who had cut off almost all contact with his parents. A calculated ditching to assist him in his efforts to better himself.

There was some truth in that, and Robert had never said otherwise. He had something to prove and didn't want to be held back by his past.

But the truth, which he would never reveal, was that his parents had distanced themselves from him after learning what he'd done back then. How ambitious and ruthless he was. How amoral when the situation demanded it.

Or perhaps it was the disappointment in their eyes that had pushed *him* away.

'You've become someone I don't recognise,' his mother had said, her face pained with confusion.

To which Robert had glibly replied, 'That's the whole point. I've changed.'

Sometimes he regretted his glibness. Perhaps if he'd properly explained to his parents why he'd done what he had, they might have understood.

But he hadn't, and his parents' incomprehension, together with his changing circumstances, had gradually driven a wedge between them.

He'd realised their relationship was on shaky ground when they weren't impressed with the big house he'd bought after marrying Barbara, who was considered a catch.

He'd expected – hoped even – that they'd be proud of him. But instead, they'd seemed faintly disapproving as they stood in his hallway – the size of their entire ground floor – with their mouths open like goldfish out of water.

'Why do you need all of this space?' his father had asked. 'It'll cost a fortune to heat.'

After a few more, increasingly awkward, visits, he'd stopped inviting them round entirely. And now it was far too late to try again.

Robert pulled his jacket tighter around him and sat down on the wooden bench that faced the sea.

Far below, Heaven's Cove was waking up and, at the top of

the village, he could make out his big house, which made him feel better. *It was all worth it*, he told himself. All of the hard work and striving and sacrifice.

He was someone in the village. Someone who mattered. Someone with a thriving business who gave back to his local community through voluntary work on various committees. Someone who didn't *need* an MBE, even though the thought of turning it down made his heart hurt.

He could have dealt with that hurt in private. But then Leo had read his letter and now thought his father was an idiot.

Did Leo believe the reason he'd given for turning the honour down?

Robert decided to call in to their shop later, to make sure that everything was good between him and his son. That would also give him a chance to check up on the work Terry was doing and see how Leo was coping with the upheaval.

But he would have to avoid that woman's shop next door while she had that dress on display. He couldn't bear to look at it because every gleam of sunshine on the delicate embroidery and every ripple of silk made it hard to breathe.

His mind suddenly catapulted back fifty-five years to 1970. She had looked so unbelievably beautiful wearing that dress as she posed for photographs in Heaven's Cove churchyard.

The wind was making his eyes water. Robert wiped them with the sleeve of his jacket and sat, quietly, looking out across the waves.

15

EMMA

Emma glanced surreptitiously at her watch and began to bite her lip. It was way past eight o'clock now and Leo would be furious.

But she was still feeling knocked off kilter by Carl's call, and she couldn't abandon Rosie anyway. The poor woman looked as if she was about to collapse from exhaustion.

Emma placed a cup of tea in front of the young mum, who was sitting on the nursery floor, watching Alfie kick and complain in his cot.

'I don't know where he gets his energy from,' said Rosie, cupping the hot drink in her hands before yawning loudly. 'You're very good to me, Emma. I'm so glad you're here.'

'I'm happy to be of help,' said Emma although, in truth, she felt fairly useless. She'd walked Alfie round for a while, rocking him gently. But sleep still seemed the last thing on his mind. 'Look, I don't want to up and go but I—'

'You've got a business to run and we're holding you up.' Rosie put a hand to her mouth. 'I'm sorry. I'm so tired, I forgot.'

'It's OK,' Emma reassured her. 'I would stay longer but I promised Leo—' She broke off when insistent knocking on the front door echoed through the house. 'Oh, Lord,' she murmured quietly. 'Here we go.'

'Who on earth's that?' demanded Rosie. 'I'm not even dressed yet.'

'I can get it,' said Emma, her heart starting to pound.

She hurried down the stairs and pulled the door open. There, standing on the doorstep, as she'd feared, was Leo.

He'd ditched the jeans of yesterday and was back in his suit, but his pale cheeks were flushed with the exertion of hurrying up the cliff path and dark locks of hair had fallen across his forehead.

He looked furious and also – Emma registered it before batting the stupid thought away – hot, in both senses of the word.

'Good morning,' she said. 'I thought it might be you.'

She groaned inwardly because for some reason – nerves, probably – her greeting had sounded uber cheerful. Which was both inappropriate and unwise when Leo very clearly wasn't.

'Easy to guess, was it?' he snapped. 'When you should have been meeting me outside your shop' – he consulted his watch – 'almost thirty minutes ago. And yet here you are, at home.'

'I know and I'm very sorry.'

'You're sorry. Again.'

'Yes, again. I apologise but my alarm didn't go off.'

'That old excuse? My alarm went off before seven so I'd be waiting to meet you at the time we'd arranged.'

'Good for you,' said Emma, who was rather fed up with being harangued on the doorstep by Leo. This was the second time this week.

'I've apologised for being late,' she added stiffly, 'and, quite frankly, I don't know what else you expect me to do. Was it worth rushing up here and hammering on the door when there's a baby in the house who's trying to sleep?'

Leo had the grace to look shame-faced at that, as Emma had

hoped he would. But her attempt to take the wind out of his sails was foiled by Rosie appearing behind her.

'Don't worry about it, Leo,' she told him. 'Alfie wasn't sleeping. I'm beginning to think he'll never sleep again.'

To hammer home her point, Alfie, in Rosie's arms, began to wail. His tiny face screwed up and he yelled as if his world was ending.

'I'll grab my cardi and we'll get out of your hair,' said Emma, over the cacophony. 'Wait there, please, Leo, and I'll only be a minute.'

She ran up the stairs, two at a time, pursued by Alfie's wails which were petering out by the time she climbed the attic stairs, and had stopped completely when she descended them again. The house was blessedly peaceful.

Emma hurried along the landing, to the top of the stairs and came to a halt. Peering over the bannister, she couldn't believe what was happening in the hall.

Leo had taken off his jacket and was cuddling Alfie close to his chest. The baby's cheek was against the white cotton of his shirt and Alfie's eyes were closed.

Leo was murmuring something close to the baby's ear, and Rosie was beaming with a look of relief etched across her face.

'It's a miracle! Leo is a bona fide baby whisperer,' she hissed when Emma padded down the stairs, wincing at every creak of wood. 'Do you think, Leo, that you could put him down in his cot for me? I'd be eternally grateful.'

Leo nodded carefully so as not to disturb Alfie, who, adorably, had started to snore. He looked like a doll in Leo's large hands.

There was something about a broad-shouldered, perennially grumpy man holding a little baby as if the infant was made of glass that made Emma's heart contract.

Leo caught Emma's eye over the top of Alfie's head and gestured with his chin that he was going upstairs. She waited as he climbed the stairs slowly and disappeared along the landing with Rosie following.

A minute later, he and Rosie were back.

'He's flat out,' Rosie whispered to Emma, even though the sound of their conversation wouldn't carry to the nursery. 'Leo's amazing! He has a very soothing manner with babies.'

Shame about the abrasive manner he has with his neighbours.

The words echoed through Emma's head but she kept her mouth shut. Not only would they sound curmudgeonly, but she'd glimpsed another side to Leo.

Perhaps he had a softer heart than he let on.

16
———

EMMA

Leo walked swiftly across the clifftop, with Emma hurrying to keep up with him.

'Can you slow down a bit? Please,' she puffed after a while.

Leo stopped and breathed out slowly. 'I want to get my stock moved into your shop before my father turns up.'

'Why?'

'I just do,' said Leo, doing up a button on his jacket. He looked so ill at ease, the penny suddenly dropped.

'Have you told him about our arrangement? That you'll be working out of my shop for a few days?'

Leo swallowed. 'Not exactly. I meant to tell him but there hasn't been a right time.'

Emma groaned quietly. Robert wasn't likely to be happy about their arrangement, given his antipathy towards her a couple of days ago.

But it was Leo's problem to sort out, she reasoned, as she fell into step with him.

They walked on in silence, across the clifftop that was scattered with spiky gorse topped with bright yellow flowers.

'Do you know a good jeweller in Heaven's Cove?' she asked after a while.

'Why?' he demanded, without breaking stride.

'I thought I might show them the lost wedding ring and see if they can tell me anything about it.'

'You're still obsessing about that, are you?'

Emma raised an eyebrow. 'Obsessing isn't quite the way I'd put it. But yes, I'd still like to find the ring's owner – the B or R of the inscription.'

'Because?'

'Because the whole thing is intriguing, don't you think?'

Leo made a harrumphing noise which Emma took to signal irritation, so she decided to say nothing more about it.

She figured they'd finish the rest of the journey in silence. She wasn't going to try making conversation again, not after the morning she'd already had.

But Leo suddenly asked: 'How long will you be staying with Rosie?'

Emma shielded her eyes against the sun which had just peeped from behind the cloud.

'I'm not sure. I'm looking for somewhere to rent in the village but everything's a little out of my price range so far.'

Hideously out of her price range was more truthful. Most local flats were let to tourists and the price of decent available accommodation was prohibitive.

She should have checked it out better before airily deciding that a shop premises being vacant in Herring Lane was fate: a sign that her future lay in Heaven's Cove. That mindset was like dropping coins into a well and making wishes, she thought ruefully. It was magical thinking that evaporated when faced with reality.

'I didn't think Rosie was taking in paying guests at the moment,' said Leo, swerving round a large boulder on the path.

'She's not, but I knew her mum from years ago. Well, I sort

of knew her. It's a long story. But I saw online that Driftwood House had become a guesthouse so I rang to see if I could stay there, when I knew I was opening the shop.'

'And you found out it was temporarily closed.'

'That's right. I was so sorry to learn that her mum had died. But Rosie remembered me and offered me a room anyway.'

'That was kind of her.'

'It really was.' Emma paused, not wanting to break any confidences, but Leo had been so good with the baby. 'I think she likes having another mother around because being a first-time mum can be challenging.'

'Particularly if the baby doesn't sleep.'

'Exactly.'

'That baby certainly has a good set of lungs on him.'

Emma glanced across at Leo. His brow was set and he was concentrating on the path down to the village, which was steep in places.

'You seem good with babies,' she ventured, realising that she knew nothing about this man who got annoyed about bags left in the street, but gently rocked a crying baby to sleep. 'Do you have kids of your own?'

Leo stopped so suddenly, she almost barrelled into his back. He looked out across the sea, at dark clouds massing on the horizon.

'It's going to rain later,' he said. 'The wind's in the right direction to bring those clouds towards land.'

Emma swallowed. Had she said something wrong?

She was about to change the subject when he said quietly, 'I almost became a dad. My fiancée fell pregnant nine years ago but she had a late miscarriage.'

Emma wasn't sure what to say. The atmosphere between them had shifted.

'I'm sorry. That must have been devastating.'

'It was. I don't think about it too much these days, but

holding Alfie made me wish...' He trailed off, still staring into the distance.

'For something that might have been?'

'For some*one*.' He pulled in a deep breath of air. 'Anyway, I don't know why I told you all of that.'

He started walking again, his pace brisk, and Emma hurried to keep up.

Leo had revealed a chink in his armour and let her in, if only for a few seconds. And it made her wonder if she should reveal something of herself too – because if they were going to be working in close proximity for the next few days, they needed to be getting on better.

Emma thought for a moment because there was so much she could tell him. How she'd been devastated by the discovery of Carl's infidelity. How she'd ploughed almost everything she owned into her new business that was going from bad to worse. How she felt washed up and washed out.

But it was too much, too soon, so instead she settled on: 'My ex-husband and daughter think I'm crazy.'

She regretted her words immediately. How on earth would telling him that her nearest and dearest questioned her sanity improve their relationship? But it was too late.

Leo gave her a sideways look. 'Really? You strike me as antagonistic, forgetful and hideously unpunctual. But I wouldn't have said you were crazy.'

Emma blinked. 'Thank you... I think.'

'How old is your daughter?'

'Thea's twenty-four and works in a nursery and is busy with her own life, which is as it should be. I'm assuming that, like Thea, you're an only child too.'

'Why would you think that?' he shot back, sounding defensive.

'Only because no one – and by no one I mean Belinda – has mentioned your parents having another child.'

Leo's shoulders visibly softened and he replied: 'No, there's only me, though I used to long for a sibling.' He shook his head. 'Again, I'm not sure why I'm telling you that. Perhaps you should have gone into counselling, rather than the fashion business. My shop would be a damn sight drier if you had.'

'I bet your father doesn't think I'm in the fashion business.'

'You probably don't want to know what my father thinks about you or your business.'

Leo stopped still and looked back across the clifftop. When Emma followed his gaze, she spotted a man standing near Driftwood House. He cut a lonely figure, standing at the cliff edge, his face turned towards the sea. There was something familiar about his profile.

'Is that your father over there?' she asked.

'I don't know. Maybe,' said Leo.

'It looks like him. Does he enjoy going for early morning walks?'

'Not particularly. It probably isn't him.' Leo turned back towards the village far below. 'Come on or we'll never get my stock moved in before the first customers arrive.'

He set off at such a fast pace, Emma had no chance of keeping up. But she didn't follow for a moment anyway. She was watching the lone figure in the distance.

The man suddenly turned towards her and then turned away, but not before she'd seen more of his face.

It was definitely Robert. And judging by the way he turned so swiftly and marched off in the opposite direction, he didn't want to be seen.

Emma watched Robert hurrying off in one direction and his son hurrying off in the other.

There was definitely something going on between them, but she was facing enough challenges of her own and couldn't get involved in anyone else's.

17

LEO

Leo squinted at his water-soaked appointments book. Gerald Wellburn was due in this afternoon for a fitting, if he was reading the smudged ink correctly.

Fortunately, Gerald was one of their more amenable customers, and therefore unlikely to complain about the cramped facilities in Emma's shop.

Emma had cleared a corner of the store for him but space was limited and the changing room they shared – basically, an alcove with a curtain drawn across it – was small. And many of his customers weren't.

That's why waistcoats were so popular with clients ordering new suits – they covered expanding waistlines beautifully.

Leo glanced across at Emma, who was staring at the laptop she'd placed near the till.

He envied her online stock system and the database of customers that she was starting to build up. And seeing her tapping away, with information at her fingertips, had made him all the more determined to drag his father into the twenty-first century.

Their paper-based system was old-fashioned, as was Jacobson-Jones Gentlemen's Outfitters. There was so much he wanted to do with the business but it had never felt like his. Perhaps that would change when his father retired – if he ever did.

Leo huffed when his finger went through a water-damaged page of the appointments book, and Emma glanced up.

'Problems?'

He extricated his finger and smoothed down the torn paper. 'Nothing major. Oh, by the way, you might want to pay Jason a visit.'

'Who's Jason?' she asked, smoothing a hand over her thick, fair hair that curled under where it hit her shoulders.

'You said this morning that you wanted to ask a jeweller about the wedding ring you found. Jason runs the jewellery shop near the bakery, before you get to the sea wall, and he'd be the best person to ask. He's a qualified silversmith and knows his stuff.'

Emma closed the lid of her laptop and gave him a straight stare.

'Thanks for the recommendation, but I'm surprised you're helping me. This morning you said I was obsessed with the ring.'

Leo tilted his head from side to side to free up the tension in his neck.

'On reflection, obsessed possibly wasn't the right word. You appear to be overly concerned about the owner of the ring, who probably intended to donate it or she'd have turned up looking for it by now. But if you want to waste your time trying to track her down, that's up to you.'

'Right.' Emma's eyebrows were heading for her fringe. 'Well, thanks very much.'

She opened the laptop and began tapping again on the keyboard.

Leo went back to deciphering the appointments book but watched Emma out of the corner of his eye.

Several people had come in that morning and enjoyed a good browse through the clothes on the rails. And she'd made a few sales.

He'd listened to her chatting to villagers and tourists and had been struck by how many proffered personal information: medical appointments they were on their way to, why they'd moved to Heaven's Cove, how long they were on holiday, what hopes they had for their children. She certainly had a way of drawing people out.

Leo thought back to what he'd told her on the clifftop, about Anna and their lost child. He rarely spoke about what had happened, and the memory, along with holding Alfie, had sparked a deep sadness in him.

Did the loss still feature in his father's thoughts? he wondered. Was he thinking about what he'd lost – his wife and his grandchild – as he stood on the clifftop this morning?

Or was he more focused on the MBE that, for some unfathomable reason, he was turning down?

It had definitely been Robert standing there in the pale morning light, even though Leo had claimed not to know for sure – not wanting to field questions from Emma about what his father was up to. His father who never went for early morning walks.

There was something strange going on with him. And it had all started since he'd seen the wedding dress, which was hanging right now on the other side of the shop.

Leo scrutinised it carefully. The fabric was beautiful, the cut of the dress divine, and the tailoring exquisite. Everyone who came into the store admired it and asked about the bride who'd worn it on her big day.

Lettie had just stepped into the shop and, predictably, was making a beeline for the gown.

'Wow! Look at this dress. It's stunning.' She laughed. 'Sadly, it would be totally inappropriate for me to wear that to the wedding I'm going to in a fortnight's time. I think I'd upstage the bride. But I've looked everywhere for something to wear and I can't find anything suitable in my price range. Nessa told me you have some lovely clothes in here, and you're my last hope.'

He watched as Emma spoke with Lettie, a relative newcomer to the village who had already settled in like a local. She'd founded the Heaven's Cove Cultural Centre and lived with Corey, who fished for a living and was a member of the village lifeboat crew in his spare time.

Emma was showing her a rack of elegant dresses.

'You should try this one,' Emma urged, holding up what looked to Leo like an unflattering shapeless dress made of sludge-green jersey.

'I'm not sure.' Lettie picked up a more flouncy dress in navy satin. 'This one's in my size and I was going to try it on.'

'That's a lovely dress,' said Emma, leading the way to the changing room. 'But just humour me and try this one on too, will you? I think it'll suit your shape and complement your fabulous red hair.'

Lettie took both dresses into the changing cubicle and emerged a few minutes later in the navy creation.

'That looks good,' said Emma, as Lettie turned to see herself in the floor-length mirror on the wall. 'It fits well.'

It looked perfectly fine, Leo thought. A safe and unremarkable choice.

'Yeah.' Lettie wrinkled her nose. 'It'll do for the wedding. Definitely.'

When she went back into the changing room, Emma called after her: 'Don't forget to give the other dress a try, too, if you've got the time.'

A group of noisy tourists went by outside and Leo glanced

through the open shop door, wondering when his father would appear. He hadn't come in yet and Leo was dreading his arrival.

He wished now that he'd mentioned his arrangement with Emma when he'd gone to see his father last night. That might have taken the heat out of the whole thing, and avoided him blowing his top when he spotted his son in 'enemy territory'.

Though there was no way Robert would ever approve of his gentlemen's outfitters sharing space with a second-hand store. Even though it was the only workable option, and Emma's shop was actually quite nice when you looked at the place properly.

But it was all about appearances, when it came to his father. Showing everyone that he was a cut above.

Leo was so busy with his thoughts he'd forgotten about Lettie until he heard Emma's sharp intake of breath. He glanced up and his mouth fell open.

Lettie had tried on the nondescript dress thrust upon her by Emma, and she looked amazing. The sludgy green of the fabric, nothing special on the hanger, was just the right shade to bring out the vibrant redness of her hair, and the fit of the dress complemented her slender figure perfectly.

'What do you think?' Lettie asked, her eyes shining.

Emma opened her mouth, then closed it again. 'I think... wow!'

'It's OK, isn't it?' Lettie admired her reflection in the mirror. 'What do you reckon, Leo?'

Leo blinked, caught unawares. 'I reckon... well, I reckon it's better than OK. You look fabulous in that.'

'Thanks.' Lettie's cheeks flared pink and she beamed as she did another twirl in front of the mirror. 'I'll definitely take this one, Emma. Thank you so much for pointing it out. I'd never have tried it on if it wasn't for you, and it's just perfect.'

After she'd paid for her purchase and left, Leo commented: 'You have a good eye for choosing what's right for your customers.'

'Do you think?' Emma's cheeks went as pink as Lettie's had been. 'I don't have many talents, but I've always been good at matching people with things – clothes, shoes, jobs, partners.'

'Partners?'

'I hooked up two of my friends with each other, back when we were younger, and they're still going strong. Mind you, I didn't do so well when it came to me.' She glanced down at her bare left hand.

'I'm sorry about your divorce,' said Leo awkwardly, hoping that was the right thing to say. 'If I'd known the other day that your divorce had just come through, I wouldn't have made a fuss about the bag being left outside your shop.'

'How could you have known? Nobody here knows anything about me.'

'Except Belinda.'

'Except for Belinda, who will, before long, have wheedled my entire life history out of me,' Emma agreed, suppressing a smile.

She had kind eyes that sparkled when she smiled. As if she was about to tell a joke that would bring the house down.

'I can come with you to see Jason at the jeweller's, if you like,' he said quickly, before he could change his mind. 'If you'd like someone to introduce you, that is.'

He thought she might refuse, and she did hesitate, but then Emma said: 'That would be really helpful. Thanks. Maybe we could close the shop for half an hour at lunchtime and nip along to see him?'

'Sure.'

'Seeing as you're coming with me to the jeweller's, I'll make you and me a cup of coffee, shall I? I would ask Maisie but I'm not sure I can stomach her speech about bosses exploiting the working class.'

Leo grinned. 'I'm not sure why you keep her on.'

'I like her,' said Emma simply. 'She reminds me of my daughter.'

After she'd disappeared into the back of the shop, Leo wondered how it felt to be newly single after decades of being married. Scary, he imagined. And lonely.

Perhaps it was better, like him, to have never married at all. Even though it intrigued Belinda, who often commented on his love life, or relative lack of it. She appeared to think he was a catch, which surprised him.

Who would choose to spend their life with a middle-aged, set-in-his-ways bachelor who liked listening to Metallica at top volume, and who, when compared to his 'wonderful' father, was often found wanting?

It was not as if he'd had good role models for marriage in his parents. They'd argued throughout his childhood but, although apparently unhappy together, would never have countenanced using divorce to bring their union to an end.

'What would the neighbours say?' Leo could imagine his father, for whom public perception was everything, asking his mother that very question.

So they'd stuck it out until the very end. And he'd got used to living alone in his cottage that overlooked the sea.

'I presumed you take milk in your coffee.' Emma was coming back with two steaming mugs in her hands. 'And I haven't brought the sugar but I can get some if you want me to.'

'No, white and sugar-free is good for me.'

She thrust the mug into his hand and he gave her a smile.

It was only a cup of coffee but it felt like a minor peace offering.

18

EMMA

Jason's shop, set back from the sea wall, was a treasure trove of silver and gold. Precious metals glinted in the sunshine streaming through the window, and diamonds split the light into mini rainbows.

'What a gorgeous shop,' breathed Emma, taking in every sparkle.

'I'm surprised you haven't been in here before,' said Leo.

He was taller than Carl, and rangier, and she felt dainty standing beside him. *Dainty?* she scoffed to herself. Since when did a mid-forties divorcee with cellulite qualify as dainty?

'Do you prefer vintage jewellery?' he asked, running his fingers across the glass-topped counter.

'I'm not fussy. *Any* kind of jewellery does it for me. But I don't have the money to spend on non-essentials at the moment.' Emma gazed covetously at a beautiful silver pendant, set with a glowing ruby. 'More's the pity.'

Her engagement ring was a ruby, set in platinum and surrounded by diamonds. She'd stopped wearing it when Thea was small – it scratched her baby's soft skin when she was changing nappies – and she hadn't got back into the habit of wearing it.

The glittering ring had always seemed a little ostentatious in the school playground, while she waited for Thea to come out, all bright-eyed and runny-nosed.

'Emma, this is Jason who owns the shop.' Leo's deep voice interrupted Emma's cascade of memories. 'Jason, this is Emma who's just opened the shop next to ours, selling second-hand...'

He glanced at her and raised an eyebrow.

'Leo says second-hand but I like to call the clothing I sell pre-loved vintage fashion.'

Leo nodded. 'Yeah. That.'

'It's good to meet you,' said Jason, holding out his hand.

A balding man in, she guessed, his sixties, Jason was wearing a long leather apron and had his shirtsleeves rolled up. His grip, when he shook her hand, was firm and warm.

'So, you're the woman everyone is talking about,' he said, giving her a grin.

'Everyone? Why? What have I done?'

'You're a newcomer which is enough for tongues to start wagging locally. That's the curse of living in a small, close-knit community. But don't worry. In around twenty years, you'll be accepted. I've been here for almost fifteen now and people are finally starting to come round and not refer to me as an out-of-towner.'

When he grinned again, Emma decided that she liked affable, cheerful Jason.

'Anyway, how can I help you?' he asked, turning to Leo. 'I heard your shop's had to close after a flood. That's bad luck.'

'Yes, it's a pain,' said Leo, fortunately not going into detail about how the flood had occurred. 'But I'm sharing space with Emma for a few days, so I can continue to trade as usual.'

'What a good idea. I bet your dad's thrilled with Emma's neighbourly assistance.'

Was he being sarcastic? Emma wasn't sure, but his remark seemed genuine, so she took it as such. 'Robert hasn't been in yet to see what's happening.'

'When he does come in, I'm sure he'll be happy with the arrangement,' Leo assured Jason, although the line between his eyebrows told a different story.

'So, how can I help you two?' asked Jason, taking a seat on the stool behind the counter.

'We don't want to hold you up—' Leo began, but Jason shushed him with a wave of his hand.

'I've been squinting all morning at a pair of tricky earrings I'm making so I'm glad of a break.'

'In that case, Emma's found a wedding ring which she'd like to return to its owner, if she can. We wondered if you might take a look at it.'

'Sure. Hand it over.'

Emma opened the zipped pocket of her handbag and gave Jason the heavy ring.

He studied it for a moment and then pulled a folding silver magnifying glass from his pocket. He peered through it, at the gold ring resting on his palm, before looking up.

'It's a lovely old ring. Gold, 22 carat, a good weight. It has some wear, and I guess you've seen the inscription inside?'

'*B & R Aeternum*,' said Emma. 'I don't suppose you have any idea who B and R might be?'

'Afraid not. From the general wear on the ring, I'd say, if the wedding took place locally, that it was well before my time here. It's a shame that the hallmark has been eroded, although...'

Jason fished in a drawer beneath the counter and brought out a larger magnifying glass. 'I can see more detail with this one, which might help.' He bent his head over the ring and inspected it closely. Then he smiled.

'Aha! That's done the trick. There's a leopard's head which tells me the gold was hallmarked in London and I can just make out the date letter which tells us this ring was made fifty-seven years ago in 1968.'

'So,' said Emma, doing the maths in her head, 'The bride might be in her seventies, at least.'

She imagined the ring being slipped onto the bride's finger in the swinging sixties, long before she was born.

'I wish there was a way of knowing if the wedding happened around the time that the ring was made.'

Jason puffed air through his lips. 'There's no way of telling but, in my experience, jewellers like to move their stock on as quickly as possible. The engraving, *B & R Aeternum*, looks old so it was probably done at around the same time that the ring was made. B & R, whoever they might be, were likely the people who bought the ring from new, and the bride wore it for years, until the engraving began to erode.'

Jason got to his feet when a customer came into the shop. 'I'm afraid that's all I can tell you, but I wish you well in your search for the missing bride.'

~

After they'd thanked Jason and said goodbye, Emma and Leo walked back through the village.

'Thanks for suggesting I see Jason and for coming with me,' said Emma, holding her handbag tightly against her. The ring was nestling inside, safely zipped back into the inner pocket.

'Unfortunately, it hasn't taken you any further forward,' said Leo, pointing at the well they happened to be passing. 'Perhaps you should make a wish that the missing bride reveals herself. I think that's the only way that we're' – he corrected himself – 'that you're going to find her.

'Also,' he added, 'there's no evidence that the bride actually lives in Heaven's Cove. Or ever did, for that matter.'

'That's true,' Emma agreed. 'But I'm guessing that she lives here because she left her bag of clothes outside my door.'

'Perhaps she was driving through and spotted your shop. Or it could have been left by someone else – a relative or carer. Perhaps the woman who owned the dress and the ring – and we're assuming it's one person who owned both – is dead.' Leo grimaced. 'It's a possibility.'

'I know.'

'Look, you could try putting a few lines about all of this in the village newsletter. But you might have to accept that the owner of the dress and ring will never be found.'

'Perhaps,' said Emma. 'But I'm not ready to give up yet.'

Leo's exhale sounded like a sigh. 'I've only known you for a short time but I didn't think you would be.'

'Newsletter!' said Emma, coming to a standstill. 'What a good idea.'

'Is it?' Leo stopped and doubled back to her. 'Not everyone reads the local newsletter, and who gets it depends on how diligent the kids are that are paid to deliver it. Some dump them in the high hedge behind the mini-supermarket, which drives my father mad. He heads up the newsletter committee.'

Of course he did. Was there anything in this village that didn't involve Robert Jacobson-Jones?

'I didn't mean the newsletter, though a mention in it might work,' said Emma, shifting from foot to foot with excitement. 'But you suggesting the newsletter reminded me of how people in Heaven's Cove would have got local news fifty-seven years ago – newspapers! And local newspapers might have carried reports of local weddings.'

'I suppose they might,' said Leo slowly. 'So what are you going to do – trawl through every wedding that's mentioned from 1968 onwards with a bride and groom whose initials start with B and R?'

Emma grinned. 'That's exactly what I'm going to do, and I'm going to wish for good luck in finding my missing bride.'

She took a twenty pence piece from her purse, went to the well and dropped it into the darkness. Then she looked at Leo, almost daring him to comment.

He held her gaze for a moment before shaking his head.

'Heaven's Cove has a tiny library but you'll probably need to go to the bigger one in Callowfield. Do you have a car?'

'No but I'm sure I can get there on the bus.'

'Have you used local public transport yet? Heaven's Cove isn't like London, with its twenty-four-hour travel network. Round here, you're lucky to get a couple of buses a day between Heaven's Cove and Callowfield.'

'Then I'll get a taxi.'

Emma folded her arms, to show that she meant business.

'It'll cost a fair bit to get there and back by taxi. Is it really worth it to find the owner of a ring who's possibly deceased and, even if she's still breathing, is clearly not bothered that her ring's gone?'

Leo had a point. Was she using this search as a displacement activity? she wondered. Something to take her mind off the fact that she was running a shop in a place she hardly knew, with family and friends a long way away.

Maybe. But, if that was the case, it was working. It was harder to focus on how scared she was when she was concentrating on solving the mystery of the missing bride instead.

'I think it's worth it,' she said, unfolding her arms and pulling her shoulders back. For once, she felt strong and resolved and brave.

19

EMMA

Ten minutes later, Emma was not feeling strong or resolved or brave. Robert had just walked through the door of her shop and all she was feeling was cross with herself for being unsettled by his arrival.

'Leo!' he declared. 'There you are. Terry said this was where you were but I couldn't believe it. What are you doing here, in this place?'

The way Robert said 'this place', as though there was a nasty taste in his mouth, ramped up Emma's irritation. What had she done to provoke such animosity? Apart from flooding out his business, wrecking his electrics and causing the closure of his shop.

She sighed quietly, hoping that Maisie's mistake wasn't going to cost her a fortune and make her life a misery.

Fortunately, Heavenly Vintage Vavoom was empty of customers and Leo, who was rearranging his stock, said calmly: 'Hello, Dad. I meant to tell you that Emma kindly offered space in her shop so that we can continue to trade.'

'Kindly doesn't come into it when she caused the problem in the first place.' Robert grimaced. 'What will people think,

Leo? This is not exactly the sort of establishment that attracts our type of customer.'

'And what type of customer is that?' asked Emma.

It was hard to believe that a charmless man like Robert was deemed worthy of an MBE. And seeing as he was, surely he should be in a good mood after receiving news of the honour?

Emma was tempted to blindside him by congratulating him on the award. But that would mean admitting that she'd spotted the letter left out on the side in their shop. And he'd only berate her for invading his privacy, and accuse her of spying or something.

'Actually, Emma's shop has an interesting section of clothes for men, and it's attracting all sorts of customers,' Leo piped up.

Emma looked at him in amazement, grateful for his support but surprised by it.

'That might be the case, however I'm sure they're not *our* sorts of customers,' Robert replied, sounding like the snob he patently was.

He glanced across the shop and his eyes fell on the wedding dress. It might have been Emma's imagination, but he appeared to deliberately turn his back on it. Then he moved closer to Leo.

'I tried to call in fifteen minutes ago but the shop was shut. What if a customer had come by to collect an order, or place one, while you were gallivanting off for lunch?'

'We always take a lunch break in our shop, Dad, and there was a notice on the window saying we'd be back soon.'

'Couldn't you have left that young girl in charge so the shop stayed open?'

'Maisie needed a lunch break too,' said Emma, annoyed that she was having to justify the way she ran her own business.

'Leave it, please, Dad. We only nipped out to see Jason, to ask him about the ring I mentioned to you last night. The one that Emma's trying to reunite with its owner.' He turned to her. 'Why don't you show it to him?'

He wouldn't be interested, but Emma fished in her handbag for the ring and held it out to Robert.

'It was in the same bag as the wedding dress but I think the owner must have dropped it by mistake. It has an inscription inside: *B & R Aeternum.*'

Robert stared at the ring gleaming in her palm. But when she went to pass it over to him, he stepped back, knocking into a rail of vintage blouses which swayed back and forth.

'I can't believe you're wasting time on a wild goose chase when you have a new business to run,' he declared. 'It's perfectly ridiculous.'

He hurried to the door and left the shop, without another word.

'Weird,' said Emma to herself, carefully returning the ring to the pocket inside her handbag.

Leo went to the door and watched his father walk off along the lane. Then he turned to Emma, his jaw set.

'I can take you to the library in Callowfield if you like.'

Emma blinked, surprised by him again. 'Why would you offer to do that, when you agree that I'm on a wild goose chase?'

'I've got a few things to pick up in Callowfield so I was just being neighbourly.' Emma didn't reply because he hadn't been overly neighbourly up to now. 'We can sort out a time and I'll give you a lift. If you want, that is?'

Emma still hesitated. The thought of spending more time in Leo's company wasn't terribly enticing. But the prospect of battling with a sporadic public transport system, or spending a fortune on taxis, was worse.

'Thanks,' said Emma, making up her mind. 'If you're sure.'

˞

The next day, Leo's car pulled up at the foot of the cliff that led to Driftwood House. He leaned across and opened the passenger door.

'Hop in,' he told Emma, who was waiting for him. 'Have you been up to the moors yet, since you arrived?'

'No,' Emma replied, sliding into the passenger seat. 'I haven't had a chance. Why?'

'I thought I might go to Callowfield the long way round so you can see what you've been missing. If that's OK?'

Emma agreed that it was, feeling awkward about being in such a confined space with a virtual stranger.

She stole a glance at him as he drove along the lanes that led out of the village. He was back in his jeans again and a slouchy grey sweatshirt that looked old and soft.

Emma was tempted to stretch out her fingers and touch the sweatshirt material. But she carefully folded her hands into her lap instead.

She wasn't used to spending time with a man who wasn't her husband, and she wasn't sure if the uncomfortable atmosphere she sensed in the car was all in her head, or if he was feeling it too.

'Thanks again for giving me a lift to the library,' she said after a while, as the car climbed higher and the lanes narrowed. 'Don't you have anything better to do on a Sunday?'

'No. My friends are all busy with their families.' He said it lightly, but there was an edge to his voice. 'What about you? Are you expecting any visitors?'

'Probably not until I've sorted out somewhere else to live. I can't expect Rosie to put up with any more people descending on her. Anyway, my daughter's always busy with her partner and her friends. And my ex-husband is busy with the new woman in his life.'

Why had she told him that? Emma wished she could take back the words but Leo kept his eyes on the road.

All he said, as he negotiated a tricky bend in the road, was: 'Ah, I see.' And then they lapsed back into silence.

Soon, Emma and Leo were on Dartmoor. And, as Leo pulled his car to the side of the track, to allow a van to go by, Emma gazed out of the window.

There was nothing for miles, save for expanses of green, littered with slabs of weathered grey granite. The land rose in places, into peaks topped by rocky outcrops.

'It must be bleak here in winter,' she said, squinting into the hazy distance. 'But beautiful when it snows, with none of the grey slush we get in London.'

'I love Dartmoor in all weathers,' said Leo, pushing his car into gear and pulling slowly away. 'Wind, rain, sleet, snow... it changes with the seasons and it's peaceful.' He glanced across at her. 'Is it too quiet after the hubbub of the city?'

'Not at all,' said Emma, marvelling at the open space. Acres and acres of it, with scrubby sheep and wild horses its sole inhabitants. The moor had a timeless stillness that touched her soul.

Touched her soul, indeed! Emma smiled at her own pretentiousness and lowered the window to allow a moorland breeze to cool her face.

Nothing had ever seemed still in London. Even on days when she was stuck at home, daydreaming about owning a fashion business, there had been phone calls to field, family arrangements to make, and Carl's life to sort out.

'It's not that much farther to Callowfield,' said Leo.

He winced when the car hit a large pothole but Emma settled back in her seat while the car trundled on, enjoying a feeling of freedom. For the first time in decades, she had no one to answer to except herself.

The road began to dip and they descended into a valley that had a pretty river at the bottom. Ahead of them lay houses, and a sign welcoming them to Callowfield which declared that the town had been mentioned in the Domesday Book of 1086.

The outskirts were scattered with modern housing. But the cottages became older, with more of them sporting thatched roofs, as Leo's car made its way towards the centre of Callowfield.

'Where's the library?' Emma asked as Leo pulled into a quaint High Street, edged with tasteful shops and dotted with cafés. 'Are you sure it's open for a few hours on Sunday mornings?'

'I'm sure.' He pointed straight ahead. 'It's there, in the old town hall. And I've just spotted a parking space. Excellent!'

He reversed into an on-street gap while Emma gawped at the beautiful old town hall. The pale stone building had huge arched windows and an imposing double-width black front door.

'I won't be too long but please don't wait for me,' said Emma, opening the car door and enjoying a rush of fresh air. 'I can get the bus back.'

'I brought you and I'll take you home,' said Leo. 'I'll come into the library with you.'

'There's really no need. You said you had things to do.'

'I can do those after the library, while you have a look round or get yourself a cup of coffee. Is that all right?'

Not really, thought Emma, wondering if Leo considered her so gormless, he believed she'd never manage to find the old newspapers she wanted without his help.

Or perhaps Leo *was* intrigued by the mysterious ring and wedding dress after all. Even if he did his best not to show it.

20

LEO

The library wasn't as peaceful as Leo had expected. A group of mums with babies were sitting in a circle, near the children's books, singing about a teddy bear that wanted to go to sleep.

Judging by the yawns and dark shadows under their eyes, plenty of the mums wouldn't have minded a nap themselves.

'It's hard work being a parent,' said Emma, following his gaze. 'Poor Rosie looks exhausted a lot of the time. Happy with sweet little Alfie, but knackered.'

'That's not surprising.'

Leo felt another pang of sadness that he'd never experienced parenthood, and never would now. That particular ship had sailed, much to his father's disappointment. Robert had built a mini dynasty in Heaven's Cove and had expected a grandchild to carry on the family business.

Leo thought back over his romantic history: several girlfriends, a few more serious than others, and then the engagement to Anna – and the baby who never was. He'd put the sorrow behind him but holding little Alfie seemed to have rekindled some of the emotion he'd felt back then, and the pain was lingering.

'Leo.' Emma's voice cut through his memories. 'Are you concentrating on these records? Because I'm beginning to see double.'

He blinked and focused anew on the screen where they were going through copies of the *Heaven's Cove Courier* – a newspaper long defunct.

Emma had trawled through all of 1968 and 1969, searching through reports of local weddings, and was now on to 1970.

But the whole thing was taking far longer than Leo had anticipated. Which was partly because people in Heaven's Cove appeared to be doing little else, fifty-five years ago, other than getting married. But also because Emma kept salivating over the fashions that women pictured in the newspapers were wearing.

Not for the first time, Leo wondered why he'd offered to drive Emma to the library. And he kicked himself for insisting that he come inside to help her look for the elusive bride.

His dad was right. It was a wild goose chase, and yet... Leo thought back to his father's bizarre reaction to the wedding dress and the lost wedding ring. And now he was turning down an honour that had been bestowed upon him by the King.

There was something unsettling going on, and Leo couldn't shake the feeling that Emma's so far fruitless search played a far bigger part in it than he realised.

So he would help her trawl through old newspapers, until she was satisfied she'd done everything she could, and then she would step away from it. And so could he.

He would accept his father's somewhat odd current behaviour for what it probably was: a driven man's emotional reaction to imminent retirement, or an unemotional man's reaction to the anniversary of his wife's death.

'How many years of newspapers are you planning to go through?' he asked.

Emma sat back in her chair and tapped her fingers on the

desk. 'I don't know. This wedding might not even have taken place in Heaven's Cove though the good news is that, if it did, it'll be in the local paper. They seem to have reported on every single marriage, and they've even included names of the guests.'

'There was no social media back then for sharing photos of your big day. Local newspapers were like the Instagram of the 1970s.'

Leo leaned forward to look at the latest wedding picture that Emma had on her screen.

'I've made a list of the brides and grooms with the initials B and R that I've come across,' she told him. 'There are only three couples so far – Betty Jefferson and Richard Collis, Barbara Brown and Raymond Baglin, Birdie Fairburn and Ruben Smith. But Betty and Barbara aren't wearing the right dress, and this is Birdie's photo. Look.'

When Emma enlarged the grainy black and white photo, Leo squinted at the smiling bride and groom. Birdie's dress, though flouncily pretty, was nowhere near as magnificent as the discarded wedding gown hanging in Heavenly Vintage Vavoom.

Emma scored a line through Birdie's name and began scrolling again through pages of news from Heaven's Cove life half a century ago: the businesses opening and closing, the storms that battered cottages, the people now long gone.

More weddings were reported but none involving a B and R, until Emma reached September 1970. She stopped scrolling, her hand hovering over the computer mouse.

'Here's another one,' she said, picking up her pen and writing down *Beatrice Farleigh-Addison and Richard Charnley-Smythe, 12th September*.

'I think there's a photo too,' said Leo, catching a glimpse of a picture at the bottom of the screen. He grabbed the mouse and scrolled until the photo came into view.

'Oh!' breathed Emma. 'We've found her.'

Beatrice and her new husband were pictured standing by the gate of St Augustine's Church, with an enormous yew tree behind them. Richard looked resplendent in a dark morning suit, with a cravat around his neck and a handkerchief poking from the top pocket of his waistcoat.

But his bride was the focus of the photograph. It was hard not to be drawn to such a striking young woman in such a magnificent dress.

'That's *the* dress,' said Leo, reading their names again. Beatrice and Richard. *B & R Aeternum*.

The bride and groom were flanked on either side by unsmiling relatives.

'Everyone looks very serious,' said Emma.

But Leo hardly heard her. He was feeling relieved that the R in question wasn't Robert Jacobson-Jones.

That was what had been bothering him, he realised. A nagging *what if* in his subconscious: what if the mysterious R, linked for ever with Beatrice in the ring's engraving, was his own father and that was why he'd reacted so bizarrely to the abandoned wedding dress and ring but refused to discuss it.

But there was no secret first wife.

Leo decided it had been ridiculous to even countenance the idea, and unkind of him not to be more sensitive to his father's feelings.

'I think I owe my father an apology,' he murmured.

'Why?' asked Emma, turning away from the screen.

'I questioned his reaction to the wedding dress and ring. But now I think he was simply remembering my mother and he's not the kind of man to show his emotions. So I feel—'

Leo stopped talking and leaned closer to the screen.

'You feel what?' Emma asked gently.

But Leo didn't answer. Something had caught his eye in the back of the wedding photograph. A shadowy figure was lurking behind the wedding party, partly hidden by the yew tree.

Leo tilted his head and looked closer.

'What is it?' Emma asked. 'What can you see?'

'That person there.' Leo touched the screen, leaving a fingermark. 'Who do you think he is?'

Emma peered at the picture. 'I don't know. There's a lot of shadow, although the face…' She glanced at Leo and back again at the screen. 'To be honest, he looks a bit like you.'

'That,' said Leo, 'is because he's my father.'

21

EMMA

Could the young man pictured behind the wedding party really be Robert Jacobson-Jones? Emma peered again at the photo, wondering if Leo was joking. Though why would he joke about his father being at the missing bride's wedding? Perhaps he was simply mistaken.

'Are you sure?' she asked, scouring through the guest list that was beneath the picture.

But Leo had got to his feet and was already heading for the door.

'Let's go,' he said loudly, over his shoulder.

Emma smiled awkwardly at the young member of library staff sitting nearby who seemed annoyed by Leo's hasty exit.

'Sorry,' she mouthed, switching off the computer and gathering up her things. Where on earth was he going?

She found him outside, sitting on a wooden bench in the shade of an oak tree. Nearby, a crocodile of children in hi-vis jackets was chattering past, and an unseen motorbike was revving in the distance.

'That was an abrupt exit,' said Emma, sitting beside him and stretching out her legs.

'I needed some air.'

Leo turned his face to the sky and closed his eyes as sunlight glinted on strands of silver in his dark hair.

'So,' said Emma, grateful for the breeze on her skin. The library had been hot and stuffy. 'Do you really think that's your dad in the photo?'

Leo nodded, but kept his eyes closed. 'I've seen photos of my dad from around that time. He'd have been... what, in 1970? About twenty? The man in the photo looked around that age.'

'But your dad's not on the guest list. I had a quick skim through it and he's not mentioned.'

Leo opened his eyes and looked at Emma. 'It's him,' he said bluntly.

'O-K,' Emma replied slowly, trying to make sense of it all. 'So, if that is your dad at Beatrice and Richard's wedding, that might explain his reaction to the wedding dress. It's very memorable and he recognised it.'

'Then why didn't he say so?'

That was the million dollar question and one that Emma couldn't answer.

'Perhaps he's trying to protect Beatrice, the bride?' she ventured.

'Protect her from what?'

'I don't know. From being found?'

'Why though? That doesn't make sense.'

Emma had to agree, but nothing about the missing bride was making sense. Uncovering Beatrice's identity appeared to have simply widened the mystery, and put Robert centre stage.

'Has your dad ever mentioned Beatrice or her husband to you?' she asked, shooing away a seagull that had landed on the bench.

'I don't think so. But my dad doesn't talk a lot about the past.'

'Perhaps he's simply forgotten that he was at Beatrice's wedding. It was a long time ago.'

Although if that was the case, why had the wedding dress rattled him so much? He'd looked frightened, as if he'd seen a ghost.

The expression on Leo's face told Emma he was thinking the same thing – even though he'd been reluctant, at first, to admit that his father's reaction had been odd.

'Look, he either forgot about the wedding or he's keeping it quiet for some reason. Nobody tells everything about themselves,' said Emma gently. 'Even husbands and wives keep things from each other.'

In Carl's case, it was the fact that he was meeting up regularly with Selena for clandestine sex sessions. Emma breathed out slowly, trying to keep her focus on the here and now, as Leo shifted on the bench until he was facing her.

'The thing about my father, Emma, is that he's an open book. A stalwart of Heaven's Cove, an honest and upstanding citizen of the village. In fact, he's so well thought of he's been given—'

He winced and pressed his lips together.

'He's been given an award in the King's Birthday Honours List?'

Leo's jaw dropped. 'How on earth do you know about that? It's a secret.'

'I'm sorry but I couldn't help seeing the letter about an award when I was in your shop. I only glanced at it as I walked past. It had been left on the side so was hard to miss. Sorry,' she added again for good measure, sure that Leo was about to accuse her of invading his family's privacy.

But all he said was: 'It's an MBE, and he's not going to accept it.'

That was the second big surprise of the morning for Emma.

'Why not? He seems the kind of man who wouldn't... well, you know,' Emma finished lamely.

'Wouldn't what?'

'Look, I don't really know your dad but, from what I've seen and heard about him, he doesn't seem the kind of man to turn down an MBE.'

'That's just it. He's not. Appearance is everything with my father, and he'd love the pomp and ceremony and... and' – Leo searched for the word – '*kudos* involved in having such an honour.'

'Did he tell you why he's turning it down?'

'He says that he doesn't think he deserves it.'

'But it sounds as if you don't believe that.'

Leo shook his head. 'I'm not quite sure what I believe at the moment. So little is making sense.'

He wiped the back of his hand across his mouth. 'If I'm levelling with you, before we saw that wedding photo, it crossed my mind that the B and R engraved in the ring might be my father and the missing bride.'

'Did you really think that Beatrice had been his secret wife?'

Leo's mouth rose at one corner. 'No, not really. It was only a fleeting thought. But what if my father and Beatrice had a fling and that's why he's skulking suspiciously at her wedding?'

'I'm not sure he was skulking.'

'He was hiding behind a tree.'

Emma had to agree that it did look rather suspicious, and he hadn't been on the guest list either. But gate-crashing an ex's nuptials still didn't explain why he claimed not to know anything about her half a century later, unless...

'I'm assuming that Beatrice's wedding was before he married your mum,' she said tentatively, and was relieved when Leo nodded. At least he wasn't a cheat, unlike Carl.

'It was ages before my parents got married. They tied the

knot in 1977 and had only met two years before that. My mother was the perfect catch, apparently.'

'So what are you going to do about this?' Emma asked. 'Will you tell your dad about the wedding photo?'

Leo bent his head and stared at the ground for a moment.

'I don't know. Probably not, and I'd be grateful if you'd keep all of this, including the MBE, to yourself.'

'I won't say a word. But now that I know the bride's name...'

'You'd still like to find her and give her back the ring?'

'I would. It seems the right thing to do. But I don't have to mention you or your father, and there'll be no reason for her to think that the two of you have been involved in any way. When I find out where she lives, I'll simply give back the ring that she's lost. Does that sound all right?'

'Yeah, thanks,' said Leo, his voice flat. 'And then everything can get back to how it was, before any of this happened.'

Before I came to Heaven's Cove and put a cat amongst the pigeons, thought Emma, wondering if she would ever fit into this beautiful, close-knit part of the world.

22

ROBERT

Robert looked at his watch and blinked to bring the gold hands into focus. It wasn't long past nine in the morning but he felt as if he'd been up for hours. Probably because he *had* been up for much of the night.

He wasn't a man to succumb to insomnia. He worked hard, slept deeply and rarely woke in the witching hours. But last night he'd woken every hour, on the hour, with a feeling of dread in the pit of his stomach.

They'll find out. That's what had kept spinning round his head on a loop. *If they dig deep enough, they'll find out and soon everyone will know.*

Finally, he'd accepted that further sleep was impossible, so he'd got up at 5.30 for the day.

He'd stood in his living room, staring at the seascape painting that Barbara had hated, and thinking about what was hidden in the safe behind it.

And then he'd sat in the conservatory that Barbara had loved and watched a pale sun rise above the village. It had scored the sky pastel pink and burnished orange as he'd decided that action was required to keep his shameful secret buried.

That's why he was now standing outside that woman's shop, steeling himself for what had to be done.

Taking a deep breath, Robert pushed open the door and stepped inside.

Leo was standing in the corner of the shop that he'd been allocated. Emma was talking to a customer near the tiny alcove that passed for a changing room.

'Dad. What are you doing here?' Leo had an unfamiliar expression on his face, a mixture of surprise and something else that he couldn't make out.

Robert took a good look around him and caught sight of the wedding dress, which looked more beautiful every time he saw it.

But this time he'd steeled himself not to react. Not to picture Beatrice wearing it as she walked down the aisle all those years ago. Not to feel again as he'd felt back then.

'Are you all right, Dad?' Leo asked.

'Of course,' Robert replied, noticing that the shop had changed, even in the short time since he'd last been in here.

The chrome rails were full of stock and more gilt-framed paintings had been put up on the walls.

Robert still expected the place to smell of mildew and sweat, which he associated with old, discarded clothing. But the overwhelming smell today was vanilla, presumably from the candle that was burning next to the till.

Everything looked clean and fresh under the bright lighting. And even the small area set aside for Leo looked rather good. Leo had a table, with his till at one end, and there were a couple of mannequins nearby, wearing suits.

'I thought I'd call in to make sure everything is ticking over efficiently,' said Robert, giving Emma a curt nod.

He didn't recognise the woman she was with – a tourist, probably, who had an armful of clothing and was chatting away to Emma as if the two of them had been friends for years.

'Everything's going well,' said Leo. 'Our customers have been very understanding about our temporary change in circumstances. And Terry's happy with how the work's going in our shop. Well, as happy as Terry can be. You know what he's like.'

It wasn't Robert's imagination. His son was definitely being a little cool with him, but there was no way Leo could suspect anything. Not yet. He was probably still confused about his father turning down the MBE.

Robert thought about the reply he was about to send, declining the award, and swallowed. But he couldn't afford to be distracted from what had to be done right now.

'Do you think I could use the facilities while I'm here?' he asked in as jaunty a voice as he could muster. 'I would call in to our shop but I don't want to disturb Terry when he's hard at work. He's so easily distracted.'

Leo glanced at Emma, who was still deep in conversation with the customer, and wrinkled his nose.

'I'm sure Emma won't mind. The toilet's at the back of the shop, past the kitchen.'

Robert was tempted to snipe that he'd be sure to turn the bathroom tap off carefully when he was done.

But now wasn't the time for point scoring. So he made his way to the back of the store where Maisie, a rather sulky-looking teenager, was letting loose with a steamer. Clouds of vapour were rising into the air as she did her best to de-wrinkle a long skirt made of pink cheesecloth.

Beatrice had had a dress made of cheesecloth, back in the late 1960s. But it was pale blue, which matched the colour of her eyes. He remembered lying on the grass, near Driftwood House, gazing into those unmistakable eyes which were streaked with silver grey.

'Looking for the loo?' Maisie enquired, stopping to mop her hot face with the back of her hand.

Robert gave her a half-smile and walked past into the kitchen area and on to the bathroom. This was the source of the flooding that had caused so much trouble.

He tutted again at the inconvenience of it all, before giving the bathroom a swerve and approaching the coat hooks near the back door.

Was it here? He felt sure that she wouldn't keep it on the shop floor, but what if he was wrong?

Robert delved behind the two jackets that were hanging up and was relieved when his fingers closed around leather. A brown handbag was hanging from the hook that was closest to the back door.

After glancing around, to make sure no one had followed him, Robert took the handbag from its peg and opened the zip.

Barbara's bag had always been crammed to the brim, with bulging purse, packs of tissues, lipsticks, a hairbrush, emergency biscuits and reading glasses.

In contrast, Emma's bag contained only a small purse, a mobile phone, a comb, a lurid key ring that said 'MUM' in orange letters, and a tube of hand cream.

Robert unzipped the inner pocket of the bag and prayed that Beatrice's wedding ring was in the same place where he'd seen Emma put it before.

He was in luck. His fingers hit smooth, cool metal and he smiled with satisfaction as he pulled out the ring and slipped it into his trouser pocket.

What he was doing was wrong but what choice did he have? Emma was meddling in something that was far bigger than she could possibly understand, and her doggedness was unsettling the status quo. The sooner it all stopped, the better.

Robert had closed the handbag and just finished rearranging the jacket back over it when he became aware of Maisie. She was standing several feet from him, near the door to the bathroom.

'All right?' she said, giving him a straight stare.

'Yes, I'm perfectly all right, thank you,' Robert answered, keeping his breathing level. 'I accidentally knocked a jacket off its peg so I was replacing it.'

Maisie nodded, and he gave her a smile, feeling a cold prickle of sweat on the back of his neck. That had been a close call.

He moved swiftly past the teenager and went back to Leo. Emma was still chatting to the tourist, who was now wearing an elegant fitted shift dress in maroon silk.

'Looks like another happy customer,' said Leo, tilting his head towards her.

'More to the point, how are *our* customers?' said Robert, glancing back at Maisie, who had followed him onto the shop floor. 'Are they happy?'

'They seem to be. Mr Brellasham Senior and River have been in this morning to collect their orders, and Warren Daleton has placed a new order for a linen suit and silk tie.'

'Warren? He's never shopped with us before.'

'He came into Emma's shop with his family and ended up looking at what we had to offer while his wife was browsing. Emma persuaded him to try on the charcoal-grey linen, which he wasn't sure would suit him. But he liked it so much, he ordered it on the spot.'

'Really?'

'I've made a few sales over the last day or so when tourists have come in with their girlfriends or wives and looked at our clothes while their other halves have been browsing.'

'Good.'

Robert glanced at Emma but felt too uncomfortable to catch her eye. Not when he'd just been ferreting about in her handbag.

'What are you up to today?' asked Leo.

'This and that. I have a committee meeting at the cultural

centre this afternoon and a Friends of Heaven's Cove Library meeting this evening. Though I'm not sure the place is large enough to be called a library.'

Leo looked down at the counter where he was folding a white shirt. He seemed to be taking a long time fiddling about with just one garment.

'I was at the library yesterday,' he said. 'The one in Callowfield.'

'Why's that?'

'Emma was researching some stuff. I had to go into Callowfield anyway so I gave her a lift.'

Robert blinked, not sure what to say. He didn't want his son getting too pally with the woman who'd flooded their shop. And what sort of 'stuff' was she researching at Callowfield Library? He could only hope that he'd taken possession of the wedding ring in time.

Leo was giving him a funny look, as if he was waiting for him to say something.

'I haven't been to Callowfield for ages,' Robert ventured.

No one needed to know that but he wasn't sure what else he was expected to say about Leo and Emma's jaunt to a library.

'Oh,' he added. 'Don't forget that I'll be in Plymouth for a business conference this coming weekend, leaving Friday and arriving back early Monday evening.'

'Right.' Leo ran a hand across his jaw. 'I had forgotten. Do you need to go?'

'It's an excellent networking opportunity and I've been invited to speak on the Sunday about building a small business into a successful enterprise from scratch.'

Robert was looking forward to it. He enjoyed public speaking, and the invitation highlighted how much he was respected as a trustworthy businessman, even outside the confines of Heaven's Cove.

His mind strayed back to searching through Emma's

handbag for a ring that wasn't his. But he refused to give it head room.

'Will you keep an eye on everything, including Terry, while I'm away?' he asked Leo. 'He said he's going to work over the weekend, if need be, to get the job finished.'

'Of course. Terry can moan for Britain but he seems to be doing a grand job.'

'Good, good,' said Robert absent-mindedly, concentrating on walking to the door while not catching sight of the wedding dress. 'I'll be off then.'

He stepped into the lane and closed the door behind him. He was desperately in need of fresh air because the thought of taking the wedding ring was starting to make him feel nauseous.

What had he done? Robert walked through Heaven's Cove, hardly noticing the tourists thronging the narrow pavements.

And he purposely walked straight past Patricia Maunder, who was trying to attract his attention. She probably wanted to complain again about children playing ball on the village green opposite her cottage.

'How rude,' he heard her tell the friend she was with. 'That man can be very pompous and self-important at times.'

Was that how people saw him? he wondered as he reached the lifeboat station and sat down on the sea wall.

He'd never have been called pompous or self-important back when he was plain 'Bob' from the Jones family who lived in Heaven's Brook. Before his life became consumed with committee meetings, financial plans and stock orders.

A sudden longing to be back with his family, when he was younger and life was simpler, hit him like a blow, making it hard to breathe.

'Don't be stupid,' he muttered to himself, taking shallow breaths. 'I was nothing back then. A nobody. And now I'm a great success.'

He repeated that a few times, to make himself feel better.

If people thought him sometimes pompous and self-important, so be it. They were probably envious of his standing in the village.

Robert looked out to sea, across the waves that were swelling towards shore. He loved this place, with its endless sky and twisting lanes and close-knit community. He was happy with his life. How could he not be when he'd sacrificed so much for it?

He pushed his hand into his pocket and felt the smooth gold of Beatrice's wedding ring. The precious metal that had touched her skin for fifty years while she'd been away in far-flung places.

Did the appearance of the dress and ring mean that Beatrice was back in Devon? He looked around him nervously – desperate to see her face after all this time, but dreading it equally.

He'd kept his distance for half a century now, resisting the temptation to find out how and where she was.

Though he had searched online for her name in a panic a couple of days ago, when a terrible thought had struck him: perhaps her ring and dress were in Emma's shop because she'd passed away.

Fortunately, there had been nothing about her demise on the internet. Just a few mentions of her diplomat husband which he'd closed down without reading.

He had allowed himself to check out her parents though, and had found that her father was still listed as living in the grand old house, ten miles away, that Robert remembered from so long ago.

He sat on the wall for a while longer, watching as the lifeboat launched, causing a wall of water to slosh against the stones and splash his shiny shoes.

If only he had the courage to throw the wedding ring into the waves. Then this painful reminder of the past would be gone for ever. But he couldn't bring himself to do it. Not when it belonged to her.

With a creak and groan of old joints, Robert heaved himself to his feet and started walking towards his house. He didn't feel proud of himself for taking the ring but he'd get over his bad behaviour. Just as he had in the past.

23

EMMA

Emma thanked the taxi driver and watched him drive away until the car vanished in the distance.

It was deathly quiet out here. In Heaven's Cove, there was usually the sound of waves crashing against the quayside, or seagulls squawking, or wind whistling around the eaves of Driftwood House.

But the outskirts of the tiny village of Heaven's Boon were peaceful this evening, with no one around. The silence was so complete, it seemed odd – almost spooky, thought Emma, pulling her jacket more tightly around her.

So she'd better get started, because the sooner she achieved what she'd come here to do, the sooner she could get back to Rosie's noisy and comforting home.

Emma double-checked the address she'd noted in her phone and opened the garden gate of the house in front of her.

It was a very grand building, just as she'd imagined it would be from the address she'd found online for the Farleigh-Addison family: Heaven's Boon Manor.

What she hadn't anticipated was that the lovely old house

would be on the market. A 'For Sale' board had been hammered into the earth by the high stone wall that edged the property.

'Just a smidgen outside my price range,' murmured Emma, whose only affordable option so far in Heaven's Cove was a cramped flat above the chip shop, or a bedraggled cottage that even the estate agent had agreed needed 'loads of work'.

It looked as if she'd be imposing on Rosie's hospitality for a while yet. Which at least meant she could give her a hand in the evenings, before Liam got home. Last night she'd looked after Alfie while Rosie had a bath, and she'd become a dab hand, all over again, at changing nappies. But their arrangement couldn't go on for ever.

Parking that worry for the moment, Emma walked along the gravel path to the front door which was flanked by white pillars. Was she about to come face to face with the elusive Beatrice?

Emma's rap on the brass door-knocker sounded like gunshots as she began to fish in her handbag for the wedding ring. She felt surprisingly nervous at the prospect of meeting Beatrice. And she had to remember not to mention Robert or his son, because she'd promised Leo that she'd keep them out of it.

No one was coming, so Emma knocked on the door for a second time, wondering if the 'For Sale' sign meant Beatrice and her family had already moved out and she'd have to begin her search all over again.

'Hope not,' she murmured, still rooting through her handbag. But the ring wasn't there.

'Oh, for goodness' sake.'

Emma pulled the zipped inner pocket of her bag inside out and, seeing it was empty, began to pile everything in the handbag onto the front step.

What would Beatrice think if she did open the door to find a strange woman surrounded by a pile of personal items? How would she react when Emma told her that the lost wedding ring she'd been about to return was lost again?

Emma suddenly wanted to cry – for Beatrice, whose ring was nowhere to be seen, and for her marriage which had crashed and burned. The important things in her life had slipped through her fingers, and she couldn't even keep hold of something precious that belonged to someone else.

Think, Emma, think.

Emma tried to stop panicking and go through everything logically. She was sure she'd placed the ring in her handbag for safekeeping. She turned the bag upside down and a shower of dust and tissue flecks drifted down onto the step. Perhaps she was mistaken and the gold ring was on her bedside table at Driftwood House or under the counter at the shop.

Fortunately, in the circumstances, no one appeared to be in at Heaven's Boon Manor, so she would have time to find it. But that meant she'd had a wasted journey.

Cursing, Emma piled everything back into her handbag and went out again into the quiet lane.

No cars had passed since she'd arrived and, when Emma pulled out her mobile phone to call for a taxi, she realised there was no signal.

'Damn!' Emma pushed her phone back into her handbag.

There were several things she didn't miss about London – pollution, rammed Tube platforms and the regular wail of emergency service vehicles, for a start. But she longed for the expansive mobile coverage she'd once enjoyed, rather than the patchy service in this neck of the woods.

I miss Thea, too, thought Emma forlornly, deciding to ring her daughter when she got back to Driftwood House and a signal. In the meantime, perhaps there was a public phone box in the heart of Heaven's Boon that she could use to summon up transport.

She began to trudge along the lane towards the centre of the village that was in the middle of nowhere.

Leo might have given her a lift out here, she supposed, but it had seemed presumptuous to ask him. They were getting on better but were hardly fast friends. Plus, there was a chance that Emma's worst-case scenario might be true.

That scenario had popped into her mind on their way home from Callowfield Library the other day: what if Robert was being evasive about Beatrice because they'd had a child together? What if there was a secret son or daughter out there that no one knew about?

It wasn't likely. But even a small chance of Leo coming face to face with an unknown half-sibling was best avoided.

Heaven's Boon was a fraction of the size of Heaven's Cove, which seemed like a thriving metropolis in comparison. But it still had a pub on the ambitiously named Grand High Street, which was little more than a slightly wider lane.

Emma popped her head round the front door. 'Is there a phone box anywhere near here, please?'

The stout, middle-aged man propping up the bar – the pub's sole customer – stopped drinking his pint and stared at her.

'A public phone box?' she tried again.

The elderly woman behind the bar put down the glass she was polishing. 'Afraid not. Is it an emergency?'

'No, not really,' said Emma, stepping inside the pub which smelled of lager and fried food. 'I need to call a taxi and my mobile phone can't get a signal.'

'There's no signal around here,' said the man unhelpfully but he redeemed himself by adding: 'I'm sure Maureen here will let you use the pub's landline, won't you, Maureen?'

Maureen agreed that she would and passed the phone to Emma, who made her call.

'Long to wait?' asked the man, wiping beer foam from his bottom lip.

'Only five minutes because they've got a car already in the area.'

'That's good. Have you got far to go?'

'A few miles. I'm in Heaven's Cove.'

'Too far to walk then.' The man gestured towards the gleaming optics behind the bar. 'Do you fancy a drink while you're waiting? You can keep me company.'

'That's kind of you but no thank you,' said Emma, wondering if the man was being kind or trying to pick her up. She dismissed that notion immediately. The chances of him trying to pick up an unremarkable ageing divorcee like her was unlikely.

'What brings you to Heaven's Boon?' he asked. 'Visiting someone, are you?'

'I've been to the manor house, trying to find the Farleigh-Addisons, but there's no one there.'

'That's 'cos they're all gone,' said Maureen from behind the bar. 'Mrs Farleigh-Addison died a few years ago and the colonel's in his mid-nineties now and has gone into a home recently. Dementia. It's very sad.'

'I didn't realise that.' Emma perched on a high stool with her handbag on her lap. 'What about their daughter, Beatrice? Is she still around?'

Maureen stopped wiping a cloth across the stained bar top and sniffed. 'She lives abroad with her husband. Has done for as long as I can remember. But I expect she's back and forth at the moment while the house is up for sale. Why are you looking for them?'

'I found something that Beatrice lost that I want to return to her,' said Emma, feeling sick all over again because she wasn't sure where the lost ring was. 'Do you know where I might find her?'

'You could try the house again on a different day,' said Maureen. 'But other than that, I don't know. The Farleigh-Addisons always kept themselves to themselves and weren't around much. They were always off abroad or staying at the Lavender Orchid.'

'What's that?' Emma asked, noticing through the window that her taxi had pulled up outside.

'Some kind of fancy hotel in London. If they were ever asked to take part in anything local, their reply was, more often than not' – Maureen dropped her rich Devon accent and adopted a snooty voice – '"We'd love to but I'm afraid we'll be at the Lavender Orchid that weekend."'

The man nursing his pint laughed. 'They weren't short of a few bob and that house will sell for mega-bucks, I reckon.'

Emma agreed that it would and headed for her taxi, after thanking both of them for their help.

In the back of the car, as it made its way towards the coast, Emma stared out at the high hedges that lined Devon's lanes.

It had been quite a day. She'd come close to finding Beatrice but had failed. Which was just as well because she'd lost her precious wedding ring.

Emma rifled in her handbag for a tissue because her eyes were prickling. This was the second wedding ring she'd 'lost', one way or another, in a week. It made her seem very careless.

She rubbed her thumb across the fourth finger of her left hand. It felt odd now there was nothing there. No cool, smooth gold against her skin.

What if the divorce had never happened? thought Emma as the car crested a hill and she spotted a ribbon of blue sea.

This was a game she often played for the sole purpose, she'd decided, of torturing herself. She imagined herself, a little older, surrounded by Thea and grandchildren. Sitting at the dining room table of their immaculate home, with Carl stooping to kiss her on the cheek.

Only this time, a different scenario popped into her head. Five years on, just her and Carl, eating lunch in silence, surrounded by photos of Thea and Henry enjoying themselves in exotic, far-flung locations.

Carl sitting with his head in his iPad as usual but stopping scrolling for long enough to ask if his shirts had been washed. Then, casting a critical eye over whatever she was wearing, and asking archly, 'Don't you think you're too old for flared trousers?' As if she was a great disappointment to him.

Emma stopped daydreaming, put her tissue away and looked out of the taxi window.

The cottages of Heaven's Cove were coming into view now, with lamplight shining from windows as the sky darkened.

The village looked beautiful, sitting in a fold of the land. It was bordered on one side by the high cliff that was topped by Driftwood House, and on the other by a wooded headland that stretched out into the water.

Emma exhaled slowly as the *what if*s of her daydreams faded further and reality pushed its way in.

This was her home now, and the site of Heavenly Vintage Vavoom – the fledgling business that was completely hers.

Her new life was terrifying but, she realised with a rush of emotion, it was exciting, too. And best of all, she didn't need anyone else's permission to live it in whichever way she chose.

Emma's thumb strayed again to the bare fourth finger of her left hand. The slight indentation that had persisted after she'd taken off her wedding ring had all but vanished.

Did Beatrice's fourth finger bear a similar imprint of a marriage? she wondered, berating herself again for being careless enough to misplace such a precious piece of jewellery.

Maybe the ring was in her bedroom at Driftwood House or somewhere in the shop. She certainly hoped so. But if it wasn't – if the ring was lost for good – her and Leo's search for the missing bride had been in vain.

24

LEO

It had been almost a week now of sharing shop space and, much to Leo's surprise, it wasn't proving to be as awkward as he'd feared.

At first, he and Emma had skirted around each other, apologising profusely every time one of them got in the other's way. Which was often in such a relatively small space.

But they'd both started settling into the new arrangement and were talking a little, in between customers.

Leo had been impressed by Emma's knowledge of vintage fashion and her manner with customers, including his. Some sartorial advice she'd offered to local accountant Henry, who'd come in to enquire about a suit half an hour ago, had helped to secure a sale. The advice on cut and colour for his physique that she'd given him had been spot on.

He also had to admit that he was enjoying the ambience at Heavenly Vintage Vavoom. The shop, with its whitewashed walls, sparkling chrome rails and vibrant clothing was much brighter than his store. There, amongst the dark wood and dour suits, he sometimes felt like an old fossil.

Right now, Emma's shop was quiet so he was taking a break,

which involved perching on the end of the table and staring out of the window at the passing tide of people. There was a lot on his mind.

But Emma, in contrast, was a ball of energy. She'd seemed wound up since arriving at work and she was currently pulling everything out from under the till counter. Stock books, spare printer cartridges, and folders filled with documents were spread around her, as she knelt with her head under the counter, out of sight.

'Emma,' Leo called softly.

There was a bang as she straightened up and her head hit wood. 'Ouch.' She rubbed at the side of her scalp. 'Did someone come in?'

'No. Sorry, I didn't mean to make you jump. I just wondered what on earth you're doing.'

Emma grimaced and got to her feet. Today she was wearing a sky-blue shift dress that Leo guessed was an original from the 1960s. It suited her.

'I'm looking for something. Actually...' She pushed a lock of hair behind her ear. 'Look, I've lost Beatrice's wedding ring. I didn't know how to tell you because the ring and the wedding dress over there seem to have caused a fair amount of... I'm not sure what the right word is?... issues.'

Leo raised an eyebrow because 'issues' definitely didn't cover it. Surprises, maybe. Or a general feeling of things being out of sorts, though you didn't exactly know why.

'The last time I saw the ring,' he told her, 'you were putting it in your handbag.'

'Which is where I thought it still was. But when I got to the Farleigh-Addisons' house, it had gone.'

'Whoa! Hold on. When did you go to see them, and what happened?'

'Yesterday evening, I went to their house... well, mansion really, in Heaven's Boon. It's enormous.'

'Did you see Beatrice?' Leo asked lightly, even though his stomach had started churning.

It was so frustrating. He couldn't get that woman's wedding photo out of his mind, even though neither he nor Emma had mentioned it. The subject seemed to be out of bounds.

But he'd lain awake last night picturing his young father lurking behind the yew tree. And he'd even begun to wonder if there might be a half-brother or -sister out there somewhere – the result of a fling between his father and the bride. Though he would never admit that to Emma.

It was unlikely because he couldn't imagine his father ever abandoning a child. But perhaps Robert Jacobson-Jones feared that a less than shiny past might ruin his sterling reputation in Heaven's Cove. And Leo had begun to realise that he knew his father far less well than he'd thought.

'I didn't see anyone at the house,' said Emma, bending to put the folders back under the counter. 'The place is up for sale and no one was there. Apparently, Mrs Farleigh-Addison died a while ago and her husband, the colonel, has dementia and has gone into a care home.'

'What about Beatrice?'

'She's lived abroad with her diplomat husband for years, but that's all I could find about her online.'

That was all Leo had found too, but he didn't say so.

'The details were scant, to say the least,' Emma added. 'She's like a ghost.'

'Or a spy,' said Leo and then coughed to cover his embarrassment.

A spy? Really? Beatrice was elusive with an unsentimental streak – or she'd never have given away her wedding dress. But that didn't make her a female James Bond.

'Are you going to carry on trying to find her?' he asked.

Emma shook her head. 'There's no point when I haven't got

a ring to return to her. I can't believe I've lost it, after all the fuss I made.'

'Have you looked everywhere?'

'I've turned out my handbag, scoured Driftwood House and searched the shop, but it's gone. I feel awful about it.'

'Things get lost so don't beat yourself up,' said Leo, feeling an unexpected wash of relief.

The dress was still hanging in the corner, attracting the attention of everyone who came into the shop. But now the ring was gone for good, perhaps he could forget his dad being weird and everything could go back to normal.

Emma finished organising everything under the counter before checking her mobile phone for the hundredth time that morning.

'Are you waiting for a call?' Leo asked, standing on tiptoe to enjoy a glimpse of blue sea from the window.

'Not really.' Emma puffed air through her lips. 'Well, actually, I'm hoping to hear from Thea. We spoke last night when I got back to Driftwood House and she sounded a little off.'

'Is something wrong?'

Emma winced. 'I don't know. She says not but I can tell something's not right. Call it mother's intuition. I messaged Carl, my ex-husband, to see if he thought Thea was upset about something. But he always says she's fine, whatever's going on.'

'It's good that you and your ex still speak though.'

'Yeah.' Emma grimaced. 'We kind of do.'

'Anna and I haven't spoken in years,' said Leo, wondering, even as the words came out, how the conversation had taken such a personal turn.

'That must be hard.'

'It was at the time, when our relationship ended. But we've both moved on. I've heard from friends of friends that she's living near Leeds now, with her husband and two small children.'

'How do you feel about that?' Emma asked softly.

'I'm genuinely happy for her.'

Which was the truth. He didn't want Anna to be miserable. But claiming that they'd both moved on from their split felt like a lie. He'd got over the heartbreak, but little else had changed since they'd gone their separate ways. He was still here in Heaven's Cove, living alone and working for his father.

'That's good. It's best not to be bitter which, after more than twenty years of marriage and only a few days of divorce, I'm still working on, to be honest.' Emma gave a rueful smile. 'Where do the years go? It seems like only yesterday that I was meeting Thea from school in my charity shop vintage bargains and dreaming of opening a business just like this one.'

'And you did it.' Leo glanced at Maisie, who'd begun steam-cleaning a 1970s trouser suit at the back of the shop and was earwigging shamelessly. 'I imagine you were the best-dressed mum in the playground.'

Did that sound flirtatious? Maisie was giving him plenty of side-eye.

He tried again. 'What I mean is, with your fashion sense and your ability to spot a bargain online, I should think you stood out compared to the other mums.'

Emma smiled. 'I loved scouring charity shops for pre-loved clothing, and I got hooked on eBay and other online sites when Thea was growing up. So I did look a bit different. But Carl wasn't happy about it. He thought my clothes choices reflected badly on him and he was worried about what people would say.'

Carl sounded like an insensitive, controlling arse, Leo decided. Though he didn't proffer that opinion, figuring that the divorce was too raw for Emma to take it well. But, with any luck, she'd come to the same conclusion one day.

'At least now you can build up your business in any way you see fit,' he said instead.

Emma nodded. 'What about you? Did you always want to go into the family firm?'

'I'm not sure it was a conscious choice. Joining the business was never insisted upon. It was simply expected, I suppose. My father had worked immensely hard to build it all up and it was expected that I would join him.'

'Expected by him?'

'By everyone really, but yes, it was expected by my dad. This business has been his life since he was a young man.'

Emma said nothing and Leo wondered if, like him, she was thinking about Robert skulking in the back of a wedding photo fifty years ago.

'Anyway,' he said, wanting to move on from the troubling photograph, 'I suppose I've had an easy life with a ready-made job handed to me on a plate.'

'It doesn't sound particularly easy to me,' said Emma. 'Living up to other people's expectations can be hard, especially if what they want isn't what you might have chosen for yourself.'

Leo had a sudden urge to grab Emma and kiss her. Everyone else went on about how lucky he was to be a part of the family business. They didn't seem to realise that, though he recognised and appreciated his good fortune, he sometimes had mixed feelings about it.

'Thanks. I—'

'Do either of you wanna coffee?' called Maisie, cutting across him.

Leo and Emma locked eyes. This was a first. Maisie did the work she was asked to do but rarely interacted with them, even when Emma tried to involve her in conversation.

'That would be lovely,' said Emma. 'Thank you.'

'Yeah, cheers, Maisie. I'll have one too.'

When the teenager scuttled off towards the kitchen, Emma

sat down heavily on the stool next to her till. She looked so tired and defeated all of a sudden, Leo felt sorry for her.

'It's a shame you didn't get to return the ring,' he said, standing up from the table and stretching his legs.

'Yeah. It's a shame I lost it. I just hope Beatrice won't turn up one day looking for it.'

'I doubt she will if she hasn't turned up already.' Leo paused. 'So her family home is impressive, is it?'

Leave it, Leo! yelled his inner voice. *Just forget Beatrice and whatever link there may or may not have been between her and your father.*

But it was like an itch that he had to scratch.

'It's a lovely old house, right on the outskirts of the village. It's quite isolated and Maureen told me that Beatrice's parents didn't mix much with the other locals.'

'Who's Maureen?'

'The woman behind the bar of the pub in Heaven's Boon. She let me use the pub's landline to call for a taxi.'

Emma hadn't asked him for a lift last night, which was probably just as well, thought Leo, who had no urge to come face to face with Beatrice or any of her family.

'Maureen made the family sound very snooty and said the colonel and his wife were usually abroad or staying at a hotel that had a peculiar name.' Emma thought for a moment. 'The Lavender Orchid, that's it. She said they were often at the Lavender Orchid in London.' She gave him a searching look. 'Are you all right?'

Bells had started going off in Leo's brain as he remembered what his father had mentioned the other night about that London hotel where he'd once worked.

'I think it was named after an exotic flower... something purple.'

Leo grabbed his mobile and began to search for the hotel. There was a Lavender Orchid hotel in Hamswood Grove.

Wasn't that the area of London that his father had mentioned?

Leo clicked on the link for the hotel and a magnificent old building appeared on his screen.

Enjoy a luxurious stay at the Lavender Orchid which has been the choice of discerning guests for the last 130 years, he read.

'What's the matter?' Leo glanced up from his phone into Emma's concerned face. 'You look like you've seen a ghost.'

'Not a ghost exactly, but an echo from the past.'

'I have no idea what you're talking about.'

Leo's eyes flicked to the back of the shop, but Maisie hadn't returned from her coffee quest.

'You said that Beatrice's parents often stayed at a hotel called the Lavender Orchid.'

'That's what I was told. Do you know the place?'

'No, but I think it might be the London hotel where my father worked as a butler to VIP guests when he was young.'

Emma's hand flew to her mouth. 'Did he tell you that he worked there?'

'Not exactly. He says he can't remember what the hotel was called, but he thinks it was named after an exotic purple flower. He also said it was in the Hamswood Grove area, which is where the Lavender Orchid happens to be.'

Leo waited for Emma to tell him he was being ridiculous. He was making assumptions and had got it wrong. But all she said was: 'How long did he work there?'

'For a couple of years, as far as I know. Then he came back to Heaven's Cove and opened his business.'

'When was he at the hotel?'

'From the end of 1970 onwards, I believe.'

'So from around the time of Beatrice's wedding.'

'Yep.'

Leo read a little more about the Lavender Orchid and then

pushed his phone into his trouser pocket. Emma was still sitting on the stool, watching him.

'So what are you thinking?' she asked. 'Coincidence?'

'Probably, yeah.'

Leo scratched absent-mindedly at the back of his neck. It had to be a coincidence, didn't it? But the coincidences were stacking up: Robert's odd reaction to Beatrice's wedding dress and ring, his lurking appearance in her wedding photo, the fact that he appeared to have worked at the same hotel her parents frequented, and his reluctance to talk about his time in London.

And now he was turning down his MBE, an honour that he'd have fought tooth and nail for just a short while ago. Before he first saw the wedding dress and everything began to change.

'Can you ask your father about all of this?' Emma asked.

'There's no point. He'll just clam up.'

'So that's that then.'

'I guess so.'

Leo moved back behind his table and began to unfold and refold shirts. They didn't need folding again. They were perfectly folded the first time. But he found the repetitive movements soothing.

He smoothed non-existent wrinkles from another shirt and made a decision.

'I'm going to London,' he declared. 'I'm going to visit the Lavender Orchid and see if they can tell me anything about my father's employment there.'

'Leo, it was fifty years ago,' said Emma quietly.

She'd moved to the other side of the shop and was standing in front of the glorious wedding dress.

'I know. It's probably a wild goose chase, but you know all about those.'

'You're right. I do.' Emma slowly traced her fingers across the lace bodice of the exquisite gown. 'When will you go?'

'On Sunday, while the shop's shut,' said Leo, making plans

on the hoof. 'I'll catch a direct morning train from Exeter and come back early to late evening. Why? Did you want to come with me?'

It was only a throwaway line. Something to say while his brain fizzed, trying to work out if this London trip was inspired. Or the worst idea ever.

'Where did you say the Lavender Orchid is?' Emma asked.

'Hamswood Grove. Why?'

'No reason.' She pulled her lips into a tight line and went quiet. Then she said: 'OK.'

Leo's brain stopped whirling. 'OK, what?'

'OK, I'll come to London with you on Sunday, if you meant what you said when you invited me?'

'Sure, if you want to. But why? You don't have to, just because I gave you a lift to the library.'

'I know, but you helped me out and now I'd like to help you. I can see if Thea's around and meet up with her, too. I'd love that because I haven't seen her for a few weeks.'

'Great. OK, then. I'll look into booking us some tickets.'

Leo tried to smile but the potential fallout from what he was planning had suddenly hit him. All he could think was *Dad will kill me if he finds out what I'm doing. And he'll kill me twice over if he realises that Emma is involved.*

But, he realised, he was too far in to step back now. There were so many coincidences – and the Lavender Orchid link between his father and the Farleigh-Addisons was a coincidence too far.

Now it was time to untangle them all and uncover the answers that he felt, in his bones, were waiting to be found.

25

EMMA

Emma stepped outside Paddington station and blinked at the onslaught to her senses.

A red bus was passing, its windows peopled by the blank faces of travellers, and workmen on scaffolding opposite were shouting good-natured insults to one another. Horns were sounding in the distance and the aromas of various cuisines mingled into a thick smell that made her stomach rumble.

Welcome to London. Welcome home.

Only it didn't feel like home. She'd been gone for less than a month but already the city felt different. And so did she.

When Emma had left London, she was separated from her husband and scared about starting a new business. Now she was a divorcee whose shop had been open for three whole weeks and, apart from an unfortunate flood, her business was doing surprisingly well.

She was also travelling with a man who, a month ago, she'd never even met, and was helping him to find out more about his father's secretive past.

'Not boring now, am I,' she murmured to herself, imagining Carl's expression if he knew what was going on.

'What did you say?' asked Leo, who'd been double-checking the time of their return train on his phone.

'I said here we are, in the Big Smoke.'

She cringed inwardly at calling the city that. It made her sound like a hick from the sticks. But Leo didn't notice. He was too busy staring at a weather app on his phone.

'It looks like the bad weather we went through is going to skirt London, which is good news.'

Emma agreed that it was and tucked the umbrella she'd brought with her under her arm. The weather had been horrendous on their train journey up from Exeter – howling wind and torrential rain – but the skies had brightened as they'd approached London.

The two of them had talked during the trip – small talk about their childhoods and favourite TV programmes. But most of the journey had passed in silence while she read her book and he read a newspaper.

What they were going to do in London had hardly been mentioned. As if they were both slightly stunned that they were doing it at all.

Plus, Emma hadn't told him the whole truth about why she'd accompanied him to the city.

She was burning with curiosity to find out more about Robert's intriguing past – a past that included skulking in the background of Beatrice's wedding photo, and working at a hotel that the woman's parents had frequented. That was all true enough.

But there was another reason why Emma was here today, and it wasn't to meet Thea. Disappointingly, her daughter happened to be away from the city this weekend.

'Wow. This is like Heaven's Cove in summer, with bells on,' said Leo, wincing as a crowd of tourists pushed past him.

Emma stepped back so the gaggle, led by a woman bellowing into a microphone, could get by. She was used to being shoulder-barged off the pavement but Leo, who seemed so rooted and sure of himself in rural Devon, looked out of place amidst the city bustle.

'Taxi or Tube?' she shouted, above the din of a drill which had started up at roadworks nearby.

'Taxi,' yelled Leo, pointing at one coming towards them and sticking out his arm.

They sat in the back of the black cab in silence as it moved at a glacial pace through the busy streets, both of them lost in their own thoughts.

Emma was feeling overwhelmed with nostalgia. But her life here already had a nebulous quality when she tried to picture it. A time when she'd been married to Carl, with a head full of dreams and days full of responsibilities.

Now she was responsible to no one and her dreams were more concrete. But it was hard to shake off the past.

Her fingers went automatically to where her wedding ring used to be and, when she saw that Leo had noticed, she pretended to be scratching her hand.

Was Beatrice also missing her wedding ring? Emma wondered, feeling another pang of guilt at losing it. Did Beatrice realise that the ring had dropped into the bag with her wedding dress? Presumably not or she would have contacted Emma by now.

The ringing of Leo's mobile phone jolted Emma back to the present.

'It's my father,' said Leo, a frown creasing the skin between his eyebrows. 'What does he want?'

'Does he know that you're in London?' Emma asked, but Leo was already answering the call.

'Hello, Dad. How's your trip going?'

Emma could hear the tinny buzz of a voice on the line but couldn't make out what Robert was saying.

'Uh-huh.' Leo was nodding. Then he winced. 'Me? No, I'm not in the village. I had a few errands to run.' He listened again as the taxi crawled along in nose-to-tail traffic. 'Actually, I've come in to... um, Exeter for a few things but I can give Terry a ring later to see if he's finished the work.'

That answered Emma's question. Robert was completely in the dark about their London trip.

Leo bit his lip. 'No, we haven't returned the ring to its owner yet. Actually, Emma's misplaced the ring which she's upset about.'

He listened to his father a little longer before ending the call.

'I don't like lying to him about where I am,' he told Emma, pushing the phone into his jeans pocket. 'But I can't tell him I'm on my way to the Lavender Orchid. He'd think I was snooping.'

Which they were. Leo closed his eyes. 'Oh, I don't know, Emma. This seemed like a good idea back in Heaven's Cove. Now I'm not too sure.'

'We'll be back later today and your dad will be none the wiser,' said Emma, trying to sound reassuring.

She peered out of the window. They were moving along roads that Emma had never travelled before, and yet they looked familiar because she'd seen them on Street View.

There was the artisan café with tables on the pavement, the achingly cool wine bar, and Edwardian houses set back from the street.

It wasn't stalking. Not really. Emma had never been in person to the house where Carl and his new girlfriend lived. But she'd looked it up online, obviously, out of curiosity.

And hearing that the hotel Leo planned to visit was in the same area – almost – had prompted an urge to see their new neighbourhood in the flesh. It had seemed like fate.

This was where Carl and Selena walked, probably hand in

hand. It was where her daughter visited, though she rarely mentioned her trips to see her father – apart from letting slip that Selena was 'up for a laugh' and 'good fun to be around'. Descriptions that had hit Emma hard.

Her maternal self-esteem had taken another dent when Thea had said she couldn't meet up with Emma today. Though her daughter had a genuine excuse – she was currently seventy-five miles away, spending the weekend with Henry in the Cotswolds.

Apparently, another mini-break to Cheshire was planned for next month and, while Emma was glad that Thea was enjoying herself, she couldn't help wondering if and when she might make it to Heaven's Cove to see her mum.

Emma leaned her cheek against the glass of the cab window and stared at the world outside.

Perhaps Carl and Selena frequented the wine bar the taxi had just driven past. Or ate at the gastro pub, festooned with hanging baskets, that highlighted an 'oysters and champagne breakfast' on its chalkboard.

Emma didn't want to see her ex-husband and his new love cosying up. But she did want to put some flesh on the bones of her divorce. To make it real, however painful that might be. At the moment everything had a dreamlike quality: her new life in Heaven's Cove, her fledgling business, even her sort-of friendship with the man next to her, who seemed kind of lost himself.

'I think we're here,' said Leo as the taxi came to a halt. He stared through the window at an eye-catching building made of pale Portland stone. 'This is where my father worked all those years ago.'

Pushing thoughts of Carl aside, Emma peered at the hotel whose impressive entrance was flanked by olive trees in huge terracotta pots. It was a far cry from her modest shop in a village lane. Yet there was a link between the wedding dress currently hanging in her fashion store, the discarded wedding ring, and this grand metropolitan building – she just knew it.

But would they be able to find out what that link was?

'Come on,' said Leo, sounding resolved. 'Let's get this over with.'

26

LEO

The reception area of the Lavender Orchid Hotel had a faded grandeur that hinted at past glory: flocked wallpaper and framed paintings of Constable-esque countryside; pale pink sofas with squat wooden legs, and an enormous walnut reception desk, with fringed art deco lamps at either end.

'Can I help you?'

The woman behind the desk gave them a cheery smile. She was wearing an unflattering burgundy waistcoat and a trailing silk scarf which had the hotel logo printed on it. A badge pinned to her chest proclaimed that her name was Branka.

'I hope so.'

Leo suddenly wasn't sure how best to explain why he and Emma were here. He should have thought this through properly beforehand. Emma would think he was an idiot. But the call in the taxi from his father had thrown him.

Lying to his father had made him uncomfortable, and this whole trip was making him nervous. Plus, there was something about what Robert had said that was niggling at the back of Leo's mind.

'Do you have a room booked?' Branka asked.

She had an accent and Leo found himself wondering how far from home she was. When Emma coughed beside him, Leo got his nerves under control.

'No,' he said firmly. 'We've come up from Devon for the day to ask if you have any information about a man who used to work here a long time ago, as a butler to your well-to-do customers.'

'*How* long ago?' asked Branka, her smile fading. 'I'm not sure I can tell you anything. Are you from the police?'

'No. Absolutely not. We're shopkeepers.' Leo took a deep breath because this wasn't going too well. 'My father, Robert Jacobson-Jones, worked here in the late 1970s and I thought it would be good to see where he'd worked and, hopefully, to find out more about his life back then.'

'Can't you ask him?' Branka asked, before her hand flew to her mouth. 'Oh, forgive me. Has your father passed away?'

Leo caught Emma's eye then he looked away. 'My father's not with us today,' he said ambiguously.

'I'm so sorry.' When Branka's face crumpled in sympathy, Leo felt bad for misleading her.

'It's OK. I just wondered if you had any documents from that time that we could look at? So we can piece together his years in London, before he returned home to Devon.'

Branka thought for a moment, biting her lip.

'It would mean a lot,' Leo added.

He was a terrible son for implying that his father was dead, just so he could snoop on his past. But it had been a long journey from Heaven's Cove and he couldn't face it being for nothing.

Branka regarded him closely. Then she twisted her mouth. 'It was many decades ago but I think there are staff employment books from that time. I don't think there is anything else.'

'Would it be possible for us to take a look at the books?' Emma asked beside him.

'You can't take them away,' said Branka fiercely.

'No, we won't.' Emma pointed to a corner where there were two armchairs and a coffee table. 'We could have a look at them over there and you'll be able to keep an eye on us.'

Branka's fierce expression faded as the phone began to ring. 'OK. You sit down and I'll see what I can do. I can't see any harm in it.' She turned to Emma. 'When was your father here?'

'Oh, he's not my dad. He's Leo's. But we think he was here from 1970 for a couple of years.'

Branka answered the phone while Leo and Emma sank into the comfy armchairs in the corner. Emma pushed her handbag and umbrella under her chair and leaned back with her eyes closed.

'Thanks for helping to persuade Branka to let us see the books,' said Leo, stretching out his legs.

'You're welcome.' Emma opened her eyes. 'Though I think it was implying that your dad had kicked the bucket that twisted her arm.'

Leo winced. 'I know. I'm going to hell for that one, aren't I?'

'Probably,' said Emma, but she smiled as golden light, falling through a stained-glass window, dappled across her face and hair. She seemed to be glowing. Leo leaned forward, towards her.

'Here you are,' said Branka, dropping an armful of books bound in black leather onto the coffee table. A cloud of dust rose into the air. 'These are all we have from the time period that you specified.'

'Thank you,' said Leo. 'That's very kind of you. We won't be long and then we'll leave you in peace.' He glanced towards the dining room just visible through beautiful art deco-style doors. 'Are we able to order a coffee?'

'I can arrange for a cafetière to be brought to you.'

Branka bustled off, and Leo and Emma began to go through

the old ledgers which listed members of staff, work rotas and holiday entitlement.

When the coffee arrived, with tiny almond biscuits shaped like stars, Leo paid with a credit card and the searching continued.

Ten minutes later, Leo had leafed through so many lists of names and dates, his head was beginning to ache. He suddenly sat up straighter.

'I've found him,' he declared, pushing the book he was looking at towards Emma. 'Here's his name, in late October 1970 and it says he was taken on as...' He squinted at the tiny writing. 'A kitchen porter. Is that right?'

'It's a perfectly good job,' said Emma, putting down her gold-rimmed coffee cup.

'Yes, it is, but my father told me he worked as a butler. That's all he told me about his time here, but he seemed definite about that.'

'Perhaps he was promoted after a while. I'll see if I can find him six months on.' Emma selected the correct ledger and began flicking through its pages. 'Here he is again, still on the work rota for the kitchens. When did he leave the hotel and return to Heaven's Cove?'

'I'm not sure but he started his business in April 1973, so it must have been before then.'

Leo found the ledgers for winter and spring of that year and began to look through them. There was his father, still marked on the kitchen rota, until 19th March when his name was crossed out. Leo flicked ahead but his father's name wasn't written on any further pages.

'It looks as if he'd gone by mid-March that year.'

'Was he still working in the kitchen?'

'That's what the book says.'

Leo closed the ledger. All he'd learned about his father so far on this trip was that he'd embellished his role at the hotel.

Though surely a white lie was no reason to be so secretive about his time here.

On the one hand, this journey to London had been a waste of time. But on the other, he realised that he was happy spending time with Emma. The more he was with her, the more he enjoyed her company.

She was exasperating sometimes, and she found him exasperating too. She'd made that clear. But mostly she seemed smart and kind, and brave to be starting out on her own.

She was also stylish and rocked the vintage clothes she wore. Leo stole a glance at her. Today she was in a 1950s red polka-dot dress with a full skirt, that made her look chic and cool and very attractive. Carl, he decided, was an idiot.

'Have you found what you wanted?' Branka, who'd been keeping a beady eye on them, had walked over. 'Has it been helpful?'

Leo smiled at her. 'Sort of. It's told us a little more about when my father worked here, but it doesn't tally with the information I already had.'

'Tally?' Branka enquired, flummoxed for the first time.

'It doesn't match what Leo had already been told,' Emma explained.

'Ah, then perhaps you should speak to Carmel, who's worked here for over fifty years. She might have known your father.'

'Would she still remember him?' Emma asked.

Branka gave her a blank stare. 'I have absolutely no idea.'

'But it's worth a try. That would be great,' said Leo. 'Is she here now?'

'I'm afraid not. But she will be at work tomorrow morning.'

Leo's heart sank at the news. They'd arrived a day too early.

'Does she live nearby? Could you let me have her phone number?'

Branka's mouth pulled into a tight line. 'That will not be possible.'

'OK.' Leo ran a hand across his chin. 'Could you perhaps call her yourself and ask if she might speak to us?'

This suggestion prompted Branka to fold her arms. 'Carmel doesn't like to speak on the phone, and I don't want to interrupt her day off. She's not a young woman and she needs her rest. It would not be fair.'

'I think Branka has been more than helpful already,' Emma said quietly, and she was right. Leo knew he was pushing his luck, but there was one more question that had to be asked. He glanced at Emma, who nodded, as if she could read his mind.

'Actually,' he said, as Branka started gathering up the ledgers, 'could I just check, have you had any guests staying here with the surname Farleigh-Addison?'

'Information about guests is strictly confidential,' Branka snapped before hurrying off to answer the ringing phone.

'Oh, well. It was worth a try,' said Leo, getting to his feet and shaking out his legs.

'Definitely, although we're no further forward on that one.' Emma wrinkled her nose. 'It's got to be more than a coincidence that your dad worked in the London hotel that the Farleigh-Addisons have visited regularly.'

Leo nodded because it was that link which had pushed him into making this trip. Not that this visit had particularly helped. The tie between his father and the Farleigh-Addison family seemed murkier than ever.

'Do you know, I could do with a walk to stretch my legs,' said Emma, standing up and hunching her shoulders up and down. 'I feel very achy.'

'Good idea. We were sitting on the train for ages.'

'Oh, you don't have to come with me.'

Her voice was higher than usual, as if she was stressed.

Leo frowned, wondering if Emma was growing tired of him.

'Seeing as you can't meet up with Thea, I thought we could get some food together.'

'What, here?' She glanced at the dining room and its tables topped with crisp white linen and gleaming silver cutlery. 'The restaurant's very fancy and Michelin-starred, according to the hotel's website. It's probably pricey too.'

'I'm sure it's amazing, but I was thinking more of finding a little bistro somewhere, maybe by the river? But if you have things to do, I can have a wander on my own,' he told her, feeling bizarrely disappointed.

Emma's face softened. 'No, that's fine. Actually, I know a nice area not far away where we might find somewhere suitable.' She stood up and brushed hair from her forehead. 'It's only a few minutes away on the Tube.'

'That sounds good. Lead the way.'

They left the hotel, waving to Branka before they joined the hubbub on the street outside. The wind had picked up and dropped chocolate wrappers were swirling in a frantic dance across the road.

'I think the bad weather we encountered on our way up to London might be heading for the city after all,' said Leo, turning up the collar of his coat.

The sky had darkened and the temperature had dropped, but, for the moment, there was no rain.

He stopped walking and took one look back at the Lavender Orchid before he and Emma disappeared underground into the relative warmth of the Tube station.

His father had walked this street in the early 1970s and worked in that grand building for two years. As a kitchen porter or as a butler? Who cared? No one, apart from Robert Jacobson-Jones, for whom appearance and social standing had become everything.

That could explain why his father didn't like to talk about his time in London. But there was something else going on, something bigger, thought Leo as he was buffeted by people rushing to catch the Tube.

The Farleigh-Addisons' frequent stays at the hotel, plus his father's odd reaction to Beatrice's wedding dress and ring were nagging at him. And then there was Robert's phone call to him in the taxi on the way here.

What was it about that call, thought Leo, that was still niggling at the edge of his mind?

27

EMMA

'Did you say you know this area?' Leo asked.

'Yeah, I do a bit.' Emma glanced around her nervously.

'It looks familiar. Didn't we drive through here in the cab on our way from the station to the hotel?'

'Yeah, I think so,' said Emma, being deliberately vague.

She'd been on edge since emerging from the Tube station into Hamsell Green High Street and taking the road opposite which led away from the shops.

'I only ask because you seem to know where you're going but I think the cafés are in the opposite direction. It's just houses along here.'

'I'm sure I saw a bistro pub in this road, on the map on my phone,' lied Emma.

She wished she was on her own. But Leo had looked taken aback at the hotel by her suggestion that they go their separate ways for a while. And she supposed it *had* seemed peculiar when they'd come up to London together.

She could have pretended that Thea had got back to the city from the Cotswolds earlier than planned, so she could go off without him. But making up a meeting with her daughter would have been weird. Though not as weird as what she was doing right now, which was basically attempting to spy on her ex-husband.

'OK,' said Leo, sounding puzzled. 'Let's go a bit further.'

They walked on in silence, as Emma scanned the street which was lined with cherry blossom trees, and tried not to hurry. She had an urge to put on her sunglasses. But that would look decidedly odd on such a grey day, and it would also fail to disguise her should Carl suddenly appear.

I'm a rubbish spy, thought Emma, realising in a panic that she'd taken leave of her senses. Nothing would be achieved by this outing, other than more heartbreak and a further drain on her confidence. Her family already thought she was losing her mind, and turning up outside Carl's house wouldn't disabuse them of that notion.

'I think we should go back now,' she declared, turning on the spot and starting to retrace her steps.

She realised that Leo wasn't following and, when she turned, he was watching her but hadn't moved.

'Are you coming?' she asked, hurrying back towards him.

'Nope. Not until you tell me what's going on. You made a beeline for this particular road but it's purely residential. You seem to be looking for something.'

Emma's shoulders slumped. She was a worse spy than she'd imagined if Leo had picked up so quickly on her irrational behaviour.

She gazed into the distance for a moment, weighing up what to tell him. She was so tired of everything right now.

'Carl lives somewhere in this road,' she blurted out, regretting her candour immediately.

'Carl? You mean your—'

'Ex-husband Carl? Yes,' said Emma, wincing. 'He lives in this road with his new partner.'

'Ah.' Leo scuffed his foot against the kerb. 'And you wanted to see where they're living.'

'I did.'

'Why?'

'I don't know,' said Emma miserably.

But she did know, and Leo knew that she was lying. She could tell by the disappointment written on his face.

'OK.' She pulled in a deep breath. 'My life doesn't seem real any more. Carl and I were a couple for over twenty years. We had a child together. Then he decides that he loves someone else and moves in with her. Just like that. Easy-peasy. Meanwhile, I move across the country and set up a new business in a tiny village by the sea where nothing is familiar and some people are... less than welcoming. It's been a lot for me to get my head around.'

'So you thought it would help you to accept the situation if you saw Carl's new home.'

'New love nest,' said Emma, impressed by Leo's swift grasp of the irrational workings of her mind.

'Love nest?' snorted Leo. 'Who calls it that?'

'Carl has, a couple of times.'

Leo grimaced. 'Well, I know he was your husband and all that, but *love nest*? Is his new partner younger than him, by any chance?'

'Yeah, almost fifteen years younger.'

'Classic mid-life crisis.'

'Yes!' said Emma, feeling somewhat vindicated. 'I said the same but he wouldn't have it.' She gave Leo a sad smile. 'Oh, come on. Let's get out of here before I'm spotted and he realises what a pathetic creature I've become.'

'You're not—' Leo began, but Emma was focusing on a house whose front door had just opened, and someone was coming out.

'Get a move on,' she urged, pushing her arm through Leo's and almost dragging him back along the road.

'Is that them?' he asked, looking over his shoulder.

'I have no idea. I don't know which number they live at. But I can't have Carl seeing me pacing up and down outside his house. What would that look like?' She tightened her jaw, feeling like crying. 'What on earth was I thinking? I'm an idiot who's living in the past.'

He glanced sideways at her as they reached the High Street but said nothing. He obviously thought she was an idiot too.

They were a good distance from Carl's 'love nest' by now but neither of them pulled apart as they walked along the High Street and turned into a park that led down to the river.

'I see a café!' Leo declared, disentangling his arm from hers. 'Let's eat.'

The café, overlooking the river, was almost full but the waiter managed to find them a small table that was pushed up against the window.

While they waited for their food to arrive, Emma watched the people walking along the river. Trees were bending in the fierce breeze and the grey of the sky mirrored the water.

What if Carl and his new love wandered past right now? thought Emma, putting her elbows on the table and her chin in her hands.

Carl would spot her and do a double-take, she daydreamed. *Isn't that Emma?* he'd wonder with a pang of regret. *She's moved on from me so quickly, she's out having a meal with a handsome man.*

Emma looked across the table at Leo. Yes, he *was* handsome. She hadn't thought so at first. When he'd scowled, all she'd noticed were frown lines and his combative attitude.

But here, away from Heaven's Cove, he seemed softer and the lines around his eyes hinted at smiles and laughter. There was the faintest shadow of stubble on his chin and a few freckles across his cheekbones.

'Why are you staring at me?' Leo asked, self-consciously wiping his mouth.

'Sorry. I was just thinking.'

'About what?'

'Nothing in particular,' said Emma, before swiftly changing the subject.

Having a meal together felt strange and Leo seemed to be feeling as awkward as she was. Carl could talk to anyone about anything. He was charming in all social situations. But Leo apparently didn't feel like making small talk right now.

Perhaps he was regretting coming to London with an idiot who'd dragged him to her ex's road under false pretences, and had then fled from the scene of the proposed stalking. He seemed dour and out of sorts.

Emma's hope that the two of them were getting on better was wavering, and her mood dipped even further when raindrops began to patter against the window. A solid greyness had descended over the park which was swiftly emptying of people.

'I think we'd better get the bill and go to the station,' said Leo, handing over his empty plate to the waitress who'd arrived to clear their table.

'Sounds good. It's been a tiring day. I'll probably sleep all the way back on the train.'

An emotion flashed across Leo's face. Relief, Emma decided, that he wouldn't have to talk to her for hours on end. Coming to London with him had been a terrible idea and he probably couldn't wait for the day to be over.

'Let's head back to Devon,' said Leo, holding the café door open for her to go out. 'Where's your umbrella, though you might have trouble using it in this wind?'

Emma's heart sank because she could picture exactly where her umbrella was, and it wasn't in the café.

'I left it under my chair at the Lavender Orchid,' she told him, mentally kicking herself.

'That's a shame,' said Leo, his words snatched away by the wind. Although it was an early evening in spring, it might as well have been January. Rain was still falling and the sky was almost black with storm clouds. 'Let's get to the Tube and, if everything's running OK, we've got time to stop at the hotel on the way to Paddington station and still catch the Exeter train.'

He hurried off and Emma ran to keep up with him. Clearly, Leo couldn't wait to be back home and shot of her.

28

EMMA

Branka was still manning reception when they walked back into the Lavender Orchid, and she eyed the damp incomers warily.

She's worried we're back for more information, thought Emma. Or maybe she was more concerned about the raindrops dripping from their wet hair onto the tiled floor.

'Hi,' said Leo, leaning against the desk. 'Sorry to bother you again but Emma left her umbrella when we were here a few hours ago.'

'Would it be this one?' enquired Branka, bending down to pick up an umbrella that she waved in the air.

'That's the one. Thank you so much for looking after it for me.'

Emma took the brolly and tucked it under her arm. There was no point in trying to use it in the swirling gale outside but she was glad not to lose it. The umbrella had been a present from Thea.

'We'd better get a move on, Leo, or we'll miss our train.'

Branka leaned forward. 'Are you getting the train back to Devon this evening? I think that's where you said you've come from.'

'Yes, Devon. That's the plan,' said Leo, pushing his hands into the damp pockets of his jeans.

'You haven't heard the news then.'

Branka tapped on her keyboard and pushed the screen of her computer monitor round so that Emma and Leo could see it. She pointed at one of the lead stories on the BBC News website.

Rail travel chaos after landslide – all trains between London and Devon have been cancelled this evening after a landslip caused by torrential rain blocked the main line.

Rail chiefs say no trains will run to Exeter from either Paddington or Waterloo stations until 9 a.m. tomorrow morning at the earliest. Tickets for today's trains can be used instead on tomorrow's services.

'Great.' Leo's shoulders slumped. 'How do we get back to Heaven's Cove?'

'Coach!' Emma declared, frantically looking up late coaches to Exeter.

There were only three on a Sunday night. One had already been cancelled 'due to adverse weather conditions' and the other two, if they did end up running, were fully booked.

'People have got in ahead of us,' said Leo, studying her phone over her shoulder. 'I should have checked the trains earlier.'

But you were too busy dealing with me having a mini-meltdown about my ex-husband.

Emma tried to push that from her mind and think logically about the situation they were in.

'Maybe we could rent a car and drive back to Heaven's Cove?' she ventured.

'That'll be tricky at this time on a Sunday, and I don't have my driving licence with me anyway. Do you?'

'Afraid not.'

Outside, car headlights reflected in the large windows of the hotel as they drove past, through puddles. The storm was showing no signs of abating.

'All in all, I think we need to find a hotel,' Emma said, already working out how early they could be back in Devon tomorrow once the trains started running again. With any luck, she'd be able to open the shop by early afternoon, so only miss a morning's trade.

Branka cleared her throat theatrically. 'You are currently *in* a hotel and it's a very good one. However, all of our rooms are taken, I'm afraid. There are a number of conferences and events this weekend and many large companies have made block bookings at the hotels in this area. You might find it difficult to get accommodation anywhere decent nearby.'

Maybe it was Emma's look of dismay, or Leo's slumping shoulders, but Branka added, 'However...'

She tapped at her keyboard and peered at the screen. 'We do have space for you both but it's not in our premium accommodation. We don't often rent out rooms at the back of the building, but it's an emergency, I suppose.'

She looked up at the two of them. 'Would that be acceptable? The charge will be minimal, in the circumstances.'

Emma turned to Leo, who shrugged and said: 'That sounds like our best option. We have a bed for the night and then, fingers crossed, we can get a train tomorrow morning back to Devon.'

'I guess so.'

Emma hadn't planned on an overnight stay but she could sleep in her underwear, and she had lipstick and mascara in her handbag. After everything she'd been through in the past few weeks, an unexpected sleepover wasn't going to floor her.

Branka took some details from the two of them before calling over a colleague to take over her reception duties. 'I will show you where to go because it's not easy to find. I'm about to leave anyway so it's not a problem.'

Emma and Leo followed Branka into a lift which took them to the top floor and then along a corridor which became increasingly shabby the farther they walked.

'The management have plans to refurbish this end of the hotel. They have had for some time, but you know how it is.' Branka rubbed her thumb across her fingers. 'Money, money, money. There's never enough.'

She stopped outside a door at the corridor's end and slid a key card into the lock. There was a beep and she pushed the door open.

Leo and Emma stepped into the room which had a double bed, a long sofa beneath the window, a small fridge and a fitted wardrobe. Everything looked tired and worn, including the en suite bathroom just visible through an open door.

'We keep this room made up for any staff who have to stay over unexpectedly so it's not perfect but it's clean,' Branka told them, running her finger along the window ledge and inspecting it for dust. 'There are some guest toiletries in the bathroom, including toothbrushes, and clean towels. Will this room do?'

'It will,' said Leo. 'Thank you. Is my room next door?'

Branka blinked. 'This is the room for both of you. You're a couple, no?'

'No,' said Emma quickly. 'We're not a couple.'

Branka's eyebrows knitted in confusion. 'Forgive me. It's my mistake. I thought—'

'We're friends,' said Leo firmly. 'That's all.'

Friends? thought Emma. Or simply people thrust together in trying circumstances who were making the best of it? They had come up to London together but her trip, though prompted by her burning curiosity about Robert's link to Beatrice's family, had also involved an ulterior motive.

Emma remembered walking along Carl's road and shuddered at what a stupid idea that had been.

Leo caught her eye and frowned. Did he think she was shuddering at him describing them as friends?

Branka had moved towards the door. 'There is a problem if you are not willing to share a room. There is no other suitable room that is ready. I am giving you this one out of the kindness of my heart.'

'And we're very grateful,' said Emma. She glanced at Leo. 'What do you think?'

'I think it's getting late, the weather's horrible and this is the only option available. So I'm willing to take the sofa. Or we can go and find somewhere else.'

Emma suddenly felt weary to her bones. The last thing she wanted to do was traipse around London in a storm, looking for a different hotel. And at least sharing one low-cost room at the Lavender Orchid would impact less on her finances.

Leo had been a perfect gentleman so far – once they'd got past the flooding incident and the tearing her off a strip at Driftwood House for being late. So it might be awkward and a little embarrassing sharing a room. But they were adults, and it was only for one night.

'This will do,' she said, making a snap decision. 'If you're OK with that, Leo?'

Before Emma had finished speaking, Branka had hurried to the door.

'Good. All sorted then,' she said, stepping into the corridor. 'My shift is over. Sleep well.'

Then the door closed behind her and it was just the two of them, alone in a hotel room in the middle of London.

29

LEO

As the door clicked shut, Leo took a deep breath. This didn't have to be awkward because they were both adults. Grown adults who were friends. Sort of. He'd noticed Emma's reaction when he'd described them as friends to Branka.

'At least staying over means I might get to have a quick word with Carmel in the morning,' he said, mostly to fill the silence. 'She might be able to tell us what the hotel was like when my father worked here, and maybe she'll even remember the Farleigh-Addisons staying here.'

'Yeah. That would be great,' Emma replied, with a smile that didn't reach her eyes. 'It'll be amazing if she remembers your dad.'

'It will, definitely. Amazing.'

There was another silence, thick and heavy, that seemed to hang in the stale air.

'If it's OK with you, I think I'll have a bath,' said Emma suddenly, heading for the en suite. 'I feel grimy after a day in the city.'

'That's fine with me. I might watch some TV for a while.'

'Right. See you in a bit, then.'

She went into the bathroom and closed the door.

Well, that wasn't at all awkward, thought Leo wryly, opening the window a crack to let in some fresh air. He sat on the edge of the bed and started pushing buttons on the remote.

The TV fixed to the wall sprang into life and he channel-hopped until he came across a football match. He wasn't a huge football fan but doing something so mundane made his current situation seem less unfamiliar.

Plus, the sound of the bath filling and then the occasional splash as Emma moved in the water were almost drowned out by football chanting and cheers.

After a while, Leo found a spare duvet at the top of the wardrobe, pulled the curtains to block out the storm, and made himself a bed on the sofa.

It wouldn't be the most comfortable of nights, but it would do. And once they got back to Heaven's Cove, he'd soon be able to move his stock back into his own shop.

Emma came out of the bathroom after a while, followed by billows of steam. She'd put her clothes back on but her cheeks were flushed.

'There's lots of hot water and everything seems clean,' she said, glancing at the TV. 'Do you like football?'

'Sometimes. I used to play for the Heaven's Cove team when I was a boy. My father sponsored the team and was chairman of the local league.'

Emma sat down on the opposite side of the bed. 'That was good of him.'

Leo nodded, though that was during his father's social climbing years – when he'd joined anything and everything and had worked his way up to head several local organisations. He'd rarely been home and Leo – then a young child – had hardly ever seen him.

Before long, everyone was commenting on how wonderful

Robert was. How focused on benefiting the village. A pillar of the local community. A local boy made good.

But Leo would hear him moaning about all that he was expected to do and all the 'sacrifices' he was making.

'It's simply a means to an end, Leo,' he would tell him. And young Leo didn't know what he meant at the time. But he did now.

He saw how his father revelled in being an important man in Heaven's Cove. A man who rarely mentioned his humble beginnings and who *never* spoke about his time in London in the 1970s, working as a kitchen porter.

How sad that his father hadn't been happy the way he was. What had instilled in him such a strong drive to be 'someone'? he wondered.

And why had he never talked about Beatrice and her wedding and his apparent links to her family who had stayed so often in this hotel? He'd had the perfect opportunity to say he knew Beatrice, after spotting her wedding dress in Emma's shop, but he'd stayed silent.

'Anyway,' said Emma, rubbing her feet along the thin carpet. 'I'm tired so I might as well go to bed. I am happy to have the sofa, you know.'

'No, it's fine. I've made up a bed and I'll be all right. It's only for one night.'

'Well, it's good of you.' Emma smiled at him. 'I don't suppose you've come across a dressing gown anywhere, have you?'

'Afraid not. Why?'

'I could do with something to sleep in but that's OK, I can sleep in my clothes.'

Leo looked at her dress which would crease like crazy. He could suggest she sleep in her underwear but that would sound beyond creepy. Then a solution hit him.

'What about my sweatshirt? I can sleep in my T-shirt.'

When Emma looked doubtful, Leo pulled off the sweatshirt and threw it onto the bed near her. 'It's there if you want it. It's up to you.'

Emma picked up the dark grey top and ran her hands across the thick, soft cotton. Then she went into the bathroom.

A few minutes later she emerged and Leo made a great show of focusing on the TV as she came out, legs bare beneath the sweatshirt. She hurried across the room and got into bed, under the duvet.

Leo went into the bathroom next, did his teeth, and got under the duvet on the sofa. Only then did he pull off his jeans and throw them onto a chair nearby.

'Did you want to watch the football?' he asked.

'No, thanks.'

'I can channel-hop for something else if you feel like watching telly.'

'You watch something if you'd like but I think I'm going to have an early night. It'll do me good.'

'Sounds like a sensible idea.'

When Leo pointed the remote at the TV and switched it off, all that could be heard was the sound of the storm outside. Rain bashed against the window and gusts of wind whistled past the hotel.

'Shall I turn out the light or are you going to read for a while?' Emma asked.

When Leo said he was tired too, she reached out and flicked the light switch above her head. The room was plunged into darkness.

Emma's voice came out of the black. 'Are you *quite* sure you're comfortable on that sofa?'

'Absolutely,' Leo lied, pushing at his pillow and wrapping the duvet around his legs. His feet reached the end of the sofa and he propped them up on the sofa arm.

'Good night, then,' said Emma.

'Good night.'

Leo lay on his back for ages staring at a chink of light coming through the curtains. The wind had eased and now he could hear the low drone of traffic outside and the occasional shouts of people going by.

London never truly slept. There was always some drama happening, some crime taking place, some love story unfolding, some drunkard stumbling down a busy street.

It was so different from Heaven's Cove where the early hours were thick with a silence that made his ears hum.

His cottage wasn't close enough to the harbour to hear the sea. Though on some nights, when the wind was strong and the tide was high, he was aware of the rhythmic boom of waves hitting stone. He found the sound comforting – a never-ending cycle, whatever else was going on in the world.

The sky was different in the city too. Light pollution gave the night sky a matt blackness, even when it was cloudless. Whereas, in rural Devon, the heavens were studded with a billion brilliant stars.

That was why he'd gone back to Heaven's Cove after university. That and his father's expectation that he would take over the family business one day.

He'd made plans to move on from the family firm and Heaven's Cove after getting engaged to Anna, who'd never taken to village life.

But then her pregnancy had ended so tragically and Leo had become for ever associated, in Anna's mind, with the child she'd lost. He got it and understood that grief could change people. But that hadn't made losing her any easier. His whole future had disappeared in a maelstrom of grief and sorrow, and it had knocked the stuffing out of him.

Leo shifted his position on the sofa to get more comfortable.

Dwelling on the past and how life might have been was

pointless. As pointless as it was for Emma to focus on what her ex-husband was doing.

He thought back to their trip along her ex's street this evening. The Emma he knew – albeit not very well – was spiky at times, yet brave enough to forge a new life for herself after her divorce.

But as she grew closer to Carl's *love nest* – Leo still couldn't help rolling his eyes – she seemed to shrink and become vulnerable. As if the life force was being sucked out of her.

Leo gave a wry smile in the darkness because he was being dramatic. She'd wanted to walk along that street. After all, it had been her ulterior motive for accompanying him to London. Leo pulled the duvet higher over his chest and tried to ignore a gnawing sense of disappointment.

'Are you awake?' Emma's voice was quiet, unsure.

Leo cleared his throat. 'I am. Can't you sleep?'

'No, even though I'm really tired.'

'It's the excitement of the day,' said Leo, wondering if the real reason for Emma's sleeplessness was thoughts of Carl just a few miles away.

'That's probably it.' Emma paused. 'Are you sure you're all right on that sofa? It can't be good for your back.'

'My back's fine, or it will be after a shedload of manipulation.' Leo laughed. 'No, honestly, there's no problem with my back.'

'So do you think you'll be able to sleep?'

'Definitely. As soon as I've removed this metal spring from my right calf.'

'Oh, for goodness' sake.' There was a whooshing sound and Leo laughed again as a spare pillow from Emma's bed hit him in the solar plexus and he batted it onto the floor. 'I really don't mind swapping.'

'I'm only joking. The sofa isn't too bad at all, and it's only for a few hours anyway. Try to get some sleep or we'll both be knackered in the morning.'

There was silence for a minute, then Emma said: 'It must be weird to think of your dad working here all those years ago.'

Leo put his hands behind his head. 'It is. I can picture how the Lavender Orchid was back in the 1970s and imagine him here.'

'This place is pretty posh now, with all the polished wood and stained glass. But you can see how impressive it must have been in years gone by. There's a real sense of luxury – a hangover of grandeur from the past.'

'That's a good way of describing it. My dad must have been overawed when he first arrived here. It's so different from anything in Heaven's Cove.'

'Do you think the staff used to sleep here, at the back end of the building?'

'Perhaps. It's certainly the less salubrious part of the hotel.'

Leo lay quietly for a few minutes, thinking about his father as a young man and wondering if he'd ever been in this particular room. The darkness almost seemed like a heavy curtain, dividing the 1970s and now, that he could pull aside. And he would step back fifty years and see his kitchen porter father, when he was young and full of dreams – before he became someone else.

Leo breathed out slowly and said: 'Thank you for coming with me to London, on my wild goose chase, and I'm sorry it's turned into a longer trip than you expected.'

'That's not your fault, unless you had a hand in the landslide that stopped our train.'

'I have fingers in many pies,' said Leo before wincing because that didn't really make sense.

But Emma laughed anyway. He liked her laugh, and the fact that he'd prompted it. But something else was on his mind.

'Can I ask you something?'

There was a pause before Emma answered: 'I guess so. It depends what it is.'

'I wondered if seeing the street where your ex-husband is living now was helpful.'

'Not really.' Leo heard the bed creak when Emma moved. 'I'm sorry. I should have told you what I had in mind.'

'You *could* have told me.'

'I was worried that you'd try to dissuade me, though, actually, I kind of wish you had now. I can't believe I thought that spotting my ex and his partner in their new home would be anything other than awful. There's no fool like an old fool, eh?'

'Excuse me! I'm pretty sure that I'm older than you.'

This time, Emma's laugh sounded muffled, as though she was trying not to cry, and Leo scrabbled around for something to say that would take her mind off her hopeless ex-husband.

'I would like to speak to Carmel tomorrow if I get the chance. Just to see if she remembers my dad. So far, this trip has been almost a total bust when it comes to finding stuff out.'

'Why do you think your father doesn't want to speak about his time here?'

'Probably because he was a kitchen porter rather than a butler to VIP guests as he's claimed. Being somebody special is very important to my dad. Always has been. And working in a kitchen probably didn't fit the narrative that he's spun about himself.'

He hadn't meant to say so much. But it felt easier talking candidly about his father to Emma when he couldn't see her face. The darkness was a shield, protecting him from watching Emma's expression change as her poor opinion of his father took a further nose dive. She didn't seem the kind of woman who'd have much truck with snobbery.

'I can see that it might not match his idea of who he is now,' said Emma slowly. 'But surely it highlights his drive and ambition to work his way up? Plus, being a porter must have been really hard work. It's impressive what he's been able to achieve since, so I still can't see why he would be as secretive about his time here as you say he is.'

'Me neither,' said Leo, appreciating Emma's compassionate take on the matter.

His father had been less than welcoming to Emma. As had he, initially. Yet she was still able to consider Robert's successes and assess him with kindness.

The wail of an emergency vehicle speeding past outside cut through their conversation.

'Look,' said Leo, 'we really ought to try and get some sleep.'

'Agreed,' said Emma. 'Sleep well.'

'You too.'

Leo snuggled down into his pillow but, a good while later, when sleep was still far away, he heard bed springs squeak and feet pad on the thin carpet.

'All right?' He pushed himself up on one elbow.

'Yeah, sorry to disturb you. I was almost asleep but realised I need the loo again. Go back to sleep.'

Go back to sleep? If only.

Leo was aware of a dark shape moving past him and then there was a thump as something hit the floor hard.

'Ow!'

'What happened?'

Leo fumbled for his phone and, turning on the torch, arced it across the room. Emma was sitting on the floor, next to a pillow, massaging her ankle.

'Oh, no.' Leo threw off his duvet and hurried over to her. 'Did you fall over the pillow that I pushed off me? I'm so sorry.'

'I did, but seeing as it's the pillow I'd aimed at your head, it's fair enough,' said Emma, rubbing her ankle. 'You weren't to know that I'd trip over it, like an idiot.'

'Can you move your toes?' asked Leo, gently brushing his fingers across her foot.

'I think so. The only thing that's badly hurt is my dignity.'

'Well, fortunately for you, I only heard your fall. I didn't see it.'

'Just as well when I'm only half-dressed.'

Her smile faltered as they both became aware that she was in an oversized sweatshirt and he was in boxers and his T-shirt.

'Well, this is awkward,' she said, giving a tight laugh.

'You're in luck because it's so dark we can't see each other,' said Leo, even though he could make out Emma's long, bare legs in the glow of his phone light.

'I can't see a thing,' Emma insisted.

As she got slowly to her feet, Leo put his arm around her shoulder, led her back to the bed and sat down beside her.

'Are you sure nothing's broken?'

'Absolutely,' she answered brightly. 'As Carl used to say, I'm making a fuss about nothing. Though he did say that when I slipped on ice and broke my elbow.'

He sounds like a top bloke. Leo realised that his fingers had clenched into his palms, and he uncurled them.

'However,' Emma continued, 'on this occasion, it's true because my ankle is feeling better already.'

'In which case I'll move the pillow so you don't do another nose dive.'

'Thanks, and I'll try heading for the bathroom once again, only this time without the OTT drama.'

Leo had said he was going to move the pillow. Emma had said she was going to head for the bathroom. Only neither of them moved.

Leo registered that his thigh was pressed hard against Emma's – his bare skin against hers. It had been so long since he'd been this close to a woman that he liked. And he really did like Emma – with her unabashed fashion style, her courage in striking out on her own, and her kind heart.

He liked the compassion in her big blue eyes, the way she

swung her hips when she walked, and her thick fair hair that flicked up at the ends, however many times she smoothed it down.

And he thoroughly disliked her ex-husband, a man he'd never met whose bad behaviour had caused her pain.

'Emma,' he said gruffly.

She turned towards him, her face in shadow. 'Yes?'

'I...' He blinked, unsure of what he wanted to say. How could he articulate a feeling that he didn't fully understand? 'I... I don't know.'

She smiled, her eyes not leaving his face. 'It's late.'

'I know.'

But still neither of them moved as a clock on a church tower far away began to toll. It was midnight already. The witching hour when things that seemed impossible in the light of day took on a new energy.

Leo wasn't sure who moved first. Who leaned in towards the other. But his lips brushed Emma's, and then they were kissing. Tentatively at first, and then more passionately as her arm slid around his neck and his hand found her waist.

A door banged shut further along the hotel corridor and the two of them sprang apart, as if an echo of his young father had just barged into the room.

Leo's phone had shifted on the bed during their kiss, and Emma's face was now in complete darkness.

She got to her feet. 'I think I'd better... um...'

'Yeah.' Leo grabbed his phone. 'I'll move that pillow.'

He picked the pillow up off the floor and placed it back on the bed as Emma padded across the carpet. By the time she came out of the bathroom again, Leo was back on the sofa, under his duvet, and lying with his eyes closed. He heard springs squeak as she got back into bed.

'Good night, Leo,' said Emma, as if nothing had happened between them.

'Good night, Emma.'

Leo turned over and tried to sleep but he couldn't stop thinking about the kiss they'd just shared. He ran a finger across his lips and tried to slow his breathing.

The kiss probably hadn't meant much to Emma, whose emotions were heightened after chasing down her ex, he reasoned. But it had meant something to him. It had made him feel more alive than he'd felt for a long time.

'Emma?' he said softly after a while. 'Are you still awake?'

But there was no reply. Only the slow, heavy breathing of a woman who was fast asleep.

Leo turned over on his lumpy sofa and only fell asleep as pale dawn light began to filter through the cheap curtains.

30

EMMA

When Emma stretched out and yawned, her hands hit against a headboard that shouldn't be there. Where was she? She blinked in the morning light, in an unfamiliar bed, and groaned quietly as memories started sliding into her mind.

London. The Lavender Orchid Hotel. Stalking her ex-husband. Landslips and cancelled trains. Staying over. And then... kissing Leo.

What on earth had she been thinking? What had he?

She glanced across at the sofa but the duvet had been thrown back and Leo was nowhere to be seen.

She hoped that he'd slept OK. But mostly she hoped he didn't know that she'd been awake when he'd softly called out to her in the early hours. That she'd feigned sleep, not because she didn't want to answer him. But because she'd been afraid of what might happen if she did.

Emma hadn't kissed a man other than Carl for years, and, after his betrayal, she'd thought she never would. That she would never want to.

But that midnight kiss with Leo had been surprising and wonderful and terrifying, all at the same time.

She hadn't wanted it to end, and yet she was too scared by her own feelings to let it happen again.

The bathroom door suddenly opened and Leo emerged, fully dressed apart from his sweatshirt that she was still wearing. Emma instinctively pulled the duvet up to her chin.

'Ah, you're awake,' he said, with an awkward smile. 'I've checked online and they reckon trains will be running to Devon from mid-morning.'

'That's good news,' Emma managed, her throat feeling parched.

'So, I was planning to go down and grab some breakfast and give you space to get ready. Then, we can hopefully speak to Carmel before we head to the station. What do you reckon?'

'Sounds good. I'll see you downstairs.'

'Right.' Leo went to the door and looked back, his fingers on the door handle. 'Look... what happened last night. I know you're upset at the moment, with the divorce and everything, and I'm really sorry if I overstepped the mark.'

'No, you didn't.' Emma swallowed. 'At least, if you did, I did too.'

'There's some strange magic around being in an unfamiliar hotel room at midnight, huh?'

He gave a lopsided grin that lit up his face. He looked younger and warmer, and so attractive. Emma swallowed again.

'That must be it. But no harm done?'

'Definitely not. Two consenting adults, and all that.'

He held her gaze across the room and Emma suddenly found it hard to breathe. She hadn't been kissed in such a long time, especially not by a man who found her desirable. A man who didn't criticise the way she dressed, or belittle her dreams.

Leo had stopped smiling but was still looking directly into her eyes. He let go of the door handle and had taken one step towards her when his mobile phone rang loudly from his trouser pocket.

'Damn,' he exclaimed, glancing at the screen and then stabbing at it to silence its insistent rings. 'I've no idea who that was. A scammer, probably. If it's important, they'll leave a message.'

But the spell had been broken and both of them knew it.

'Breakfast?' said Emma briskly.

'Yes, breakfast. I'll see you down there.'

'Give me fifteen minutes.'

After Leo had gone and she heard his footsteps disappearing along the corridor, Emma lay back on the bed and covered her eyes with her arms.

The cotton of Leo's sweatshirt was soft and carried a faint smell of him. Emma inhaled an aroma of citrussy soap and the subtle spice of an expensive aftershave.

She wasn't sure what was going on between the two of them. But with time and proximity, could it become something? Perhaps she was simply flattered by his attention. Or – though she hated to admit it, even to herself – maybe she was trying to get even with Carl.

Emma sat up and swung her legs out of bed. Whatever may or may not be going on, both she and Leo had been hurt in the past so it was wise to tread carefully.

She pulled Leo's sweatshirt up and over her head, folded it neatly, and went into the bathroom.

∼

By the time she got downstairs, Leo was biting into a piece of toast – his second if the crumbs on his plate were anything to go by. Another plate nearby bore traces of scrambled egg and bacon.

'The food here is *good*,' he said, pushing a white china teapot across the table towards her. 'There should be enough left in there for you.'

'Thanks.'

'Is your ankle all right this morning?' he asked, reaching for a third slice of toast and not catching her eye.

'Yes, thanks. It's much better.'

'That's good.'

He began to butter the bread, still with his head down, while Emma poured herself a cup of tea. She took a sip and tried not to grimace. She liked what Carl called 'builders' tea' but this was more perfumed, and probably far more expensive.

'Do you want the menu or will you be attacking the breakfast buffet?' Leo asked.

Emma glanced at the long table at the back of the room that was groaning with food – a variety of cereal, chopped fruit in crystal bowls, individual servings of yogurt in china ramekins, and croissants and other pastries under glass domes.

'I think the buffet will do for me,' Emma decided, after glancing at the menu and noticing the cost of ordering à la carte.

She was still worried about how much the electrical repairs in Leo's shop would deplete her savings.

Leo dabbed crumbs from his lips with a starched white napkin.

'I'm still hoping to have a word with Carmel before we head for the trains, which are due to start running again from eleven, according to the National Rail website.'

'Eleven? That's later than they were saying yesterday. We won't be back in Heaven's Cove until mid-afternoon at the earliest, which means we'll both miss out on a day's trading.'

'I know. It's a shame. I'm just glad that my father won't be back in Heaven's Cove, from his conference, until early evening so he won't know the business is shut.' He wrinkled his nose. 'Could Maisie maybe open your shop for you?'

When Emma widened her eyes at him, he laughed. 'All right. Maybe that's not my best ever idea. Why do you keep her on when she's so...?'

'Oblivious?' Emma volunteered.

'That's one way of describing her unique approach to shop-keeping.'

'I like her. She reminds me of Thea at that age, and I think she's been through a fair bit in her short life.'

'You appear to have a very soft heart.'

'Which isn't always an asset in business, I know.' Emma gave a rueful grin. 'But Maisie's getting better at helping out in the shop, and she's turning into a whizz with the steamer – if I can get her to look up from her phone for long enough.'

As their conversation continued, the kiss last night wasn't mentioned. But when their fingers brushed, as they both went for the teapot at the same time, Leo's cheeks flushed and her heart began to hammer.

Honestly, Emma, she told herself sternly, *you're not a teenager any more.*

She got up and went to the buffet table and, as she filled a bowl with cereal and yogurt, she resisted the urge to look back and see if Leo was watching her.

He was right about the food. It was *very* good, and Emma went back after finishing her cereal to nab a buttery croissant.

Leo seemed easier to talk to this morning which meant that breakfasting together was less awkward than Emma had been expecting.

They'd just got on to the subject of dealing with difficult customers, when Branka came bustling over.

Today she was in a cream blouse but wearing the same unflattering burgundy waistcoat, with her name badge pinned to her breast.

'Good morning.' She gave them both a perfunctory smile.

'Hello, Branka,' said Leo, putting down his tea cup. 'We didn't expect to see you this early.'

Branka waved her hand dismissively. 'I don't mind hard work. My shifts change from day to day and I am used to it. I trust you both slept well?'

Emma assured her that they had, ignoring Branka's raised eyebrow. Had she guessed what had happened between the two of them?

'I wanted to let you know,' said Branka, leaning closer, 'that Carmel has arrived and I have explained to her the situation. She's not sure if she remembers your father but she would be amenable about speaking to you.'

Emma grinned at Leo across the table. Perhaps they were finally going to get some answers, rather than snippets of information – about long-ago weddings and hotel jobs and lost gold rings – that simply posed more questions.

'That's great, Branka, and very kind of both of you,' said Leo, taking the napkin from his lap and folding it. 'Could we speak to her now, do you think?'

'You can. Please follow me.'

Branka led them to a small office, set back from reception, where an elderly woman with hair dyed a jarring shade of orange-brown was rifling through a pile of receipts.

'You must be Carmel,' said Leo, advancing with his hand outstretched. 'I'm Leo and this is Emma.'

'Yeah,' said Carmel, shaking Leo's hand. 'Branka has told me all about you, and about your dad who worked here in the early 1970s. I'm not sure I remember a Robert.'

'It is a long time ago,' said Emma, taking one of the seats that the older woman had pointed to. 'We didn't think anyone who was working at the hotel back then would still be here.'

'They keep me on, rather like a mascot,' said Carmel in a cockney accent. Her face, bathed in light from a small window, was a maze of lines. 'I took time off when I had my children but I came back. And now I've got grandchildren and three great-grandchildren, but I still work two mornings a week, helping them to sort out office paperwork mostly. The extra money's nice, and it stops my brain from shrivelling into a husk.'

'I'm sure it does,' said Emma, who'd already taken a shine to Carmel.

She had a practical, no-nonsense air about her that Emma admired, and kick-ass style when it came to fashion. This morning the elderly lady was wearing a tweed skirt that looked like between-the-wars vintage, a chain necklace made of large gold links, and yellow Doc Martens that encased her narrow ankles.

Carmel followed Emma's gaze and winked at her.

'My grandchildren never know what I'll be wearing from one day to the next. It keeps them on their toes. Now, how can I help you both? What do you want to know?'

'Just anything you might remember about my father, please,' said Leo, sinking onto the chair next to Emma's. '*If* you remember him at all.'

'He's not dead, is he?'

Leo glanced at the open door to make sure Branka was out of earshot before replying.

'No, he's still alive and doing well in the little village we come from in Devon.'

'That's good to hear.'

'But he doesn't speak much about his time in London and I thought it would be nice to know more. I have a photo of him if that would help.'

When Carmel nodded, Leo took a small black and white photograph out of his wallet and passed it over. The head and shoulders photo was grainy but it was the same young man pictured at the back of Beatrice's wedding snap. And the resemblance to Leo was even more noticeable.

Carmel studied the photo, then she sat up straight, the bracelets on her wrists jangling.

'I *do* remember this man. We used to share a ciggie outside and have a moan about the management. The hotel's no-smoking now but back in the '70s we enjoyed regular cigarette breaks. You say he was called Robert but I knew him as Bob. He was working in the kitchen and I was part of the housekeeping team.'

'That's wonderful that you remember him,' said Leo, smiling broadly. 'Do you know if he worked anywhere else in the hotel?'

Carmel's brow furrowed into deep lines. 'I'm not sure but I doubt it. The chef back then – a temperamental man from France, named Monsieur Moreau – was territorial about his staff.

'There was no chopping and changing. Not like there is today when staff are supposed to be jacks of all trades. Using the computer, waiting tables, filling in on reception, raising invoices and making beds. There aren't enough staff, in my opinion, thanks to a raft of redundancies a few years back. A cost-cutting measure that hasn't gone well. I was surprised they kept me on. Though I've been here so long they probably can't afford to pay me off.'

'So, you think my father worked in the kitchen the whole time he was here, then,' said Leo, gently bringing Carmel back to the point. 'Did he have much to do with your VIP guests?'

'Heavens, no! The hotel manager back then, Mr Benedict Carruthers, ran this establishment with a rod of iron and only select staff came into contact with the more well-to-do guests. I wasn't allowed anywhere near them. Still wouldn't be.'

She laughed, showing a row of such perfect white teeth, Emma guessed they must be false.

'We had film stars staying here back then, you know. And politicians and the landed gentry. I would see them in the distance occasionally which was a thrill for a young girl brought up in a two-up, two-down in Hackney.'

'I'm sure it was.' Leo leaned forward. 'My father was here for about two years, wasn't he?'

'I can't remember any dates but I know Monsieur Moreau had a lot to say when he left so suddenly.'

'Do you know why he left?' Emma asked, but Carmel shrugged.

'Who knows? An argument over something stupid, a love affair gone wrong, or a better job somewhere else. Could have been anything. I missed our chats over a ciggie, though.' She gave a throaty chuckle. 'I haven't told you much, have I. I'm sorry about that.'

Leo smiled, although he must have been feeling as disappointed as Emma. 'You've been very generous with your time, Carmel, and we appreciate it. It's lovely to meet someone who knew my father all that time ago.'

'Send him my best wishes,' said Carmel, getting to her feet. 'From one old soul to another.'

'I will,' Leo assured her, though Emma knew the chances of Leo mentioning being at the hotel, let alone meeting Carmel, were slim.

Near the door to the office, Emma spotted a black and white photo of vintage film star Cary Grant on the wall. Her mum had had a soft spot for the good-looking actor which meant that Emma had grown up watching his movies.

'Did he stay at this hotel too?' she asked, pointing at the framed picture.

'He did, a few times, though I never saw him. Most of our guests weren't famous but they had money – they needed it to stay here. The landed gentry would make a beeline for the Lavender Orchid when they were in town. They liked their comforts.'

Emma looked again at the photo which had been taken in the hotel's reception area, with a couple of staff members lurking in the background.

Emma's mind flitted back to the photograph in the 1970s newspaper at Callowfield Library. Beatrice's wedding photo with young Robert peeping out from behind the yew tree in Heaven's Cove churchyard. And, more recently, Maureen's observation in the Heaven's Boon pub about Beatrice's family: *'They were always off abroad or staying at the Lavender Orchid.'*

'We do have one more question, Carmel,' said Leo, glancing at Emma as if to say 'over to you'.

'This is a long shot, Carmel, but do you happen to know if a woman called Beatrice Farleigh-Addison, or perhaps Beatrice Charnley-Smythe, has ever stayed here?' Emma asked. 'It's quite an unusual name so I just wondered...'

'Charnley-Smythe doesn't ring a bell, but Farleigh-Addison?' Carmel's lipsticked mouth twisted as she thought back over the years. 'I'm pretty sure there was a Colonel Farleigh-Addison and his wife who were guests. Perhaps the wife's name was Beatrice. I don't know anything about them. But I do remember the fuss they caused.'

'What kind of fuss?'

'The wife's ring was stolen from her room, or so she said. There was a complete hoo-hah about it because the reputation of the hotel was at stake. It was in the newspapers and everything.

'Old Carruthers was beside himself, 'specially 'cos he believed the colonel's wife had misplaced the ring or lost it somewhere else. He had some harsh words for her behind the scenes. But the couple weren't much liked round here anyway. Ideas above their station, is how Mr C described it. *Calls himself a colonel but I bet he never saw action in the war,*' said Carmel, mimicking her old boss. 'Mr Carruthers fought on the Normandy beaches during the D-Day landings and he didn't take kindly to officers with airs and graces.'

'Can you remember when all this happened?'

'It was donkey's years ago. Actually...' Carmel's gaze became unfocused as she stared into the distance. 'I do believe it was early 1973.'

'How can you be so sure?'

'Pink Floyd.'

'Um...' Emma stared at Carmel, nonplussed.

'Pink Floyd? The best band in the world. Their groundbreaking album *The Dark Side of the Moon* was released in the UK on the sixteenth of March 1973 and I'd planned to be first in line at the record shop, only all the staff were called in by Mr C after the so-called theft. I was fuming.'

'I bet.'

Emma could imagine a young Carmel, desperate to get her hands on new Pink Floyd vinyl and incandescent at being thwarted.

'Did Leo's father ever come into contact with the colonel?' Emma asked, an idea half forming in her mind.

The ledgers had shown that Robert had left the hotel not long after the theft, which was probably purely coincidental. But what if it wasn't?

She noticed Leo giving her a sharp look, his jaw tight. Was he following the same train of thought?

Carmel chuckled. 'I very much doubt that Bob and the colonel ever mixed. Upstairs, downstairs. I know things are different now but, back then, it was very much two worlds that never collided. Bob wouldn't have been anywhere in the hotel, save for the kitchen and wine cellars. Mr Carruthers would have had his guts for garters otherwise.'

'Can you remember which newspaper the story was in?'

'I expect it was the *Evening Standard*. I remember Mr C raging that the whole of London would have read about it. I'd never seen him so angry. We all kept out of his way for days.'

'Is Mr Carruthers—'

'Dead,' said Carmel bluntly. 'Heart attack as he walked over Tower Bridge, three days after he'd retired. Such a shame.'

'Did Mrs Farleigh-Addison ever get her ring back?'

'No idea. But they were loaded and soon got over it. It

certainly didn't put them off staying here again, though I think the discount from Mr Carruthers on future stays helped.'

Leo was quiet after they'd bid Carmel goodbye and gone back to their room, to collect their belongings. But in the lift, on the way down to reception, he turned to Emma.

'Why did you quiz Carmel about Mrs Farleigh-Addison's missing ring?'

Emma blinked. He was making it sound as if she'd questioned Carmel aggressively. 'I don't think I *quizzed* her. I asked her about it because I was interested.'

'Is that because of the link there appears to be between the Farleigh-Addisons and my father?'

'Yes, but I was also generally interested in what had happened. And the timing of it all.'

Emma's words hung in the air between them as the lift juddered to a halt on the ground floor.

'Even if my father and the Farleigh-Addisons did know each other, which seems likely from that old wedding photo,' said Leo – not moving even though the lift doors had opened – 'it's unlikely they'd have met at this hotel. From what Carmel said, my dad would have been confined to the kitchens, and the colonel didn't sound the type to be fraternising with staff anyway.'

'That's true.' Emma hesitated, wondering whether to continue. 'It's a shame that his wife's ring went missing, that's all.'

'Things go missing every day,' said Leo, his voice clipped. 'You've just lost Beatrice's wedding ring.'

Ouch! Emma swallowed as a fresh wave of guilt swept over her.

'That came out more harshly than I meant,' said Leo. 'But what I'm trying to point out is that misplacing things happens every day.'

'I realise that.'

'And the fact that my dad was here around the same time that the colonel's wife's ring went missing is coincidental.'

'I didn't say it wasn't,' said Emma, even as the half-formed idea in her mind started to take more shape. But it couldn't be true, could it?

Leo lapsed into silence again as they left the hotel, after splitting their discounted bill.

They walked to the Tube station and sat together on the train as it carried them deep beneath the streets of the city. Leo stared out of the windows at the darkness, seemingly lost in thought.

They'd stopped in a station, not far from Paddington, when he turned to Emma.

'When you were questioning Carmel, were you thinking that my father might have stolen that ring from the colonel's wife?'

Emma looked around her. Fortunately none of their fellow travellers were taking any notice of this awkward conversation. Most of them had headphones on or were staring fixedly at their mobile phones.

'No.' Emma breathed out slowly. 'I was simply trying to get the sequence of events right in my head. Your dad was working at the hotel around the same time as the Farleigh-Addisons were staying there. They presumably knew each other, even if they didn't meet. Then, the wife's ring is stolen, or so she says, and your dad leaves soon afterwards.'

'Which, no doubt, was purely coincidental.'

'I'm sure,' said Emma, wishing she'd never opened this can of worms. 'I was just trying to make sense of it all.'

Leo folded his arms as the train hurtled through the black tunnels.

'My father didn't use money from a stolen ring to set up his business in April 1973. He didn't need it because he set up his business with a bank loan and, no doubt, with the money that he'd earned during his two years at the hotel. That's why he left when he did. He'd earned enough to make his dream of setting up his own business come true. And you, of all people, should applaud him for that.'

'I do.'

Emma was kicking herself. Of course Robert hadn't stolen the colonel's wife's ring and sold it. He was a respected local businessman who was looked up to by people in Heaven's Cove.

He was also an unwelcoming neighbour and a man who, as far as she could glean, kept secrets. But that didn't mean he went around stealing other people's belongings.

'Sorry,' Emma said, breathing in hot underground fumes.

'Look, I imagine you dislike my father, and I can see why you would,' said Leo, leaning forward so his words could be heard above the screeching of the train's brakes. 'But it's a big step from dislike to harbouring the idea that he's a thief who built his business on stolen jewellery.'

Leo impatiently brushed hair from his eyes. 'You have no idea how much work he's put into getting where he is today. How much family time he's sacrificed. He's always been honest to a fault, and I trust him.'

'I really am sorry,' said Emma. 'I didn't mean to imply anything awful. Of course your dad's not a thief and I'm sure he's a good man. I mean,' she added with a smile, as their train pulled into Paddington station, 'his son seems pretty decent.'

But she wasn't sure he heard her, as he got to his feet. And the damage was already done.

Emma tried to make conversation during their train trip back to Devon. But, while Leo was polite and made small talk, he seemed to have folded in on himself. And she couldn't even glimpse the man who had sat beside her on the bed at midnight and kissed her.

31

LEO

Leo knew something was wrong. He knew his father was keeping secrets, and he knew that family secrets were often best left undisturbed. But he couldn't stop thinking about his conversation on the Tube with Emma.

The woman he'd shared a kiss with just last night – a tender, wonderful moment that he was having great trouble not thinking about – believed that his father might have stolen Mrs Farleigh-Addison's missing ring.

It was a theory that she'd swiftly denied, but it had hit home, in spite of his protestations about coincidence. That was partly because he was hurt that she could think so badly of his family. But mostly because, much as he hated admitting it to himself, a tiny part of him wondered if Emma might have a point.

The ring that had gone missing from the Lavender Orchid in 1973 was on his mind. And there was something about Beatrice's lost wedding ring that was niggling at him too.

On their way to the hotel in London, when Robert had rung him, he'd asked about the wedding ring and, when told it was lost, he'd commented: 'That's such a shame, but I suppose you can stop looking for its owner now.'

At the time, Leo had thought little of it because he'd been consumed with guilt for snooping behind his father's back. And Robert was right. There was no point in looking for the owner of a ring that had disappeared.

But now, as he sat alone in his cottage, he remembered their exchange in a different light.

'That's such a shame,' his father had said when told about the lost ring. But he'd sounded unsurprised and almost happy about it. As if that was what he wanted: no ring, so no search for the missing bride. The bride whose wedding he'd attended fifty-five years ago, although he claimed to have no knowledge of it. The bride whose dress had caused him to stop in his tracks decades later, lost for words.

Leo went back to the *Evening Standard* online archive and continued searching for the story that had enraged the hotel manager, Mr Benedict Carruthers. And a few minutes later, he found it.

The headline declared: GOLD RING MISSING FROM SCREEN STARS' HOTEL

Leo took a deep breath and read on: *A gold and garnet signet ring, belonging to the wife of Colonel Horace Farleigh-Addison, has gone missing from a hotel favoured by stars of the silver screen.*

The ring went missing from the colonel's room at the prestigious Lavender Orchid Hotel in Hamswood Grove on 15th March. The police have been informed.

Colonel Farleigh-Addison, who lives in the picturesque Devon village of Heaven's Boon, complained that the ring had been stolen on Thursday morning from a bedside nightstand. He said it had once belonged to his daughter, who now lives abroad, and therefore had sentimental as well as financial value.

Mr Benedict Carruthers, manager of the Lavender Orchid,

said the loss of Mrs Enid Farleigh-Addison's ring was a mystery that he hoped the police would soon resolve.

Film stars who have stayed at the hotel since it opened more than eighty years ago include Marlon Brando, Cary Grant, Debbie Reynolds and Audrey Hepburn.

Leo read the article again before closing the lid of his laptop. Outside his sitting room window, a yellow moon was rising in a navy sky scudded with cloud.

The article confirmed what Carmel had remembered. The signet ring had been stolen – or perhaps Mr Carruthers was right and it had merely been mislaid.

Maybe the colonel's wife had found it later, hidden in the folds of her clothes, or at the bottom of her suitcase where it had fallen from the nightstand.

Leo could imagine the conversation: *'Look what I've found, Horace. Should we inform the hotel?'*

'Heavens no, Enid. Not after the fuss we made and insisting that the police be involved. We'd never be able to return to the place, and I've secured us a discount on future stays now.'

And years later, suspicion was now falling on a man – his father – whose only 'crime' at the time had been working all the hours God sent to earn enough money to start a business.

Coincidences happened all the time in life, Leo told himself, feeling horribly guilty.

His father could be a difficult man but he'd given Leo a stable upbringing and constant employment in a family business. That business was buckling after not keeping up with modern times. But it was still testament to Robert's hard work and determination over the decades – and he deserved a son who fully believed in him.

Leo grabbed his jacket and set off at a swift pace for his father's house. The salted breeze smelled fresh after the polluted atmosphere of London, and the light of the moon lit his way across the ancient cobbles. A lone seagull flitted overhead, spectral-white against the dark sky.

He would speak to his father, apologise for going to London without telling him, and generally clear the air. If there were some things in his past that he wanted to remain a secret, so be it.

Everyone had secrets of some kind. He'd never told his father how close he'd come to leaving Heaven's Cove and the family business nine years ago, with Anna.

But when he reached Robert's house at the top of the village, there were no lamps shining from the windows. And the house felt empty when he opened the front door and stepped inside.

'Dad?' he called out, even though it was clear that no one was home.

'Mum?' he said more softly, feeling his eyes prickle.

His mother had been gone for exactly two years now and Leo had learned to live with her absence. But still, on entering the house that had once been her home, he found it almost shocking that she was no longer there.

He smiled at her photograph on the hall table and went into the sitting room where Robert had a calendar that kept track of his hectic life.

Switching on the lamp, he peered at the calendar and huffed with irritation. He should have remembered that the Royal National Lifeboat Institution meeting was this evening, and his father would be there. That meant their difficult conversation would have to wait until tomorrow.

Leo sat down and looked around the room which smelled of sandalwood polish. Sylvia, Robert's cleaning lady, must have been in recently because everything was tidy – except for the large seascape painting that hung above the fireplace. It was slightly at an angle.

Leo got up and went across to the painting that his mother

had always complained about. He could almost hear her, at his shoulder, saying: *'What's the point of having a painting of the ocean when you can look out of the window and see the real thing?'*

Art was one topic on which his parents disagreed. One of many. They had little in common, other than a shared child, and were leading more or less separate lives by the time his mother became ill.

Leo had asked her once why the two of them had married. What had prompted Robert to propose? She'd immediately replied: 'Status,' which he hadn't understood at the time. But, as he'd grown older, he'd recognised the differences in their backgrounds.

His mother came from a well-to-do family who farmed on the western edge of the moor. Whereas his father's background – as much as Leo could glean – was far more humble. He'd been raised in a small cottage on the outskirts of Heaven's Brook by his mum, who took in laundry, and his dad, who was a labourer.

Had his father really married for status rather than for love? Leo hoped not, for his mother's sake.

While Leo was adjusting the seascape painting, he remembered that his father's safe was hidden behind it. Was that why the painting had been moved? So that his father could gain access to it?

Leo hadn't sneaked a look in the safe since he was a teenager. He'd been hoping to find diamonds and bags of money back then. Perhaps even a gun – he'd been heavily into spy novels at the time. But he'd been thoroughly disappointed.

All Leo had discovered was a pile of boring documents, relating to the house and pension entitlements, which he'd soon got tired of rooting through.

Leo stood still as a statue for a few seconds before carefully lifting the painting off the wall and leaning it against the stone fireplace. Then he put the same combination of numbers into the safe that he'd memorised as a teenager.

To his surprise, the door of the safe swung open.

'Still got it,' murmured Leo, feeling like a master safe-breaker.

Inside, there was a teetering pile of documents – probably the same ones from almost thirty years ago. And, as Leo went to close the door, the top of the pile fell forward and scattered across the carpet.

'Damn.' Leo stooped down to scoop them up, hoping that his dad hadn't filed them in order.

He'd come here to apologise for prying into his affairs in London, and here he was, with his hand in his father's safe. Talk about making matters worse!

Leo was shoving the documents back when he noticed a small fabric pouch. It was at the very back of the safe and had only become visible when the papers had fallen out.

Leo stood in his father's sitting room, still as a statue. He should walk away from all of this. Pretend he'd never opened the safe and leave before his dad returned from his meeting.

But, instead, he pulled out the pouch which was made of soft red velvet. He guessed that it held the diamond solitaire pendant that his mum wore all the time, or her gold bracelet.

But when he loosened the drawstring and tipped the bag up, a ring fell into his palm: a gold signet ring with a large red garnet at its centre.

'Oh my God,' he breathed, staring at the ring as if it was about to explode.

This had to be the ring that had gone missing from Colonel Farleigh-Addison's bedroom at the Lavender Orchid. The ring that Emma had implied his father might have stolen.

It turned out that she was right.

Leo's breathing sounded deafening in the quiet room as he

contemplated what to do next. He was finding it hard to take in that the missing ring he'd just read about in the *Evening Standard* was now nestled in his palm.

'Put it back for now,' he muttered, trying to stay focused. That would give him time to work things out.

But when he dropped the ring back into the velvet pouch, there was a clink of metal against metal.

Leo pushed his fingers to the bottom of the bag and pulled out another ring – this one a plain band of yellow gold.

It has to be Mum's, thought Leo, turning it over in his hand. But then he spotted an unmistakable engraving: *B & R Aeternum.*

Leo thrust the ring into the pouch, pushed it into the safe and slammed the door shut. With shaking hands, he hung the painting back on the wall and left the house, almost at a run.

As he hurried along the street, his toes caught on cobblestones and he almost tumbled down the hill.

'Slow down. Slow down,' he recited to himself, easing up his pace.

He was heading for his cottage, which was on a lane that led out of the village. But when he reached home he kept on walking until the lights of Heaven's Cove were far behind him.

It was dark up here, with no streetlights. Moorland stretched into blackness way ahead. But there was enough light from the moon for him to see his way.

Ten minutes later, he reached a group of standing stones. These markers of ancient times were scattered across the moor, but Leo had always particularly loved the five tall stones that stood here, high above Heaven's Cove.

No one knew for sure why the pitted stones had first been set into the earth millennia ago. Perhaps they were part of a Bronze Age ritual, or an attempt to understand the stars.

But Leo didn't care about the reasons. All he cared about

was the feeling of comfort that they'd given him since he was a young boy. A feeling of being at one with nature and at peace with the earth.

His father had never understood why his son wanted to spend time up here, 'in the arse-end of nowhere'. And that, Leo realised in a moment of clarity as the wind picked up and began to whistle between the stones, was because all that his father truly valued was spending time with people who could be of use to him.

People with whom he could network and forge connections, and persuade to vote for him in various elections to chair organisations.

That was probably one reason why he'd spent so little time with Leo as a child. What use had he been to his father's ambitions back then? Though now, as the adult heir to his father's precious business, he had value again.

Leo sat on the cold grass and leaned against the tallest stone which felt rough against his back. He curled his fingers into his palms, imagining the weight of the gold and garnet signet ring, and thought about how little he really knew his father.

Robert Jacobson-Jones set great store by his excellent reputation around Heaven's Cove. But all the while, his respectable life had been built on the foundations of a criminal act. He'd kept the evidence of that crime locked away in his safe for decades.

And then, almost more shocking to Leo than discovering the stolen garnet ring, was finding Beatrice's lost wedding ring too. His father must have stolen it to stop Emma's search for the missing bride from continuing.

Two thefts, more than fifty years apart. But why? What hold did Beatrice have over Robert Jacobson-Jones? If only Emma had been able to track her down, they might have found out.

Leo closed his eyes and thought of Emma, as the wind swirled and eddied around the stones.

What would she think of his father if she found out the truth? And, by association, what would she think of him?

32

EMMA

As Emma approached the Farleigh-Addisons' house for the second time, she noticed that the 'For Sale' sign in the garden had been replaced with another saying 'Sold'.

It wasn't surprising. This was a gorgeous house that she'd snap up herself if she hadn't come out of her divorce with barely enough money – after setting up her business and putting by some savings – to rent a ramshackle cottage with no sea views.

There would have been more money from their London house sale for her and Carl to share if only the property hadn't been so heavily mortgaged. Divorce had proved expensive, which meant that Emma's current accommodation options were limited.

The tiny flat above the chip shop in Heaven's Cove – a possibility – had been taken already. And although she'd spotted an affordable cottage in an estate agent's window yesterday, it looked a bit of a dump.

In contrast, the colonel's house had definitely been well cared-for over the years. Window frames looked freshly painted, brickwork re-pointed, and even the brass letterbox and doorknocker were gleaming.

The house wasn't as impressive as the Lavender Orchid, but what it lacked in glamour, it made up for in charm and character. The Farleigh-Addisons had presumably enjoyed their jaunts to the capital, thought Emma, but they must have been happy to come home.

Though no one seemed to be home now. The place appeared emptier than ever, with its curtain-less windows, and Emma spotted a pile of flyers on the hall tiles when she opened the letterbox and peeped inside.

Fortunately, she didn't need to speak to anyone. After the trip to London with Leo, and how badly that had ended, she'd decided her quest to reunite a woman with a ring, that she possibly didn't even want, was done – especially since the ring in question was still missing.

She'd also come to the decision that Robert's bizarre reaction to the wedding dress, and his time at the Lavender Orchid, were best left alone. There was no point in falling out with Leo even more. It was awkward enough already after their London trip, and the kiss that neither of them had mentioned since.

But, in all conscience, if Beatrice *had* accidentally dropped the ring into the donation bag, Emma couldn't leave her in the dark, for ever wondering what had happened to it.

So she'd written a note that she hoped someone – the estate agent or the new owners of the house – would get to Beatrice, explaining that her ring had been found and then lost again. But if the note never reached her, so be it. She'd done what she could.

Emma pushed the envelope through the letterbox and had turned to leave when the front door was pulled open.

'Can I help you?'

Emma swung round in surprise. The woman at the door was tall, slim and elegant. Her white hair was swept into a chignon at the base of her neck, and the wide-legged navy trousers and cream blouse she was wearing screamed style and money. She suited the house.

Emma glanced at the woman's left hand, which was clutching the flyers and her note. She wasn't wearing a wedding ring.

'Beatrice?' she asked tentatively.

The woman's bright eyes narrowed. 'That's right, but I'm afraid you have me at a disadvantage. You appear to know who I am but I don't think that I know you.'

'My name's Emma and I'm so pleased to have found you,' she said, a smile spreading across her face. Then, remembering what was in the note, her smile faded.

'Have you been looking for me?' asked Beatrice, tilting her head to one side.

'I have. I've explained it all, actually, in my note.'

'This one you've just posted through the door?'

When Emma nodded, Beatrice said: 'How mysterious,' before placing the flyers on the telephone table, opening the envelope and pulling out a piece of paper.

'Dear Beatrice,' she read aloud. 'My name is Emma and I run Heavenly Vintage Vavoom, a clothing shop in Heaven's Cove. I also sell donated clothes in aid of a local charity, and I believe that you donated some clothing recently, including your wedding dress.'

Beatrice looked up. 'That's correct. But I made the donation anonymously and assumed the proceeds from the sale would go to the charity. How did you know that the clothes were from me? I deliberately didn't include my name and I don't appreciate you turning up on my doorstep. If you're hoping to sell the clothes in your shop for profit, my answer is no. I want all the money to go to the children's centre.'

'I'm definitely selling all the clothing you donated in aid of charity,' said Emma quickly. 'That's not why I'm here. The rest of the note explains it, but I found a wedding ring at the bottom of the bag, underneath the wedding dress, and we've been trying to return it.'

'Oh.' A flicker of a smile crossed Beatrice's face. 'In that case, I owe you an apology. You've been very kind.'

'Not really.' Emma swallowed, wishing Beatrice had read the rest of the note. 'The truth is that I found the ring and noticed the engraving inside which, along with the wedding dress, helped to identify you.'

'How?'

'We found a photo from your wedding in an old copy of the *Heaven's Cove Courier*, which gave us your name. That's how we managed to track you down.'

Track you down? That made her sound like a proper stalker. Emma winced, but Beatrice's smile had grown.

'That sounds very clever and enterprising of you. I realised that the ring was gone but I've been wearing it for so long, I never actually notice it any more. So when I discovered it wasn't on my finger, I had no idea how long the ring had been missing.' She absent-mindedly rubbed the fourth finger of her left hand. 'It was very kind of you to return it.'

'Not really,' said Emma, wishing she'd made a swifter departure from Beatrice's house. 'I did find your ring but I'm afraid that we've managed to—' She stopped because her carelessness was nothing to do with Leo. '*I've* managed to lose it.'

Beatrice blinked. 'Oh, I see.'

'I've no idea where it's gone. I'm so sorry. But I didn't want you driving yourself crazy trying to find it.' Emma knew she was gabbling but she wanted to get this out, and then she could leave. 'I might come across the ring somewhere and, if I do, I'll get it back to you. Like I say, I'm really sorry. I should have looked after it better.'

'As should I. The fault was initially mine, and I appreciate your explanation about what's happened since.'

Beatrice was taking it very well and Emma's shoulders

relaxed at her generosity. She seemed a nice woman, but sad. There was an air of melancholy about her and a calm resignation over Emma's carelessness.

'I see that your lovely house has been sold,' said Emma, not so keen to bolt now that her message had been delivered and received so well.

'It's my parents' home which has been bought by a retired couple who want space for their visiting children and grandchildren. It'll be good to have some laughter again in the house. My mother died some years ago and my father, the colonel, has dementia, sadly. He's just moved into a residential home where he'll get the care that he needs. It's hard but it's for the best.'

Beatrice's bottom lip wobbled and Emma wondered if she was explaining the situation for Emma's benefit or to comfort herself that the right decision had been made.

The older woman swallowed before continuing: 'I've lived abroad for decades but I'm here for a short while, sorting out my parents' things and the belongings I kept here, and making sure the house is ready to pass on to its new owners. I'm an only child, so organising everything falls on me.'

'It's never easy selling a house that holds memories,' said Emma, thinking of the home she'd shared with Carl.

Now the two-bed semi belonged to a family from Belfast, Carl was living with Selena in a London love nest, and she was lodging in Devon with a young couple whose baby rarely slept. How had her life changed so radically in such a short period of time?

'It sounds as if you have experience of losing a house full of memories,' said Beatrice with a sympathetic tilt of the head.

When Emma gulped, momentarily too full of emotion to speak, Beatrice changed the subject.

'You said "we".'

'I'm sorry?' said Emma, not keeping up.

Beatrice pushed a stray strand of hair back into her chignon. 'You said that *we've* been trying to return the ring.'

'Yes, that's me and Leo who works in Jacobson-Jones Gentlemen's Outfitters which is next door to my shop. I flooded his business – by mistake. Actually, it wasn't me. It was...' Emma stopped, not about to name Maisie, and remembering she'd planned to keep Leo's name out of all this. But she'd burbled on without thinking, and it was too late now. The beans were spilled. 'What happened with the flood doesn't matter. But Leo saw the ring and he's helped me to find you.'

The pink in Beatrice's cheeks was fading to white, and she placed her hand on the doorframe to steady herself.

'Are you all right?' asked Emma.

Beatrice let go of the doorframe and breathed out slowly. 'I felt wobbly for a moment but I'm fine now, thank you.'

Packing up this big house on her own was apparently taking its toll on Beatrice. Unless... was it mentioning Leo that had shaken her?

'Was there anything else you wanted to know?' Emma urged gently. But when Beatrice stared at her feet without replying, Emma realised it was time for her to go. 'Look, if you're sure you're OK, I'd better head back to Heaven's Cove.'

At that, Beatrice lifted her head. 'Is Leo Bob Jones's son? Leo is an unusual name and I'd heard—' She pulled her lips into a thin line.

'Well...' Emma hesitated. 'Leo's dad is Robert Jacobson-Jones, who I'm assuming is the same person.' She could imagine Robert, or rather, Bob, double-barrelling his surname, just for show. 'I think you might know him? Or have known him?'

'What has he said?'

Beatrice's tone was sharp and Emma quickly reassured her, 'Nothing. When Leo and I came across your wedding photo in the paper, we spotted his father lurking in the background.

Sorry. I don't mean lurking. He was in the back of the shot, that's all. Not in the main party.'

'No, he wouldn't have been.'

'Wasn't he invited?'

Emma knew this wasn't her business and she should keep her nose out. But she was suddenly tired of people keeping secrets and, a divorce down, fed up with always holding her tongue.

That was what she'd done during her marriage and it hadn't done her any favours. Carl had still poured cold water on her dreams and, ultimately, had an affair with someone he'd once described admiringly as 'sparky'.

That description of his new girlfriend had instilled a deep rage in Emma that, she now realised, had yet to fully lift. He'd spent their marriage pushing her down and then had the temerity to complain that she was too quiet. Too 'downtrodden', as if she was a tatty old mat by the back door.

'Bob wasn't *not* invited to my wedding,' said Beatrice enigmatically. 'I rather hoped he'd be there. I rather hoped…' She trailed off and stared at Emma. 'Are *you* all right? Now you don't look well.'

'Sorry. I've had a tricky couple of weeks and talking about weddings has stirred up a few things.'

It was Beatrice's turn to stare pointedly at Emma's left hand. 'Separated, are you?'

'Divorced, actually. Newly divorced and I'm striking out on my own.'

'Is that why you've opened your shop?'

'Yes. I'm starting a new life in Heaven's Cove.'

'And how's it going so far?'

Emma thought of leaving everything and everyone she knew behind, of trying to sell vintage clothing to strangers, of flooding out the shop next door, of Leo…

'It's up and down,' she managed.

Beatrice gave her a sympathetic smile. 'This part of Devon is a funny old place. The people here take a while to accept you but, when they do, it's a great area to put down roots.'

'Though you haven't lived here for years, you said.'

'That's right. My husband, Richard, and I moved abroad almost immediately after we were married. He worked as a diplomat so we went wherever his postings took him. I'm fortunate in that I've seen many parts of the world.'

'It sounds wonderful.'

'In many ways it was. In other ways...' Beatrice sighed. 'My husband and I separated last year.'

'I'm sorry to hear that.'

Beatrice waved away Emma's concern. 'A separation had been on the cards for some time and we've both made new lives for ourselves.'

'Yet you were still wearing your wedding ring?'

'Old habits die hard, but it was time to take the ring off, which is why I didn't make a fuss when I realised that it was missing.'

That made Emma feel a whole heap better about losing it, but she empathised with Beatrice's dilemma. It had taken her until the day of her divorce to finally take off the ring that Carl had slipped onto her finger more than twenty years earlier.

'How long have you been back in Devon?' Emma asked.

'Not long, and it feels very odd because I've hardly been here for years. My parents, and latterly just my father, always came to see me, wherever I was living. They enjoyed the break.'

'I expect you've missed home though.'

Beatrice looked up and caught Emma's eye. 'I have, and I've particularly missed some of the people. But it was better to stay away and make my life wherever my husband and I were posted. That was the best way, I found, to avoid homesickness. Are you homesick for what you've left behind?'

'A little. I mostly miss my daughter but we speak—'

Emma had been about to say 'regularly', but that wasn't true. Thea seemed increasingly distant these days and had sent the briefest of replies to the last two of Emma's WhatsApps.

'Sadly, Richard and I were never blessed with children. It must be hard for you not to see her.'

'It is. Thea's got her own life in London.'

'Then I suggest that you take a break from your shop and pay her a visit as soon as possible.'

Would Thea even want that? Emma nodded anyway. 'I will, but for now I'm concentrating on building up a successful business. That's my dream.'

She bit her lip, fearing that she sounded ridiculous. Beatrice had lived all around the world, probably throwing high-class dinner parties for visiting diplomats and the rich and famous.

Whereas, her dream was running a tiny vintage fashion shop in sleepy Heaven's Cove.

But Beatrice reached out and patted her arm. 'It's good to have a dream and to make it come true, don't you think? I didn't always manage that with my dreams, so I wish you the best of luck with yours.'

'Thank you,' said Emma, wondering what dreams Beatrice had missed out on. Her life sounded exciting but perhaps it hadn't been all diplomatic pomp and privilege. She'd not had children, which seemed a regret, and her marriage obviously hadn't been happy – at least not recently.

There was a silence, broken only by the sound of a tractor trundling past, along the lane.

'Anyway, I'd better not keep you,' said Emma, taking a step back from the front door. 'Again, I am sorry about losing your wedding ring and I'll return it if I come across it. How much longer will you be in Devon?'

'Only for a couple more days. But let me give you my email address.' Beatrice grabbed a pencil from the hall table and scribbled on the back of the note from Emma. 'There you go. You can contact me if you find the ring but please don't worry if it's gone for good.' She put out her hand. 'It was very nice to meet you, Emma.'

'You too,' said Emma, clasping Beatrice's hand and shaking it.

She'd only just met this woman but there seemed to be a connection between them. *Two women who are both disappointed in love*, thought Emma ruefully.

She'd turned to leave when Beatrice said: 'How is Bob, or rather, Robert, keeping these days? I haven't seen him for years.'

Emma turned back. 'He's doing very well, I think. He has his business next to mine and he seems to head every organisation in the village.'

'He sounds busy.' Beatrice cleared her throat. 'And is he happy?'

That was a difficult question for Emma to answer.

'I guess so,' she said slowly. 'He's been grumpy with me but that's probably because I flooded his shop. I imagine that's enough to put anyone in a bad mood.'

Was that sufficient for Beatrice? Emma hoped so because what else could she say? *I don't think I've ever seen Robert smile, and he's been a pain in my backside since I arrived in Heaven's Cove*? Probably not.

'Flooding the premises doesn't sound the best way to introduce yourself to a new neighbour,' said Beatrice. 'But I do hope that Bob has had a good life.'

'His wife died a couple of years ago, but he has his business and his son and his standing in the village, so he has a lot.'

'That's good to hear.'

With that, Beatrice bade Emma a second goodbye, went back into the house that would soon no longer be hers, and closed the door.

Emma stood for a second, imagining Beatrice growing up in this grand house. Her parents must have been so proud of her, marrying a diplomat and travelling the world – living the dream. Though they must have missed her and they'd never experienced the joy of grandchildren.

Dreams are funny things, thought Emma as she set off on the bicycle she'd borrowed from Maisie. *They don't always turn out as planned.*

Her mind turned to Beatrice's reaction to Leo's name, and what the elderly woman had said about Robert being at her wedding five decades ago: *'Bob wasn't* not *invited.'* What on earth did that mean?

'Stop thinking about it!' Emma told herself, pedalling furiously and cursing every time her bike hit a pothole.

She'd never know why Robert was so spooked by the old wedding dress, or why he rarely spoke about his time at the Lavender Orchid. But that, she determined, was absolutely fine. Now she'd delivered the note about Beatrice's missing wedding ring, it was finally time to leave the whole mystery well alone.

33

ROBERT

Leo was not in a good mood. Robert realised that the minute he entered Emma's shop to speak to his son about the repairs being done next door.

He wasn't in the best of moods either. But his 'Good morning' to Leo – which he proffered fairly cheerily in the circumstances – was met with a quiet 'Hello'.

'What's the matter with you? You've got a face like a bulldog chewing a wasp.'

Not everyone liked his predisposition for straight talking. But then not everyone had worked so hard to build a life for themselves or had made the sacrifices he'd made. He had no time for beating around the bush.

Leo gave the hint of a smile and said, 'I'm fine.'

Robert knew from his late wife that 'I'm fine' sometimes meant the opposite. But it wasn't surprising if Leo was unhappy in here.

Hadn't he advised Leo against working in this second-hand clothing store that today smelled of... Robert took a deep breath, still anticipating a stink of mothballs and body odour. But a waft of something vaguely citrussy hit his nostrils, which wasn't unpleasant at all.

And the merchandise – vibrantly coloured clothing hanging on shiny chrome rails – gave the shop a boutique vibe.

Robert gazed around him. He had to admit, albeit grudgingly, that this place didn't look too bad.

'Did you come in for anything specific?' Leo asked, not looking up from his accounts book.

Robert ignored his son's question. 'Where's that woman?' he asked, glancing across the shop and spotting the sulky teenager. She caught his eye and gave him a straight look that made Robert falter.

She'd been loitering about when he'd taken the wedding ring from Emma's bag. But she hadn't seen anything. He was sure of that. She was simply giving him the vacant stare that so many youngsters seemed to employ these days.

'*Emma* has gone to the bank so it's just me and Maisie,' said Leo, nodding towards the teenager, who was disappearing into the stock room.

She shut the door behind her with a slam that made Robert wince. Quite why that woman – Emma – kept her on was beyond him.

Emma must have a kind heart, which was to her credit, he supposed, but it would do her no good in the long run. She would be out of business in no time if she couldn't stand up to her staff or competitors.

Robert leaned against the counter and watched his son as he added a figure to the account book and rested the pen against his bottom lip.

'Has Mr Greyson come in for his suit?' he asked, once it became clear that Leo wasn't going to initiate a conversation. 'He needed it urgently for a family wedding on Saturday.'

'Yes, he came in yesterday.'

'Does it fit well?'

'Perfectly.'

'So he's pleased with it?'

'Very pleased.'

'Good.'

'My conference speech in Plymouth went down very well, if you're interested.'

'I never doubted that it would.'

Leo went back to his accounts. He appeared to be paying extreme attention to every figure. And he'd still not looked properly at his father, as if he couldn't be bothered to register his presence.

'I can see you're out of sorts today,' said Robert, 'but Terry's getting on well and says we can be back in our own shop tomorrow, so that'll cheer you up.'

'Great,' said Leo, his tone flat.

Robert felt irritation building in his chest. He wasn't used to people being off with him like this. Everyone in the village treated him with respect, and respect was the very least he expected from his own son.

'What's going on?' he demanded. 'Tell me now.'

Leo looked up at that. 'We need to have a chat but this isn't the place or time. Perhaps we could meet up after work.'

'I have a meeting of the village hall steering committee at six thirty and, as the chair, I'll be missed if I don't turn up.'

'Of course you will because, as you've always told me, you're a very important man.'

Robert blinked at what sounded very much like sarcasm in Leo's voice.

'I'm not sure I like your tone, Leo. You should show me more respect.'

'Respect?' Leo actually snorted. 'That's rich, coming from you.'

'What on earth is your problem,' said Robert coldly.

'Working here, with that woman, is having a very bad effect on you and your mood.'

Leo slammed the accounts book shut and dropped his pen onto the table.

'*That woman* is called Emma and my mood has nothing to do with working here. The thing is I *know*, and I'm not quite sure what to do about it. *That's* my problem.'

'What do you know?' asked Robert, a sense of unease creeping over him.

Leo glanced behind him at the closed stock room door.

'I went to see you last night and, when I realised you were out, I went into the sitting room and noticed that the painting above the fireplace was askew.'

'So what?' barked Robert, panic sparking in his brain.

'When I was adjusting the painting, I saw the safe and I opened it.'

'How dare you open my safe,' blustered Robert. 'That's private.'

'I shouldn't have opened the safe but I did and guess what I found at the back of it?'

Robert closed his eyes briefly, his mind doing somersaults. There was no point in reasoning this out. Damage limitation was needed, pronto.

'I imagine, from your demeanour, that you found the wedding ring,' he said. 'Look, I can explain. I found it on the ground outside, where Emma must have dropped it. So I put it away for safekeeping.'

'Which you failed to mention when I told you on the phone that the ring had been lost.'

'That's because I hadn't found it by then,' said Robert, his breathing growing more shallow as he tried to stay one step ahead.

He was getting too deep into this lie but he didn't know

what else to do. He'd never expected Leo to rifle his safe while he was away from home. Leo never did that kind of thing.

'So you're telling me that, when we spoke on the phone, you knew nothing about the whereabouts of the ring?'

'Absolutely. I found it in the street, outside this shop, on my way home after the conference. I should have mentioned it immediately but I completely forgot. It's just a ring.'

Robert hated lying to his son. But hadn't he, in effect, been lying to everyone for years? He wasn't the honest, respectable and honourable man that they believed him to be.

Robert forced his mind away from such damaging and self-defeating thoughts and tried to focus on what Leo was saying.

'OK. We can discuss it later.'

'Or let's not,' said Robert, his voice growing louder. 'If you have something to say, I'd rather discuss it now.'

That wasn't the case at all. He'd rather that the ring was never mentioned again. That small gold band had caused him pain half a century ago and it still had the power to wound him.

He should have disposed of it, after taking it from Emma's handbag. He should have dropped it into the waves and let it sink to the seabed. But he hadn't been able to throw it away, because it had once belonged to her.

However, Leo obviously wasn't going to let the subject drop, and he couldn't wait on tenterhooks for it to be brought up again. Better to get it over and done with now, he reasoned.

'Come on,' he said, surprised by how loud his voice had become. 'Let's have this out right now.'

'Have what out right now?'

Robert spun round. Emma had walked in off the street and was standing there, with her hands on her hips.

'Nothing,' said Robert.

But Leo leapt right in. 'My father was telling me how he found the wedding ring that you lost.'

'Really? You found it?' Emma's face lit up. 'That's amazing. Where was it?'

'In the street outside,' said Robert quickly. 'Where you must have dropped it.'

There was a snort from the back of the shop. The teenager had come out of the stock room and was standing with her arms folded.

'Maisie?' said Emma. 'Is everything all right?'

'Of course everything's all right,' huffed Robert.

But the girl followed this up with another snort, as if she was going down with a cold.

Then, she said: 'I saw you.' She repeated it again, looking directly at him. 'That day, I saw you.'

'I beg your pardon?' he blustered, cold dread seeping through him.

'What did you see?' Emma asked.

'I saw him looking in your bag that was hanging on the hook out the back,' said Maisie, her cheeks turning red.

'When was this?' Leo asked as Robert thought frantically about the best way to respond. Deny, deny, deny, he decided.

'You must be mistaken,' he said, trying to sound both incredulous and relaxed, which wasn't easy. 'As I said, I found the ring in the street outside, young lady.'

Young lady was a faux pas, he realised too late as Maisie's lip curled at what she presumably found condescending. It was hard to know what to say to young people these days.

'Nope,' she said forcefully. 'I'm not mistaken. Not at all. I saw you going through Emma's bag and I was pretty sure you took something out and put it in your pocket.'

Emma's mouth had fallen open. 'But why didn't you tell me at the time?'

''Cos I'd already flooded his shop out and I thought he'd really go off on one if I accused him of nicking something. Plus, it would be my word against his, and the whole village thinks he's like a king or something.'

Robert noticed a look pass between Emma and his son.

'I mean,' added the teenager, whom he'd hardly ever heard speak before, but who now seemed intent on doing nothing but. 'Who would believe *me* rather than the great Robert Jacobson-Jones?'

'I would,' said Leo quietly.

'Really?' bellowed Robert.

A quote from a performance of *Julius Caesar* that he'd once sponsored at the castle ruins rang in his head. *Et tu, Brute?* Why wasn't his son standing up for him?

'How can you believe this child, who is patently mistaken, over your own father?'

'Because,' said Leo, so quietly that only he could hear him. 'I found something else in the safe. Something that related to a visit Emma and I made recently to the Lavender Orchid in London.'

Robert hadn't heard the name of that place in years and it hit him like a hammer blow. He opened his mouth to speak, to bluster his way out of the situation, but no sound came.

It felt as if his lives were colliding: the carefully curated life he lived now and the life he'd lived before. The person he once was, before he'd left him behind for ever. Robert suddenly had an almost overwhelming urge to cry.

'This is ridiculous,' he managed to blurt out as tears blurred his vision.

He had to get out of this shop before he let himself down. He was Robert Jacobson-Jones, who headed countless organisations in the area and was respected far and wide.

He couldn't be seen crying in public. And while Leo and Emma might not spread news of his humiliation around Heaven's Cove, he couldn't be sure that blabbermouth Maisie would keep it to herself.

'This is a travesty and I'm not staying to be insulted,' he said, blinking rapidly as he rushed for the door.

He gulped in deep breaths of fresh air after stepping outside, and started hurrying along the street.

Past the business he'd worked so hard to build up. Past the poster for the local summer fair that declared: *Officially opened 3 p.m. by Robert Jacobson-Jones*. Past a friend coming out of the bakery who tried to attract his attention by waving at him.

He couldn't stop or his life would unravel. A torrent of memories was coming at him now. Memories that he'd managed to suppress for years.

He rushed on until he reached the foot of the cliff and then he began to climb. Up and up the narrow path until he could see Driftwood House in the distance and hear the boom of water hitting land far below.

He scarcely noticed the ache in his knees or the stones under his shoes because, in his mind, the past had come alive.

His son had found the ring that Robert had stolen when he was someone else, and now that life had been resurrected and was running parallel to the here and now.

In that parallel life, Beatrice was walking down the aisle, so beautiful in her stunning silk dress, with a circle of blue delphiniums holding her veil in place. And he loved her. He loved her so much.

But the man waiting to meet her at the altar wasn't him.

The man turning to watch his bride walk towards him was Richard Charnley-Smythe. A man with a double-barrelled surname, a gold-plated education, and sterling prospects.

But Richard didn't love Beatrice the way that he did. Robert could see it in his eyes. There were no tears as his bride approached, no gasp of wonder when he took in how beautiful she looked. All Robert saw was the man's smile of satisfaction, and his glance around the church to make sure everyone present was impressed.

That was when Robert should have taken action. When he should have grabbed Beatrice's hand and begged her to run away with him. Run away from duty and family expectation, and choose life with a man who truly loved her.

But he'd been a coward back then. Too scared of his own shadow to cause a scene. Too frightened that he could never measure up. Too beaten down by Colonel Farleigh-Addison and his haughty wife, who had laughed in his face when he'd asked them for permission to marry their daughter.

He hadn't been good enough then, but he'd made up for it since. He'd shown them exactly what he could achieve.

His successes might not measure up to Richard and his diplomatic appointments across the world. But the irony was that, had he been the man to marry Beatrice, she would have stayed in Devon and the colonel and his wife would have seen far more of her over the years.

But, instead, he'd gleaned from snippets of overheard gossip that she'd followed her husband around the globe and had rarely, if ever, returned to Devon. If her parents wanted to see her, they had to go to her.

Robert slowed his pace across the cliff after he stumbled and almost fell. Driftwood House was behind him now and he'd started descending towards the inland hamlet of Heaven's Brook.

He wondered why was he returning to this place, which was little more than a cluster of cottages. But his feet kept on walking, almost as if an unseen hand was pushing him towards his past.

The cliff descended less steeply on this side and the grass became a gentle slope as he approached the thatched cottage where he'd been born seventy-four years earlier.

It didn't belong to his family now. Not that it ever had. His parents had always been tenants, scratching to put food on the table and shoes on their son's feet.

They'd worked hard to provide for him. *And how did you repay them?* said the little voice in his head that kept him awake at night.

'Look what you've done to your mother.' That's what his father had said after they'd uncovered his crime at the Lavender Orchid in London – the hotel that Leo had recently visited. A visit that he and Emma had made together, that was what his son had told him.

Robert held onto the wall that fronted the cottage where he'd been brought up, and bent over to catch his breath.

Emma had gone with Leo to the hotel, which meant that she also knew – or soon would – what he had done all those years ago. His humiliation was complete.

Robert gulped, still trying to catch his breath. No, he was wrong. His humiliation wouldn't be complete until everyone in Heaven's Cove knew that the man they respected was little more than a common thief. A man whose success was built on criminality and deception.

'Are you all right?' A young woman had opened the cottage door and was hurrying along the garden path, her face creased with concern. 'Do you need some water?'

And a part of him had so expected it to be his mother – so wished it was – that Robert felt his knees go from under him and he sank down onto the wall.

'Stupid,' he muttered to himself.

His mother had died decades ago, not long after his father. But it was as if a door had been opened to the past, and he'd stepped right through it.

And now he could weep that the woman leaning towards him, with sympathy in her eyes, was not his mother, who had loved him.

That's why she'd been so disappointed after learning he'd stolen the ring from the hotel. After finding it in his suitcase when she'd gone to unpack it, to help him settle in after returning from London.

And her disappointment and upset were matched by his father's anger.

'You know what some folk think of us already, Bob,' he'd thundered. 'Because we're poor, they look down on us and say we can't be trusted. And now you've gone and proved them right. Why? Because you're still mooning over a woman who can't be yours? You need to grow up and accept your station in life.'

So he had grown up, but he hadn't accepted anything. Instead, he'd used money from pawning the ring, and the bank loan he'd secured off the back of that, to set up his business and start climbing the social ladder.

Thank goodness he'd been able to get the ring back after a while. But the damage was done and he'd grown apart from his parents while distancing himself from his impoverished background, and they'd distanced themselves from the man he was becoming.

Yet they'd taken his secret to their graves. They'd never reported their son for being a thief because they were so disappointed and – he could suddenly see it so clearly – because they had still loved him.

The woman from the cottage, the woman who wasn't his mother, was talking to him.

'Are you feeling unwell?' she asked. 'Is there someone I can call for you?'

Robert shook his head because there was no one to call. His parents and his wife were dead, his son was hugely disappointed in him, and he wasn't sufficiently close to anyone in Heaven's Cove for them to come to his rescue. They respected him, he realised, but they didn't particularly like him. Was that a successful life well lived?

Robert stood up and forced a smile at the woman who had the humanity to care about a stranger.

'Thank you for your concern. I felt a little unsteady but I'm much better now.' He swallowed. 'I used to live here, you know, back when I was a kid.'

'Really? We've not long moved in and I've started looking into the history of the cottage, and the people who once lived here. What's your name?'

Robert hesitated. It usually tripped off his tongue: Robert Jacobson-Jones. His name for almost fifty years, since he'd decided to become a different man.

'Bob,' he said. 'My name's Bob Jones.'

34

LEO

Leo was sitting in the garden at the back of the shop when Emma found him. He'd retreated there after his father's abrupt departure, needing time to think. Though he'd been doing nothing but think since discovering the two missing rings in his father's safe last night.

Surely, there had to be a good reason why the two rings were there, hidden away. A logical, innocent reason that would explain everything and put their world back to rights.

But he couldn't find one, and Maisie's bombshell that she'd seen Robert stealing the wedding ring from Emma's handbag had been the final nail in the coffin. The truth was he didn't know his father at all.

'Are you all right?' Emma sat down beside him on the edge of the wooden planter that was in dire need of some planting.

Leo nodded and stared at the ground. The atmosphere between the two of them had been strained all morning but not for the reason that Emma believed.

She presumably thought he was still smarting after she'd implied his father was a thief. When, in reality, he was wondering whether to tell her that it seemed she'd been right about his dad all along.

He felt pulled in two directions. On the one hand, shouldn't he be loyal to his father and keep his transgression quiet? But, on the other, didn't Emma deserve to know the truth because the two of them had embarked on this search together?

He was so desperate to talk to her about what he'd found in the safe. It was too big a secret to keep to himself. Yet he worried about what Emma's reaction would be.

It was all horribly complicated, but then Maisie's revelation had taken the decision out of his hands anyway. Emma now knew that Robert was a thief and if she thought less of his son because of it, there was nothing he could do.

'This isn't the most comfortable of seats,' said Emma, shifting about. 'I could do with a couple of sun loungers, though Maisie would spend all her time out here then.'

'Probably,' Leo agreed, grateful to Emma for even attempting small talk in the circumstances. 'Look,' he said, deciding to get it over with. 'I'm so sorry that my dad went into your bag and took the wedding ring. It's unforgivable.'

'If Maisie's right.' Emma batted away a fly that was buzzing round her face. 'Perhaps she didn't see what she thinks she did.'

Again, Emma was standing up for his father, who didn't deserve her generosity.

Leo sighed. 'I'm pretty sure that Maisie saw exactly what she said she did.'

'Really? What's made you change your mind about your dad? Why would he go into my bag and take the wedding ring?'

'Because he's done it before.'

Surprise sparked in Emma's eyes. 'What do you mean?'

'I mean,' said Leo, clearing his throat, 'that you were right when you suspected my dad of taking the signet ring from the Lavender Orchid fifty years ago.'

'How do you know? Did he tell you?'

'No.' Leo took a deep breath. 'But I found the garnet ring in his safe last night, along with the missing wedding ring.'

'Oh.'

That was all Emma said. She sat quietly alongside him, as a stray cat stretched out on the paving stones.

'Aren't you going to say "I told you so"?'

Emma glanced at him. 'Why would I be so unkind? What you've discovered has obviously hit you for six.'

'I just...' Leo stopped to compose himself and tried again. 'I still don't understand it. If he stole the ring to fund his new business, why has he still got it? I could ask him, but I don't trust him to tell me the truth. I just want to know why he's so embroiled in the lives of Beatrice and her family.'

Emma ran a finger round and round her lips, then she said: 'You could always ask her.'

'Ask who? Beatrice? I'm not sure how to find her.'

'But I am. She was at her parents' house yesterday when I called round to drop off a note about her wedding ring. I was going to tell you about it, only we haven't been on the best of terms since... well, you know... what happened in London.'

Did she mean since she'd accused his father of theft? Or since they'd shared a kiss in a dark hotel room?

Leo felt the muscles in his jaw tighten as he tried to keep his emotions in check. Everything around him was a mess: his relationship with his father, his business, and what, if anything, he might have had one day with Emma.

'Your dad might not want to tell you the truth. But maybe he would tell Beatrice,' said Emma.

'But how do we get him to her house?'

Emma screwed up her eyes as the sun appeared from behind a cloud. 'Maybe we don't. Maybe we ask Beatrice to come to his house instead.'

'She'd never agree.'

'Probably not, but I'm fed up with trying to second-guess

everything and everyone. Perhaps we should give her the choice. She asked after your dad when I was with her and she seemed to care about what had happened to him. What do you reckon?'

Leo put his head in his hands and massaged his temples. Getting Beatrice involved might make the situation worse. But the secrets his dad was keeping were festering and breaking down any trust between him and his son.

Leo lifted his head and nodded. 'Yeah, let's give it a go.'

To his surprise, Emma slid her hand over his and curled her fingers into his palm. And her skin was so warm and her touch so comforting, he wanted to pull her into his arms. He wanted her cheek to rest against his chest as he held her.

'Emma! Emma! Come quick!'

When Maisie ran into the garden, Emma pulled her hand away, but not before the teenager had clocked that something was going on.

She narrowed her eyes while Emma was jumping to her feet, but repeated, 'Come quick.'

'What on earth's the matter, Maisie?' demanded Emma, already rushing for the door. Leo just caught her saying, 'You haven't flooded anything else, have you?' before they both disappeared inside.

Leo stood up, shook out his legs and held the palm of his hand to his cheek for a second, before following them into the building.

By the time he reached the front of the shop, Emma was embracing a young woman with blonde hair who was sobbing on her shoulder.

'What's going on?' he whispered to Maisie, whose face was a picture of bemusement.

'Dunno. That woman rushed in, asked for Emma and, when I said she was out, she burst into tears. I only meant she was out in the garden but I didn't get a chance to explain. She went off on one and started crying so loud, I thought she was having a breakdown.'

'Do you think she might be Emma's daughter?' Leo asked, noticing how tenderly Emma was stroking the woman's hair.

'Oh, yeah.' Light dawned in Maisie's eyes. 'Could be, I s'pose. But whoever she is, she needs to stop going round alarming people.'

'She's upset.'

Maisie folded her arms. 'We're all upset, about one thing or another. But we don't all lose control in the middle of a shop. It's been, like, totally random here this morning.'

'Perhaps you could go and put the kettle on?' said Leo soothingly. 'I think we're all going to need a cup of tea.'

Maisie scowled but sloped off to the kitchen as the young woman pulled away from Emma and wiped the back of her hand across her nose.

'I'm all snotty and disgusting,' she gulped. 'But I'm so happy to see you, Mum. It's been awful.'

'What's been awful?' Emma brushed hair from her daughter's eyes. 'What on earth's the matter? You're scaring me.'

'Sorry.' Thea's bottom lip wobbled again. 'Henry has dumped me, and I hate my job.'

When she began to sob again, Emma pulled her back into her arms and her eyes met Leo's, above Thea's head.

'Sorry,' she mouthed.

'It's OK,' he mouthed back, feeling as if he was intruding on a private family matter.

He'd decided to go back out into the garden and leave them in peace, when Thea pulled away again and took the tissue that her mother was proffering.

'I'm so sorry, love,' said Emma, close to tears herself. 'We need to sit down and have a proper chat about everything. But how did you get here?'

'We drove down together. He's parking the car,' Thea gulped.

'Who is? Henry?'

'No.' Thea tilted her head towards the man who was hurrying into the shop. 'Him.'

Leo immediately knew it was Carl. He'd imagined what Emma's ex looked like, and this man looked nothing like it. He was taller, broader and looked less like a weasel, for a start. But it was apparent from the shock on Emma's face that her former husband had just reappeared in her life.

'Em,' he said, a broad smile lighting up his face.

'What are you doing here?' Emma managed, her voice tight and strange.

'Thea wanted to see you and I did, too. The truth is…'

The smile had gone and Carl's eyes had started glistening. 'The truth is, I've made a terrible mistake, Em.' He clasped his hands together. 'Will you take me back?'

35

EMMA

When Emma was ten and suffering from flu, she'd had a fever dream filled with fantastical creatures and irrational happenings. The dream was so bizarre, she'd never forgotten it.

And what was happening right now felt very similar: a confluence of outlandish events that was making her feel divorced from reality, and very overheated.

First of all, Thea, who'd wanted little to do with her for weeks, had appeared out of the blue and was now leaning against her, a tear-streaked, snotty mess.

Leo, minutes after disclosing that his father had stolen two gold rings fifty years apart, was watching open-mouthed from a corner.

And Carl, the man who'd ditched and divorced her, was publicly admitting he'd made a mistake and begging to be taken back.

Outside, people were bustling past and shouts echoed from the quayside. But inside Heavenly Vintage Vavoom time seemed to stand still.

'Say something,' urged Carl. 'I know this is a shock, Em, and perhaps we should have rung ahead to let you know we were on our way. But aren't you pleased to see us? Aren't you pleased to see me?'

Emma blinked, feeling as if she was emerging from a trance.

'I can't deal with this now, Carl,' she insisted, putting her arm around Thea's shoulders. 'Our daughter's upset and she's my priority.'

'It's OK, Mum.' Thea brushed tears from her cheeks. 'I think you need to talk to Dad first and we can speak later. He's got to go back to London this afternoon but I'm staying for a few days.'

Where was she staying? Emma parked that concern for now and turned to her tear-stained daughter.

'I'm not sure your father and I have much to talk about, Thea, and I'd rather know how you're doing.'

'No, really. It can wait.' Thea gulped. 'I needed a hug from you and a cry, and I feel better for that. A bit. But we'll have lots of time to talk later. *Please* speak to Dad and listen to what he has to say.'

Emma swallowed, not sure she wanted to listen to Carl but Thea was looking at her so pleadingly, she couldn't refuse. And he had driven all the way from London to the Devon coast.

'OK, but the two of us need to go somewhere private. And what about you, Thea? Are you going to sit and wait for me here?'

Maisie, who'd just appeared from the back of the shop, made a strangled noise and eyed Thea nervously. It was clear that leaving her daughter here wasn't going to work. But what else could she do?

Leo stepped forward. 'What about the pub, Thea? I know it's early but it sounds as if you could do with a drink.'

'And who's this?' asked Carl, folding his arms.

'This is Leo,' said Emma.

'So you're the famous Leo I've heard so much about.'

'I mentioned him once.' Emma began to massage her

temples. It felt as if a band was tightening around her head. 'Leo and his father run the shop next door.'

'Yet he's in yours.'

'There was a flood so Leo has been working out of my shop for a while. Thea, would you be OK going to the pub while your father and I have a chat?'

Thea dabbed at her eyes with a tissue. 'I guess so. I could murder a vodka and lime.'

'Good. That's settled if, that is, you don't mind, Leo?'

Emma sounded brisk and realised she'd automatically slipped back into family organiser mode. It didn't take long.

'I don't mind at all,' said Leo, walking over and giving Thea a sympathetic smile.

'Are you sure?' Emma felt a wave of gratitude towards him – the only person in the room offering solutions rather than problems. 'What about your customers?'

'I'm sure Maisie can deal with them, and if they're here to collect an order, if she takes their name and contact details, I can drop the orders round later.'

Was he really going to trust Maisie with his precious family business? That was beyond kind of him.

'I don't know, Leo. You don't have to.'

'It's all right, Emma.' Leo briefly touched her arm and smiled. 'Family emergencies come first.'

'And we've had a *lot* of them this morning,' muttered Maisie.

Emma ignored her as she made up her mind and took hold of Thea's hand. 'OK. Go and have a drink in The Smugglers Haunt, love, and I'll come and join you in a little while, once your dad and I have chatted.'

Thea nodded and followed Leo out of the shop.

'Is it a good idea, her going off with a strange man?' asked Carl, running his hand along a rail of vintage dresses.

'He's not strange. He's being extremely helpful.'

Emma turned to Maisie as a couple of people walked into the shop and began to browse.

'Carl and I can't talk here so I'd be grateful if you could hold the fort for half an hour, please?'

Maisie sniffed. 'I s'pose, but I *was* taken on as a retail assistant, not the manager.'

'I'm sure a little extra can be added to your pay packet to reflect the increased responsibility. Would that be all right?'

'How much?'

Emma briefly closed her eyes, marvelling at teenagers' ability to be self-centred, even when the world around them was collapsing.

'I'm not sure, Maisie. As much as I can afford after I've paid for the unfortunate flooding incident. Is that acceptable?'

'Yep.' When Maisie dipped her head, her dark hair swung across her reddening cheeks.

'And please don't forget that Leo wanted you to take down details of any of his customers who call in to collect their orders.'

'Cool.'

Emma supposed that meant Maisie would do what Leo had asked. She desperately hoped so when he was being so accommodating. She turned to Carl, who was standing quietly, watching.

'Right, let's go and find somewhere peaceful where we can talk without being interrupted.'

'Is it sensible leaving that girl in charge of the shop?' Carl asked as they walked along the street, past Jacobson-Jones Gentlemen's Outfitters.

'I hope so. I don't really have much choice, do I?'

'Come on, Em. You're not annoyed with me for turning up, are you? Thea was upset and desperate to see you.'

'And I'm grateful to you for bringing her down. But you burst into my shop and asked me to take you back. What do you expect me to do with that when we're actually divorced now?'

'I was overwhelmed by the sight of you, Em, looking like a proper businesswoman in your own shop.' Carl glanced sideways at her as they walked past the wishing well and onto the lane that led towards the beach. 'I've missed you so much.'

So much that you shacked up with Selena and signed the divorce papers, thought Emma. But she kept her mouth shut until they reached the beautiful cove that gave the village its name.

As Emma had hoped, grey skies and a stiff breeze had discouraged tourists from having a beach day and the sands were almost empty.

'It's freezing!' Carl complained, when Emma led the way to the rocks at the foot of the cliff. 'Couldn't we have found a tea shop or café?'

'The caffs will be heaving with tourists, and we need somewhere where we won't be overheard,' said Emma, shuddering at the prospect of Belinda listening in. Her family meltdown would be all over the village by tea time.

She sat down on a flat rock facing the sea and gestured for Carl to sit next to her but, instead, he started pacing up and down.

'Right, I need to say this.' He swallowed. 'The truth is, I've made a terrible mistake, Em. Will you take me back?'

Word for word what he said in the shop, Emma noticed. Had he rehearsed it?

The first time he'd said those words, the breath had been knocked out of her. This time, she simply felt odd. As if she was floating outside her body and watching this bizarre scenario unfold. Carl, the man who'd betrayed her and broken her heart, was begging her to take him back. Now what should she do?

'This isn't great timing, you know,' she ventured. 'Not with our divorce becoming final a few days ago.'

'I get that, totally, but it was the divorce coming through that made me realise just how big a mistake I've made.'

Carl spluttered and wiped away sand that had been whipped by the wind into his face. Behind him, grey waves were crashing onto the shore.

'Honestly, Em. I'm telling you the truth.'

He gazed at her beseechingly, an expression Emma remembered so well from their years together. She could never resist his 'puppy dog face', which was what Thea had christened it when she was a child.

But should she believe his claim that he was now a repentant ex-husband? Leo had believed that his father was a law-abiding, upright citizen, and look how that had turned out.

'Say something, Em,' Carl pleaded. 'I'm freezing my bits off here.'

'What about Selena?'

'Oh, I knew she'd come into it.'

A hot surge of anger shot through Emma, insulating her against the chill wind.

'Of course Selena's coming into it. You had an affair with her, which prompted our divorce, and now you're living together on a perfect little street lined with cherry blossom trees.'

'I don't think—' Carl paused. 'How do you know about the cherry blossom trees?'

'Thea mentioned them,' said Emma quickly, mentally kicking herself for even hinting at that ridiculous stalking episode during her trip to London with Leo. 'Anyway, that's hardly the most important detail, is it?'

'Agreed.' Carl took a deep breath. 'What's most important is I think Selena and I are breaking up.'

'You *think* you're breaking up?'

'No.' Carl winced and waved his arms above his head to shoo away two noisy seagulls. 'We are definitely breaking up.'

'Does Selena know?'

'Not exactly, but I think she'll be relieved. Oh, Em, it's awful. It was all exciting at first, her and me. But she's so young.'

'There's no need to rub it in.'

'That's not what I'm doing. I'm explaining that we've got nothing in common. She's never heard of Simple Minds, Em, one of the best British rock bands in the world.'

His face crumpled in disbelief. 'She listens to K-pop bands and watches *terrible* reality shows. Not that she's in much because she's desperate to go out *all* the time. I want to sit in front of the telly some nights and watch re-runs of *Succession* but she's raring to hit the clubs. I've tried keeping up with her but I'm exhausted, Em. Completely exhausted.'

When he paused, Emma wondered if he was waiting for her to sympathise. If so, he'd be waiting a long time.

Carl blinked furiously as another blast of sand scoured his face. 'Plus, she insisted we get matching tattoos,' he continued, 'and it really hurt.'

He pulled up his shirtsleeve to reveal a black bulbous stick inked on his forearm.

'What is *that*?' Emma asked, leaning forward for a better look.

Carl shrugged. 'It's supposed to be a microphone representing rap and hip-hop, which Selena's also very into, though I don't like it much. *And* she keeps buying me clothes that Thea says are too young for me, but when I wear my usual stuff, she rolls her eyes.'

'You used to criticise me all the time for what I was wearing.'

'Did I?' Carl sucked his bottom lip between his teeth. 'Sorry, Em. I probably wasn't a brilliant husband and I sometimes took you for granted, but I've learned my lesson. I really have. I think you look amazing today, and I'm very proud of you for setting up your own business. The shop's great – I didn't realise that second-hand clothes could look so good.'

'Pre-loved vintage,' murmured Emma automatically.

'What did you say?' Carl finally stopped pacing and sat down beside her, on the rock. 'Never mind. All I want to know is what you think.'

'I don't know what to think, Carl. You broke our wedding vows and you broke my heart.'

'I know, and I'll spend the rest of my life making it up to you. I promise. So let's give *us* another chance, Em, for both our sakes and for Thea.'

'Please don't bring Thea into this.'

'But she's a huge part of it,' said Carl, grabbing hold of Emma's hand. 'She wants us to get back together. And you still love me, I can tell.'

Did she still love Carl? After their break-up, Emma, completely distraught, had longed for him to do exactly what he was doing now. But a lot had changed since then, especially in the last few weeks.

Yet the pull of being a family again was strong, and surely they owed it to Thea to try? Emma still had feelings for Carl – she couldn't wipe out the decades they'd spent together. But her emotions were so tangled, she couldn't even begin to make sense of them.

'I need time to think,' she said, pulling her hand from her ex-husband's and standing up abruptly.

'I get that,' said Carl soothingly, also getting to his feet. 'Even good news can take a while to sink in. But it will sink in, and then you'll realise that we're meant to be together.

'We can get another place in London, close to Thea, who needs you, and I'll support you to open a second-hand clothes shop up there, where you'll have far more customers than in a poky little place like this. Doesn't that sound amazing?'

When Emma stayed silent, Carl's face clouded over. 'Is

your lack of enthusiasm anything at all to do with that Leo bloke?'

'No, absolutely not,' Emma asserted. 'How could it be? I hardly know him.'

'I thought as much. He looked a bit of a tosspot in that suit.' Carl smiled. 'Look, I've got to get back to London. I postponed a load of meetings to drive down because Thea was so upset and desperate to be with you. Plus, I wanted to see you and say all that face to face, but' – when he glanced at his watch, his left eyelid began to twitch – 'I need to head off, like, right now 'cos it's going to take me a good while to get back.'

'Does Selena know you're here?'

Carl's eyelid began twitching at twice the speed.

'No, I couldn't see the point in telling her. I don't need that kind of grief and she'll be none the wiser if I'm back on the road within the next half hour. But I'm telling the truth that it's all over between Selena and me, Em. You're the only woman for me, always have been, and you could be joining me in a few days' time, once you've closed everything up here. You could come back to London with Thea. I know you want to, and she's too upset to travel on her own.'

He leaned forward and slowly kissed Emma on the lips. 'Now, can I get off this windswept beach and back to civilisation? You'll look after Thea, won't you?'

'Of course I will.'

'And you'll be in touch?'

'Yes, I will.'

'Good. It was great to see you again, Em.'

When he reached out and stroked her cheek, Emma leaned towards him. She'd loved him so much once upon a time. Surely she could again?

Carl gave a low groan, as if he couldn't bear for the two of them to be parted, before walking off the beach without looking back.

Emma walked to the sea's edge, to where the waves were sucking at the sand, and turned her face into the wind.

What a morning! It had been one revelation after another – Robert's sticky fingers when it came to gold rings, Carl's apparent desperation to be reunited with her, and Thea's heartbreak.

Oh God, she needed to go and rescue Leo from weeping Thea and do her best to help her grieving daughter.

Emma turned away from the sea and began hurrying across the sand.

∼

The Smugglers Haunt was rammed with tourists escaping the poor weather. But Emma quickly spotted Leo and her daughter sitting in a nook near the fireplace.

Thea was nursing a drink and Leo was sitting back in his chair, with a half-empty pint glass in front of him. He spotted Emma across the pub and waved.

'Hello.' Emma sat on the chair next to Thea and put her arm around her shoulders. 'How are you doing?'

'I'm so glad to be with you, Mum. I can't believe what Henry's done, and I can't face going to work.' She sniffed and rubbed at her nose with a shredding tissue. 'I feel better for a drink though.'

Emma glanced at the empty glasses lined up beside her, all of them topped by a slice of lime speared on the rim.

'How many have you had?'

'Not enough. Did you speak to Dad?'

'I did.'

'And?' Thea dabbed the disintegrating tissue across her cheeks which were still blotchy from crying. 'What did you say?'

'Nothing definite. Look, why don't we go back to the shop

and you can have a rest out the back while I find somewhere for you to stay? I'm assuming you haven't arranged anything?'

'I've just been dumped by Henry. Sorting out accommodation wasn't top of my to-do list.'

'Understandably,' said Emma placatingly, not wanting to provoke a fresh storm of tears in the pub. She glanced around but, fortunately, Belinda was nowhere to be seen.

'I need the loo before we go.'

Thea pushed back her chair and wound her way through people congregating at the bar, towards the *Ladies* sign.

'Thank you so much, Leo.' Emma leaned across the table. 'I'm so grateful to you for taking Thea off like that. Has it been OK?'

Leo puffed out his cheeks. 'Yeah. She's upset but she wants to talk to you about it all. I didn't mean for her to have so many vodkas but she insisted.'

'It's all right. I know how headstrong my daughter can be at times.'

'A little like her mother?'

'I have no idea what you mean.' Emma smiled, grateful for Leo's attempt to lighten the mood.

'So.' Leo stared into his pint glass, suddenly serious. 'Are you going, then?'

'Am I going where?' Emma blustered, but Leo regarded her coolly.

'To London with Carl. It's obvious he wants you back. He literally said so while I was standing there, and Thea has told me a bit about his intentions.' Leo ran a finger down his pint glass. 'She said he needs you.'

'I don't know what I'm doing,' said Emma, realising it was true. She had no idea what to do for the best – the best for Thea and Carl, the best for her. 'I need to make up my mind.'

'Right. Of course.' Leo waved at Thea, who'd just come out of the Ladies' and was looking disorientated. 'If I'm no longer needed, I suppose I'd better be getting back to the shop.'

'I rang Maisie on my way here and she seemed to be coping well.'

'Thank goodness for that.' Leo's mouth lifted at one corner. 'I had visions of her telling customers to take a hike, and shutting up shop. At least my father won't have been calling round to wind her up.'

'No, probably not. Not after what happened earlier.'

Thea had almost reached them but Leo leaned across the table and said urgently: 'Look, you've got a lot on your plate. Just forget what I told you about my father and I'll sort it out myself.'

'Are you sure?'

'Is he sure about what?' Thea asked, pushing her arms into her jacket with great difficulty. The vodkas were starting to hit home.

Leo caught Emma's eye as he straightened up in his chair. 'Why don't you take Thea back to Driftwood House and I'll watch the shop for you.'

'I can't do that.'

'Yes, you can. I mean, with me there and Maisie, what could possibly go wrong?'

When he smiled, Emma found herself smiling back, even though she felt wrung out after such a difficult morning.

She'd miss Leo when she left Heaven's Cove. Because she was leaving, she suddenly realised, whether she went back to Carl or not. How could she pack her heartbroken daughter back off to a job she hated in London while she swanned around in Devon, running a second-hand clothes shop?

It was time to be realistic and to face up to the fact that dreams didn't ever come true. Not when real life was waiting in the wings, ready to barge in and drag people back to their responsibilities.

36

EMMA

'He told me that he loved me, Mum.'

'I know, sweetheart,' said Emma soothingly, keeping an eye on the ground. She wanted to comfort poor Thea but a tipsy woman and a cliff path were not a match made in heaven.

'Don't get too close to the edge,' she warned, putting her hand beneath her daughter's arm and steering her away from the drop.

'He takes me to the Cotswolds for a mini-break which was really romantic. But apparently the whole thing was some kind of test, to see if he still loved me and wanted to spend time with me... and I failed.'

Emma stopped walking when Thea burst into uncontrollable sobs.

'You didn't fail at anything,' said Emma, gently, pulling her daughter close. Even though Thea was all grown up and independent, it turned out that she still needed her mum sometimes. 'If Henry doesn't appreciate how wonderful you are, he doesn't deserve you. Men can be idiots sometimes.'

'They really can,' Thea agreed, her voice muffled in Emma's shoulder.

'I know it feels awful right now but you will get through this. I promise. And one day, you'll look back and think, *That was a dreadful time but it all worked out for the best and I came out of it stronger.*'

'Do you think so?'

Thea pulled away and wiped her face with a tissue that Emma fished from her pocket.

'I do, and we mums know these kinds of things.' She put her hand back under Thea's arm. 'Look, we're almost at the top now. Let's get there, safely, and then we can sit on the bench and have a proper chat.'

When they reached the bench that faced the sea, Thea dropped onto it as if she was completely done in, and Emma sat close beside her.

'When did Henry tell you this?' she asked, patting her daughter's hand.

'Last night.' Thea gave an enormous gulp. 'He was very decent about it all. Henry *is* decent. That's one thing I like – liked – about him.'

Emma waited for the crying to resume, but Thea stared ahead, dry-eyed. She was cried out, Emma realised – an exhausted state that she'd reached two days after discovering that Carl was cheating on her.

'What exactly did Henry say?' Emma asked gently.

'He said that he still loved me and always would – blah, blah, blah – but he wasn't *in* love with me and he couldn't see us having a future together so it was better to end it now. I cried, and so did he.'

'Do you think he might change his mind?'

'Nope. When Henry makes a decision, that's it. He's not like us. He never second-guesses himself or does U-turns. He just puts his head down and moves on. So, that's that.'

'I'm so sorry, love.'

'Yeah, me too.'

Thea huffed, a picture of misery.

'So what happens now? What would you like to happen?'

'I don't know but I'd like to stay here for a few days, if that's all right with you?'

'It's definitely all right with me. I love having you here, but what about your job?'

'My hideous, horrible job?' said Thea, with a pout worthy of her at the age of five. 'The kids are OK but their parents are rude and demanding, my boss is difficult and does the bare minimum which means I'm drowning in admin, and a couple of the people who work there are super bitchy. I kind of dread going in every day and I just can't face it now. Not after Henry.'

'OK. Perhaps you could ask for some compassionate leave?'

'My boss would never go for that. She doesn't do compassion. But I can take emergency annual leave, which she'll go bananas about.' Thea wiped the back of her hand across her snotty nose. 'Actually, the number of kids going to the nursery has dropped so we've been asked if any of us would like to volunteer for redundancy.'

'Will you volunteer?'

'Probably, though the thought of looking for another job is terrifying.'

'Now isn't the best time to think about that,' said Emma quickly when Thea's bottom lip began to wobble. Perhaps her daughter wasn't as cried out as she'd assumed. 'You can work out what happens next when you get back to London. There's no rush.'

'Won't you be coming back to London with me?' Thea implored, her eyes huge in her tear-blotched face. 'Are you going back to Dad?'

Emma gazed across the sea, towards the smudgy horizon. A part of her craved the familiarity that being back with Carl would provide.

'I haven't decided yet. Your dad and I loved each other for a long time but it's complicated. I hope you understand.'

'I do understand, and do you know what, Mum, I owe you an apology.'

'Why?'

'I blamed you a bit for the split between you and Dad, though you probably haven't noticed.' Oh, Emma had noticed, but she kept her face neutral. 'I know Dad went off with Selena and that's, like, really awful. But I thought you must have done something wrong to make him do that. But *I* didn't do anything wrong with Henry and yet he's still left me.'

'Sometimes relationships simply run their course and no one is to blame.' Emma gave a rueful smile. 'Though I think your dad found me a bit boring at times.'

'That's because he didn't let you do anything. I love him – he's my dad – but he can be a controlling, misogynistic dinosaur at times. Don't you think?'

Emma mumbled noncommittally, wondering if Carl was aware of how Thea perceived him.

'Dad reckoned you were crazy to set up your business down here, and so did I, but Leo's told me how great you are with customers and what a good eye you have for what sells.'

'Did he?'

'Yeah, he said you're a natural.' She paused. 'He seems nice.'

'Mmm, he is.'

Thea gave her a straight look and then opened her eyes wide.

'Whoa, look at that view! It's all so *open* down here. You can see for miles.'

'It's beautiful, isn't it?'

And it was, even though dark clouds were hurrying across the sky. The waves were a maelstrom of different greys today – from smoke and pewter to slate and charcoal. And the sea wind on Emma's face made her feel rooted and alive. She could grow to love this place, but she wouldn't have the chance because Thea needed her in London.

That's okay, she told herself. *I can restart my business in the capital.* But she knew it wouldn't be the same. She would miss this spectacular view, and this peaceful village and its people – some more than most. Had Leo really praised her business flair and called her a natural?

'Mum!' Thea was waving a hand in front of her face. 'Mum, come on. I'm getting cold.'

Emma's concentration snapped back to her daughter. 'Let's walk on then, to Driftwood House. Do you remember it from our holiday here years ago? You and I came up onto the cliffs but it started raining and we got soaked. The lady who lived there took us in to get dry.'

Thea properly looked at the house for the first time and tilted her head to one side. 'I do remember. She had a little girl who showed us round, and we played together.'

'That little girl, Rosie, now has a child of her own. Come on, let's go and have a reunion.'

～

Twenty minutes later, they were in the comfy sitting room at Driftwood House. Rosie, much like her mother almost two decades earlier, had welcomed them with open arms. And now they were sipping tea – Emma in the chair that faced the window, and Thea and Rosie sitting on the Persian rug. Alfie lay between them, kicking and gurgling.

The girls carried on chatting while Emma sat back and watched. It warmed her heart to see them getting on so well, although their reunion felt bitter-sweet with Rosie's mum, Sofia, missing.

But Emma couldn't concentrate on what they were saying.

Her mind kept returning to Maisie's bombshell, shortly before Carl and Thea had turned up, that Robert had stolen Beatrice's wedding ring from her handbag. She'd thought the teenager must be mistaken – the whole thing was some horrible mix-up.

But then Leo had dropped bombshell number two, that his father had also stolen the gold and garnet ring from Colonel Farleigh-Addison's room at the Lavender Orchid. What was it with the pompous man and rings that didn't belong to him?

The buzz of conversation and Alfie's squeals dimmed as Emma went over what she'd said to Leo while they sat together in the back yard of her shop. *'Your dad might not want to tell you the truth. But maybe he would tell Beatrice.'* Then she'd offered to contact her in the hope of getting the two together.

Emma massaged her temples at the very thought of getting more embroiled in the mystery that somehow linked Beatrice and Robert across half a century.

She'd vowed to keep out of it, after coming face to face with Beatrice at her parents' house yesterday. But that was before Maisie had dropped bombshell number one, and Leo bombshell number two, and she'd witnessed just how confused and upset Leo was about his father's actions.

He deserved some answers – but he'd have to get them on his own because, fortunately, she *could* walk away from the whole thing now that Carl and Thea had turned up so unexpectedly. She could take the train back to London, for good.

'Mum?' Thea's voice jolted Emma out of her own head. 'Rosie asked where I'm staying in Heaven's Cove for the next day or two.'

'Um... I'm not sure yet but there's a B&B down by the harbour.'

She could ask, perhaps, if Thea might sleep in her room – they could share the double bed. However, it seemed a cheek in the circumstances, seeing as Emma had already outstayed her welcome.

But Rosie was beaming. 'No, you must stay here,' she said. 'We've got spare bedrooms because we're not open for guesthouse business at the moment.'

'Are you sure?' Thea asked, looking happier than she had all day.

'Definitely.'

'It's very kind of you, if you're sure,' said Emma. 'Thea will pay her way, like I do, and she can always share the top room with me if that's more convenient.'

'No, absolutely not,' said Rosie. 'It won't take me five minutes to freshen up one of the bedrooms, and it'll be good practice for when the guesthouse reopens.'

'Which is when?' asked Thea, wiping dribble from Alfie's chin.

'It's supposed to be in three weeks' time. I've started taking bookings again, although it's going to be chaos here, with Alfie in tow. I can only hope that his sleep pattern has improved by then. Liam will help out as much as he can but it's a busy time on his family farm right now and he's working all hours there. Oops!' She lifted Alfie up and sniffed. 'I think this baby needs a new nappy.'

'I'll do it,' Thea insisted, while Rosie fetched the changing mat. 'Working in a nursery, I'm a dab hand at changing babies. I must have changed hundreds in my time.'

Now was a good time to disappear, Emma decided, heading for the door. She'd done her fair share of nappies twenty-five years ago, and she'd leave the young ones to it.

The house was peaceful as she climbed the stairs, and all she could hear when she lay on her bed was the wind whistling through the eaves and a dull thud of waves hitting the cliff.

It would be different when she got back to London with Thea. Bright lights, wall-to-wall sound, people everywhere. She'd loved all of that once, but now the buzz of the city had palled.

I'll soon get back into the swing of it, she told herself, wondering if she had the courage to go it alone. Or if the prospect of being a 'safe' couple again, with Carl, would be too tempting.

The trouble was, every time she thought of Carl and tried to picture him, an image of Leo swam into her head. And when her ex-husband had kissed her on the beach, her mind had flitted back to the Lavender Orchid at midnight, and a very different kiss.

'Stop it!' said Emma out loud, swinging her legs off the bed and sitting up.

She grabbed her phone and started scrolling but the distraction didn't work. Now she was picturing Leo sitting in The Smugglers Haunt and leaning towards her.

'Just forget what I told you about my father and I'll sort it out myself.'

That's what he'd told her, and it made sense to keep out of it, especially as she'd soon be leaving.

But Emma had said she'd help, and, after he'd been so caring with Thea today, she would keep that promise, she decided. It would be the last thing she could do for Leo, before she left for good.

Emma opened her email and picked up the note she'd taken to the Farleigh-Addisons' house. She turned it over, to check the email address, and then she began to write: *Dear Beatrice...*

37

ROBERT

Robert was sitting in his conservatory, looking out over the village. But he hardly noticed the kittiwakes circling, or the sea sparkling in sunshine now that yesterday's thick clouds had cleared.

It was mid-morning but he hadn't bothered with breakfast, or a cup of tea either, even though he could desperately do with one.

He had no energy for anything, other than to sit and do something that he had avoided for a long time – think.

There was a meeting of the summer fair organising committee this afternoon but he didn't have the heart to go. He would give his excuses and see if they could manage without him.

Of course they will, whispered through his mind. *You're not half as important as you think you are.*

'Not important at all,' he said out loud into the still, quiet room.

He could see it more clearly now, as if blinkers had fallen from his eyes. He wasn't the great Robert Jacobson-Jones, local man made very good.

He was simply Bob Jones, who had messed everything up: his marriage to long-suffering Barbara which had, in some ways, been a union of convenience for both of them; his relationship with his son, who had lost all respect for him now he knew his father was a common thief; and his business which, he had to admit, was losing money hand over fist.

Leo had been right all along, that the business needed to adapt to changing times. But he hadn't listened. He hadn't properly listened to anyone for a long time.

Everything had been drowned out by his driving ambition which was fuelled by a thirst for revenge.

'Well, here you are, Bob. You've got just what you wanted, and it's nothing but damn lonely.'

He leaned forward, with his head in his hands. There had been a fork in the road fifty-five years ago, on Beatrice's wedding day, and he had taken the wrong turning.

Many in Heaven's Cove saw him as a good man with a big heart... for now. But the truth was he had acted badly and hurt people, and it was only fair that he got his comeuppance, which might be viewed as karma.

Robert closed his eyes as memories of the Lavender Orchid Hotel came at him like poisoned darts. He would stop hiding, and make himself remember.

But someone was knocking at his front door. He ignored the intrusion at first, but the knocking continued, loud and insistent.

'For goodness' sake!' Robert's eyes snapped open. 'Can't I even have a breakdown in peace?'

He hauled himself to his feet and traipsed into the hall, across the muddy footprints that remained after yesterday's walk to Heaven's Brook.

'What is it?' he demanded, wrenching open the front door.

Leo and Emma were standing side by side on his doorstep,

and Robert's irritation morphed into an emotion that felt very like fear.

'Why are you here?' His voice sounded brittle and odd, and he deliberately softened his tone. 'You have a key, Leo. You could have let yourself in.'

'I thought it best to knock because we have someone with us and we weren't sure...'

His words tailed off and he and Emma exchanged a glance before he stepped to one side.

A woman was standing behind him. A tall, slim woman with her hair pulled back from her face. And Robert's breath caught in his throat as he recognised her blue eyes that were streaked with silver. Her hair was snow white now, and the soft skin on her face lined. But he would know Beatrice anywhere.

'Hello, Bob,' she said with the hint of a smile. 'It's been a long time.'

And the way she said his name – just as she had before everything changed and he became Robert – almost unravelled him.

'Your son and Emma persuaded me to come and see you. I hope that was all right.'

When Robert gave a curt nod, still unable to speak, the three of them stepped inside and Beatrice and Emma followed Leo into the sitting room.

Robert had a sudden urge to flee. He could slip out of the front door and never come back. But he knew in his heart that the time had come to face his past, and make amends if that was even possible.

Beatrice was perched on the sofa when he went into the sitting room, her hands twisting in her lap.

'We're off,' said Leo, not catching his eye. 'We'll leave you two to talk in peace.'

'No, please don't go.' The words were out of Robert's mouth

before he realised he was going to say them. 'You deserve to know what's been going on, Leo.'

He looked at Emma, the woman whose arrival in Heaven's Cove had kick-started the events which had led to this. He'd strongly disliked her to start with, but now couldn't really remember why.

'You, too,' he added.

'Are you sure?' she asked, her eyes flicking to his son.

'I'm very sure.'

What was the point in hiding any more? He needed to atone for what he'd done, and what better way to start than with a semi-public confession?

As his son and Emma took a seat in the corner of the room, Robert turned to Beatrice.

'So how are you?'

It was an anodyne question. One he might have asked of anyone he met in the street, but Robert didn't know where to start. How could they cover the last fifty-five years in one conversation?

When Beatrice's reply, 'I'm doing well,' was equally bland, Robert decided that cutting through any inhibition and awkwardness was the only way.

'Is that right?' he asked. 'You gave away your wedding dress.'

Beatrice smiled. 'Still straight talking, I see.' Her smile faded. 'The dress was in storage at my parents' house and I couldn't see the point in keeping it any longer. However, I didn't realise that donating the dress would lead to this.' She shrugged. 'To us.'

'No, the whole situation is rather overwhelming.'

'I had no idea that you would ever see the dress, let alone remember it.'

Beatrice clasped her hands together and glanced around the room – at the cream velvet curtains, the polished floorboards and the antique furniture inherited from Barbara's parents.

'It looks as if you've done well for yourself since we last met, Bob.'

'I heard on the grapevine that you've done well too, moving in diplomatic circles in various parts of the world. It sounds exciting.'

Beatrice's face clouded over. 'It's been interesting, certainly.'

'What about your husband?' asked Robert. 'How is he?'

Beatrice looked up and caught his eye. 'Richard and I have been living apart for some months.'

'Living apart?'

'Separated,' said Beatrice flatly. 'The marriage wasn't working and hadn't been for a while.'

'I'm sorry.'

A long time ago, Robert had longed for the marriage to fail and Beatrice to return. He'd even thrown coins into the old well by the quay and wished as much.

But later, when he had a family and a business and not so much to prove, he'd hoped that she was happy with Richard.

'Anyway, enough of my marital woes,' said Beatrice briskly. 'I didn't know that you'd changed your name until Emma told me.'

Robert's eyes darted to Emma. What else had she and Leo said about him? But it was way too late now to put up a front. The truth was spilling out.

'I became Robert Jones just before I opened my business, and Jacobson-Jones when I got married. Jacobson was Barbara's maiden name.'

Incorporating her name had seemed a wonderful gesture at the time, and Barbara and her family had been thrilled. But it had suited him to have a double-barrelled surname. If it was good enough for the Farleigh-Addisons...

'I believe I saw your business when I dropped off my bag of clothing at Emma's shop. But I didn't realise that Robert Jacobson-Jones was you. If I had—'

Beatrice stood up and walked to the window that overlooked the garden. Then, she turned towards him, her face resolute.

'Perhaps I should try straight talking too. Why did you abandon me, Bob, all those years ago?'

She continued, without waiting for his reply. 'We saw each other for months, albeit in secret, and I thought we were in love. I was ready to tell my parents about us but then you ghosted me. Isn't that what young people call it these days? You didn't answer my calls or letters and seemingly did everything to keep out of my way. It was heartbreaking.'

When Robert went to speak – he had to say something, anything, to ease her anguish – she held up her hand to silence him.

'I stopped at the wishing well on my wedding day to Richard. It was traditional for brides to do that on their way to the church, but can you guess what I wished for?' Robert shook his head. 'My wish was for courage – that you'd realise how much you loved me, even at that late hour, and you'd have the courage to fight for me, and I would be brave enough to leave with you. And when I saw you in the church, I thought... I hoped.'

Her shoulders slumped. 'But it was very clear that you never really loved me.'

'I *did* love you,' Robert protested. 'That's why I came to the church. I wanted to scoop you up and run away with you.'

'Yet you didn't.'

'That's because I didn't think I was good enough for you.'

Beatrice's laugh sounded bitter. 'Wasn't that for me to decide?'

'Your parents—'

'What's it got to do with them? We decided to keep our relationship a secret at first because they were such snobs. But they'd have come round, if you hadn't simply changed your mind and decided I wasn't worth the trouble after all.'

Robert was so floored by her words, he found it hard to speak. 'You were always worth the trouble, Bea,' he managed. 'This, all of this, has been for you, in a way.'

'I don't understand,' said Beatrice, confusion flitting across her face.

Robert swallowed, remembering standing in Colonel Farleigh-Addison's intimidating sitting room, and how he and his snooty wife had completely humiliated him.

'Did you know that I asked your parents for your hand in marriage? Did they ever tell you?'

Robert could tell from the shock on Beatrice's face that her parents had never let on.

'I'd decided to propose so I went to your parents and asked for their blessing because I wanted to do it properly. That was how people in their social class behaved, and I thought they'd respect me for it. I thought it would make them see past my worn clothes and lack of money.

'But they laughed in my face and told me I was delusional if I thought I was good enough. They sneered about my upbringing and said I'd never amount to anything. I was a nobody, and it wasn't fair to hold you back from the glittering life you could have. They convinced me that I would only make you miserable and you would end up hating me for it. That's why I backed off. I wanted the best for you. Better than me.'

'Oh my God.' Beatrice's hand flew to her mouth.

'Then, a few days later, Richard came on the scene: the son of an acquaintance who had all the right breeding and was going places – presumably your parents pushed the two of you together. I couldn't compete with that so I stayed away. So you could have the glittering life you deserved. That I wanted you to have.'

'But I didn't really want Richard. I wanted you.'

'Yet you married him quickly enough,' said Robert, trying to keep the pain out of his voice. 'You were engaged only a few weeks after your parents had seen me off.'

'I thought you'd given up on me. I was upset and confused when you suddenly went cold on me. So I took the easy way out and did what my parents wanted. I always seem to have done what they wanted.' Beatrice swallowed hard. 'Anyway, it was all right in the end. Richard's a good man in many ways, and I was content with our life together for a long time.'

Robert did his best to smile. 'I'm glad,' he said, which was true because he'd only ever wanted her to be happy. That was what had guided his actions back then.

'I feel so angry about what my parents did. I want to have it out with them.' Beatrice's hands had balled into fists that she banged against her sides. 'But it's half a century ago now, my mother's dead and my father has dementia and doesn't always know who I am. There's nothing I can do. It's far too late.'

'I was angry, too,' Robert admitted, feeling the need, after so many years of saying nothing, to confess everything. 'I was so humiliated by them that I vowed never to feel inferior again. That's why I've worked so hard to become a successful businessman, and build a family, and be *somebody* who no one can look down on. But now I wonder, at what cost?'

He glanced at Leo, who was sitting very quietly, next to Emma. What on earth did the two of them think of him now?

'My son and Emma have obviously told you... *things* about me. But have they mentioned what I did a very long time ago in London?'

Beatrice frowned. 'I don't know what you're talking about.'

This was it. The final revelation that would disgust the

woman he'd once loved and make her realise that her parents had been right all along: he would never have been a suitable husband.

Robert moved to the painting above the fireplace and carefully took it down from the wall. Then he opened the safe and pulled out the red velvet pouch at the back.

He pushed his fingers into the soft bag and, taking hold of Beatrice's hand, dropped gold into her palm. As she studied the object, deep furrows appeared between her eyebrows, and then she looked up, her beautiful eyes wide.

'This is... I'm sure that this is—'

'It's the signet ring that you always wore, that you gave to your mother when you moved abroad.'

'But it was stolen from the Lavender Orchid.'

'I know because—'

Robert paused because once this was said, any enduring fond memories Beatrice might have of him would be eradicated. As would his standing in the local community when the news got out, as it invariably would.

He couldn't expect Emma to keep it quiet, not after the way he'd behaved. He regretted being so unwelcoming to her now, and not simply out of self-interest. She was probably more of a decent human being than he was.

'How do you have this ring?' Beatrice was whispering, as if she was afraid of the answer.

Robert took a deep breath and began to talk about the life he had done his best to forget.

'I needed to earn money, to start my own business, so I worked at the Lavender Orchid for a couple of years in the early 1970s. I chose the hotel so carefully. I wanted to come into contact with what I considered the right kind of people – basically, upper-class people with money and status. I wanted to learn, I suppose, how to be like them. And the Lavender Orchid was always in the newspapers because Lord Somebody or Other was staying there, or some rich film star.

'I thought I could become a butler or concierge but, surprise, surprise, Bob Jones from Heaven's Brook was deemed only fit to work in the kitchens.'

He wiped a hand roughly across his face.

'I stayed anyway. The head chef was a nightmare but I got on all right. Then, one day, your parents paid a visit to the hotel. Their first, apparently. I spotted them in reception.'

'What happened?' breathed Beatrice, her face pale.

'I kept out of their way. Can you imagine their reaction if they'd seen the man who'd wanted to marry their daughter working in a hotel kitchen?'

Robert shuddered. He'd imagined Colonel Farleigh-Addison's smug reaction many times.

'But how did you come into possession of this ring?' asked Beatrice, turning it over in her fingers.

'I sneaked into their room while they were out. I wanted to see if there was a letter from you in their belongings. Something that told me where you were and how you were doing. I'd heard nothing of you since you'd married Richard and moved abroad.'

'But you stole the ring instead.'

Robert nodded, feeling unutterably miserable. 'It was lying on the nightstand, next to the bed, so I took it.'

'Why would you do that? The Bob I knew wasn't a thief.'

'I'd been at the hotel for almost two years but hadn't managed to save enough to convince a bank manager to give me the loan I needed to start my own business. I was so frustrated, working all hours and getting nowhere. Though I'm not trying to make excuses for what I did.'

Robert breathed out slowly to steady himself. 'Anyway, I stole the ring and pawned it to top up my savings. And it worked. I got my loan and came back to Heaven's Cove and set up my business.'

Emma's voice sounded from the edge of the room. 'But you've still got the ring.' She winced at him. 'Sorry, I know this doesn't have anything to do with me, but how come the ring is in your safe, after all these years?'

Robert blinked because this had everything to do with Emma. Everything had been turned upside down since she'd arrived in Heaven's Cove.

'I couldn't bear to part with it,' he told her. 'The ring had belonged to Beatrice and I wanted it back. My business did well very quickly, so I bought it back from the pawn shop.'

'But you didn't return it to my mother,' said Beatrice, her expression hard to read.

'I thought about doing that but your parents had moved on from the theft, and even posting the ring back to them anonymously could have opened a can of worms. *You've got away with it*, was my thinking, so why tempt fate?'

'And you were angry with them, in any case.'

'Yes, I was angry,' said Robert, feeling a rush of curdled fury in the pit of his stomach. 'In my eyes, they'd taken you away from me and ruined my life, so the least I was owed was the ring you'd once worn.'

'Oh, Bob.'

Beatrice's eyes were glistening which troubled Robert. He didn't want to make her cry. He'd wanted to strike back at her parents, not at her. But maybe her tears were pity for the pathetic man she now knew him to be.

'What about my wedding ring?'

Ah yes, his second theft. When Robert emptied the velvet bag into her palm, her fingers closed around the ring that Richard had placed on her finger in St Augustine's Church fifty-five years ago.

'I took that too,' he said, glancing at Emma. 'I apologise to you and to Emma and my son. After recognising your wedding dress, I realised the ring was yours too. Did you mean Emma to have it and sell it?'

'No. It must have fallen off while I was filling the bag with my donated clothes.'

'Your ring sparked a quest in my son and his...' Robert was unsure how close his son and Emma had become, and decided to play safe, 'his friend to find out who the ring belonged to. But every question took them closer to finding out about us and what I'd done after your wedding.'

'So you took that ring, too,' said Leo, 'hoping that no ring meant we'd stop searching for its owner.'

'That was my plan, but it didn't work out that way.' Robert sank onto the nearest chair, feeling drained. 'I don't expect any of you to forgive me but I've lived with the shame of this for decades and, for what it's worth, I'm truly sorry.'

He put his head in his hands, expecting them all to leave. Who would want to spend time with a man whose life was a morass of lies and deception?

But, after a few moments, he felt something brush his hair and when he looked up, Beatrice was standing close. She'd slipped the garnet ring onto the little finger of her left hand, but her fourth finger remained bare.

'Bob,' she said, kneeling down beside him. 'You've got yourself into such a mess.'

'I'm sorry,' he whispered. 'Your parents were right about me.'

'No, they weren't. I just wish I'd been stronger and had never tried to keep our relationship a secret from the start. I wish I'd had the guts, back then, to go my own way and make my own decisions. I wish you'd talked to me, but I should have found you and made you tell me what was wrong.'

'The fault is all mine, Bea.'

'No, it's not.' When she placed her hand on his, the gold of her garnet ring felt cold against his skin. 'We both messed up, but it's all in the past now. It's gone, and you have to let it go.'

When Robert looked at her, with tears in his eyes, she smiled. 'You were always enough for me, Bob.'

And her words, her forgiveness, felt like salvation.

38

LEO

When the sound of the front door closing echoed through the house, Leo went to the window.

Emma and Beatrice were walking along the garden path with their heads bent together, seemingly deep in conversation. Which wasn't surprising, he supposed, when they had something so elemental in common: they were both separated from men they'd once loved. Though there might yet be a happy reunion on the cards for Emma.

Would she go back to Carl? he wondered. The man patently didn't deserve her. But she hadn't said anything about him or London while they'd waited for Beatrice to arrive in Heaven's Cove.

Leo could have asked, but he'd figured it was none of his business – even though they'd shared a midnight kiss in a hotel room. A kiss that neither of them had mentioned since.

So instead, before Beatrice arrived in a taxi, he'd enquired about Thea. Then, they'd made small talk, about the weather and tide times and the history of the village. Emma's imminent return to London had been off the table.

'Well, it's been quite a morning,' said Robert.

Leo turned from the window. The seascape, so disliked by his mother, was back on the wall and everything in the room had returned to normal. His father had even plumped the cushions where Beatrice had been sitting.

Yet the atmosphere was still charged, as if the strong emotions unleashed were circling with nowhere to go.

Leo groaned quietly. Bringing Beatrice and his father together had been a gamble. And, while it seemed to have gone relatively well in the circumstances – he'd been concerned that his father might storm out – the next few minutes were bound to be tricky.

It was Robert who spoke first.

'You ambushed me,' he said. 'In my own home, you ambushed me.'

Leo swallowed. 'Yes, I did, but I did it with the best of intentions. I could tell something was very wrong with you and it had something to do with Beatrice.'

'That was quite a leap to make.'

'Was it, Dad? A ring stolen from Beatrice's parents was in your safe, you claimed never to have seen her wedding dress even though you were at her wedding, and you went into Emma's handbag and stole the woman's wedding ring. It all came down to Beatrice.'

'I had some... history with Beatrice but I was doing OK.'

'No, you weren't. You've been behaving oddly ever since you spotted her wedding dress in Emma's shop. You've seemed... I don't know, haunted.

'Plus, you're turning down your MBE, an honour that ordinarily you'd be thrilled about. Anyway, we thought—' Leo stopped, not wanting to drag Emma into this any more than she had been already. '*I* thought that, if you faced your demons, it might help you. Not that Beatrice is a demon. What I mean is...'

He stopped and tried again. 'You and Beatrice were obviously linked in some way, and the secrets you were keeping were badly affecting you. Sometimes, it's better if secrets are aired.'

'Well, they've certainly been aired this morning. Every single last one of them has been hung out to dry.'

'Do you feel any better for it?'

'No,' his father snapped. Then he breathed out slowly and added, more softly, 'Yes, actually. And once I'd got over the shock, it wasn't unpleasant, seeing Bea again. But that doesn't mean it was the right thing to do. How did you find her?'

'Good ol' detective work,' said Leo, trying to ease the tension.

'You went to the Lavender Orchid.'

'Yes, and I'm sorry I did that behind your back but I was worried about you and I needed answers that you weren't going to give me.'

'Is that where you first found out about the stolen ring?'

'Yes, Carmel mentioned the theft when we were talking to her at the hotel.'

'Carmel?' Robert thought for a moment. 'The same Carmel who I used to nip out for a ciggie with all those years ago?'

'The very same. She's still working there, part-time.'

'Heavens! She must be as ancient as me.'

Leo smiled. 'She's doing well and she sent you her regards.'

'Does she think that I—'

'No, she doesn't think that you stole the ring. It seems that no one ever found out.'

'Fortunately, no one saw me going in or out of the colonel's room and I'd had a few run-ins with the head chef, who was a horrible, shouty man, so no one was particularly surprised when I upped and left.'

Robert's face collapsed into a grimace. 'I can't believe I'm talking about any of this with you, Leo. You must hate me.'

'Of course I don't hate you. What I've heard today made me sad more than anything. You've spent so much time and effort trying to prove yourself to Beatrice's parents and other people like them. But they don't care, Dad, and they're also horrible, snobby people. You were always far better than them to begin with.'

'It's kind of you to say so, but I'm the one who turned out to be a thief. I lived down to their expectations.'

'Look, I don't condone what you've done but I can understand it. Basically, you've got yourself into a complete tangle about who you are and your own self-worth. You've been trying to boost your self-esteem in, ultimately, very unhealthy ways.'

Had he strayed too far into what his father deemed 'navel-gazing idiot speak'? Anna had always been into it but Leo felt uncomfortable with the whole touchy-feely tone of this conversation – even though it was probably long overdue.

He braced himself for his father's derision, but Robert simply asked: 'How did you persuade Beatrice to come here this morning? Did you paint me in a bad light?'

'We explained that you seemed troubled, particularly since seeing her wedding dress, and she didn't need much persuading. She still cares about you.'

'So she came along to the ambush and I painted *myself* in a bad light.' Robert took a step forward. 'You say you don't hate me, Leo, but I'm so sorry that I'm not the man you thought I was.'

'Thank goodness for that.' Leo shoved his hands into his pockets. 'Do you realise how hard it is to live up to a parent who's a high-achieving paragon of virtue?'

'I wouldn't say I—'

'A while back,' Leo interrupted, 'I overheard two people in the pub discussing what a shame it was that I wasn't more like you. Apparently I don't share the same marvellous community spirit and must, therefore, be a great disappointment to my family.'

Leo had been bottling up that hurt for some time and it felt good to say it out loud.

'Quite honestly,' he continued, 'since I was a child, and you were always out doing good deeds, I've had a nagging feeling that I'll never measure up and I'm not good enough.'

The words were tumbling out but Leo stopped abruptly when his father's face crumpled.

'That's how I've felt for a long time.' Robert's voice sounded choked. 'But I never wanted the same for you, Leo.'

'It's all right. I feel way good enough now because, although I might not belong to as many committees and organisations as you, I can honestly say that I've never stolen two gold rings and stashed them in my safe.'

Robert stared at his son, as the clock on the mantelpiece began to strike eleven. Then his mouth twitched and he laughed, as Leo had hoped he would.

'You're right,' he said, wiping away tears that were trickling down his cheeks. 'You're a far better man than me, Leo, and I'm immeasurably pleased about that. I know that your mother was always very proud of you.'

Talk of his mother took the wind out of Leo's sails. What would she have made of Beatrice and her husband's unrequited passion? Perhaps she *had* known all along.

'There's one thing I need to ask about Mum,' said Leo gruffly. It was a question he'd wanted to ask for a long time. 'Did you love her, or did you marry her for what she could bring to the marriage?'

'Do you mean financially?'

'No, I mean status-wise.'

Any hint of laughter had vanished from Robert's face. 'I did love your mum once,' he said slowly, 'and she loved me too. At least, for a while. It wasn't a grand passion. It was convenient and safe and practical. But sometimes love is like that. It's not always fireworks that fizzle out once the flame dies.'

'Do you think your relationship with Beatrice would have fizzled out, if you'd grabbed her hand in the church and the two of you had run off together?'

Robert shifted in his chair and sighed. 'Who knows? Perhaps. I felt consumed by it as a young man, and I suppose I've been consumed by it in one way or another ever since. What a waste.'

When he put his head in his hands, Leo patted his father's shoulder.

'It wasn't all a waste, though. You might not have always acted legally—' That prompted a snort of rueful laughter from his father. 'But you built up a business that provided for your family and will be mine one day. And you've done a lot of good for the village.'

'How?' Robert asked, raising his head. 'I was busy trying to be the best at everything – head of this committee, chair of that organisation – and, deep down, it was all for my own benefit.'

'But those committees and organisations have raised money for charities, and put on events enjoyed by the community, and have made life better for people around here.'

'That doesn't change the fact that I did it for the wrong reasons.'

'Does it matter when the outcome was the same? You've helped to make life better for the locals and tourists in Heaven's Cove. That's something to be proud of, isn't it? Perhaps, after all this time, you need to give yourself a break.'

Robert looked up, tears in his eyes. 'You're being far kinder to me than I deserve, Leo.'

'You're simply a flawed human being, like the rest of us,' said Leo, thinking about things he'd got wrong in his own life.

He'd been so caught up in his own grief after Anna lost their baby, perhaps he hadn't been understanding enough about hers. And then there was Emma… he'd been so unwelcoming at first that, by the time he realised how special she was, it was too late.

'I'm not sure the community in Heaven's Cove will be as kind when they find out about my nefarious past,' said Robert.

'*If* they ever find out. Beatrice isn't going to say anything and neither am I. We can tell Maisie that the wedding ring she saw being taken has been returned, with no harm done. And Emma won't tell anyone.'

'Are you sure about that?'

Leo nodded. 'Completely. I haven't known Emma for long but decency comes off her in waves.'

'Decency is an admirable quality in business so perhaps she'll succeed after all with her second-hand clothes.'

'Pre-loved vintage.'

Robert blinked. 'I stand corrected.'

'Anyway, Emma won't be around long enough to spill your secrets because she's moving back to London.'

'Why? We haven't always seen eye to eye but she's always struck me as tenacious. I didn't see her as someone who'd cut and run.'

'She isn't, but her ex-husband wants her back and, even if she decides not to rekindle their relationship, she misses her daughter, who's having problems, so she'll go back to be nearer to her. She'll probably be glad to see the back of Heaven's Cove. The village has been full of nothing but conflict and secrets since she arrived.'

He tried to say it all lightly, as if it was of no consequence to him, but his father wasn't easily fobbed off.

'You like her, don't you?' he said.

When Leo went to protest that of course he liked her, he liked everyone, his father held up his hand. 'No, I mean, you *really* like her.'

Leo opened his mouth to deny it, but the time for secrets was over. He nodded miserably.

'Yes, I like her a lot. She's funny and kind and she's full of courage.'

'Does she like you?'

'I thought so. When we were at the hotel...' He trailed off and ran a hand across his face. 'I don't know, and how could I compete with an ex who's been an important part of her life for two decades? I certainly couldn't compete with her daughter, and I wouldn't want to. So she'll be going.'

'When?'

'Soon.' Leo suddenly felt weary to his bones. 'Look, Dad. I need to go. Terry's finished the electrical repairs so I've moved our stock over, from Emma's store, and we're ready to reopen the shop.'

He waited for his father to complain that the shop was currently closed, during trading hours. But the rebuke didn't come. Instead, Robert got up and walked with Leo to the front door.

'I'll see you later, Dad. I expect you'll be calling in to the shop?'

'No, not today. I'm sure you can manage without me.'

The two men stood for a few seconds, in silence. There was often an awkwardness when Leo left the house because he'd find himself waiting, though he wasn't sure what for.

'Right then, I'll be off,' he said.

But before he could move, his father stepped forward and pulled him into a hug.

Leo blinked with surprise, feeling stiff in his father's arms. Even as a child, hugs between them had been rare, and their relationship had suffered because of his father's absences.

As he let himself relax into the embrace, his father murmured, close to his ear, 'I'm proud of you, Leo. You could never disappoint me.'

39

EMMA

Emma was in the hall at Driftwood House, carrying a pile of sheets, fresh off the line, when a gentle knocking on the front door caught her attention.

She poked her head round the sitting room door and smiled. Rosie and Liam were sitting close together on the settee, cooing at Alfie, who was sitting on Thea's lap.

It was too contented a scene to disturb so Emma put the sheets on top of the hall table and opened the door herself.

'Hello. Can I help you?'

Her smile froze when she saw who was on the doorstep.

'Hello, Emma,' said Robert, brushing away hair that had blown into his eyes.

As always, the clifftop was breezy, and puffs of white cloud were racing across a blue sky.

'Were you looking for Rosie?' Emma asked, mentally crossing her fingers.

Her heart sank when he said quickly, 'No, actually, it was you I wanted to see.'

He was probably here to tear her off a strip for turning up with Beatrice yesterday morning.

'Is there somewhere we could speak?' he asked, when she just stood there like a lemon.

'Actually, I'm here with my daughter at the moment,' she managed.

'It won't take long.' He swallowed. 'Please. It's important.'

And he looked so pained, Emma grabbed her jacket from the coat stand in the corner.

'We can talk outside,' she told him, quietly closing the front door behind her.

'That's good of you,' Robert said, leading the way out of the garden and onto the clifftop. He started marching off, with Emma hurrying to catch up.

'You walk as quickly as your son,' puffed Emma after a while. 'You've both got longer legs than me.'

'I want to put some distance between us and the house.'

He came to an abrupt halt and, shielding his eyes from the sun, stood facing the huddled cottages of Heaven's Brook in the distance.

'Look,' said Emma, keen not to prolong this encounter any longer than necessary, 'I know why you're here. You're worried that I'll tell people about what I heard yesterday morning, when Beatrice was at your house. But you don't need to be concerned. I'm not the kind of person who spreads gossip.'

'So my son says.'

'In any case, I'm leaving Heaven's Cove. I'll be going back to London very soon.'

'Yes, Leo told me that too.'

Emma felt her shoulders relax because at least Robert and his son were still on speaking terms following yesterday's 'intervention'. She'd imagined all sorts going on between them – from icy silences to screaming matches – while she was putting Beatrice into a taxi afterwards.

'Actually.' Robert cleared his throat. 'I wondered if you might be persuaded to consider staying on.'

'I... I don't know what to say. I thought you'd be delighted to see the back of me.'

'You'd think that would be the case,' said Robert, 'but in reality...' He breathed out slowly. 'We haven't always got on too well.'

That's an understatement, thought Emma, but she kept her mouth shut.

'I feel that much of that was due to me, although you flooding my shop was a provocation. It was foolish in the extreme and—'

Robert pulled his lips into a thin line, as if attempting to dam a torrent of accusation.

He appeared to mentally regroup before adding: 'However, I haven't been as welcoming as I might have been and I'm here to apologise for that.'

Emma blinked with surprise at yet another unexpected apology. First, Carl had said sorry for being such a rubbish husband, though not in as many words. Then, Thea had apologised for being distant following her parents' separation, and now this. Though Robert's mea culpa surely had an ulterior motive.

'You really don't have to worry,' she told him. 'I promise I'm not going to say anything about you to anyone.'

'I appreciate that, but it's not the reason why I'm here.' He looked back at Driftwood House, as if he was concerned they might somehow be overheard. 'The truth is, I've done a lot of soul-searching since you and Leo ambushed me with Beatrice.'

Emma winced. Ambushed was a strong word, but he had a point.

'I suppose it was an ambush, though we did it for the best of reasons. I'm sorry if we overstepped the mark.'

'I'd overstepped the mark a long time ago,' murmured Robert, almost to himself.

'Do you think you'll see Beatrice in the future?' Emma

asked, suddenly feeling brave because soon she'd be leaving Heaven's Cove and would never see Robert again.

He shrugged. 'I don't know. Perhaps, if she agrees to it. But rekindling old relationships is never easy, is it? You should know that from dealings with your ex-husband, who, I understand, wants you back.'

Emma raised an eyebrow. 'It seems that Leo has been telling you quite a lot about me.'

'Not really. He didn't say much at all, but I got the gist. So what are you going to do about your ex?' Robert demanded.

Emma had to laugh at the sheer chutzpah of the man. Beatrice had been spot on when she'd remarked on his penchant for straight talking.

'I don't know,' she told him.

Which was true. Carl had texted her a few times over the last twenty-four hours, and she got the feeling he believed it was simply a matter of time before she fell back into his arms. But she hadn't made any decisions.

'So you don't *have* to leave.'

'Robert, why are you asking me to stay?'

'It seems a shame to cut and run, and my son appears to be enjoying having you as a neighbour. So I wouldn't be... let's say, dismayed if it turned out that you'd be remaining in the village. Also, if your decision to go is being influenced by financial affairs, you should know that you won't be receiving a bill for the flood repairs.'

Out of the many surprises recently, this was one of the biggest. Emma realised that her mouth had fallen open, and she closed it with a snap.

'Leo pointed out that our electrics needed upgrading anyway,' Robert continued. 'So it would be unfair to charge you for the work.'

Emma smiled. 'That's very kind of you, Robert' – words that she'd never expected to come from her lips – 'but I insist on paying my way. You might get the money in instalments, but you will get it.'

'I'm sure we can come to some arrangement, if you insist.'

'I do,' said Emma. 'My decision to leave Heaven's Cove has nothing to do with finances, or with my ex-husband, for that matter. My daughter, Thea, is having some problems in London and I want to be there, to support her.'

'I understand. We need to do right by our children when we can.' Robert took a deep breath, as if he was psyching himself up. 'Which is why I need to make sure that you realise how much my child will miss you if' – he corrected himself – 'when you go. I haven't been the best of fathers to Leo but he's turned out to be a kind and decent man, thanks to his mother, no doubt.'

'Does he know that you're talking to me today?' asked Emma, aware of her heartbeat.

She suddenly wished it was Leo here right now, saying how much he would miss her. Though all that would cause was more pain.

'No,' huffed Robert. 'He would be mortified at my meddling. But life hasn't always been easy for him. He was heartbroken when he and Anna split up, after they'd lost the baby so late in the pregnancy. That was...'

When Robert bowed his head, Emma reached out and placed her hand on his arm.

'You lost your grandchild, too.'

Robert nodded, unable to speak for a moment. Then, he swallowed and raised his head. 'What I'm trying to say is, he hasn't seemed particularly interested in anyone since Anna. But there's a spark between the two of you. I can see it.'

Emma blinked, feeling close to tears. 'I like Leo a lot. More than is good for me. But everything has got very complicated here' – she pushed away a memory of Leo's kiss – 'and at least in London I'll be closer to my daughter.'

Robert held Emma's gaze for a moment, then he pointed towards Heaven's Brook.

'Do you see that cottage down there, the one with a red door? That's where I was born and raised.'

'It's very different from Beatrice's family home. How did the two of you meet?'

'On the beach when we were both eighteen.' Robert smiled at the memory. 'She was sunbathing and reading a book, and I was showing off by diving off rocks into the sea. Until I misjudged it and gashed my forehead.

'She provided a towel to stem the blood, told me I was an idiot, and that was that. We met up for months in secret, at the beach and the castle ruins, and we went for long walks on Dartmoor. I was soon hopelessly in love with her, even though it was obvious that we moved in different circles and she was wary about telling her parents. I decided that I'd ask her to marry me, and you know the rest. Anyway' – he did up another button on his jacket – 'I think we've heard quite enough about my past.'

But Emma had one more question and nothing to lose by asking it because soon she'd be gone.

'Forgive me, but why did you go to the church when Beatrice married Richard?'

'I had a fantasy of grabbing her hand and urging her to run away with me. But I couldn't do it. Her parents had convinced me I'd ruin her life, and perhaps I would have done. We'll never know.'

Robert scuffed his shoes into the grass, seemingly lost in his memories.

'I need to get back,' said Emma gently. 'I didn't tell anyone that I was going out.'

'Yes, you don't want them to worry.' Robert held out his hand. 'It was good finally getting to know you, Emma.'

'And you, too, Robert.'

She took his hand and shook it, realising that she would miss this flawed, often irascible man, as well as his son.

'Oh,' he called out, as she walked away. 'I wish you good luck in London if you restart your business, selling pre-loved vintage clothing.'

'Thank you,' she called back, feeling amused. Better late than never, he'd finally accepted what her business was all about. 'Have you turned down that MBE yet, by the way?'

He shook his head. 'I'm psyching myself up to do it.'

'Then don't. I think you should accept it. What happened was a long time ago and it only still lives in your head. No one is going to find out.'

'Even if it all stays secret for ever, I don't deserve the award.'

'Of course you do. You belong to a gazillion committees, and what was it that Maisie called you, the King of Heaven's Cove? If anyone deserves it, you do. Just think about it.'

'I will,' he promised, giving her a wave.

As Emma hurried back towards Driftwood House, her mind flitted over the last few weeks. A new business, an old wedding dress, two stolen rings, secrets from long ago, and Leo.

She would never forget her time in Heaven's Cove, or the people she had met here. And it broke her heart to go.

40

EMMA

Emma sat on the sand and pulled her knees up under her chin. It was freezing out here as the first rays of dawn lit up the horizon but Driftwood House, though warm, had felt confining when she'd woken in the early hours.

The old house had creaked and groaned while she'd sat up in bed, going over and over the decisions she had to make. And at last, as the clock nudged towards 5.30, she'd thrown some clothes on, left a note to say where she was going, grabbed a torch and slipped out of the sleeping house.

The boom of sea crashing against rock had filled the air as she carefully made her way down the cliff path in the dark. Then she'd walked through the village, waving to the fishermen whose boats were pulling into the quayside after a night's work, and made for the beach.

When she'd last been at the beach, Carl had urged her to return to him. But she wanted time here on her own, to psych herself up for what had to be done.

Emma wrapped her arms around her legs and looked out over the sea which was turning to molten silver as the horizon grew brighter.

She'd always known that Heaven's Cove was a special place – from the moment her friend's mother had regaled her with tales of the village years ago. The family holiday she, Carl and Thea had spent here had only reinforced that opinion. And even the goings-on since she'd arrived a month ago couldn't dent the beauty of the Devon seashore. There was something about the wide-open space before her, and the timelessness of it all, that seeped soothingly into her soul.

Carl would say that was ridiculous, thought Emma, taking a deep breath and pulling out her phone. She knew what had to be done and didn't want to waste another minute.

Carl's phone rang for a good thirty seconds before it was answered.

'Emma?' he asked blearily. 'Is everything all right?'

'Yes, it's fine.'

'Is Thea all right?'

'I think so. Still upset, understandably, but she's doing well.'

'Then why the hell are you ringing me at six o'clock in the morning?'

Emma glanced at the sky which was turning salmon pink and gold. 'I have something I need to say to you and it couldn't wait.'

'I can understand that, babe,' said Carl, his grumpiness instantly banished. 'Being apart is killing me too. When are you coming back?'

Emma breathed out into the chill morning air. 'That's what I wanted to tell you. I'm not coming back. Not to you, anyway.'

The silence that came down the line was broken by screeching seagulls skimming the waves.

'Carl? Are you still there?' she asked after a few moments.

'Of course I'm still here.' His grumpiness had returned. 'What do you mean you're not coming back? I came down to Devon and threw myself at you. I apologised and everything.'

He lowered his voice to a whisper. 'I told you my relationship with Selena was a mistake and begged for your forgiveness.'

'Which I appreciated, and I've thought long and hard about it. But I've come to the conclusion that it wouldn't work, Carl, you and me back together.'

'Why?'

'Because I deserve better.'

There, she'd said it, and it felt as if a weight she hadn't realised she was carrying had been lifted from her shoulders.

'That's a bit harsh,' said Carl, with a familiar sulkiness in his voice.

'Maybe, but I'd never be able to trust you, after what you've done, and you've never supported my dreams.'

'I said you could open your second-hand clothes shop in London after you came back.'

'It's pre-loved vintage, Carl. Pre-loved vintage, which is my passion and has been for a long time.' Emma tried to relax her shoulders because she was getting irritated. 'Look, I'm sorry if things aren't working out with Selena, I really am, but I don't think I'm the answer you're looking for. If I came back to you, it would only be because I crave familiarity and the feeling of security that comes with it. And you're just looking for a way out of the mess you've made. Are you at Selena's now? Is that why you're speaking so quietly?'

'Yeah,' he admitted grudgingly. 'I haven't got round to telling her yet that it's over.'

'Or you're hedging your bets, in case I decided not to come back?'

'Well, what about you? I bet you're not coming back to me 'cos of that idiot Leo in his stupid suit.'

'It's nothing to do with him,' said Emma quietly.

'Yeah, I bet. Are you in a relationship with him?'

'No.'

'Has he kissed you?'

Emma hesitated but replied, 'Yes.'

She could have denied it but the time for lies between her and Carl was long gone.

'Ha, I thought as much. You like him.'

'So what if I do? We're divorced, Carl, which means I can like whoever I want. But the decision I've made about you and me is for no one except myself. We had a good life together, mostly. But times have changed. *We've* changed, and I can see that we wouldn't be happy together any more. I wish you nothing but the best, Carl, and we'll always be linked because we share Thea. But I need to move on, and so do you.'

Emma stopped talking, feeling drained. While she'd been putting the final nail in the coffin of her reunion with Carl, the sun had risen fully above the horizon and she turned her face towards its rays.

Far away in London, she heard a woman's voice calling out: 'Carl, who are you speaking to on the phone at this time of the morning?'

'It's a work thing,' he called back before whispering, 'We'll talk about this more, later.'

'If you like,' said Emma. 'But I'm not going to change my mind, Carl, and you'll thank me for that one day.'

'Whatever,' he hissed before ending the call.

Emma pushed the phone into her jeans pocket and sat watching waves curl on the sand. The air was warming in the pale sun, and the breeze held a sharp tang of brine and, she mused, fresh beginnings. She'd taken some huge steps recently and, difficult as the last phone call had been, it felt like another stride towards the new life she'd hoped for.

'Here you are, Mum.' Thea dropped down onto the sand beside her. 'I was worried when you weren't in your room and then I saw your note. Why on earth did you decide to walk to the beach at the crack of dawn?'

'I had a lot to think about,' said Emma, turning to face her daughter. Thea, wrapped in a thick jumper and scarf, still looked fragile, but the dark circles beneath her eyes were fading and there was colour in her cheeks. Heaven's Cove was suiting her.

'Were you thinking about coming back to London?' Thea asked, brushing sand from her jeans.

'Yes.' Emma paused. She'd planned to tell her daughter later today, but she supposed that now was as good a time as any. 'I've decided not to go back to your father,' she said in a rush, keen to get the words out.

Thea looked towards the horizon, her jaw set. 'I kind of knew that you wouldn't because you seem different since you've been here.'

'How do you feel about me saying no to your dad?'

'I don't blame you. Dad had his chance but blew it when he went off with Selena. She's nice enough but she's not right for him.'

'And neither am I. Not now.'

'Yeah. It's sad though.'

'I know. It's really sad, but lots of relationships come to an end and life goes on,' said Emma, linking her fingers through her daughter's.

Thea gripped her mum's hand tightly. 'Yeah, I know I'll get over Henry but it feels horrible at the moment.'

'I expect it will for some time, but you're right that you will get over him and you'll go on to meet a special someone who truly deserves you. Or, if you want, you'll build an amazing life on your own.' Emma swallowed because what she was about to say was going to be harder than turning Carl down. 'There's something else I wanted to discuss with you.'

'You're not coming back to London with me, are you?'

Emma gave her daughter a sad smile. 'No, I'm not. I love you, Thea. You're the most important person to me in the whole world and I'll always support you in whatever you do. But I can do that from Devon. I'm always on the end of the phone, and I'll come up to London to visit you often, or you can holiday down here whenever you like. You don't need me to be around the corner any more, because you're grown up now with your own life and it's time I fully accepted that.'

'And time I fully accepted that you have your own life too?' asked Thea, wrinkling her nose.

'That too,' said Emma, giving her daughter's hand an extra squeeze. 'Heaven's Cove is bonkers. You have no idea what's been going on since I arrived. But I've fallen in love with the place and I'd like to stay.'

'For Leo?'

Emma shifted in the sand until she was fully facing Thea. 'No, not for Leo. He's a nice man but things have got complicated between us.'

She was going to explain more, about the kiss that was never mentioned, and the secrets they'd uncovered about his father, but she decided against it. Thea had enough going on in her own life, without hearing about her mother's fledgling relationship that had withered as soon as it had begun.

So, instead, all Emma said was: 'I'm staying for me, Thea, and maybe that sounds selfish but it's what I need to do right now.'

When Thea pulled her hand away, Emma's heart sank. She couldn't bear a rift with her daughter. But then she felt Thea's arm snake around her shoulders and she was pulled into a hug.

And it felt as if the roles of mother and daughter were reversed when Thea said quietly in her ear: 'Well done, Mum. I'll be cheering for you all the way.'

41

LEO

It had been three days since the meeting between Beatrice and his father. Which meant it had been three long days since he'd last seen Emma.

Leo leaned against the counter in his newly wired shop and scrolled through the T-shirts on his laptop screen.

He wanted to expand the range of clothing they had on sale and branch out into more casual wear. With any luck, that might attract more tourists and boost their income. But it was impossible to do anything with his mind flitting all over the place.

Leo rolled his neck from side to side and counted to ten.

He was trying so hard to concentrate while serving customers and ordering stock and going about his everyday life.

But so far he'd failed miserably, even though his life was just the same as it always had been, and he'd been contented enough then. Not happy, exactly. But not unhappy either.

For years, he'd coasted along as the seasons changed in Heaven's Cove – spending time in the pub with his friends, enjoying walks across the wild moors, and doing up his cottage that overlooked the sea.

But all of that had been before he knew Emma existed. Before she'd appeared in his life like a whirlwind and shaken everything up.

Now the tragedy was that he knew what he was missing, and would carry on missing when she went back to London.

Leo tried to clear his mind and began scrolling again, but thoughts and images kept assailing him: Emma, in her black 1950s dress, her face bright with wonder at Dartmoor; Emma, lost and vulnerable outside her ex-husband's house; Emma's warm lips on his at the Lavender Orchid.

Leo gave up and slammed the lid of his laptop shut.

This was why he'd been keeping out of her way. What was the point in making more memories of her to torment him when she was gone?

But he couldn't help wondering how she was. How she was coping with heartbroken Thea, and what decision she'd made when it came to her cheating ex-husband.

He was sure she'd be happy to head back to London and relieved to leave Heaven's Cove behind for good. He couldn't blame her when she'd not seen the best of village life. Stolen rings, dysfunctional families, and secrets and lies were hardly likely to make a newcomer want to stay.

But he hoped that she would miss some of it – the beach at sunset, the castle ruins shrouded in mist, the wide-open sky that seemed to go on for ever. Perhaps she might even miss him, though he doubted that.

His thoughts returned again to the kiss which neither of them had mentioned since. He'd felt nervous about bringing it up, but what if Emma had simply been too embarrassed to talk about it?

Perhaps she'd found the whole thing mortifying. Or maybe cheating Carl was a better kisser than he was, and Leo's romantic lunge was the final straw that had ultimately pushed her back into her ex-husband's arms.

'Oh, for goodness' sake!'

Leo began to pace up and down in front of the shop door. He knew he was being ridiculous, but being cooped up in here was driving him crazy.

Then do something, said the little voice in his head that had become deafening over the last few days.

Leo made a decision and, turning the door sign to 'Shop Closed', he strode out into the spring sunshine.

He planned to walk past Heavenly Vintage Vavoom and, if Emma was there, he would go in and wish her well before her return to London. Because he did wish her well. He wanted only the best for her, which was why he hoped so fervently that she would turn down her no-good ex and forge her own path.

Then, when she was gone, he could return to his normal life and the memories would fade over time. They would still scratch at him occasionally, as memories of Anna and his lost child did from time to time. But he would survive.

Feeling resolved, he walked past Emma's shop and glanced in. But she wasn't there, and the place, usually vibrant and full of life, looked abandoned. Most of the shiny chrome rails had been stripped bare.

He doubled back and went to the shop doorway. Maisie was standing in the middle of it all, staring at her phone screen with a vacant look on her face.

'Hey, Maisie!' When she didn't move, he called her name again more loudly and she startled.

'You made me jump,' she whined. 'I almost dropped my phone and the screen's already cracked.'

'Sorry, but I noticed that most of the rails are empty.'

'Yeah, the clothes are being packed up.'

'And what about Emma?'

'She's gone...' said Maisie, looking back down at her phone and pushing her finger across the screen.

Leo stepped away from the doorway as disappointment

speared his heart. He'd known that Emma was leaving, but she'd gone before he'd had a chance to say goodbye.

He'd expected removal vans and boxes in the street that would alert him to her imminent departure. And in his heart of hearts, he'd hoped that she might call into his shop to bid him farewell.

But the truth was she thought so little of him, she'd gone back to London without a backward glance. She was done with him and with Heaven's Cove which had offered her little more than conflict, secrets and angst since she'd first arrived.

He walked on, blinking hard as his eyes watered. That was it then. He'd never see Emma again.

42

EMMA

Emma fished a pound coin from her purse and dropped it into the well. A few seconds later, there was a distant splash when the coin hit dark water. But before she could make a wish, she spotted Leo in the distance.

Her breathing grew shallow as she raised her arm and put it straight back down again. Should she call him over?

He was sloping along with his head bent and, in spite of Robert's protestations that his son would miss her, Emma wasn't so sure. Leo seemed to have been avoiding her for the last few days. But then, hadn't she been doing exactly the same?

It was understandable, because he had a business to run. While she'd had decisions to make and couldn't afford to be distracted.

No, that's not it, thought Emma. What loomed between them and was keeping them apart – like a high fence neither could clamber over – was the kiss in the Lavender Orchid hotel room.

She hadn't wanted to bring it up in case he was embarrassed – or worse, mortified. And the longer it had gone unmentioned, the higher and more topped with barbed wire the fence had become. Which was a pain when she couldn't stop thinking about the kiss and remembering how wonderful it had been.

It was going to be difficult, working next door to each other. But she'd reassured herself that, in time, the tricky memory would fade and they'd move past it to become business acquaintances – people who made small talk about customer footfall and the weather. In the meantime, it was probably best to keep out of his way.

'Emma?' Leo's voice rang across the cobbled square and he squinted into the sun. 'Emma, is that you?'

It seemed whether or not to attract his attention had been taken out of her hands.

When Emma gave a half-wave, feeling horribly self-conscious, a smile lit up Leo's face and he looked so handsome, standing there in his shirtsleeves, she felt wobbly. Putting their kiss behind her wasn't going to be as easy as she'd hoped.

'What are you doing here?' he asked, hurrying over.

'Making a wish,' she replied, trying to sound breezy. 'I haven't actually got around to wishing yet, although I've paid for it already.'

Emma cringed. Why had she said she'd paid for it, as if she was remunerating the wishing well gods for their service? Leo seemed a practical man who wouldn't hold much truck with anything mystical.

Fortunately, he ignored her remark. 'I thought you'd packed up already and left Heaven's Cove for London,' he said, running a hand through his hair.

'What, left for good? Why?'

'I poked my head into your shop and Maisie said you'd gone.'

'Yeah, gone to the bank to get some change.' Emma rolled her eyes. 'Did Maisie have her head stuck in her phone, by any chance? She can't string a sentence together when she's engrossed in her social media feeds.'

'She *was* looking at her phone and seemed distracted.'

'There you go then.'

'I see.'

Leo stepped aside so a couple of tourists with dripping ice creams could get past, and then lapsed into silence. His smile had gone and he seemed awkward all of a sudden, just like her.

'So, how's Thea doing?' he asked after a few moments.

'Still heartbroken but she's doing well, considering, and being with Rosie and Alfie has been a tonic. I know Thea works in a nursery but I hadn't realised quite how good she is with babies. Heaven knows why. I was never a natural. I found the whole thing hard going, though I missed the baby stage when Thea got older and didn't need me so much.'

Emma stopped talking, aware that she was wittering on and remembering how Carl often berated her for gabbling when she was nervous.

'I'm sure you were a great mum,' said Leo. 'Still are,' he added quickly. 'And I guess she's going to need you while she's getting over her broken relationship.'

'Yeah, I'll be giving her all the support I can until she gets back on her feet.'

Leo scuffed his shoes against the cobblestones. 'And what about Carl? How is he?'

'He's OK, I think. He says he's planning to move out of the house he's been sharing with Selena.'

The house that I ill-advisedly went searching for with you when we were in London together.

Emma dug her nails into the palm of her hand, trying to stop herself from thinking about that day because it would invariably lead back to memories of the kiss. The kiss that she had to forget if she and Leo were ever going to get on as neighbours.

'So you've decided to go back to him, then,' said Leo. His tone sounded peculiar – upbeat but almost strangled. He swallowed and held out his hand to shake hers. 'Well, I really hope it'll all work out for you, Emma. You deserve the best and I wish you well.'

'Thank you, but, actually, after careful consideration of Carl's offer, I've turned him down.'

'So, you're not getting back together again?'

Leo's soulful hazel eyes searched hers.

'No, our life together has come to the end of the road.' It felt peculiar but oddly liberating to be saying that out loud. 'We wouldn't make each other happy. I can see that now, and it's time to move on with our lives. Separately.'

When she glanced at Leo's hand, which was still outstretched, he pulled it back.

'Does Carl know?'

'I rang him.' Emma closed her eyes briefly, remembering that call from the beach at dawn. 'He didn't take it too well, but he'll come round. It's funny. I usually flip-flop after making a decision – have I got it right or made a total pig's ear of the whole thing? – but, this time, I know I'm not going to change my mind.'

'Well, for what it's worth, I think you've made the right decision. You can make a good life for yourself and Thea back in London.' Leo looked past her, at a glimpse of blue sea and the wooded headland beyond. 'I see you're packing up the shop,' he said, his jaw tight.

'That's right. I'm expecting a big delivery from a vintage clothing wholesaler and I'm making space. I want to rejig the shop and make it even better' – she paused, not sure how Leo would take the next bit of information – 'seeing as I'm staying in Heaven's Cove.'

She braced herself for Leo's reaction, but all he did was stare at her, as if he couldn't quite believe what she was saying. Then, he asked: 'What about Thea? You told me you need to give her support.'

'I do, and I'm going to give her as much as I can. But she's an adult now and I've realised we don't need to live in each other's pockets. She's got her life and I've got mine. We can speak on the phone, and I dare say I'll be making lots of trips to and from London.'

'So, are you *definitely* staying?' he asked, still sounding as though he could hardly believe it.

'Uh-huh.' Emma nodded, upset that Leo seemed floored by her plans, even though she understood why he'd be keen to see the back of her. She was the woman who knew his family's dark secrets. The daft divorcee he'd been stupid enough to kiss after they'd been thrown together.

'Look, you don't have to worry,' she told him. 'I'll be careful not to flood your shop again, and I'll keep out of your way, and your dad's. We never have to speak about what's gone on over the last few weeks, and you won't even know I'm around. We'll simply be business acquaintances.'

'Oh, right.' Leo took a step backwards. 'If that's what you want.'

'I think it's for the best.'

'Absolutely.' He shook his head. 'Anyway, it's good to know that you're staying, Emma, and I'm glad that Thea's OK.'

He sounded stiff and formal – just as he'd been the first time they'd met.

Emma tried to smile. 'Thanks... Well, I suppose I'd better get on.'

'Yeah, sure. Get to the bank before the queues build up.'

'They could do with more staff.'

'They really could.'

Emma knew she should go, but her feet stayed rooted to the spot, as if the wishing well gods had put a spell on her.

The two of them were making small talk. That's how it would be from now on. But, suddenly, Emma couldn't bear the awkward tension between them a moment longer – and wasn't prepared to put up with it.

She was a woman who'd survived infidelity, moved across the country, started her own business, turned down her ex-husband's offer of a reconciliation, and realised her daughter was adult enough to stand on her own two feet.

Whatever Leo says about the kiss, however much he regrets it, I can cope, thought Emma, remembering what Beatrice had told Robert during their first meeting in half a century: 'We should have talked to each other.'

Before she could change her mind, Emma blurted out: 'We need to talk about the kiss. The one at the Lavender Orchid when we had to share a room. The one that happened at midnight after I'd fallen over.'

'I know which kiss you mean,' said Leo, a flush of colour spreading across his cheeks.

'It's just that we haven't talked about it and that wouldn't be a problem if I was leaving, but now that I'm staying it's kind of the elephant in the room and... everything.'

Emma tailed off, cursing the sudden feeling of invincibility that had prompted her to bring the subject up. Of course she'd cope if Leo told her he regretted every moment of their kiss, but she'd still be crushed.

It had been two decades since she'd kissed anyone other than Carl, and she liked Leo. *Really* liked him. But what if he saw her as a poor, pathetic divorcee and he'd simply been trying to make her feel better about herself? A kiss to boost her confidence.

'Say something,' Emma demanded, desperate to get the next few minutes over with.

'I thought you didn't want to talk about it,' said Leo, glancing around them, probably checking that gossipy Belinda wasn't lurking nearby. 'That's why I've been keeping out of your way for the last couple of days.'

'I thought *you* didn't want to talk about it either – and ditto with the keeping out of the way stuff.'

'But the thing is' – Leo stopped, his cheeks growing pinker – 'though we haven't talked about what happened that night at the Lavender Orchid, I can't stop thinking about it.'

'Me, neither.' Emma took a deep breath to gather up the little courage she had left. 'So what exactly *do* you think about it?'

Leo ran a hand across his face. 'What do *you* think about it?'

'No, bagsy you first.'

Bagsy you first? Emma groaned quietly. Rather than coming across as an assertive woman making her way in the world, she was regressing to the playground.

A slow smile was spreading across Leo's face. 'Bagsy?' he said, raising an eyebrow.

'Yeah, OK, that sounds stupid.' Emma's shoulders dropped and she looked into Leo's eyes. 'Look, I just want to know what you thought about the kiss, and you can tell me the truth – even if you thought it was dreadful and you regret it and you wish you'd never even met me. I can cope, and then we can move on and be neighbours who chat about customer footfall and the weather.'

'Do we *have* to chat about customer footfall and the weather?' Leo grinned but then his smile faded. 'You're right that we should talk about what happened at the Lavender Orchid. I've been avoiding it because I thought *you* regretted the whole thing. But, actually, with my dad and Beatrice, we've both seen what happens when two people don't talk so, here goes.'

He swallowed and pulled himself up tall. 'I think, in the words of Maisie, who is possibly the worst shop assistant in Heaven's Cove, by the way, that our kiss was totally awesome.'

'Really?' gasped Emma, breath catching in her throat.

'Yes, really. What about you?'

'Same. Mutual. Ditto.' Emma groaned again. She never

used the word 'ditto' but now she'd used it twice in the last two minutes. 'Sorry, what I mean is—'

'I know exactly what you mean,' said Leo, his eyes shining. And when he reached out his hand and cupped Emma's cheek, she leaned into him. 'I'm so glad you're staying,' he whispered into her ear.

A young couple suddenly appeared from around the corner and Leo dropped his hand when they started walking across the square.

'Have you made your wish yet?' he asked, nodding towards the well. Then he gave her a wink that made her heart pound.

'Not yet, but I'm about to make one now.'

Emma screwed her eyes up tight and wished with all her heart.

When she opened them again, Leo's arm was outstretched over the well and a two-pound coin was gleaming in his palm. He dropped the money into the darkness.

'I assumed you didn't believe in all that kind of nonsense?' said Emma, feeling fizzy all over from the excitement of the last few minutes.

'On this occasion, I'll make an exception.'

He closed his eyes and then opened them with a smile.

'What did you wish for?' she asked.

'I think – I hope – that I wished for the same thing as you.'

'I think you might be right,' said Emma, finding it hard to breathe as he gently pushed a stray strand of hair behind her ear. 'So what happens now?'

Leo glanced around the square which was starting to fill with tourists. A coachload must have been dropped off at the quayside.

'I guess we both go back to work right now and take it from there. Perhaps I could start by taking you out to dinner tonight, to celebrate your continuing presence in Heaven's Cove?'

'I'd love that.'

Leo's wide smile made her feel warm inside.

'Excellent. It's a date.'

When he held out his hand Emma slid her fingers between his and, as they walked through the village together, she realised that she felt truly happy for the first time in a long while.

She'd had a rocky start in Heaven's Cove. The mysterious wedding dress, missing rings and unwelcoming locals had combined to make her doubt her decision to move to this beautiful coastal village.

But now Emma knew that she'd been right to follow her dream. She glanced at Leo, who was grasping her hand tightly. She'd chosen a new kind of life for herself and, so far, things were working out just fine.

EPILOGUE
FIVE MONTHS LATER

Emma pulled the steaming mug of coffee close to her chest and leaned on the doorframe of Heavenly Vintage Vavoom. She enjoyed standing here, watching people go by, including lots of locals who often waved to her as they passed.

Carl still insisted on referring to Heaven's Cove as 'that sleepy little village' but, in reality, the place was buzzing, especially at the height of the summer season. A stream of tourists in shorts and T-shirts slapped along in flip-flops, and plenty of them called into her shop.

A family group was browsing the packed rails at the moment, but Maisie was hovering nearby in case they needed any help.

'All right?' Emma mouthed at her, and the teenager gave her a thumbs up. She still had her moments – last week she'd refused to serve a woman who'd apparently 'disrespected' her – but, overall, Maisie had settled in well and Emma enjoyed her company. She'd certainly needed her help during the school summer holidays, now that business was so brisk.

'Hey, Mum.'

Thea's shout caught Emma's attention and she waved at her

daughter, who was walking past with Alfie in his pushchair. Thea steered the pushchair towards her and Emma beamed at Alfie, who was giving her a gorgeous toothy grin.

'How's it going?' Emma asked, bending down to stroke Alfie's soft cheeks.

'Good, thanks.' Thea pushed hair from her tanned face. 'Rosie's got a gaggle of guests booked in at Driftwood House so Alfie and I are making ourselves scarce for a few hours. I thought I might take him to the soft play session in the village hall.'

'Isn't that run by Dougie?'

'Is it?' said Thea, not catching Emma's eye. 'I'm not sure. It might be.'

It was, and Thea knew it. But she was being very coy about her attraction to local man Dougie, whose business involved running children's activities across the region.

Perhaps nothing would come of it, but at least Thea had stopped grieving over Henry – she didn't have the time, now she was looking after Alfie.

For the hundredth time, Emma thanked her lucky stars that her daughter had decided to remain in Heaven's Cove rather than return to London. Rosie's genius suggestion that she stay on as Alfie's live-in nanny seemed to be benefiting everyone: Rosie had lost her haunted sleep-deprived look and had more time to run the guesthouse, Liam was able to help his parents out on the farm without feeling guilty about leaving Rosie, and Thea was besotted with Alfie, who was thriving.

The new arrangement had also saved Emma from a shed-load of absent mum guilt, because she could see and support her daughter regularly.

'Anyway, I'd better be getting on because the play session starts soon,' said Thea, keen to avoid any more talk of Dougie. 'Are you still OK for me to come round for tea tomorrow?'

'Yeah, definitely. Is six thirty OK? I'll make us a shepherd's pie and we can eat in the garden, overlooking the sea.'

Thea raised an eyebrow because 'overlooking the sea' was an ambitious description. The tiny cottage Emma was renting on the edge of the village only had a sea view if you stood on tiptoe in the garden and squinted. But after decades of London brick and concrete, that glimpse of water first thing in the morning always got Emma's day off to a good start.

'Six thirty sounds great, Mum,' Thea confirmed, turning the pushchair around. 'I'll see you then. Say goodbye, Alfie.'

When she bent down, took hold of Alfie's arm and waved it at Emma, he giggled.

'Bye, baby.' Emma waved back vigorously, eliciting more giggles, before Thea walked off towards the village hall.

After they'd disappeared from view, Emma leaned back against the doorframe, feeling at peace as sun filtering through the branches of a nearby silver birch dappled across her skin.

It had been a hectic few months since she'd made the decision to stay in Heaven's Cove rather than abandon the village and return to London. But life was settling into a rhythm that suited her and made her feel grounded.

'Slacking off again, are you?'

Emma smiled at the sound of his voice – a voice which was so familiar to her now. She glanced up the lane and saw Leo walking towards her, his scattering of grey hairs, amongst the brown, glinting in the bright light.

He looked relaxed and cool in his grey cotton chinos and blue T-shirt. He'd ditched the work suits shortly after his dad had properly retired. That was change number one. Others had followed swiftly, including stocking a range of more modern men's clothing, painting all his dark-wood shop fittings white, and updating the shop's street frontage.

The changes seemed to be working with sales on the up, and Robert had been far less disapproving than Leo had feared.

Probably because he was too busy involving himself in even more community ventures now he had more time. And he was still dining out on the news of his MBE, which had been made public in June.

'Hey, you,' said Leo when he reached her. He leaned over and kissed her on the lips. 'I'm off to buy a cappuccino and wondered if you wanted one, but I see you're taking a coffee break already.'

'I am, but I'm definitely not slacking off. I'm having a quick breather after a very busy morning selling loads of—'

'Second-hand clothes?'

Emma batted his arm. 'Pre-loved vintage, I'll have you know. How's your morning been?'

'Busy, too.' Leo glanced into the shop, where Maisie was ringing through a sale on the till. 'Your place is looking so good, Em.'

Today, the shop was crammed with high-quality vintage clothing, from pre-war trousers and dresses to long gowns from the 1980s that sparkled with sequins. Beatrice's divine wedding dress was long gone – snapped up by a local bride-to-be who paid a handsome price that went to the local children's centre. She'd be wearing it when she walked down the aisle at St Augustine's Church in a fortnight's time.

'You've done wonders with your business,' said Leo. 'I'm so proud of you.'

Once upon a time, when she'd been someone else, Emma would brush off any sort of compliment with a deprecating comment. But now she accepted Leo's praise with a smile because she was proud, too, of the business she was building up.

'That's very kind of you, Mr Jacobson-Jones. Did you see Thea and Alfie going past? They're on their way to the soft play session in the village hall.'

'The one run by Dougie?'

'Yep, though Thea claims not to know if he runs it or not.'

Leo laughed. 'Oh, I think she knows. I bumped into Dougie earlier and he asked whether I'd heard if Thea and Alfie would be there today. When I said I wasn't sure and asked why, he said "No reason," and went pink to the tops of his ears.'

'Young love,' said Emma, standing on tiptoes to give Leo a peck on the cheek, just because she could. 'Thea's coming round to mine for shepherd's pie tomorrow evening if you'd like to join us?'

'Sounds great, though I don't know why you keep paying rent on that place when you spend so much time at mine.'

'It suits me for the moment,' said Emma, who, one day, would probably take up Leo's offer to move into his much less ramshackle cottage that boasted a decent sea view. But right now she was still enjoying the novelty of living alone.

'Guess what my dad's doing today,' said Leo, waving at one of his customers who was passing by.

'Mounting a coup to take over leadership of Callowfield Neighbourhood Watch?'

'No, that's next week,' said Leo drily. 'He and Beatrice are meeting up for lunch. She's back in the country, now that she and her husband have sorted out the details of their separation, and she suggested that the two of them should meet.'

'That's brilliant, but how does your dad feel about it?'

'It's hard to tell, but I think he's chuffed that she wants to meet again. They've been emailing since they had that reunion at his house, and the fact they're communicating now has made all the difference.'

'Communication is key.'

'It certainly is. Talk and iron out any misunderstandings,' said Leo, slipping his arm around Emma's shoulder. 'Just think what might have happened if you hadn't grilled me so savagely about our Lavender Orchid kiss.'

'One, it wasn't savage, two, it wasn't a grilling, and three, we'd have probably got there eventually.'

'Got where?' asked Leo, looking down at her with a grin.

'Here,' said Emma, reaching up and kissing him on the mouth.

She was vaguely aware of Maisie shouting 'Get a room', but everything around them – her shop filled with vintage treasures, tourists ambling by, the sound of sea slapping against quayside stone, and seagulls circling – faded away as Leo slid his arms around her waist and kissed her back, as if she was the only woman in the world.

A LETTER FROM LIZ

Dear Reader,

You've reached the end of the book! If this was your first visit to Heaven's Cove, welcome! If it was a return trip, I'm delighted that you ventured back into my pretty, coastal village which harbours more than its fair share of secrets.

I've had fun bringing Emma and Leo together, and revealing the truth behind Robert's success, and I hope you've enjoyed your time with them. Thank you so much for reading their story.

Readers who are new to the series might like to know there are now eight books set in Heaven's Cove – I love writing about the village so much, I don't want to leave. All of the books are standalone stories so it doesn't really matter which ones you read first (though you will recognise a few returning characters if you read through them in order).

I'm always working on a new story idea, and signing up at the following link will mean you can keep up to date with all of my latest releases. Your email address will never be shared and you can unsubscribe at any time.

www.bookouture.com/liz-eeles

If you did enjoy *The Wife at the Last House Before the Sea* and you have the time to write a review, I'd really appreciate it.

I love getting feedback from readers, and even a brief review might encourage someone new to give one of my books a try.

You can also get in touch with me via my website or social media, if you'd like to say hello. I'll pop the details of those below.

Until next time,

Liz x

www.lizeeles.com

facebook.com/lizeelesauthor
x.com/lizeelesauthor
instagram.com/lizeelesauthor

ACKNOWLEDGEMENTS

At the end of this book, you'll find the names of the team who have contributed to *The Wife at the Last House Before the Sea* being published. I'm always humbled by how many people are involved, either directly or indirectly, in the process of turning my first draft into a proper book that reaches readers. Thank you to Bookouture and the whole team.

In particular, thank you to Ellen Gleeson, my wonderful editor who's been a huge support from the very start of this book, and throughout the whole Heaven's Cove series. I know I can always rely on her good ideas, insightful edits and spot-on advice.

I'm grateful, too, for my family and friends who are always encouraging when I'm writing. And I'll never take for granted people, like you, who choose my books and read them. Thank you so much.

PUBLISHING TEAM

Turning a manuscript into a book requires the efforts of many people. The publishing team at Bookouture would like to acknowledge everyone who contributed to this publication.

Commercial
Lauren Morrissette
Hannah Richmond
Imogen Allport

Data and analysis
Mark Alder
Mohamed Bussuri

Cover design
Eileen Carey

Editorial
Ellen Gleeson
Nadia Michael

Copyeditor
Jenny Page

Proofreader
Becca Allen

Marketing
Alex Crow
Melanie Price
Occy Carr
Cíara Rosney
Martyna Młynarska

Operations and distribution
Marina Valles
Stephanie Straub
Joe Morris

Production
Hannah Snetsinger
Mandy Kullar
Ria Clare
Nadia Michael

Publicity
Kim Nash
Noelle Holten
Jess Readett
Sarah Hardy

Rights and contracts
Peta Nightingale
Richard King
Saidah Graham

www.ingramcontent.com/pod-product-compliance
Ingram Content Group UK Ltd.
Pitfield, Milton Keynes, MK11 3LW, UK
UKHW030805170325
456354UK00002B/195